CRUEL
&
BITTER
THINGS

To Michelle,
Thanks for reading my novel!

CRUEL & BITTER THINGS

A BAD CHOICES NOVEL BOOK 1

JOSEPH SOUZA

LEVEL
BEST BOOKS

Author Photo Credit: Doug Bruns

First edition

ISBN: 978-1-68512-842-5

Cover art by Level Best Designs

This book was professionally typeset on Reedsy.
Find out more at reedsy.com

To my wife, Marleigh.

Chapter One

Gwynn knew as soon as she saw Sam Townsend that she would kill him. And it pained her, because she swore to never kill again. The object of her gaze stood in a circle of admirers, all eyes on him as he spoke. He held a cocktail in one hand while the other chopped through the air to drive home whatever point he was making. Behind him, a trio played Brubeck's "Take Five."

The sight of Townsend at this event shocked her. She noticed him the moment she'd walked into the grand room of the Custom House, built between 1867 and 1872 and Portland's most beautiful monument. It had been fourteen years since she last laid eyes on him, and she still hadn't forgotten the contours of his handsome face, his athletic build, and the charismatic smile that lit up her dorm room that fateful night he came to pick Tift up. A sophomore the first time they'd met, she had never forgotten him. Nor had her resolve waned about what she would do to Townsend if they ever met again, despite her constant prayers to cure her of these murderous desires.

She remembered the way Tift had come back to their dorm room in tears. It was late at night, and Tift had just returned from her date with Townsend, the ridiculously handsome boy who attended Crawford College, which was located fifty miles north of Brooks College. She had tried getting Tift to tell her what happened, but her friend merely lay down on her mattress in a fetal position and sobbed inconsolably. Gwynn stayed with her for over an hour before she finally broke down and admitted what Townsend had done to her. Gwynn became enraged when she learned what had happened, and she vowed that if she ever caught up with Townsend, she would make him pay for hurting her friend, and she would make sure he knew exactly the reason why.

Now, she would have the chance.

A server stopped and offered her a glass of champagne. Although she had no intention of drinking tonight, she grabbed the flute off the tray and held it conspicuously in front of her, happy to have something to keep her hands occupied.

Would Townsend remember her if she approached him?

The flesh on her arms dimpled as she thought about how she would end his life. Although there were many other people in the room, their faces appeared murky and vague. She gazed up at the second-floor balcony and the vaulted Greek ceiling, as well as the rows of dangling cylindrical lights. Staring at them kicked her out of her tunnel vision and helped clear her mind. Sparkling gold arches framed the windows and interior doors. An ornate iron rail encircled the second-floor walkway. No one was up there, but she could envision herself watching Townsend from a bird's-eye view. For a brief moment, she felt like a prisoner inside a cellblock, being watched by armed guards.

Gwynn closed her eyes and took a deep breath. She pinched the skin on her arm to remind herself where she was. Her old college friend, Sandra Clayborn, had invited her to this event. Sandra's company, Plumhurst Capital, had recently opened an estate planning division, and Sandra wanted people to spread the word to wealthy Mainers.

Gwynn prayed to God to help her make the right decision.

An unfamiliar man approached and greeted her in a flirtatious manner, but she had no desire to talk to anyone. She stepped away, her eyes fixed on Townsend. A photographer stepped in front of her, asking everyone in the vicinity if they could gather together so he could take a group photo. The people around her huddled awkwardly, strangers with drinks in hand, waiting for the photographer to finish snapping his shots so they could go back to enjoying themselves. She had no desire to have her picture taken, but it was too late now, as he'd already moved on to another group. Being in this photograph didn't concern her, as there were hundreds of other people in the room, and her connection to Townsend was tenuous at best.

She stood back against the bar, willing herself to become invisible. Every fiber in her body crackled with nervous energy as she watched Townsend captivate the people around him. Once he finished talking, his audience broke out into peals of laughter. Men slapped him on the back, and women ogled him with barely disguised lust in their eyes.

He deserved exactly what he had coming to him.

The group scattered as he sauntered to the bar and ordered a drink. The conversational hum in the room played like a movie soundtrack in her ears.

A well-dressed man came over to her, smiled, and asked if she would like a drink. She shook her head, hoping he might get the message and move on. Townsend was now talking with Sandra, and they appeared engrossed in conversation. For a brief moment, it appeared as if they were in a relationship. Gwynn thought it a good time to slip to the ladies' room and take the medication Dr. Kaufman had prescribed for her.

Leaving her champagne on the counter, she walked toward the lobby, her heels clicking against the checkered marble floor. Approaching the lobby, she looked forward to smoking that last delicious cigarette in her pack.

Her jacket hung on the lobby hook. Beads of rainwater still clung to the material. Rather than grabbing it, she pushed open the massive door and stood with her back pressed against the granite wall of the building. A light rain began to fall. It dripped loudly on the steps in front of her. The scent of the nearby harbor hung thick in the air. She pulled out the lone cigarette in the pack and lit it, noticing that her hand was slightly trembling. Her mind splintered in many directions, thinking about all the possible ways she could end Townsend's life. Maybe she would change her mind and have mercy on him, but she doubted it.

A young couple, walking arm in arm, made their way up the granite steps. They stopped and briefly kissed, staring into each other's eyes. Gwynn studied them, slightly jealous of their affection for each other, wishing she had that in her own marriage. The skies opened up, and the rain began to bucket. Down below, traffic crept along Fore Street. After throwing her butt down, she stubbed it out using the heel of her shoe, swearing it would be the last one she ever smoked.

Exhaling a cloud of smoke, she pulled out her phone and stared down at the screen. There were no messages, which meant the children at the group home she ran were all safe at the moment. She debated whether to call Tom and ask how Jack was doing, but then decided against it. Whatever else she thought about Tom, he was a good father to Jack, their five-year-old son. She felt bad that she'd recently broken up with him, but she couldn't fathom living another minute with him. As the years passed, he'd become more domineering, trying to control all facets of her life. She blamed herself for marrying Tom, despite that silly promise they'd made back in college. It had been a bad choice in a lifetime of questionable choices. She'd blinded herself to his serious character flaws back then, trying to see the best in him.

She turned and went back inside, heading downstairs to where the restrooms were located, hoping that she might run into Townsend. After finding a darkened nook in the back, she peeked her head out and monitored all the people who came and went. She opened her purse and took two Ambiens out of an orange vial, placed them on the floor, and ground them into powder with the heel of her shoe. The powder she scooped onto a dollar bill. Then funneled into a silver flask filled with whiskey.

Another two minutes passed before she heard the *tap, tap, tap* of footsteps coming down the stairs. She slipped the flask back into her purse. Carefully, so as not to be seen, she glanced around the corner and saw Townsend disappear inside the men's room.

She pulled out her compact and checked her reflection in the mirror, barely recognizing the woman staring back at her. Everything inside her felt alive and engaged, as if this was what she was meant to do.

After taking a deep breath, she strode out of the nook, praying that no one would see her slip into the men's restroom.

She went inside and closed the door behind her. Smelled the strong scent of urinal cake and stale piss. Townsend stood at the sink, washing his hands. He had the hands of an ex-athlete, strong and supple. In another time and circumstance, she wouldn't have minded them caressing her body. He looked in the mirror and smiled when he saw her, two dimples popping up on either side of his mouth. His blond hair swept back over his scalp, and his striped yellow tie was slightly undone at the neck. Only the subtlest hint of a receding hairline indicated he'd aged from that cocky guy he was back at Crawford. He smiled when he saw her. It was the same smile he flashed in their dorm room when he arrived to pick up Tift. She remembered the pang of jealousy she'd felt when she saw Tift in that gorgeous sundress standing next to him.

"Sorry, I guess I read the sign wrong," she said.

He continued to wash his hands. "Do you make it a practice to barge into restrooms and introduce yourself to strange men?"

"Only the good-looking ones," she said, noticing that he wasn't wearing a wedding ring.

"You look familiar," he said, turning the faucet and shaking the water off his hands. "Do I know you?"

"Gwynn."

"Sam." He pulled out a paper towel and dried his hands on it. "Pleasure to meet you, Gwynn, although I'm not sure this is the best place for us to be meeting."

She turned and registered herself in the mirror, still not recognizing herself. "I was watching you up there."

"You were?"

She nodded at his reflection in the the mirror.

"If I'd known I had a secret admirer, I would have upped my game."

She turned back to face him. "Guess it's not so secret now."

"No, I guess not."

He tossed the towel into the trash bin.

"What do you do, Gwynn?"

"I run a home for troubled children. You?"

"Finance. In fact, the woman who organized this shit show desperately wants my firm's business."

"Sandra?"

"You know her?"

"She's an old friend of mine."

"That woman's a shark."

"She's always been one, for as long as I've known her."

"Where do you know her from?"

"We went to Brooks College together."

He smiled. "I went to Crawford, just up the road."

"Now that's a coincidence."

"I'll say," he says. "Would you like to leave here and go somewhere else, Gwynn?"

Gwynn smiled. "I thought you'd never ask. These corporate events are so mind-numbingly boring."

"I couldn't agree more."

"Maybe you should walk out of here first. That way, you can tell me if there's anyone out in the hallway."

He laughed. "I can do that."

He opened the door and checked to see if the coast was clear. Then he waved for her to follow him. They climbed the stairs, giggling like children, until they reached the dim lobby. She stayed behind so as not to be seen.

She moved toward him once they were in the lobby. "What would you like to do now?" she whispered.

"I think you know what I'd like to do. And I'm hoping you want to do the same thing."

"I knew the moment I laid eyes on you." He leaned in close enough so that she could smell the gin on his breath.

"Then let's get out of here before some empty suit comes over and ties me up."

She stifled a laugh when he mentioned being tied up. Placing her lips against the bottom of his stubble-filled chin, she said, "Maybe I'll be the one to tie you up."

"Is that a promise?"

"Only if I can keep it." She placed her hand on his forearm and squeezed.

She stood on her toes, the lobby now empty, and kissed him on the lips.

6

He turned and snatched his coat off the hook. She lifted her rain jacket and slipped into it, flipping the hood up and over her head. They made outside, the rain falling even harder since the last time she was out there. She lifted the umbrella out of her pocket, slid it open as if cocking a shotgun, and held it over the two of them while they strolled down the street. He held out his hand to her, and she took it.

"Where to?" Townsend asked.

She squeezed his hand. "My car is parked a few blocks away."

"Are we going back to your place?" He stopped and stared into her eyes.

"Is that a problem?"

"No, but my hotel is just down the street. It has an amazing view of the water."

"When we go back to my place, I'll make it so you won't want to look at anything else."

"I like the sound of that." He leaned down and kissed her on the lips. "Besides, I don't want anyone I know to see us."

"Why? Are you married?"

"Are you?"

"I guess it doesn't really matter." She saw his expression change and didn't want to blow this one opportunity to get her revenge. "One night of mind-blowing bliss won't end our marriages."

"No, I suppose not."

She pulled him by the hand and up the side street, thinking about her son, hoping that Jack never found out about her secret activities. Her mind switched gears and she thought of Tift. She had vowed to make Townsend pay for what he had done to her back in college, and now the time had come.

She remembered the night she and Tift had stumbled back to their dorm high as a kite after attending a house party. They sat on the couch, giggling at nothing in particular. At one point, Tift leaned over, cupped her chin, and kissed her on the lips, catching Gwynn off guard. It was in that moment that Gwynn first suspected that something was off about her best friend.

After a few seconds had passed, Gwynn sat back and tried to make sense of the kiss. Yes, it felt nice. She remembered fleeing up to her room, confused at what had just happened. Had Tift been in love with her? Had she loved Tift? Was Tift messing with her head? She never viewed her friend in a sexual way, but she absolutely did love Tift, and now she was prepared to kill for her.

There were not many people out this evening, a good omen. They turned the corner, and she caught sight of her SUV parked against the curb. Gwynn thumbed the remote, and the SUV beeped to life. The lights flashed. Rain pummeled them as she closed the umbrella and opened the driver's side door. She collapsed into the seat. Townsend fell in next to her, and they laughed at the situation they'd found themselves in. Sam's skin had a veiny, pinkish glow to it from having consumed too much alcohol. She pulled her hood down, exposing her damp hair, and stared into his eyes. What would Tift think if she knew what she was planning to do? Knowing Tift, she'd probably be happy about it.

Taken aback by her growing attraction to this financier, Gwynn tried to concentrate on her plan. There was a small part of her that wouldn't mind sleeping with him, but she knew that wouldn't happen. She was still married to Tom, even if they were currently separated, and most likely headed toward divorce. The vow still meant something to her, not that she wouldn't break it if the right person came along and swept her off her feet.

"You're beautiful," he said, wiping a strand of wet hair over her ear.

"Thank you." She pulled the flask out of her purse and pretended to drink from it. Once done, she passed it over to him.

He held up his hand. "No, thanks. I've had a bit too much already."

"Come on now. Don't ruin the party." She pushed the flask into his chest. "Let's have some fun tonight."

He hesitated before taking the flask. "Sure, why not?"

"That's the spirit," she said, her hand resting on his crotch. "I'm going to do some very nasty things to you tonight, Sam Townsend. Promise you won't hold it against me?"

"Scouts honor," he said, holding up his right hand. "Wait. How did you know my last name?"

She cursed herself for messing up. "You told me your name earlier. Or have you forgotten already?"

"I don't remember telling you."

"That's because you're drunk." She laughed.

"I'm not *that* drunk."

"Drunk enough to forget that you told me your name."

He seemed to think it over. "Seriously, how did you know?"

"Are you going to make a federal case out of this?" She rolled her eyes. "Have you considered that I might have asked about you back at the Custom House? Because I was hoping we might meet up?"

Satisfied, he smiled at this response.

"Are you going to be okay with this, Sam?"

"Don't worry about me."

"Because it would be a real shame if you couldn't."

"Really?"

"Really. We're going to do things you've probably never done before," she said. "Things you've only seen on video."

"Jesus, you're a wild one."

"You don't know the half of it."

She started the ignition and pulled away from the curb. The rain assaulted the windshield, forcing her to turn the defrost and wipers on high. The heat combined with the alcohol would help speed up the effects of the Ambien in his system.

"How far do we have to go?" Townsend asked after taking another swig of whiskey.

"Relax, handsome. We'll be there before you know it."

"We have to keep this between us," he slurred.

"What kind of woman do you think I am?" She backhanded him in the midsection, seeing his chin drop briefly to his chest.

"Is it hot in here?" He loosened his tie, a bead of sweat beading up on his pale forehead.

She turned toward him. "Feels fine to me."

"I must have drank more than I thought," he said, trying to keep his head upright on his neck.

"You just sit back and rest, Sam. We'll be there before you know it."

"What's your name again?"

"Gwynn. You mean you don't remember meeting me back in college?" she said, noticing him slumped against the passenger door. "The night you date-raped my best friend, Tift?"

She reached inside his jacket, removed his cell phone, pulled out the SIM card and battery. Then she did the same to her own phone, knowing that by doing this, she could never be tracked by the police. A wave of exhilaration passed through her, but she knew not to get ahead of herself just yet. Hopefully, no one had seen her leaving the Custom House with Townsend.

Certain she was in the clear, she accelerated toward the interstate and steered the SUV up the ramp heading north. Assuming there was no traffic at this hour, she estimated that it would take ninety minutes before she got to the vacation cabin she and Tom owned.

She congratulated herself on a job well done, but she had a lot more work to do before she could relax. Paying Townsend back for what he had done was a good thing. Justice was being served.

Chapter Two

The cabin creaked while Gwynn tossed and turned on her mattress. She couldn't get any rest knowing Townsend was out there and tied to a tree. It had been too stormy to kill him right away, and she had wanted him to be awake when she did the deed.

Branches swayed in the wind and brushed up against the floor-to-ceiling windows. Once the sun came up, she'd be afforded a full view of the valley and surrounding hills. A slow-moving river cut through the valley, and in better days, she and her family would take their canoes down there, drop them in the river, and go for a long paddle. But the main reason she had chosen this cabin was its proximity to the nearby quarry.

She opened her eyes, saw darkness, and heard the rustle of branches knocking against the cabin. Glancing at the clock, she saw that it was just past three in the morning.

Rather than lay in bed, she got up and dressed. A cup of coffee would have been nice right now, but she didn't feel like making any. Instead, she walked around in the dark cabin, trying to settle her nerves. She felt fortunate to have this place as an escape hatch from the rat race. Many a nights had been spent playing board games with her family, the three of them sprawled on the floor next to the fireplace, laughing and joking. During the day, they would hike through the woods. The ski resort was just down the road, and on clear winter days, they would break out the snowshoes. Tom liked to carry Jack in his backpack and then trek over the many trails crisscrossing the hills.

Slipping into her rain jacket, she exited the house and made her way out to her vehicle. The rain beat down over the nylon material and tapped in her ears. She opened the rear door of the SUV and made a mental checklist of all the items in the compartment. She kept these in her SUV in case she might need them. Certain she had everything, she closed the back door.

The darkness of the early morning blanketed the landscape. She jumped inside and turned on the high beams. Instantly, all the trees along the road came to life, resembling goblins and evil spirits.

Was she really going to do this?

A mile passed before she turned and climbed the steep trail. She grew more nervous the closer she got to Townsend. Once she saw the clearing, she parked the SUV and shut off the engine. Jumping out of the Highlander, she retrieved the items in the back. The wind howled as she removed everything. It blew through the branches and tree limbs. Even with the SUV's headlights on high beam, she had to illuminate her surroundings with the flashlight she'd brought with her.

She pointed the beam along the wet, leaf-strewn ground as she made her way deeper into the woods, stopping when she saw him sitting against the tree. The beam of light settled on his expensive loafers first and then worked its way along his expensive suit, which was soaked from the rain. He looked up at her, his eyes squinting when the beam rested on his face. Rainwater slicked down his hairline and into his eyes. She walked over and examined his hands, which were still secured around the birch tree. His wrists bled from trying to break free from the plastic cuffs restraining them. Gwynn squatted down in front of him and ripped the duct tape off his mouth. He gulped in air and stared at her, fear in his eyes.

"Please, I have a wife and three kids at home."

"You should have thought about that before you tried to sleep with me."

He shook his head, slicks of water flying off. "I'm an asshole, I know, especially after I've had a few drinks. But that's no reason to keep me tied up here."

"Who said that was the reason I was keeping you here?"

"Look, I've learned my lesson. I'll never be unfaithful to my wife again."

"Is that the lesson you think I'm teaching you?" She laughed.

"I haven't done anything to you. Shit, I don't even know who you are."

She studied him. "I can see why she fell for you."

"Who fell for me? What are you talking about?"

"You're a smooth one, Sam Townsend. Must be easy picking up the babes with your line of bullshit."

"Please let me go back to my family."

"I know your type, mister."

"My type?"

"Rich assholes who think they can get away with everything."

"You couldn't be more wrong about that. I've worked hard for everything I've gotten in life."

She listened to the wind, wondering if there was a message buried in it. Wondering if it was trying to tell her to let him live. Townsend's expression changed when she didn't say anything, and he became angry, thrashing against the tree in an attempt to free himself.

"Just tell me what I've done to deserve this." He appeared on the verge of crying. "At least tell me how I've wronged you."

"It must have been quite a surprise to wake up and find yourself tied up here in the middle of nowhere."

"You spiked that whiskey, didn't you?"

"How else was I going to drag a big guy like you out here and then secure you to this tree?"

He peered around in the dark as if trying to determine his location.

"You won't get away with this."

"Oh, I most certainly will. Little did you know, Sam, but I've been planning this for quite some time now, and I know how to cover my tracks."

"You've been planning to kidnap me? What kind of psycho are you?"

Gwynn shrugged. "A very thorough one."

"Just tell me why you're doing this and what I've done."

She remained quiet, feeling a bit guilty for enjoying this as much as she did. Then she got up and walked around, listening to the rain beat down over her hood.

"Why won't you explain yourself to me?" he shouted.

"Okay, Sam, here it is: you raped my best friend back in college."

"Raped your best friend? That's the craziest thing I've ever heard. Besides, I don't even know who you are."

"My name is Gwynn Denning. You came into my dorm room that night, but you barely noticed me." She stared into the dark woods, wondering if jealousy was motivating her actions. "Not that I blame you. My roommate was a knockout."

"I'm sorry for not paying attention to you. It was such a long time ago."

"Not to worry, Sam. My roommate had that effect on the boys," she said. "It's what you did to her afterward that I can never forgive."

"I swear to you that I did not, nor did I ever, rape anyone back in college."

"You have no idea how hard it was dealing with her after that happened. She went to pieces, and I was the one who had to take care of her for the next few months."

"Who went to pieces? Please tell me who you're talking about."

She stared up at the sky and let the rain fall over her face. "Tift Ainsley."

"Tift Ainsley?" He thought about it for a few seconds. *The* Tift Ainsley? The movie star?"

"Yes. I was her roommate that day you came into our dorm. You honestly don't remember?"

"I don't, but I swear to you that I didn't do anything to your roommate that night."

Gwynn reached in her pocket and pulled out a clear plastic bag, the kind with cotton strings ringed through it as handles. Her entire body shivered while fingering the material.

"Please, you have to believe me," he said, staring at the bag in her hands.

"I fully expected you to deny it. Had you admitted what you'd done, I might have reconsidered what I'm about to do."

"Yes, we had sex in the back of my car, but she consented to it. In fact, she was the one who came on to me. The girl was a whack job. She wanted to hang out and talk all night. But when I told her I needed to head back to school to study, she started crying hysterically. Then I dropped her off at her dorm and flew back to Crawford, hoping to never see her again."

14

She didn't reply to this.

"What do you want me to say? That I did it and I'm sorry? Okay, I'll admit it if you just let me go home to my family."

The wind picked up and howled, causing the trees above to sway. Taking a deep breath, she wrapped the string handles around her cold fingers.

"Even assuming you're telling the truth, I couldn't possibly let you go now," she said. "You'd go straight to the police and tell them everything."

"Is this a game to you?"

"Trust me, this is no game."

"I'll never tell another soul if you let me go."

"You raped my best friend, Sam. I want to hear you admit it."

"Okay, I raped her. I did it, and I'm sorry. Is that what you want to hear?"

Standing, she whipped the bag up over her head until it filled with air. The rain pelted the plastic as she straddled his legs.

"I'm begging you," he wailed, tears in his eyes. "You'll leave three beautiful kids without their father."

"Your guilt or innocence is of little concern to me now. I have no other choice in the matter."

"You do have a choice."

"Trust me, I don't."

"Why not?"

"Because I'm a killer, Sam. This is what I do." It felt good to finally admit this to someone.

"Do you have children?"

She was taken aback by this question. "Yes. A five-year-old son."

"Then for god's sake, you know what it's like to be a parent. Please don't punish my kids for whatever you think I've done to your friend."

"Pray with me, Sam," she said.

"What?"

"Pray with me that God will have mercy on your soul."

"Fuck you!"

It angered her that he wouldn't repent and ask for mercy. She said a quick prayer for him and herself. No way she could let Townsend live and possibly put her life in jeopardy. She had her son to raise. The thought of Tom raising Jack by himself caused her to shudder in fear. Tom, with his controlling and paranoid personality. But then Gwynn remembered what Townsend had done to Tift and Tift's nervous breakdown in the months following the encounter, and she knew she couldn't allow him to get away with it. Why would Tift lie about being raped? More importantly, Gwynn didn't want Townsend to hurt other women the way he hurt Tift.

After a quick prayer, she took a few seconds to regain her composure. She sat above his knees, forcing the weight of her body down over his wet thighs. Gripping both sides of the bag, she slammed it down with a force that surprised her. Townsend cried out, his head flailing around inside the pulsating bag, his muffled pleas filling with air. She wrapped the strings around his throat until he gagged. Then she pulled back as hard as she could, remembering why she was doing this. The strings stretched, causing her to stumble back onto his ankles. She tried to stand, but he kicked her in the ribs. Gwynn managed to hold onto the two looped ends. Struggling to keep the lines taut, she reared back like a jockey reining in a thoroughbred, the tendons in her neck and arms straining. Townsend's panicked expression stared back at her through the clear plastic material. His eyes bulged as the wet bag sucked into his gaping mouth. She studied his perfect white teeth and his flaring nasal cavities. Their eyes briefly met, locking in a momentary grip of wills.

His legs kicked and spasmed, but she was far enough away now to avoid another injury. She knew her ribs would ache for days. Pulling back a few inches, she gasped for breath. The strings grew tauter the more she pulled. The pain in her ribs became a faint memory the more she exerted herself. At some point, the bag stopped moving, and his legs remained still. His eyes appeared frozen in terror. She took another step back and pulled, the loops wrapped tightly around her creased palms. Her lungs burned, and her muscles ached.

She released the two-stringed loops. Almost instantly, the muscles in her arms went slack. The physical exertion caused her hands to tremble. She began to hyperventilate. After lifting the bag off Townsend's head, she noticed a red ligature mark ringed around his throat. His lifeless eyes were open and staring off in the distance.

After a few seconds passed, she broke down and wept. A wave of remorse blew over her. It took her a few minutes before she regained her composure. She took a deep breath and tried to comprehend what she had just done. Tried to rationalize her actions.

The world was a better place now that Townsend was dead. This was what she kept telling herself as she limped back to the car. She opened the back door and carried out the two twenty-five-pound kettlebells and rope she had brought with her. With flashlight in hand, she lugged them up the path until she arrived at the quarry's edge, dropping them on the ground before returning to Townsend's corpse. There was more work to do before she could head home.

Practical matters now weighed on her as she considered how to get him out of these woods. Like how not leave any forensic evidence behind that might incriminate her. She cut the restraints on his wrists and then grabbed him by the ankles, pulling him with great effort out of the woods. Sweat streaked down her forehead and armpits. She had to stop every few seconds to take a break. The rain peppered her jacket and hood, and she was sweating profusely by the time she arrived at the quarry's edge. Instead of resting, she secured the rope around his neck and ankles. Then she looped the ends through the metal handles of the kettlebells. Once done, she placed his phone and SIM card in the pocket of his pants. When the rope was secured around him, she pushed his mud-covered body over the edge. A few seconds later, she heard a faint splash. She peered over the cliff but couldn't see anything because it was so dark.

This quarry had proved useful after all.

Gwynn returned to her car and took out the broom she'd brought with her, struggling to control the spasms quaking throughout her body. She swept over the ground imprinted by Townsend's corpse. She swept away her own gloppy footprints left in the ooze, leaving no trace of her ever being up here. To her surprise, she gazed up and noticed the first streaks of sunlight flaring over the eastern sky, and this made her happy. It was a new day, a fresh start. Taking out her flashlight, she checked one last time to see if she'd left anything behind. Certain that she hadn't, she trekked back into the woods where she'd tied Townsend to the tree and searched for anything that might lead back to her. Nothing stood out, so she headed back to her SUV and drove home.

'She's A Rainbow' by the Rolling Stones played over the radio as she navigated her way back home. Every nerve in her body pulsed and radiated. Tom would be bringing Jack home this afternoon. In anticipation of her son's arrival, she was going to bake a tray of cookies for when Jack walked through the door. She'd also purchased a new video game for his console, which meant that she would get very little rest today. It didn't matter. Sleep would be hard to come by over the next few nights. Townsend's murder would replay over and over in her head.

She drove slowly, fighting the paranoia threatening to overwhelm her. A traffic violation would place her in the vicinity of the crime, in the unlikely event that Townsend's body was ever discovered. Ring cams along the road might capture her vehicle, but they would be automatically deleted by the time anyone discovered Townsend's body, assuming he would ever be found. She thought of ways to fly under the radar, including staying off the toll roads so that the state of Maine would have no record of her ever being here.

Just under two hours later, she arrived home. Using the garden hose, she washed the mud off her tires. She then parked her car in the garage and put the SIM card back in her phone. Seconds later, a series of text messages popped up on the screen. Most were work-related, but there was one from Tom telling her that he'd be delivering Jack home earlier than expected. It was Sunday morning, but he had to go into the office early to work on a client's tax account. Gwynn realized that he'd be over in less than an hour. The change of plans upset her, before realizing that she could use this to her advantage.

As Gwynn made her way inside the house, she vowed that Townsend would be her final victim.

One of the text messages was labeled urgent. She opened it and read that Ivy, her favorite client at The Loft, had been rushed to the hospital. Gwynn had come to love Ivy, especially the way she fought for her life and encouraged the other girls to feel better about themselves. She made a mental note to call the hospital later and check up on the girl.

Gwynn wished she could spend five minutes alone with Ivy's manipulative, violent father. Now, that might be the last time she killed.

Chapter Three

Gwynn heard Tom's Mercedes pull up in the driveway. She went over to the curtain, nervous, and peeked out the window, watching Tom get out of his car. He moved to the back door where Jack was seated and unbuckled the five-year-old from his booster seat. She couldn't help but notice the forty pounds Tom had put on since they got married, not that his weight gain was the reason she'd decided to leave him. His hair was longer than usual and a bit messy. He'd let himself go this past year, and it appeared that he had no intention of changing his bad habits.

She still loved Tom, despite his many flaws, but she was definitely not in love with him. Growing up, she dreamed of the prince-in-shining-armor type of love, and falling head-over-heels with the man she hoped to spend the rest of her life with. But none of that had happened. They were always friends before lovers, before she really got to know the true Tom, which seemed highly problematic now that she reflected on it.

They'd met at Brooks College, where they quickly became friends. He excelled in academics, enjoyed trivia contests, and played lead guitar in a popular rock band that borrowed heavily from the Pixies and Nirvana. At first, Gwynn was drawn to his dry sense of humor and gentle playfulness. Unlike a lot of the boys on campus, he was nice and acted respectful toward her. Tom never pushed his political views or took a hard stance on matters. She felt completely safe around him. Free, to a degree, to be herself and express her opinions openly. But then again, she never really expected to find someone to whom she could confess all of her deepest, darkest secrets to.

Tom took Jack by the hand and started to walk toward the front door. A neighbor passing on the street called out to Tom, and Tom turned and waved.

At various intervals throughout college, Tom had tried convincing her that they should be more than just friends. But she couldn't see that happening. There were no thrills or goosebumps when she was with him. She dated other guys, never being a prolific dater, but she always ran back to Tom for a shoulder to cry on. Tom loved her deeply. Acted like a true friend when she really needed one.

They started dating at a vulnerable time in her life. It was the end of her junior year and she and her boyfriend at the time had just broken up. While crying in Tom's arms one evening, she realized that her soul mate might just be closer than she thought. Her parents had always told her that love was much deeper than mere sexual attraction, and that it was more important to be friends first. A summer abroad in Paris awaited her, and that meant a chance for love and romance. She and Tom kissed that last evening she was to get on the plane, agreeing to meet up once classes started up again in the fall.

Jack let go of his father's hand and ran off laughing, daring Tom to catch him. Tom put his hands on his hips and grimaced, shouting for Jack to stop playing around and return to his side.

Upon returning to campus that September, Gwynn knew that getting back with Tom had been a mistake. She had an "incident" while in Paris, whereby she was forced to defend herself against a predator late one night while walking along the banks of the Seine. The incident had profoundly changed her when she returned home.

Tom acted more covetous once she was back on campus, demanding to know her whereabouts at all times. He was more controlling and covetous, and she didn't like this aspect of his personality. Making matters worse, their relationship lacked the passion she had always desired.

As winter break neared, she realized that she had no other choice but to break it off with him. He confessed his love for her and claimed that she was his soul mate, and he begged for her to give him one more chance. But she held her ground and declared their relationship over. When they returned to campus after Christmas break, they resumed being friends. It felt strange to her, him acting as if nothing had ever happened, but she felt free again. Tom buried his head in his school books, played in his band, and dated other girls. He took up rock-climbing and spent weekends in the mountains with his friends. With her, he acted as he always did before they started dating. She concentrated on her academics, continued writing her dark stories for her creative writing class, and hung out with Tift. But mostly, she worked at keeping the demons at bay.

Jack made his way back to Tom, giggling, and together they made their way to the front door.

When the day of graduation came, she realized she might never see Tom again, and to her surprise, this depressed her. Despite their failed romantic relationship, she still considered him one of her best friends. They went to the college pub the night before they were to receive their degrees and proceeded to get drunk. He talked openly about his grand career plans and how he was going to make a lot of money in the business world, and someday own a big house with a white picket fence, and have a bunch of kids. It sounded like he was bragging for her sake. Later that night, after too many beers, he broke down and confessed that he still loved her. His time at Brooks had been the best four years of his life, and much of it because of his friendship with her. She held Tom in her arms and comforted him like he'd done for her so many times before. After a few more beers, they made a drunken pact: if they hadn't both met someone by the time they were thirty, they would marry each other.

The doorbell chimed.

Eight years later, they ran into each other at Gritty's Pub in downtown Portland. The year prior, Tom had left his Boston firm and accepted a job with a CPA firm in town. He was out with a group of friends when she literally bumped into him while carrying a pint of Black Fly Stout back to her table. She was expecting to meet a guy she'd met online, but he hadn't arrived yet, so she sat with Tom until he showed up. But then her date never materialized, or if he had, she hadn't expended much energy looking for him. Tom seemed different than in college, all grown up and mature, and she rather liked this adult version of him. This professional version. He looked as if he'd been working out, too. He wore an expensive tailored suit, and his long rocker hair had been replaced with a stylish business cut that suited his face. They caught up on their lives over many pints of beer.

Gwynn moved away from the window so as not to be seen. Seconds later, the doorbell rang again.

Later that night, she found herself stumbling back to Tom's apartment in the East End and then falling into bed with him. She was amazed to discover how nice it was to be with somebody she shared a rich past with and whom she could so easily talk to. Her mother had recently died of cancer, and she'd been lonely and depressed after graduating from college, struggling to resist the dark urges that had been getting stronger with time. Although sparks didn't fly when she was around Tom, being with him felt comfortable and safe. She also considered the possibility that he could help keep her demons at bay.

They were married three months later by the justice of the peace, over the fierce objections of Tom's mother. For whatever reason reason, Tom's mother and sister never warmed up to her. Never even gave her a chance to prove that she was a good person. Had they seen something in her that only she saw in herself?

Being married to Tom was far different than she imagined. She'd thought that maybe he'd matured and smoothed out those quirks in his personality. There were moments where his passivity and indecisiveness infuriated her, as if these traits were masking some deeper flaw. But then he demanded to know everything she did and where she was going. Who her friends were and who she socialized with. Sex with him was totally devoid of passion, as it was back in college. He catered to her every need, stopped playing guitar and climbing mountains, and turned into a dull corporate suit, often rambling on at dinner about the complexities of the federal tax code. She once had a vivid dream of killing him with a meat fork, although she figured that most couples had similar dreams.

Gwynn opened the door and let them in.

Jack laughed happily upon seeing her, and she scooped him up in her arms, kissing him on his chubby pink cheek. He closed his eyes and feigned disgust at being kissed by his mother, but she knew he loved getting showered with affection, especially after being away from her for a few days. Tom looked weary and disheveled as he placed the bags down on the kitchen island.

"You look tired," he said. "Rough night?"

"It wasn't the best night's sleep." She studied him for any trace of suspicion. "I could say the same about you."

He scratched his head. "You try spending half the night wrestling with the federal tax code."

"No thanks. I have my own problems to deal with."

"What problems do you have?"

"I had to attend a corporate event at the Custom House last night. It was hosted by our old college friend Sandra Clayborn."

"I haven't seen much of her since we graduated from Brooks. How's she doing?"

"Quite well, from the looks of it. She's Vice President of Plumhurst Capital."

"I never liked that bitch," he said, envious of his classmates who were more successful than him.

"I had a drink and something to eat. Then I dragged myself home and jumped into bed. As soon as I fell asleep, I received a text message that one of my clients had been rushed to the hospital."

"You should quit that shitty job and find one that pays more."

"Fortunately, you don't get to tell me what to do," she said. "Besides, I love working at The Loft. And I care way too much about those kids to just abandon them for more money."

Tom lifted Jack's bag. "I washed and dried all of his clothes. Like a dumbass, I left his video games back at my place."

"No problem. I can get those later." She turned to Jack. "So, how's my little wiggleworm?"

"I am not a wiggleworm, Mom," Jack said, giggling as she poked her finger into his belly. "You're the wiggleworm."

"Take your bags up to your room before I make you eat a bowl of wiggleworm stew."

"Okay, Mommy Wiggleworm."

She pretended to be mad and chase after him, and he sprinted away with his bags in tow. "And wash your hands while you're up there."

"He's such a great kid," Tom said. "You've done a fantastic job raising him."

"So have you."

"We're lucky to have such an amazing son."

"It's the one good thing that happened in our marriage."

"The only one?"

She realized she misspoke. "I didn't mean it that way."

"I thought we had a great marriage."

"Then you obviously weren't paying attention to my needs."

"Obviously not, but I'd love another chance to prove myself."

"We both know that we're better off as friends. The same thing happened to us at Brooks. You couldn't stand when I went out with my friends and had a life of my own."

"But we're older now and more mature, Gwynn. And don't you think Jack's better off with his parents together?"

Gwynn crossed her arms and looked away, not wanting to discuss this topic with him right now. Her mind kept returning to last night and the way she'd killed Townsend, and if she'd forgotten to cover all her tracks.

"Marrying you was the greatest day of my life," he said. "I'll go to counseling if you want. I'll change and be a better man if you give me another chance."

"You might be able to change, Tom, but you can't change me. And it's me who's been unhappy in this marriage, the way you've been controlling our money and watching my every move."

"I realize that now. It's me who needs to do all the hard work."

She sighed, wishing he'd leave.

"You're the only thing I've ever wanted in my life." Tears shined in his

25

eyes.

She felt sorry for him and didn't know how to respond to this.

"Don't say anything right now. Just think about it."

Tom opened the front door and headed to his car. She watched him for a few seconds before returning inside. While Jack put away his stuff, she poured herself another cup of coffee and recalled her previous night's activity. Sam Townsend's death continued to replay in her mind. She wanted desperately to believe that justice was served by her actions, but deep down, she knew that a small part of herself enjoyed killing him.

Her desire to kill began at a young age. Why had she been cursed with such insidious thoughts? As a little girl, she often prayed to God that He might cure her of this affliction. Her father, a beloved minister in Portland, instilled in her the belief in God's goodness. So why had God allowed her to suffer from such a crippling curse? In high school, she daydreamed about killing all the bullies and teachers who tormented the more vulnerable students. Nothing she did alleviated this crippling obsession until she started seeing Dr. Kaufman. Even with the medications he prescribed, it only dulled the sharp edges of her mania.

She sat sipping her coffee, thinking about her past.

There were times when she simply gave in and savored these thoughts to their fullest, only to be racked with guilt afterward and asking for God's forgiveness. As a child, she saw bad deeds everywhere she looked: the newspaper, on television, and on the streets where her father preached the Gospel to the various street people who had made it their home. She seemed attuned to the evil occurring in the world, especially after following the depraved story of the Muddy River Killer, who had left a trail of corpses along the banks of the nearby rivers. Her trajectory had led her to caring for children who'd been abused by the monsters who'd raised them.

It was part of the reason she took up pen and paper and began to write down the little stories germinating in her brain. Writing helped her deal with these conflicting motions. It gave her an outlet for her dark and twisted nature to fully express itself in a positive way. Even Kaufman encouraged her to journal, not knowing the true reason why she did it.

Now, as director of The Loft, she was able to help society's most vulnerable children. And she toiled long and hard to that end, oftentimes coming home late at night, exhausted and emotionally spent. Tom had complained about the long hours she put in, and this had been a frequent point of contention in their marriage. He pestered her to quit and get a better job with good benefits and regular hours. But she was not willing to let go of the one thing that gave her life meaning and direction.

She walked over and grabbed a croissant out of the box. After tearing off a buttery layer, she placed it in her mouth, savoring the morsel along with her coffee.

Despite the four murders she'd committed up to this point in time, she'd come to a tenuous covenant with her maker. Most of the time, she had no desire to kill—not even harm a common housefly—until something drastic happened, and murder was all she could think about. She only hoped that Townsend would be her last victim.

Her phone buzzed. She snatched it off the kitchen island and studied the screen. It was a number she didn't recognize. She opened the text message and read it.

I know what you did last night.

Dr. Ezra Kaufman

One Week Later

I became worried as soon as I saw the man's photograph in the newspaper. One couldn't forget such a chiseled profile. I didn't know him personally, but I do remember seeing him the night of that Custom House event. I hadn't wanted to attend, but one of the principals of the firm extended an invitation to me that I couldn't turn down. He was an old acquaintance, and my office is located across the street from the historic Custom House. My intention was to make a brief appearance, say hello, and then go directly home afterward and retire for the evening.

I stare at the missing man's face on the front page. His name was Sam Townsend and he's not been seen for a week. He came up from Boston to attend that corporate event and was never seen again. The article states that he worked in high finance and did a lot of business up here in Portland. He has a wife and three children, and his wife claims that he still hasn't answered any of her calls or texts.

The truth be told, I was there ten minutes before I noticed Gwynn, my longtime patient. I watched her from the opposite side of the room, surrounded by fellow associates who worked in the same building as I did. She looked elegant that night, dressed in an understated way that only enhanced her beauty. In therapy, she often expresses the belief that she doesn't feel pretty, but that's so far from the truth that I sometimes wonder if she's mining for compliments. Men in the room stared at her, but she hadn't seemed to notice. I was about to walk over and say hello, but then something stopped me. Her eyes were glued to someone across the room. The sheer concentration she expended on this person made me curious as to who she was staring at. I excused myself from the group and moved to another spot so I could get a better look.

It didn't take long to identify the object of her affection. Without a doubt, he was the most handsome man in the room, and for a few seconds, even I couldn't take my eyes off him. He stood in a circle of admirers, regaling them with some tale that I was not privy to. My eyes traveled back and forth between Gwynn and the Adonis she was ogling. Was it sexual attraction consuming her or something else?

By the time I had turned back to Gwynn, I noticed a man standing next to her and vying for her attention. He looked a few years older than her and was not even remotely her type. Finally, Gwynn turned and walked away. I placed my drink down and followed, hoping we could at least speak before I departed. I glanced back one last time at the well-dressed man, who now stood at the bar, ordering another cocktail. Then, I grabbed my coat and headed out.

But she wasn't anywhere to be seen. Had she gone to the ladies' room? As far as the event was concerned, I had no intention of returning inside and engaging in small talk with stock traders, accountants, and high financiers. And yet, I was concerned about Gwynn's mental state. She had that look on her face that gave me pause. I'd seen it many times before in our sessions.

So I stood across the street, hands in my pockets, allowing the rain to dampen my London Fog and fedora, hoping to be rewarded for my patience. Twenty minutes later, she emerged with the Adonis by her side. She'd recently separated from her husband, but I didn't expect her to be the kind of woman who would jump into bed with the first person she met. Yet I couldn't really blame her for choosing this particular specimen. She held his hand in her own and pulled him along the rainy Portland streets, stopping briefly to kiss. I followed a ways behind, a diminutive figure in a diminutive town, until they reached her vehicle. She climbed into the driver's seat and her Prince Charming stumbled drunkenly into the passenger side.

I watched as she sped off, turning right onto Congress Street before disappearing from sight.

Thinking about that evening, I stare down at my newspaper, certain that Gwynn was the last person to see Townsend before he went missing. My guess is that he's not coming back.

What have you done, my dear Gwynn?

Chapter Four

Although Detective Peters thought things couldn't get worse, they did when he discovered his cat dead on the floor this morning. Mango had lived to the ripe old age of seventeen. He'd adopted her before he'd met Beth, his ex-wife, and in many ways, he felt a deeper connection to his cat than he ever did for her. He was twenty when he adopted the adorable orange tabby, a present to himself for having earned his associate's degree in Criminal Justice from the community college. A month later, he'd gotten hired on by the Portland Police. Two months after that, he entered the police academy. Now, seventeen years later, he'd made it to detective. Despite all that, it seemed his career was permanently stuck in neutral.

To make matters worse, he'd lost three hundred dollars on the Patriots game last night after the kicker missed an easy field goal with seconds left in the game.

Now, he had a man's disappearance on his hands. And Portland was a town where people didn't just disappear. Two weeks ago, Sam Townsend vanished after a corporate event at the Custom House. Once Peters was assigned the case, he'd begun to compile a long list of persons to interview, which included everyone who had attended the function. He considered the possibility that it had been a random street crime, but after looking at all the facts, he rather doubted it. For starters, it was raining hard that night, and the Old Port had been relatively quiet. Townsend was a big guy, and would be difficult to overtake. He'd been an all-conference linebacker at Crawford, one of the most exclusive liberal arts colleges in the country. The likelihood of some street thugs taking him down seemed unlikely. Unless it was a professional hit. If that was the case, then where was his body? Some theorized that Townsend had gotten drunk and accidentally stumbled off the pier, but rescue divers had searched the depths off the wharf and found nothing. Nor did security cameras along the waterfront detect any evidence of Townsend walking along Commercial Street that evening. He'd scoured Townsend's personal history, and nothing struck him as unusual. If he'd been killed over money, it would have been unusual, considering that Townsend earned a healthy salary and his family lived comfortably in a nice suburb south of Boston. Maybe a business deal gone wrong? Or a drug deal? Even wealthy financiers were known to dabble in illicit activities.

He pulled up to the interviewee's house in Falmouth and studied it. Nice but not outlandish like a lot of the homes he'd already visited. He glanced down at the list and read the name of the interviewee: Gwynn Denning. Would she be another rich, stuck-up socialite like a lot of the others? Then he saw what she did for a living and thought otherwise. He sped-read through his notes and couldn't find any remote connection between her and the victim.

He exited his car and made his way up the path, eager to be done with this interview and on to the next one. With his reputation in tatters, thanks to that traffic-stop shooting a few years ago, he needed to solve this case in order to redeem himself in the eyes of his superiors.

Peters rang the doorbell and waited. A few seconds passed before the door opened. For a second, he couldn't breathe. It was not that she was the most beautiful woman he'd ever seen, but there was something about her that drew him in. Those blue eyes. The way she stood there smiling at him. The long, strawberry blonde hair and delicate features. It took him a moment to realize that she was waving him inside. For some reason, he couldn't take his eyes off her ass. Only the prospect of her catching him in the act forced him to look up.

"Are you coming in, Detective?"

"Sorry, it's been a rough morning."

"Anything I can help you with?"

32

"My cat died this morning."

"My condolences," she said. "Losing a pet is like losing a beloved member of your family."

"When you first get them, you never realize that this super cute animal will one day die and break your heart."

"It happens way too soon," she said. "Would you like a cup of coffee?"

"I'd love one."

He followed her inside, noticing that she was not wearing a wedding ring. But then he saw the action figures and trucks along the floor and realized she had a son. Unless she was divorced, it was a depressing sign for a single guy like himself. The inside of the house was a lot bigger than he expected. Rather than sit at the dining room table, she walked to the kitchen island and pulled out a stool for him. Slim and graceful, she moved easily between the island and the coffee pot. She poured two cups and then set the cups down on the granite countertop.

"I read that the missing man hasn't shown up yet," she said, sliding the cream and sugar toward him.

"He hasn't, and there's been absolutely no sign of him anywhere," he said, adding cream and sugar to his coffee before stirring it. "Thank you for meeting with me on such short notice. I know you must have a busy schedule at that home you work at."

"The Loft." She smiled, her lips glossed in an understated manner. "You've done your homework."

"Requirements of the job."

"Good work." She sipped her coffee, leaving a pink smudge on the rim of her cup. "I only wish I could be more helpful to you about the case."

"I take it you didn't know Sam Townsend?"

"The first I saw of him was when the newspaper put his photograph on the front page."

Peters took out his notebook and glanced at his list of questions, quickly eliminating most of them. Clearly, this woman would be of no help. Yet he didn't want to leave, as unprofessional as it was to flirt with one of his interviewees. But if he ended this now, he'd miss out on any chance he

<figure>33</figure>

might have with her. Besides, he had his coffee to finish, which he planned on milking for as long as possible. It had been a long time since he'd had coffee with such a beautiful and interesting woman.

"I see that you attended Brooks College. Impressive."

"The admissions officer must have taken pity on me." She laughed.

"I doubt that," he said. "Did your parents go there?"

"Oh, no. My father served in the Marines and then became a minister. My mother was a stay-at-home mom. She died of cancer when I was twenty-four."

"I'm sorry to hear that."

"Thank you," she said, lifting her cup in both hands. "The point is, I didn't come from money."

"Join the club," he said, looking down at his scribbled notes. "Did you know that the victim attended Crawford College around the same time you went to Brooks?"

"Yes, I read that in the newspaper. The campuses are over fifty miles apart, so it's unlikely I would have ever met him."

"You're probably right about that." He glanced up at her and tried not to stare. "Please don't take any of these questions personally, Mrs. Denning."

"You're only doing your job," she said. "And it's Gwynn."

"Okay, Gwynn." He liked the sound of her name. "Was your husband home when you returned from the event that evening?"

"We're technically separated. Tom had our son for the weekend and brought him back the next day."

He jotted this down to keep his hands busy, happy to discover that she was single. "In what capacity were you at that function?"

"Sandra Clayborn invited me. She's a bigwig at Plumhurst Capital. Otherwise, I never would have gone."

"And how do you know her?"

"We went to Brooks together. Plumhurst donates a great deal of money to The Loft."

"Do you ever socialize with Sandra and her husband?"

"God, no. I didn't even see her that evening because I left early. I wasn't feeling well."

"How long have you worked at The Loft?"

"Nine years now. Six as managing director."

"That must be a difficult job?"

"It's not easy at times, but it's been a lifelong passion of mine to help these children."

He looked up at her, tapping the eraser end of his pencil against the notebook page. "That's very noble of you, working with abused children."

"The same could be said of you. Seems we're addressing society's ills from different angles."

"Never thought about it like that."

"You and I are alike in many ways; we do our jobs because we love it, not for the money."

"I suppose that's true," he said, trying not to think about his sorry-ass bank account.

"When did your cat die, Detective?"

"Just this morning. I covered him with a towel and plan on taking him to the vet after work." He liked the way she held her coffee mug in both hands, the steam swirling in front of her face.

"You should give him a proper burial."

"You think."

"Of course. Animals have souls, too," she said. "When I was a young girl, I was so distraught when my dog died I couldn't even get out of bed. My father and I said a few prayers for Chester, and then we buried him in the woods behind our house. We covered his grave with some of his favorite toys and doggy snacks."

"That sounds nice," he said. "How did he die?"

"He was attacked by a neighbor's dog."

"That sucks," he said, disappointed that his cup was almost empty. Should he ask for a refill? No, better not to push his luck. "Thank you so much for your time, Gwynn."

"My pleasure, Detective."

"Please, call me Mike."

"Okay," she said. "I really must be getting back to work now, unless there's anything else I can do for you."

"No, I think I have everything I need at the moment."

She escorted him to the door and held out her hand. He took it in his own and felt a jolt of electricity shoot up through his arm. Was he imagining it, or did she feel the same chemistry as he did?

* * *

The next day, Peters drove down to Massachusetts to see if he could learn more about Sam Townsend. He'd already interviewed the man's wife last week. She traveled up from Boston: blonde, gorgeous, and entitled, and driving a black Mercedes EQS worth almost as much as he made in a year. Surprisingly, she didn't appear overly concerned that her husband had gone missing. What did that mean? A troubled marriage? Infidelity? Or was this merely the emotional shell of a pretentious Boston blue blood?

He couldn't stop thinking about Gwynn while cruising down Route 95. She'd occupied his mind all last night while he was trying to sleep. Would it be unprofessional to ask her out for coffee sometime? Clearly, she had nothing to do with the disappearance of Sam Townsend.

Townsend's house was located south of Boston, in a wealthy development along the water. Peters drove past the colonial, amazed that someone could amass that much money before the age of forty. His own bank account had less than six hundred dollars in it, a good portion of his paycheck going to paying off gambling debts and rent. If only he could achieve some degree of success in his chosen profession, being poor would be more tolerable. He blamed that scumbag he gunned down for much of his recent woes. And his divorce.

After viewing the house, he drove back up to Boston and to the skyscraper in Post Office Square where Townsend once worked. He parked in the garage, went inside, and took the elevator up to the twenty-first floor. A perky receptionist greeted him. He showed her his badge, and she escorted him to the department Townsend once managed. Before leaving, he asked the girl if she knew anything about her boss, and she claimed that she merely greeted him when he came into the building each morning.

No one had anything bad to say about Sam Townsend, but no one had anything great to say about him, either. They spoke in platitudes, saying what a devoted husband and father he'd been. Apparently, he'd made a lot of money for Trenton Capital and for himself. The pretty secretaries at his pod seemed detached and reserved, keeping whatever ugly truths they might have known about their boss to themselves. As he left the facility, Peters had the strange feeling that there was more to Sam Townsend than people were letting on.

He headed back to Portland, thinking about Gwynn when he should have been focused on solving this case. If he could somehow catch a break on this missing-person investigation, it would go a long way toward putting his career back on track. Maybe, if the planets aligned, he could get his love life back on track, too. And maybe that would be with Gwynn.

Chapter Five

G wynn's heart raced as soon as Detective Peters left the house. Had he felt the same chemistry that she had? If she had any doubt about getting back with Tom, Peters effectively slammed that door shut. She'd felt the jolt of electricity as soon as she'd opened the door, and their eyes locked. Rarely, if ever, had she experienced such a strong physical attraction to another human being, except, ironically, when she was ending their life. Of course, that was an altogether different kind of attraction. If only he'd asked her out for coffee, she would have said yes. Maybe she could call him at the station and invite him out, but that would seem tacky and desperate.

She glanced at her watch and saw that she was running late. After putting the coffee cups in the dishwasher, she jumped in her car and drove straight to the hospital to see Ivy. Her thoughts alternated between Peters and Townsend and that ominous text message that had been sent to her. As she drove, she recalled the look of terror in Sam Townsend's eyes after she slipped that plastic bag over his face. Then how the bag contracted and expanded during his final moments on earth. It gave her goosebumps just thinking about it, so much so that she had to pull over to the side of the road to collect herself. The soreness in her ribs from where he kicked her was a reminder to her that it wasn't a dream but really happened. A few minutes passed before she pulled back onto the street.

Gwynn remembered that she had an upcoming therapy session with Kaufman. What would he say at their next meeting? Would he ascribe her good mood to something else? She couldn't confess to him what she did to

Sam Townsend, nor the positive effect it had on her mood.

A mile from her office, she began to think about the first time she murdered someone. Like her first kiss, she would always remember the first time she took another person's life. His name was Mr. Teehan, and he was her freshman gym teacher and JV soccer coach. Over the summer, her friend Eadie Kane had confided in her that Teehan had done some vile things to her in the locker room one afternoon after all the other girls had gone home. A few weeks later, a girl named Caitlyn Tedeschi relayed a similar story to her in more graphic detail. Both girls were terrified that their secrets would be made public and that they'd be ostracized by teachers and students alike, so they made Gwynn swear to never tell anyone. The fact that both girls had behavioral issues didn't, for one moment, make her believe that the girls were lying. Because of their troubled pasts, she knew no one would ever believe their stories of molestation and rape by a beloved teacher.

A few months later, she arrived at school one day to learn that Eadie had taken her own life. The news devastated her, and the school brought in extra counselors that day. They allowed students to stay home if they needed more time to grieve. She remembered transitioning from shock to rage, knowing that her gym teacher was responsible for Eadie's death. A feeling of revulsion consumed her, and she knew that if given the opportunity, as unlikely as that might be, she would kill the bastard. She had no idea how to process her feelings or shape them into any cognizant plan. She just knew that she would do it if given the chance and that her sins would be forgiven.

Later that year, she learned that her gym class was to go on a school hiking trip on one of the nearby mountains and that Mr. Teehan would be one of the chaperones. The trip was optional, but she signed up for it, having hiked it many times with her father. She had no idea what she would do, but she felt like there might be an opportunity somewhere along the way. She wore extra-tight shorts and an athletic tank top. At one point, he sidled up to her on the trail, whispering where they might go to get some privacy. Gwynn remembered smiling at him and then asking what he had in mind. He explained what he would like her to do if they found themselves alone for a few minutes. When he asked where they could meet, she suggested an out-of-the-way ridge on the other side of the trail that was rarely used by hikers.

With about a hundred yards to the peak, she took off running. There were only fifteen other students on the trip, all scattered along the trail. Mr. Cantina led the way at the top, and Mrs. Pierce covered the rear, out-of-shape and sweating profusely. No one saw Teehan slip off the footpath and follow her to the opposite side of the mountain. She remembered jogging over to a clearing that gave hikers an unobstructed view of the White Mountains. Out of breath, Teehan pulled up next to her, a mischievous grin on his face. She recalled the thrill she felt standing on that edge, looking off in the distance at snow-capped Mount Washington, as well down at the jagged rocks hundreds of feet below. He cupped her cheek and kissed her. Then he placed his hands on the crown of her head and pushed her down to her knees. As he pulled down his polyester sweatpants, she swiveled him around so that his back faced the edge. It was the first erection she had ever seen, and she didn't know what to make of it.

Reflecting back on that moment, she recalled how he gazed down at her with that strange look men got before instructing her what to do. Grabbing her hand, he told her to massage his penis in a certain way. Gwynn lifted her arms, and instead of doing what he asked, she shoved him with all her might. He toppled backward, his arms helicoptering as if to prevent himself from falling. She leaned over the edge, and their eyes locked. His body fell as if suspended from a cord attached to his abdomen. Then it was over. His head exploded upon hitting the granite cropping. She thought it was one of the most amazing things she'd ever seen. Her exhilaration was quickly replaced by a brief wave of nausea.

She didn't stay long to admire her work; instead, she sprinted back to the trail and joined up with the others. What would her parents think if they knew she'd pushed a man to his death? She felt like she had done a good thing. Meted out punishment when no one else would. Teehan would never again hurt another innocent girl. Every night thereafter, she prayed for God's forgiveness, no matter how vile the crimes that teacher committed seemed to her.

The sound of her phone ringing jolted her back to the present. She turned into the hospital's parking lot and answered it.

"Hey, Gwynn. I can't believe we didn't run into each other at the Custom House."

"I'm sorry, Sandra. I wasn't feeling well and headed home early."

"Probably a good decision, considering what happened afterward."

"Yes, it's unfortunate about that missing man."

"Probably ran off to Mexico to start an avocado farm." She laughed. "What can I do for you?"

"I'd like for us to sit down and have a chat."

"A chat about what?"

"Do I have to spell everything out for you?"

"It might help if you did."

Sandra paused for a few seconds. "You knew who Sam Townsend was because you met him back at Brooks."

Gwynn froze upon hearing this. Had she not thought everything through? Had she left some loose ends?

"I remembered him when I saw his picture in the newspaper. He came into our dorm room one night to pick up Tift."

"I suppose it doesn't matter now."

"No, I suppose not."

"Tift had that effect on guys, especially the straight ones," Sandra said. "Anyways, Tift told me what Townsend did to her."

This revelation stunned Gwynn. "Did you tell the detective about it?"

"Of course not. I swore to Tift that I would never tell another soul about what Townsend did to her. I assume you made the same pledge?"

"Yes."

"I'd like you to come over to my place Saturday evening so that you and I can talk. William will be spending the night at his friend's house playing poker. They smoke cigars, drink expensive booze, and tell tall tales."

"Does it have to be this Saturday? I have custody of my son."

"You and Tom are divorced?"

"Separated."

"Sorry to hear that," she said. Sandra had, for whatever reason, always disliked Tom. And Tom hated her just as vehemently. "I strongly suggest you find a babysitter."

"Okay, I'll figure something out," she said. "What time do you want me there?"

"Five sound good?"

"Five will work."

"Plan on staying the night so we can drink expensive wine to our heart's content. I'll have Dimillo's send over some chilled lobsters and some freshly shucked oysters. We'll cap our meal off with some strawberry shortcake."

"Great. I'll see you then."

Gwynn sat in her car, wondering what Sandra knew about Townsend's disappearance. She was certain that no one saw her leave with him. Or maybe someone had, and that someone had been Sandra. If Sandra did see her leave with Townsend, why hadn't she called the police? The only way of finding out was to go over to her house Saturday night and hear what she had to say.

A ripple of anxiety swept over her. Sweating, she reached inside her purse, took a pill out of the orange vial, and swallowed it. Her mind warbled, and her vision became opaque, as if she was looking out a glass shower stall. She reminded herself that these were only thoughts and not reality. Kaufman had advised her to perform some grounding exercises whenever she started to feel this way. It meant separating her thoughts from reality. She knew the routine: touch objects in front of her. Focus on her breathing. Be in the moment.

She struggled now with the task, her mind returning to Sandra and what she had inferred. Tomorrow, she would meet with Kaufman. Then she would go over to Sandra's house on Saturday and find out what she knew.

She would do whatever necessary to stay out of prison. Jack needed her. And she needed him. Tom raising Jack would be the worst possible outcome. He would destroy her precious boy and turn him into a miniature version of himself.

Chapter Six

She sat on the bed next to Ivy and held the sleeping girl's hand in her own. Ivy looked angelic, masking the horrors she had been forced to live through during her short time on this planet. Thick bandages covered her wrist from where she had cut herself.

Ivy had come to The Loft after CPS removed her from her home, claiming it had been an unsafe place for children. There were indications of sexual and physical abuse by family members, but nothing was ever proven in court, and then the charges against her father were summarily dropped. Gwynn had no doubt that Ivy's father preyed on her and her brother. The girl had admitted as much during her intake interview. There had been questionable trips to the ER and countless visits by case managers. Yet, time after time, Ivy and her brother managed to slip through the cracks designed to protect them. And although Ivy claimed to love her parents, Gwynn knew the truth of the matter. Ivy's mother was a fragile person, too weak to stand up to her cruel husband. Women like her fell for violent, manipulative men, had no backbone, and succumbed easily to drugs and alcohol, leaving their children to bear the brunt of their bad choices.

It seemed unfathomable to think that Ivy would choose to return to such a dysfunctional home, but Gwynn understood how an abused child could have such complex feelings. No matter the violence and despair that permeated a child's home life, blood was still thicker than water.

One of the doctors came into the room and stood at the foot of the bed, staring down at her notes. For a moment, Gwynn wondered if she'd picked a bad time to visit. But then the doctor turned to her and smiled.

"She's sedated and won't wake up for a while," the woman said.

"Is she okay?"

"She'll be fine—physically, anyway. Despite all the blood she's lost, the cuts weren't too deep."

Gwynn turned and studied Ivy's profile. Under the heavy lines of black mascara and multicolored hair strands, she saw a beautiful girl with a potentially bright future in front of her.

"She's done this before," Gwynn said.

"I know. I saw the scarring."

"Her family history is not a pretty sight."

"My heart goes out to children like her. I feel so lucky to have been raised by such loving parents."

"Me too," Gwynn said, wondering how her life would have turned out had she not been given up for adoption.

"Sometimes I think that people who hurt children don't deserve to…well, I probably said too much."

Gwynn stiffened.

"I don't think she'll be waking up anytime soon, but you're welcome to stay until the end of visiting hours."

"Thank you," Gwynn said, "but I have to be getting back to the office."

"Don't worry, the nurses will take good care of her."

"I'm sure they will," she said. "Do you know when she might be released?"

"Maybe tomorrow. The day after at the latest." The doctor walked out of the room.

Gwynn brushed a few strands of purple hair out of Ivy's eyes. Resisting the urge to cry, she leaned over and kissed the girl's forehead before heading out. Once in her car, she sat quietly for a few minutes, trying to tamp down the rage consuming her. Everywhere she turned, she saw the chaos and destruction left in the wake of bad people, and it was all she could do to keep her violent urges from bubbling to the surface.

Dr. Ezra Kaufman

wynn emerged from my office in a daze. Somehow, this session seemed different from all the others. Was it because of what happened to Townsend?

Gwynn started seeing me when she was sixteen, not long after that gym teacher fell to his death. Rescuers found the teacher's body over the slab of granite, his pants down by his knees, his skull cracked open. From that they concluded that he was relieving himself when he slipped and fell.

Mostly, she talked about her struggles with anxiety and feelings of abandonment at being adopted. She talked openly about how the death of that beloved gym teacher had affected her, and how she felt her faith in God was wavering. Why, she asked, was God allowing innocent children to get hurt and sometimes die?

I knew that the abandonment issue didn't bother her as much as she'd let on, but she could tell that it intrigued me whenever she brought the subject up. At one point, I suggested that she might one day consider tracking down her biological mother and having a conversation with the woman. But she didn't care to push the envelope back then, because the truth was, getting adopted at such young age had likely saved her life. Although her mother was a quiet and reserved woman, Gwynn loved her fiercely. As for her father, a minister, she thought him the kindest and most generous man she had ever known.

So it troubled her that she harbored these dark fantasies, especially after being raised in such a loving, Christian household. For whatever reason, she came to believe that she inherited these genes from her biological parents.

Even I had to admit that her dissociative disorder and delusional thoughts might have been inherited traits. It's why I prescribed different medicines for her, and changed them whenever the effects of one medication began to diminish. It was all a delicate, chemical balancing act.

There were times when she would call me at two in the morning, sobbing, and I had to talk her through a particularly difficult episode. There were also times when she demanded that I listen to her long-winded and deluded notions. Deep down, she knows that I've always done what's best for her.

During today's session, I suggested two things that surprised her. The first was that she go ahead and try to track down her biological mother. Coming to terms with this facet of her life might help her achieve closure with the past. It was an idea she had always considered but never had the will to pursue. Then I mentioned that I'd seen her at the Custom House the night Townsend disappeared. She explained that she had a splitting headache that evening and left early. Had she suspected that I knew what she had done? If there was anyone in this world who knew her almost as well as she knew herself, it was me.

There was one last thing I added before she left. I encouraged her to keep journaling, stating that pursuing such a creative endeavor would help her work through all her emotional issues. Writing was restorative and healing. She smiled when I mentioned this, because she was extremely self-conscious about the kind of stories she was writing, stories she never let me read. But she was proud of them, informing me that she planned on converting them into scripts and showing them to her friend Tift, a successful actress out in Hollywood. I knew the likelihood of them ever getting produced was low, but at least it gave Gwynn something to work toward. It gave her a creative and restorative outlet, allowing her to channel her darkest urges in a productive way.

I stand at the window and watch as she gets in her SUV. Why do I always feel such an emptiness when she leaves?

Chapter Seven

Gwynn called Tom and asked if he'd watch Jack despite it not being his weekend to have him. He agreed to help her; he always did. Then she went upstairs and helped Jack pack his clothes and toys for the weekend.

"But I thought I was staying with you, Mommy," Jack said, looking up at her from his bed with the saddest of eyes.

"What's the matter, hon? I thought you loved hanging out with your dad."

"I do, but you said we could go to the Children's Museum this weekend and get ice cream cones at Red's after."

"Next weekend, I promise," she said. "Maybe Daddy will take you to the Children's Museum."

"He likes playing video games with me instead."

"Daddy should take you outside and get you some exercise and fresh air."

"Aunt Trish says he might move back in with us," Jack said, hands on his chubby cheeks.

"She did?"

He nodded. "I want Daddy to move back home. That way, you guys won't have to share me no more."

She sat next to him, his look of concern breaking her heart. "Don't get your hopes up, buddy, because that's probably not going to happen."

"Aunty Trish asked me if you had a boyfriend."

"You tell Aunt Trish that my only boyfriend is a little dude named Wiggleworm," she said, touching the tip of his nose. "Now grab your bag, and let's bounce."

Trish had no business asking Jack about whom she was dating. She needed to have a talk with Tom about his busy-body sister and tell her to back off.

She drove over to Tom's place, feeling guilty about leaving Jack with him in his tiny apartment overlooking Deering Oaks. She knocked on the door until Tom finally answered. He was dressed in wrinkled sweats and looked exhausted. His belly protruded from his gray Brooks College sweatshirt, making him look six months pregnant. Gwynn peered over his shoulder and saw what she could only describe as a bachelor's pad. A soiled plate sat on the arm of the couch next to a pile of dirty laundry. Empty pizza boxes rested on the trash bin. He explained that the apartment was only temporary until things became more settled between them. Tom squatted and lifted Jack into his arms.

"Hi, buddy," he said, kissing his son's cheek.

"Hi, Daddy."

"Thanks for taking him on such short notice," Gwynn said.

"No problem." Tom smiled, but it didn't appear genuine. He put Jack down and instructed him to go inside and put his bag away. "Big date tonight?"

"You're not going to start on me now, are you?"

"I know, I know. It's none of my business." He held up his hands.

"For your information, I'm going out with an old friend." She thought of telling him that she was going over to Sandra's house but decided against it. "I'll make it up to you, Tom."

"How about making it up to me by letting us be a family again."

"That's not what I meant."

"Whatever happened to that pact we made? That we would marry each other if we hadn't met anyone by the time we were thirty? Marriage is supposed to be for life."

"We never said anything about splitting up."

"I'll go to counseling if you want. I won't be so meddling if you just give me one more chance. Living without you is killing me."

"It's not that simple."

"Then what is it?"

"We both know that we're better off as friends."

"I hate that word. It's possibly the most despicable one in the English dictionary."

"I'm sorry you feel that way."

"Did you ever really love me?"

"Of course I loved you," she said, although she wasn't entirely sure now. "I certainly didn't love how insecure you were when it came to our relationship."

"I only did those things because I was concerned about your safety."

"Constantly asking me where I was going and calling me ten times a day at work?"

"It won't happen again, I promise."

"It should have never happened to begin with."

"Is there someone else? You can tell me the truth."

"There's no one else, Tom. Besides, I'm far too busy raising Jack, caring for my father, and dealing with work to even think about dating."

"At least consider what I said."

"Sure," she said more to shut him up. "Another late night at work?"

"Me and Uncle Sam have been going toe-to-toe lately. I worked on tax returns until about ten last night, and then a bunch of us went out for beers at The Kings Head," he said, swiping his greasy bangs over the back of his scalp. "Wouldn't have stayed out so late had I known I'd be watching Jack."

"You don't know how much I appreciate this."

"I might take Jack up to the cabin this weekend if I get the chance."

"Do you think that's a good idea?" Alarms went off in her head, thinking about Townsend's body resting at the bottom of that quarry.

"Beats sitting around this dump all day. Might take him fishing, too."

"Have fun if you do," she said, confident she'd covered all her tracks. "One other thing, Tom. Make Trish stop telling Jack that we're getting back together."

"I had no idea she was saying that."

"Well, she is. If you don't tell her to butt out, then I will."

"You know my sister. She's not afraid to speak her mind."

She turned and scampered back to her car, paranoid that she'd somehow tripped up and left something behind at the cabin.

Her hands trembled as she slipped behind the wheel and drove over to Sandra's house. She took a deep breath as she sped onto 295, convinced that no one knew she had killed Sam Townsend.

Not Tom.

Not Kaufman.

Not Detective Peters.

Not even Sandra—she hoped.

So, who the hell had sent her that message?

Chapter Eight

Gwynn pulled up to Sandra's house located on Cousins Island, amazed at the size of it. She'd never been here before, only heard about it from other alumni. Glancing around, she couldn't see any other homes near it. The scent of an ocean breeze blew off the water. She parked in the driveway, walked up the steps, and dinged the doorbell.

As she waited, she recalled her time at Brooks College. Like many students, they were the best four years of her life. She remembered all the hours she and Tift had spent together, sipping coffee at the college café and talking about their futures. Gwynn had opened up to Tift and told her about being adopted, as well as her various mental health issues, with the exception of the one issue she could never mention to anyone. And Tift, in turn, had told her about her absent parents and how she grew up in Malibu. According to Tift, both of her parents were distant, emotionally cold, and never around for her and her two siblings.

Moving to Maine to attend Brooks College had been the best move of Tift's life. She delighted in the people and the culture, discovering that Mainers were way more grounded than the people out in LA. To her delight, Tift even seemed to enjoy the long and cold winters. Of course, Tift would never live in Maine; she was always destined to return to the City of Angels and become a star.

The fact that Gwynn and Tift had completely different backgrounds bound them in a way like nothing else. At parties, they were inseparable and constantly watched out for each other, making sure no one spiked their drinks. Tift even got them fake IDs, which allowed them to spend many a night at the local pubs, drinking stale beer and getting to know one another better. Or else they'd go to one of the clubs in town and listen to Tom's band play. One time, when they were freshmen, Tift even got up onstage and sang a scintillating version of 'Zombie' with his band, getting a standing ovation afterwards. The first time Gwynn heard Tift sing, Gwynn was blown away by the pitch of her voice. Tift had other friends at school, but none as close as Gwynn. And Gwynn knew that the other girls at Brooks were envious of her because of their tight friendship. She'd even invited Tift to stay with her and her parents over Christmas break one year. They went ice skating at Deering Oaks, sledding down Two Lights hill, and took long, bundled-up walks around the Eastern Promenade while conversing about their favorite books and movies.

But there was something about Tift that alluded her. Yes, she was a drama queen and liked being the center of attention. But there was something else, something off-kilter about her friend that she couldn't quite put her finger on. Maybe she was too blinded by the force of Tift's personality to notice the small, disturbing warts trying to poke their way out.

Although Gwynn and Sandra hung out in the same social circle, they were never really friends. Sandra was one of the many girls in competition for Tift's friendship. Sandra acted civil around Gwynn and invited her to all the cool parties, but only as a means to get closer to Tift. To do otherwise would have alienated her, and that was the last thing Sandra ever wanted.

But Sandra wasn't the only one seeking Tift's friendship. Tift had been the object of everyone's desire at Brooks, especially the boys. Even some of the professors. In some ways, Gwynn often felt like she dwelled in her long shadow. Tift was destined for greatness someday, be that as a singer, model, or actress, and everyone knew it. She starred in all the college's theater productions and, on occasion, sang and played guitar at open mic night. Gwynn felt honored that Tift had chosen her to be her best friend—and that infuriated some of the other girls as the years wore on. Gwynn sensed that Sandra felt this way, too, despite Sandra's considerable academic and athletic achievements, which landed her at Harvard Business School and then managing partner at Plumhurst Capital.

The door opened, and Sandra appeared with a welcoming smile. She invited Gwynn inside and embraced her. Gwynn followed her up the stairs and into the home's living room. The entire eastern wall was composed of glass, giving her a full view of Casco Bay. The hardwood floors gleamed, accentuating the grains. Against one of the nearby walls was a massive stone fireplace. As someone who toiled in the field of social work, she wondered if she'd made the right career choice. Yet despite the low pay and long hours, she knew that working to better children's lives was her calling in life.

"What do you think?" Sandra spun around and held out her toned arm like Vanna White flipping a panel.

"It's breathtaking," she said, staring out at the water.

"William and I fell in love with the place the moment we laid eyes on it. Initially, we put in an offer, but someone beat us to the punch. Fortunately, their deal fell through, and we were able to swoop in and scoop it up before it hit the market again."

"Lucky for you. This house is amazing."

"We had a good deal of work done on it before we moved in, but I think it was money well spent."

"I'll say. It's so quiet out here. And it looks like you have the entire shore to yourself." Gwynn walked over to the window and stared out it, seeing a sandy beach and a long dock stretching into the bay. Tied up at the end of the dock was a small boat with an outboard motor. She couldn't see another home in any direction.

"The privacy aspect was the biggest selling point. We're out on a jetty, and the nearest house is a quarter mile away."

"You mean to say that all this beach property is yours?"

"It sure is. Every morning, I take a long swim in the bay. Except for the occasional lobster boat, I rarely see anyone else out there. It's just me and the gulls."

"You were such a good swimmer back at Brooks."

"We're not college girls anymore, Gwynn. It takes a lot to keep these figures of ours."

"Tell me about it. I struggle every day to get in my workouts."

"So sad to hear about you and Tom splitting up."

"I suppose people change as they grow older."

"He was like the chillest guy back in college. Everyone loved him."

"They sure did."

"He played a mean guitar, too." Sandra laughed. "Remember that band he played in around town? Dirt Fish? Thought they were going to be the next big thing."

"True, but we all thought they were amazing at the time, especially after a few beers." Gwynn laughed at the memory of Tom shredding chords while his long blond hair hung over his eyes.

"You're right about that. And all the girls swooned whenever his band played a Dave Matthews song," she said, gesturing for Gwynn to sit. "Would you like something to drink?"

"Whatever you're having is fine with me."

"I'll grab a bottle of Chardonnay and throw away the cap. You are planning on staying the night, right?"

She lifted her bag to show her.

"Good. I was hoping we could let our hair down and catch up on old times. William is at his friend's house for the evening, playing cards. A bunch of them get together once a month to play Texas Hold'em, drink scotch, and smoke expensive cigars."

"Remind me again how you and William met?"

"William was studying law at BU at the same time I was attending Harvard Business School. He came over to me one night at the Pour House while I was out with some friends. After a quick introduction, he commented on how beautiful I was."

"Cut right to the chase. Smart move."

"Although I was flattered, I thought him a bullshit artist and ignored him. He then handed me a box seat ticket to the Red Sox game and asked if I'd meet him there the next day. I'd never been to a Sox game before, never mind sitting in a box seat, so I took a chance on him. And that's how our whirlwind romance began. I fell in love with the Red Sox that day, too," she said.

"What a cool story."

"It is cool," Sandra said. "Are you still writing?"

"How did you know about that?"

"Tift always commented about what a great writer you were. A little twisted, but great."

"She said that about me?"

"Yes. Tift really thought you had a talent for it. Too bad you never pursued a writing career."

This backhanded compliment pissed her off. "Actually, I am writing some stories I hope to turn into scripts. I sent them to Tift, and she thinks they're pretty good."

"That's wonderful. Are they currently in production?"

Gwynn turned and stared out at the water. "Not yet, but Tift says they have potential."

"I'm sure they do."

Sandra walked over to the kitchen, which was attached to the living room, and returned with a bottle of wine and two glasses. They sat for a while, discussing their college days and all the students and professors they encountered back at Brooks. The first few glasses of wine relaxed her, but she knew she couldn't rest easy until she discovered why Sandra had invited her here. For some reason, the subject of Tift never came up. As the sun started to set, and the sky over the water turned purple, Gwynn began to relax, aided in part by the wine. She knew she shouldn't be drinking too much, knowing it interacted with her meds, but she was so at ease right now that she felt everything would be alright. Sandra had mellowed over the years and seemed less acerbic than she remembered her being in college. Still, she knew not to trust the woman.

The ocean appeared smooth and glasslike. After a brief lull in the conversation, Sandra gave her a quick tour of the house. Gwynn shuffled mindlessly through the bedrooms upstairs, each wonderfully furnished and with its own view of the bay. Afterward, Sandra showed her the kitchen and finished basement, where William's man cave was located. Another room in the basement was outfitted with a wine cellar, an elaborate bar, flat-screen TV, and a climate-controlled cigar room. At the far end, she saw a fully equipped gym that rivaled many of the professional gyms Gwynn had signed up for but rarely used. What caught her eye, however, was the assortment of kettlebells along the floor, and it reminded her of how she had pushed Sam Townsend's corpse into that quarry.

Sandra snatched a bottle out of the wine cellar before heading back upstairs.

"Would you like to eat now?"

"Maybe in a little bit," Gwynn said, sitting on one of the sofas. "I'm enjoying myself way too much to eat at the moment."

"Of course. Let me know when you start to get hungry. In the meantime, let's enjoy some of this delicious Cabernet from Caymus Vineyard." She poured some into two glasses.

"Gwynn took a sip of her wine. "This is soooo good."

"It better be for eight hundred dollars a bottle."

"Eight hundred?"

"William and I love our wine. And this is a special occasion."

"I'll say." Gwynn craned her neck toward the bay. "Do you ever use that boat tied up on the dock?"

"The Boston Whaler? William uses it to check his traps every now and then."

Gwynn laughed at this. "William lobsters on the side?"

"Oh, yes. He got his recreational license after we purchased this place. He claims it helps him deal with the stress of being a criminal defense lawyer."

"Not a bad hobby, especially when you get to have free lobster every night."

"Trust me, it would be much cheaper to go to Harbor Fish Market and buy them live. Those lobsters he catches probably cost us a hundred dollars a pound after everything is said and done," Sandra said, laughing. "We have a sailboat moored at the yacht club, but William loves jumping in the Whaler when the mood strikes him, especially in the summer when the days are warm."

"Must be nice to just go out and take a spin around the bay."

"It is. Feel free to use it come morning if you like. He leaves the key right in it."

"Thanks. I might just take you up on that."

"Just make sure you put on the life jacket. Hate to have something bad happen to you out there," Sandra said, petting the Miniature Poodle that had jumped in her lap.

Gwynn sipped her wine. "So why did you ask me here, Sandra? Not merely to wax nostalgic about our college days."

"Like I said, we didn't get a chance to talk at the Custom House."

"I know, and I'm sorry about that. I saw you were busy with clients, and then I came down with a splitting headache."

"A headache, yes." Sandra sipped her wine and smiled. "That was one fine-looking headache you came down with."

"What's that supposed to mean?"

"We've barely discussed the elephant in the room."

"And that is?"

"Tift, for starters."

Gwynn laughed. "Wasn't everything about Tift back at Brooks?"

"We can't deny that we were both competing for her friendship."

"We were young and immature back in college."

"No arguing with that," Sandra said. "What about Sam Townsend?"

The sound of his name sent a shock wave through her. "What about him?"

"Don't play coy with me."

"I swear to you I'm not."

"We both know what he did to Tift that night."

Gwynn remained quiet, staring out at the pink sky.

"That bastard hurt our friend."

"Before you called me the other day, I never knew that Tift told you about that."

"Don't flatter yourself, Gwynn. Did you really believe you were the only person Tift confided in at Brooks?"

"I never said I was."

57

"No, but you always believed that you were her most trusted confidante. I often suspected that Tift gave you your identity back in college."

"Now, that's not a very nice thing to say, especially after we've been having such a nice time this evening."

"It wasn't meant to be mean, just an observation. We were all searching for our identity back at Brooks; only some were looking harder than others."

"You couldn't be more wrong about that," Gwynn said, knowing that Sandra had no idea about her real identity or that Tift had unwittingly helped keep her real identity in check all those years.

"Am I wrong?"

"Absolutely."

"Okay, there was that complicated relationship you had with Tom. And admittedly, you were a good student, even if you did major in sociology."

"With a minor in creative writing, don't forget."

"Yes, that too," Sandra said. "But when I think back on those days, my most vivid memory of you is standing alongside Tift."

"You should refresh your memory, then, because there were a lot better things for you to recall than that."

Sandra tried not to show any emotion, but Gwynn could see the frustration building behind her eyes. "You said you still talk to Tift."

"From time to time." It was at least once a month, in fact. Sometimes more when Tift was feeling needy.

"I assume she made you swear never to tell anyone about what Sam Townsend did to her."

Gwynn nodded, wondering what Sandra was getting at. She put her glass of wine down, finished drinking for the night. "If you knew what an evil person Sam Townsend was, why did you invite him to your company's function?"

"We've been trying to get his firm's account for years now, to no avail. I'd been waiting for the right time to confront him about what he did to Tift and parlay it into a business deal."

"You were going to profit off Tift's trauma?"

"Why not?"

"That seems pretty coldhearted, even for you."

"I'm an enterprising and ambitious businesswoman," she said, refilling her glass. "Besides, I wanted to make that prick pay for what he did. The statute of limitations on that crime has expired, and we both know how traumatic it was for Tift."

"She was a basket case for months."

"At one point, some of the girls even became worried about her mental state."

"We all tried to be there for her," Gwynn said. "Still, I find it troubling that you were looking to profit from that crime."

"How else was I going to get back at him? Tift didn't want it to become an issue. And Townsend can't be prosecuted for what he had done."

"True," Gwynn said, knowing that Townsend had paid with his life.

"Do you know how much money our firm donates to The Loft each year?"

The question threw Gwynn off.

"A pretty penny. And I was going to donate a lot more from the deal I was planning to make with Townsend's firm, but I guess that's water under the bridge now that he's gone."

"He might still be alive."

Sandra laughed a bit drunkenly. "Please, we both know that's not true."

"Maybe he just ran off with one of his floozies."

"Floozies? Did he tell you he had one?"

"Tell me?" Gwynn laughed. "I have no idea what you're talking about."

"Oh, I think you do." Sandra lifted her glass and drained the rest of her wine. "I had my eye on Townsend most of the night, waiting for the right moment I could corner him and make him an offer. Then I glanced across the room and noticed that you were watching him in the same manner that I was. But why? At least I had an ulterior motive for doing so."

"I was not watching him."

"Were too."

"Can we please act like adults?"

"Then tell me why you left the Custom House with him?"

The accusation nearly floored Gwynn, but she managed to keep her composure. "I told you, Sandra, I left early on account of my headache."

"Stop lying to me and just admit what you did. Nothing you say ever has to leave this room."

Her body felt on fire. She looked at Sandra and saw someone out to ruin her life and leave Jack an orphan.

"Okay, so maybe I did leave with him. So what?"

"It's why I want you to talk to Tift for me."

"Why can't you talk to her yourself?"

"Believe me, I've tried many times, but Tift obviously doesn't want to talk to anyone these days, even the old friends she went to college with. I imagine there are many layers of red tape to reach her out in LA."

"Why do you want to talk to her?"

"Do you know how beneficial she could be to my career? Access to all her rich and famous friends out in LA, many of whom might find my firm's services helpful. But even more important to me is the breast cancer race I sponsor every summer. Did you know that it's the second biggest charitable event in the state of Maine?"

"Sure, I knew that." The event was a scenic ninety-mile bike ride from Portland to Camden and then a swim across Casco Bay.

"Then you know what a great cause it is. My mother died from breast cancer."

"My mother did, too."

"Then I'm sure Tift would agree to be a co-sponsor if you be the one to ask her. I want this charity to be number one."

"I can try, Sandra, but I can't promise you anything."

"You should do more than try. I'd hate to show that detective the photograph I took of you and Sam Townsend walking hand in hand down Fore Street. I was up in one of the second-floor offices when I snapped it, and I'm fairly certain that you'd be easy to identify, especially since you two lovebirds shared a kiss."

Gwynn realized she was screwed. "So it was you who sent me that text message."

"Of course, it was me."

Gwynn chastised herself for being so stupid and kissing Townsend on the street. Why hadn't she waited until they got back to the car?

"The kiss really surprised me, but then again, I've always sensed that there was something a little dangerous about you."

"Don't be silly."

"Trust me, there's not a silly bone in this magnificent body."

"Your mind is playing tricks on you, Sandra. Or maybe it's all the expensive wine you've been drinking tonight."

"Whatever you did to Townsend, we both know he deserved it. I don't blame you one bit if you did what I think you did."

Gwynn bit her lower lip.

"Sleep on it. You don't need to make a decision right now, but it would make it much easier on you and your family if you did agree to cooperate with me."

Gwynn considered this threat. "No, you're right. I don't see why Tift can't give something back for all the good she's received in life."

"I'm so glad we see eye to eye on this matter," Sandra said, clapping her hands together. "Look, Gwynn, I don't judge you for whatever you've done. Tift can't even begin to know what a dedicated and loyal friend you are."

"Tift never has to know about this get-together, right? Nor do the police?"

"If you help me out, our little secret will never leave these walls," Sandra said. "Now, how about we dine on some oysters and lobster before the wine does us in."

"Sounds great."

"Maybe tomorrow you'll open up and tell me what you did to Townsend."

"Maybe."

For reasons that Gwynn never understood, Tift never took a shine to Sandra. Whatever had transpired between the two of them must have really pissed Tift off. Because of this, she knew that Tift would never agree to work with Sandra, charity or no charity, which meant that Sandra would always be able to hold Townsend's disappearance over her head.

They dined on the seafood Sandra had sent over. By ten that evening, she told Sandra she was tired and ready for bed. Sandra escorted her up to her room. Because of the dark, all she could see were the lights twinkling across the harbor, as well as a lighthouse and its phosphorous beam rotating every few seconds.

"Sleep in as long as you like. I typically get up around five-forty-five and go for my morning swim. When I come back, I'll whip us up some blueberry pancakes and sausages."

"Sounds good. And thanks for a wonderful evening."

"No, thank you. I think the three of us will have a fruitful and rewarding relationship moving forward."

"Yes, I'm sure we will."

Sandra looked away as if lost in thought. "There's just one other thing that's been bothering me all these years."

"What's that?"

"Well," Sandra said, pausing. "It's about Tom."

"What about him?"

"Back when we were at Brooks, I went to one of his sets one night with my girlfriend. We had a few drinks afterward, and then Tom and I hung out for a while. One thing led to another," she said, looking down at the bed.

"What are you getting at?"

"Gwynn, Tom, and I hooked up that night."

Gwynn momentarily felt herself leaving her body.

"I'm sorry, but he told me that you two had broken things off at the time."

She stared at Sandra in silence.

"I regret having to tell you about this, but it's been eating away at me for years."

This shouldn't have bothered her, but it did; only Gwynn didn't want to give Sandra the satisfaction of seeing her with hurt feelings. "It doesn't matter now. And as you said, Tom and I had split up at the time."

"Besides, it was a long time ago when we were young and immature," she said. "I'm so glad you're okay with me telling you this, because it's been weighing on my mind all these years. I just didn't want it to be a problem between us."

"No problem at all."

"Great. I'll see you tomorrow morning, hon. Sleep well." She turned and staggered back downstairs.

Gwynn didn't bother to undress. The idea of Sandra sleeping with Tom back in college fermented in her gut like a bad case of food poisoning. She wanted to be ready when Sandra went out for her swim. She was not yet sure how she would do it, but she knew that her only option was to kill the bitch.

She set her clock for five-forty-five. Then she got up, switched off the lamp, and snuggled under the covers. She knew she would toss and turn, thinking about every possible way she could get rid of her old college classmate.

At three in the morning, she finally drifted off. Her mind wandered aimlessly until she dreamt that she was walking hand in hand with Detective Peters through a huge sunflower field. She wore only a sundress, and he was wearing a white cotton shirt with white pants and bleached white sneakers. The sun shone above them as they walked beneath the towering stalks. She gazed up and saw the giant, sad faces tilting to one side and getting ready to die. After walking a considerable distance, they settled down between some taller plants. She snuggled her head in the crook of Peters's shoulder, her hand resting on his chest. He leaned over and kissed her on the forehead. But when Gwynn looked down, she saw a tiny pinprick of red spreading over his white shirt, just above the sternum. She closed her eyes. When she opened them later in the dream, Gwynn noticed that the pinprick was now a red circle the size of a grapefruit. Had Peters died? Had she killed him? She closed her eyes again in the dream and dozed off, her head still resting against his muscular shoulder.

Chapter Nine

Peters worked at his desk late into the night, studying all the photographs from the Custom House event where Townsend was last seen. Working late never bothered him; he had nothing else going on in his life. No hobbies other than betting on horses and football games. No girlfriend, even though he sometimes got hit on at the local bar by the occasional drunk cougar. Work was all he had—and he badly needed to solve this case if he hoped not to get reassigned to a desk job filing papers.

He studied all the photographs loaded onto his laptop, finding it more difficult to concentrate the later it got on. All his thoughts returned to that encounter with Gwynn. She'd occupied his every waking moment since their first meeting, which was not a good thing, seeing as how he needed to put all his energies into finding out what had happened to this missing Boston man.

By eight-thirty, his mind shut down, and he couldn't concentrate anymore. Peters closed the file on his desk and headed to the dive bar across the street from the station. His first beer arrived as soon as he plunked his ass down on the stool. The place served cheap pub food and poured double shots passing as singles, and he liked it mostly because other cops rarely stepped foot in here except to drag out the occasional rabble-rouser. It used to be a lot rougher back in the day when Gus owned it and ran tabs for the regulars, many of whom were B&M baked bean workers getting off shift at seven in the morning. After an hour of hard drinking, the place reeked of bacon fat and molasses.

An ultimate fight played on the television screen above the bar. An hour later, after four beers, he switched to gin and tonic. On the bar sat his phone opened to his contact list. Gwynn's name appeared front and center. He badly wanted to call and ask her out on a date. Was nine o'clock at night too late to ring a woman? He couldn't come right out and ask her out. No, that would seem too forward. He needed a convenient excuse if he wanted to see her again. Tell her that he had a few more questions to ask about the case. Better to do it in the morning, during office hours, when he'd be sober and more alert. He'd regret it if he didn't at least try to meet with her again, and his gut told him that she felt the same way about him.

He rarely went out and drank like this, but when he did, he did so in style. The first gin and tonic went down easy, filling him with a warm glow. Staring up at the television screen, he watched as a bloodied and bruised fighter pummeled his opponent. He burped and glanced around the place, realizing he was one of only four people inside the bar. The hot dog he'd ordered arrived, sitting like a steaming pile of shit in front of him. He loaded it with mustard, onions, and hot sauce before letting it cool, knowing his innards would pay a steep price come morning.

How could a prominent businessman simply vanish, especially on a Friday night? He grabbed his phone and pulled up some photos from that night. There was one of Townsend standing next to Sandra Clayborn. Townsend had his arm wrapped around Sandra's shoulder, towering over her. Peters enlarged the photograph using his thumb and forefinger and saw something he hadn't noticed before. Townsend was not wearing his wedding ring. Odd, but not earth-shattering. Townsend was a handsome guy, two hours from home, and not wearing his wedding ring at a function filled with beautiful, wealthy women. Could he have met someone at that event, put the moves on her, and she ended up killing him?

He scanned the rest of his photographs before realizing that there was not a single one with Sandra and Gwynn in the same frame. That seemed odd, considering that they were old college friends. Then again, Gwynn did say she'd left early because she wasn't feeling well. Maybe she talked to Sandra beforehand. In every instance where he'd left an event early, he always made sure to check in with the person who invited him so that they would know he'd shown up. Then he would slip out the back door before anyone noticed, unless, of course, there was an open bar. Then, he would stay until the free booze stopped flowing.

Something seemed off as he picked up his second gin and tonic. Although he couldn't put his finger on what was bothering him, he was fairly confident that Townsend's body would not be found anytime soon. His thoughts began to merge like a collage, cluttered and unorganized and made worse by the booze. He downed the remainder of his drink, wondering how he'd get home.

How nice it would be to wake up next to Gwynn and inhale the odor of her lustrous hair. Gaze into those beautiful blue eyes and kiss the faded freckles over the bridge of her nose. Nuzzle closer until their lips brushed up against each other. He would give anything to have a woman like that in his life. He wouldn't need to drink or gamble if he had Gwynn Denning waiting for him at home every night.

He'd always been fussy when it came to women. His mother often said that about him. He hated dating and all the silly games one had to play to succeed in love. His heart always yearned to be with one woman.

An hour later, he downed his fifth gin and tonic and turned to leave, unsteady on his feet. Having consumed only the hot dog since noon, Peters realized he might have overdone it. He tossed some bills down on the bar, staggered out the door, and ordered an Uber. As he shuffled down Middle Street, he wondered if he had it in him to kill another human being. Then he remembered that street thug he'd shot dead after a traffic stop. The question he asked himself was this: could he carry out a premeditated murder and get away with it? And could he live with the guilt?

Chapter Ten

Gwynn bolted upright before her alarm beeped. Every muscle in her body tensed in anticipation of what she was planning to do. Fully dressed, she tossed off the covers and moved to the sliding glass door. To her surprise, it led to a private deck. She needed to devise a foolproof plan—and fast. On the stand next to the bed sat a mini coffeemaker like the kind they had in high-end hotels. In a jar next to it were packets of expensive Italian coffee that she'd never heard of. She grabbed one, split open the packet of Caffe Firenze, and poured the grounds into the filter. It smelled like damp soil. She took the miniature pot and filled it with water from the guest bathroom before pouring it into the well. Seconds later, the maker started to burp and trickle coffee into the pot, filling the room with a deliciously rich aroma.

Think, Gwynn, think! You can't leave Tom to raise your son.

While the coffee brewed, she went out to the deck and sat in one of the pricey L.L. Bean deck chairs facing the bay. It promised to be a beautiful morning as the first streaks of light illuminated over the horizon. Ten minutes passed before she went back inside and poured herself a cup of the freshly brewed coffee. Returning to the deck, she stared out at the sun-streaked sky, past the tree branches and flagpole, sipping her coffee while contemplating how she would kill Sandra.

She glanced at her watch and realized that Sandra would soon be in the water. Gwynn stared down at the dock; her eyes fixated on the rig with the outboard motor. Sandra said that William left the key in it. That could come in handy. Gwynn's mind began to formulate the first seeds of a plan.

At six-thirty, Sandra made her way down the dock dressed in a black wetsuit. Sunlight reflected on the choppy harbor. Any good thoughts she might have had for her former classmate had long ago dissipated: their shared college experience, their mutual friendship with Tift, and the deep social and work ties that bound them in Maine. All she could focus on was her plan and executing it with surgical precision. The thrill of killing Sandra excited her the more she thought about it.

Gwynn bolted downstairs into the living room and then made her way to the basement, heading straight for the gym, having seen it yesterday during the tour of Sandra's home. Searching for her tool of choice, she grabbed a twenty-pound kettlebell and returned with it upstairs. She placed it on the floor and looked through the drawers and cabinets until she found a coil of rope. When she did, she cut it into two even lengths. She moved to the sliding glass door and saw Sandra standing at the end of the deck and doing some stretching exercises. After five minutes of these warm-ups, she leaned over the dock and dove into the bay.

Gwynn stood behind the sliding glass door, watching Sandra swim out into the open water. She tied the nylon rope into a large honda knot, one of the many knots her father had taught her. Lugging the kettlebell with her, she felt like a combat soldier readying for battle. Once Sandra reached a hundred feet from the dock, she went outside and walked across the wet lawn, her arms straining to hold onto the kettlebell. Then, down the stairs until she reached the dock. It was long and narrow and at least a foot above the lapping waterline. She moved with purpose toward the end of it, searching the bay for any other vessels. The only thing she saw was a small sailboat anchored offshore, as well as a number of lobster buoys bobbing in the swells. Seagulls squawked overhead, the only witnesses to her potential deed. About a hundred yards from the pier, she noticed splashing followed by the slow, rhythmic arc of Sandra's arms churning through the water.

Time to make her move.

She climbed into the boat with the word Whaler emblazoned on the side, setting the kettlebell next to her. An oar sat under the seat, which was good to have in case the motor died. Her father once owned a small boat like this, and he'd taught her how to operate and steer it. This rig was much easier than the old two-stroke her father owned, which required far more elaborate steps to start. She lowered the engine so that the fuel would reach the carburetor, turned the key, and the engine growled to life. Gwynn gripped the tiller and directed the boat to where Sandra continued to freestyle, strategizing on precisely how she would kill her.

At the sound of the approaching motor, Sandra flipped over on her back and began to backstroke. The hood of the wet suit covered everything but her face. Sandra smiled up at Gwynn as she floated along the surface. After inferring that she had killed Townsend, Gwynn wondered why her old friend never suspected that she'd come for her next.

"How's the water?" Gwynn asked. A droning sound echoed off in the distance. She glanced up and saw a lobster boat chugging toward them. It was a good distance away, but the sight of it concerned her, and she realized that she had to finish Sandra off before someone on the lobster boat saw her.

"The ocean is beautiful this morning. Glad you decided to take the boat out for a spin," Sandra shouted, the water bobbing around her head.

"It's gorgeous out here," Gwynn said, moving closer to her.

"When I get back from my swim, I'll make us some blueberry pancakes and sausages," Sandra shouted before turning back to her stomach and doggy-paddling through the water.

Gwynn cruised alongside Sandra. Letting go of the tiller, she grabbed the first section of rope and whipped it over the woman's head. A brief scream went up as she pulled on the end of the rope and cinched it around the back of Sandra's neck. On her knees, Gwynn squeezed with all her might, keeping her legs apart in order to maintain her balance inside the boat. Sandra thrashed around, and it was all Gwynn could do to maintain her grip. The Whaler rocked perilously back and forth. If the boat capsized and Gwynn went into the bay, she was a dead woman. Struggling to hold on, she glanced to her left and saw the lobster boat slowly moving through the channel. Estimating it to be a half mile away and gaining, she yanked back the knot in her stinging hands until it pressed against the base of the woman's neck, preventing Sandra from flipping over. Water splashed up and into the boat. Remembering how Sandra blackmailed her, and threatened to separate her from Jack, Gwynn leaned back and pulled, the tendons in her arms straining to their limits.

Less than a minute later, the woman lost consciousness. Another minute without oxygen, and she would be dead. Releasing her grip, she let Sandra go, and Sandra floated on the surface. Gwynn moved quickly down her body until she held one of her feet in her hands. She tied the honda knot through the loop located on the back of Sandra's neoprene boot. Once she secured the knot, she slid the boot a few inches down Sandra's ankle so that it would eventually slip off in the current. Then, she tied the other end around the loop of the kettlebell. She glanced up and saw that the lobster boat was getting nearer. She caught sight of a six-digit number written on the stern. Along the bow, she made out the name *Lilly*. Ducking low in the Whaler, Gwynn wondered whether the captain could see her from his vantage. Finally, she lifted the kettlebell out of the boat, dropped it in the water, and watched as Sandra's lifeless body disappeared into the blueish-green bay, her hands the last to submerge.

Wasting no time, Gwynn grabbed the tiller and spun the boat around, accelerating as fast as she could back to the dock. She needed to go inside Sandra's house and get rid of any evidence she'd left behind. Did William know that she was the college friend who had stayed the night? Maybe she'd call Sandra's husband and tell him that his wife had not returned from her morning swim. Hopefully, Sandra would still be alive when that kettlebell dragged her to the bottom. That way, there would be water in her lungs when the divers found her body. The medical examiner would then have no choice but to rule it an accidental drowning. More worrisome, however, was the possibility that the captain of that lobster boat had seen what she had done.

She made a mental note to learn more about the *Lilly's* captain in the event she had to...

Glancing over her shoulder, she noticed that the rest of the bay was relatively quiet. Good thing there were no other houses in the vicinity of Sandra's home. She pulled up to the dock, her face beaded with ocean spray. It covered her tongue and filled her nostrils, and she knew she would always associate this briny sensation with Sandra's drowning. To her relief, the lobster boat continued to motor toward open water, oblivious to what she'd done. She tied the boat up and pulled herself onto the dock. A sense of accomplishment filled her, and she recalled the fierce struggle she'd experienced while gripping that rope behind Sandra's neck and then watching as her body sank into the murky depths.

She sprinted down the deck, confident that no one would ever know what she had done. She hit the lawn and dashed over the manicured blades of grass. Climbed the stairs and arrived on to the massive deck. The sliding glass door opened easily. She slammed it shut behind her, locked the door, and gulped in mouthfuls of air. The feeling coursing through her felt indescribable. Gwynn turned and surveyed the harbor, knowing she had little time to relax. Tears of joy streamed down her cheeks.

Something was at her feet. She glanced down and saw the Miniature Poodle waving its tail and staring up at her. She'd forgotten about the dog.

How dare that woman sleep with Tom. And then threaten to tell the police about her rendezvous with Townsend—and potentially leave Jack without his mother to protect him.

As she turned toward the kitchen, she heard someone keying the front door lock. Who could that be? The handle turned. Frightened, she tiptoed through the living room until she arrived at the top of the stairs. Below was the mudroom with all the coat hooks and pricey slat storage bench. On the wall hung two original Thomas Connolly paintings of various maritime scenes. She wiped away the tears as the door opened, and in walked William Clayborn, riffing through a pile of mail. Wedged under his arm was the Sunday newspaper. He looked up with a tired smile when he saw her. The Miniature Poodle ran down the stairs and greeted him. William picked up the dog in his arms and gave the pooch a kiss.

"Hey there, Chloe." He stroked the dog's head. "And hello to you."

"Hi," she said, trying to stay composed.

She hadn't planned on Sandra's husband showing up so soon after she'd

71

just drowned his wife. Her head began to spin. She needed to focus and think. *Think, Gwynn. Fast!* What in the world would she do now that he was walking up the stairs toward her?

Dr. Ezra Kaufman

Gwynn froze when I mentioned that I'd seen her at the Custom House the evening that Boston gentleman disappeared. She quickly recovered, asking me why I didn't come over and say hello. I told her I'd started to, but then she'd left for the evening. She shrugged and said nothing else about the matter, and I didn't push it, despite having seen her walk off with that man.

For years now, she's been debating whether or not she should track down her biological parents. With her father's dementia worsening, I suggested that she should finally go for it, seeing as how he would never know about it at this late stage in his life. Again, she merely shrugged and took my advice in stride. This time, however, I think she might actually do it. She's eager to learn whether or not her mental condition has been passed down through her genes.

So am I.

Her adopted father, Dave, was a friend of mine, a patient for a few years, too, well before Gwynn was even a sweet pea in her mother's womb. She started seeing me in high school, months after her gym teacher died in that unfortunate hiking tragedy. Her father claimed that the death of that beloved teacher, as well as her friend who had committed suicide, had caused Gwynn to close herself off to everyone. I informed him that I would have to see her on a weekly basis if I were to affect any real change. He thanked me, knowing how hard it was to procure my services.

The only times I saw Gwynn before she became a patient of mine was when she joined her father on his street missions. I still remember the two of them walking hand in hand among the destitute and homeless, bestowing God's blessings upon them. She was such a cute little girl, pigtailed and innocent, and not at all bothered by the blight and squalor on the streets. She had nothing to fear walking alongside her father, because he was practically worshipped by the people who patronized the soup kitchens and shelters, and he moved easily among them. He reminded me of what Jesus might have been like had he been around today: handsome, humble, and ready to spread the word of God's infinite wisdom.

Pastor Dave, who had been chronicled on television and in print, saw this as an opportunity to change lives and convince people to accept God into their heart. Gwynn had observed her father's charisma from a young age, witnessed his benevolence toward society's outcasts and downtrodden. It's the reason she chose to go into social work and care for abused children. It's why she clings so tightly to her religious convictions, falling back on them like a crutch when she's feeling down.

In that respect, she's much like her father.

It's why I can't wrap my head around the disappearance of this Boston man. But then again, maybe I'm making too much of this. Maybe I'm letting my imagination get the best of me.

We've been together for nearly twenty years now, and the basis of our relationship has not changed in all that time. When she starts to spiral, I'm always there for her. I've told her on numerous occasions that I will not provide her with any physical affections, nor will I sit and listen to her babble on about her deluded thoughts. Nor will I enable her when she becomes irrational and legitimize her fantastical notions. One of my other rules is that she is to never argue with me when I increase her meds, although she often does, until I have to remind her of our agreement.

She's fired me three times in all our years together. Then she calls a few days later and begs me to take her back. Sometimes, I think I'd be better off without her. That way, I could slip quietly into retirement, reading all the classics that I've set aside for that period in my life. But the truth is, I really don't want to lose her as a client. She's a complex and fascinating individual, and I've learned a great deal from her psychological makeup. Furthermore,

I've invested so much time and effort in her mental health that it behooves me to see how she turns out. Over the years, I've discovered that there's something mysterious and slightly dark about Gwynn. Maybe with this missing Boston man I can finally discover the truth.

She acted oddly during our last session. Her mental state seemed directly related to the disappearance of this man, although she wouldn't come right out and say it. She acted strangely euphoric, which seemed unusual considering that this state of mind occurred right after a period of deep depression. She'd been under a lot of stress lately with the disintegration of her marriage, her father's advancing dementia, the rigors of raising a young son, and the pressures that come with her position as director of The Loft. So why did her mood flip so dramatically? After checking my logs, I realized I hadn't changed her prescriptions.

Based on her life history, I'm starting to have my suspicions.

Her adopted father also experienced these dark bouts of depression, but he was adept at keeping them hidden from everyone around him.

Three people tenuously connected to Gwynn have died or gone missing. That high school gym teacher. The heroin addict father she met with when she first started working as a social worker. And now this Townsend fellow. I'm seeing a pattern emerge. But am I reading too much into this? Maybe so, but my instinct is telling me to keep my guard up. My heart, on the other hand, is telling me that I'm being a suspicious old fool.

Chapter Eleven

"**W**hat are you doing here?" Gwynn said.

"I live here." William looked up at her, holding the dog and smiling. "You must be Gwynn."

"Yes, of course you live here. This is your house." She laughed. "And yes, I am Gwynn."

"No worries," he said. "I returned home early from my poker game. A bunch of us old friends get together once a month to smoke cigars, drink scotch, and try to win a few bucks off each other."

"I know. Sandra told me all about it," she said. "How did you know who I was?"

"Sandra said she was having a friend over. I've seen you in her college pictures, and you look exactly the same as you did back then."

Gwynn was flattered by this comment but also unsure of what she should do. Had Sandra told her husband what had happened that night with Tift? Or maybe Sandra kept her word and told no one, including her husband. William seemed nice on the surface, but she knew that he made his living as a criminal defense attorney, defending murderers, criminals, and rapists. He was the best lawyer in Maine, or so people said, and he charged an exorbitant fee for his services.

"You girls have a good time last night?" he asked as he made his way onto the main floor. He placed the stack of mail on a side table.

"Yes, it was fun catching up on old times," she said, trying not to panic. "I'm a little worried, though. Sandra hasn't returned from her swim yet, and it's been well over an hour." She followed him into the living room and watched as he placed the dog down and settled on the sofa.

"Over an hour? That's nothing. Sometimes, my darling dolphin stays out there a lot longer than that. One morning, she swam to Cousins Island and back." The dog jumped up on the couch and cuddled up next to him.

"Wow. That's quite a long way."

"I'll give her credit. She keeps herself in great shape."

She felt awkward standing there, watching as he flipped through *The New York Times*. He didn't seem to mind that she was all alone with him in this large house.

"I'm so glad to be home. I nearly lost my shirt last night," he said, shaking his head.

"Sorry to hear that. How much did you lose?"

"Five dollars and fifty-five cents," he said. "We play for nickels."

"Big spenders, huh?"

"We used to play for dimes, but then the guys started to get too competitive."

"If you need a loan, I'll get my purse."

"I kept getting dealt terrible cards all night," he said. "Besides, tomorrow's the first day of my upcoming trial, and I need to spend most of the day preparing for it."

"What's the case about?" She walked around the sofa, staring up at the artwork on the wall, wondering what she should do.

"My client just graduated from medical school and was spending time with friends in the Old Port. He met a woman at one of the waterfront bars, she made a false claim about his intentions, and here we are."

She despised him already. "Do you think you'll win?"

"My chances of winning are far better than they are at playing poker," he said. "And unlike my card game, I get paid whether I win or lose, although I rarely lose when it comes to the law."

"Would you like some coffee? I was planning on sticking around and saying goodbye to Sandra."

"I would love some. But I can make it."

"No, William, you sit there and read your paper. Making coffee will give me something to do."

"There are some scones from Standard Bakery atop the refrigerator. We can have those smeared with jelly if you like."

"Wonderful," she said, staring out at the bay, imagining Sandra's body slithering along the ocean floor and dangling from that kettlebell.

He snapped open his newspaper and began to read.

"Is there a lobster boat that cruises past your house each morning?"

"Yes, the *Lilly*. Why do you ask?"

"Just wondering if the captain knows that Sandra swims in the vicinity. Hate for something bad to happen to her out there."

"Don't worry about my wife. She knows every inch of that bay."

"Will you excuse me for a second, William? I have to get something up in my room."

"Sure. Take your time."

Gwynn ran upstairs, trying to contain her panic. She knew she was being unreasonable and that Sandra's death would appear like a drowning once her body washed ashore, sans one boot. But what if it didn't? What if they sent scuba divers down there and found Sandra attached to that kettlebell? William would no doubt testify that he'd discovered his wife's classmate inside his house when he came home, acting suspicious about Sandra's whereabouts. Maybe he'd mention what Townsend had done to Tift back in college, and the police would put two and two together.

But the likelihood of divers finding Sandra at the bottom of that bay was low. Within days, the powerful tidal currents should pull her foot free from the boot and set her body adrift. Gwynn knew from studying similar cases that murder by drowning was a very hard thing to prove unless it took place in a bathtub or hot tub. She'd studied every manner of death and knew as much on this subject as a medical examiner.

But what if they did find Sandra attached to that rope? Held there by that kettlebell?

She couldn't take the chance, which meant that making William disappear was her only option. Not like it was the worst decision in the world, seeing as how he profited from keeping the worst of humanity out of prison. And the couple had no children, making her decision that much easier. But how would she kill him and get away with it? She remembered the vial of Ambien in her purse, the same pills she'd used on Townsend.

Her phone rang, startling her back to reality. She instantly realized the mistake she'd made by forgetting to remove the battery and SIM card from her phone. Should she answer it? Gwynn glanced down at the number and didn't recognize it. What if something bad had happened to Jack? She decided to see who it was. After she took care of William, she'd destroy the phone and SIM card and get a new one.

"Hi, Gwynn. It's me, Detective Peters."

"Oh, hi." Her heartbeat picked up at the sound of his voice. "I'm afraid I don't have much time to talk."

"I called to ask if we could meet this afternoon for coffee. I have a few more questions to ask you about the Townsend case."

"I'm afraid I don't have much to add since the last time we met," she said, wanting to end this call as soon as possible.

"You'd be surprised. Every small detail in an investigation matters."

She bit her thumbnail and paced around in the room. "Could we meet later?"

"How about dinner?"

"Dinner will work."

"Where would you like to meet?"

"Wherever," she said, trying to move this conversation along. "How about you come over to my house, and I'll order out."

"Let me at least pick up a pizza."

"Fine," she said. "We good here?" Gwynn picked up her bag and searched through it.

"All good."

Gwynn ended the call and headed back downstairs, eager to get on with it. After searching the kitchen cabinets, she found a bag of Peruvian single-sourced coffee. On the counter sat an expensive Breville coffee maker. She poured the beans into the well. After randomly pressing a few buttons, the machine began to grind and brew. When it finished, she crushed up two

Ambiens and poured the powder into William's coffee, stirring it until the powder fully dissolved into the liquid.

"Cream or sugar?" she shouted out to him.

"One cream and two sugars, please," he replied.

She found the sugar bowl next to the coffee maker and plopped in three cubes to hide the taste of the Ambien. Her hand shook as she poured in the cream. Placing the cup on a saucer, she brought it out to William and stood back. Instrumental jazz played through speakers hidden somewhere in the room.

"Don't forget the scones and jelly."

"Oh, yes. I'll go get them."

She got the scones and jelly, plated them, and then poured herself a cup of coffee. She returned to the room and sat across from him, her nerves on edge. His face was hidden behind the newspaper, and all she could see were his fingers gripping the edge of the pages.

"Can I ask you a question, William?"

He lowered the paper and stared at her. "Of course."

"Do you ever wonder if your clients are guilty?"

"Their guilt or innocence doesn't concern me in the least. I'm paid to win their acquittal and make the government prove beyond a reasonable doubt what they are alleging. Any less would be giving the state too much power." He sipped his coffee. "Interesting blend. What brand did you use?"

"The Peruvian single source I found in the cabinet. You don't like it?"

"No, it's okay," he said. "Just has an odd metallic taste."

"You think? I haven't had coffee this good in ages." She meant it.

"What setting did you use on the Breville?"

"Setting? I just turned it on and let it do its thing," she said. "Would you like me to brew up another pot?"

"No, this is fine." He took another sip and grimaced. "I'll have Sandra buy another brand the next time she shops."

She bit off a chunk of scone and chewed slowly. "But what if you knew with absolute certainty that your client committed the crime?"

He stared at her as if annoyed. "The state's job is to prove my client's guilt beyond a reasonable doubt, and if they can't do that, then they haven't succeeded in prosecuting their case."

"And it wouldn't trouble you that a murderer had been set free to possibly kill again?"

"I wouldn't lose an ounce of sleep over it. This is how the law works, and it's the best legal system in the world."

She took another bite of scone and felt the buttery confection dissolve over her tongue.

"You have to remember, Gwynn, I've worked many years in order to hone my skills as a defense attorney. If not for lawyers like me, the state could lock you up for any crime of their choosing, and you would have no options. Is that what you want, assuming you ever found yourself charged with murder?"

The irony of this question struck her as comical. "No, of course not."

"If you give the state unlimited power, they'll be able to convict anyone they believe threatens their grip on society."

She nodded, her decision now cemented by his apathy toward the pieces of shit who hurt and killed other people. As the scone settled in her belly, she turned and stared out at the blue-green water, half expecting to see Sandra floating on the surface.

"I can't believe your wife can stay out there for so long."

"That's my mermaid," he said, eyes returning to the paper. "Then again, she was the star freestyler on her college swim team."

"Yes, she was amazing back at Brooks. I think she was all-conference her senior year."

"Then you know how much she loves the water and wanted to live near it."

"I can see that now."

"Look, if you need to run along, Gwynn, I can just tell her you had to get going and that you wished her well," he said, trying politely to get her to leave. "I'm sure she'll understand."

"Oh, no, I'm in no hurry to return home. Besides, I have my coffee and scone to finish."

"Make yourself comfortable, then."

"Thank you, William."

"Just to let you know, it's the weekend, meaning that Sandra might be out there for a while."

"That's not a problem. I can sit on the deck and wait for her as long as I'm not bothering you."

"Don't worry about me. I'll be heading up to my office soon to start preparing for trial."

She sat back, cradling the cup of coffee in hand, wondering how long it would take for the Ambien to kick in. Hopefully, he'd finish his cup. On the outside, she appeared calm and collected, but on the inside, she was screaming at him to drink up.

The long-winded jazz solo irritated her. She picked up a section of the newspaper and feigned reading it, amused to see that she had grabbed the obituaries. Her stomach rumbled, reminding her how hungry she was despite the morsel of scone she'd eaten. Sandra had promised to make blueberry pancakes and sausage this morning, but Sandra wouldn't be doing that now. Instead, Gwynn sipped her coffee and scanned the death notices.

Her mind returned to Jack and why she needed to get rid of William. She could never abandon her son, swearing to do whatever it took to stay out of prison, even if that meant making a defense lawyer disappear.

Her mind switched gears, and she thought about her meeting with Peters that night. What more could he possibly ask her? Still, she was excited to see him, despite being upset with herself for answering his call and placing herself at the scene of the crime. How did she not remember to remove her battery and SIM card? After committing two murders in less than twenty-four hours, would she be in any shape to sit down and answer his questions? Would she be able to remain calm and collected while sitting so close to him, knowing he had the power to ruin her life? She couldn't deny the sexual attraction she'd felt that day when he sat in her kitchen.

"Would you like another cup of coffee, William?" she asked. When he didn't answer, she lowered the obituaries and saw that he was sitting back on the sofa with the newspaper spread over his chest. The Miniature Poodle slept next to him, snoring. She got up and walked over, noticing that his cup was three-quarters empty. The dog's loud snores competed with the jazz playing over the speakers. Shaking his shoulder several times, she knew he would be out for several hours.

Time to get to work. She picked up the dog and carried it upstairs, locking it in William and Sandra's bedroom. Once she was downstairs, she ran into the garage. Both bays were empty. She opened the electric garage door and sprinted out to her vehicle, parking it in the empty bay. Once the garage door closed, she grabbed the roll of masking tape and returned inside.

After taping his ankles and feet together, she pushed the coffee table aside and began to pull him out by the ankles. His head thumped against the hardwood floor, not hard enough to do any damage. But it was crucial she didn't cut him and cause him to bleed all over the place, leaving behind microscopic traces of blood for the cops to find.

Once in the garage, she took a brief rest. Then she propped him up on the footstool and climbed in the back of her SUV. Grabbing him by the arms, she struggled mightily to pull him up until he was lying in a fetal position over the carpet. After a quick breather, she grabbed his cell phone, exited the vehicle, and returned inside the house, where she found her overnight bag. She made up her bed, grabbed a rag out of one of the closet shelves, and dipped it under the faucet. Then she proceeded to wipe down every part of the house she might have touched. Making sure to be thorough, she went out to the Boston Whaler and wiped down the sides of the boat, as well as the tiller handle. The bay was quiet at this hour, but she could almost hear Sandra's voice calling out her name. Once she finished, she returned inside, thinking if she'd forgotten anything. Yes, the coffee cups and scones. She tossed them in a trash bag, planning to take them with her. She placed William's cell phone on the coffee table. Many a defendant was brought down by DNA evidence, and so she found a broom and swept clean the hardwood floor and sofa, hoping to leave no strands of hair behind. She went upstairs and did the same thing in the bedroom. Hopefully, the police wouldn't find a shred of evidence that could implicate her.

She sprinted out to her car parked in the garage, tossed the trash bag on top of William's comatose body, and then covered him over with a plastic tarp. She opened the garage door and drove out, leaving the engine idling. Running back inside, she covered her finger with her sleeve before engaging the garage door button. The motor growled, and the door began to lower. She limboed under it as it lowered. Then she drove away. In her mind, she was doing this for Jack and for all the innocent people William's dirtbag clients had screwed over.

This was not murder as much as it was self-defense, she kept telling herself.

Chapter Twelve

Gwynn decided during the drive that it was not enough to just kill William, but she needed to make him aware of his wrongdoings and see if he would repent. Which meant waiting for him to regain consciousness, as dumb as that sounded right now. Once she arrived at the quarry, she dragged him out of the vehicle and, with much effort, placed him near the edge. She took out a mini-beach chair and sat next to him. Her SUV was parked in a way so that it shielded them in the event a car passed by on the country road. A few feet away was the ledge, and she could sense the cold, lonely depths below. Years ago a company had used this pit to conduct sonar and sound tests for the Navy. She'd heard some of the locals say that it was at least two football fields to the quarry floor. Although her mind was telling her to dump his body ASAP and head home, she sat under the blue sky, sunning, waiting for him to come to.

Part of her wished she'd taken the Breville with her, seeing as how they wouldn't need it anymore. But she didn't want to profit from this act. Ridding the world of morally corrupt and violent people was its own reward.

She looked up at the sky, closed her eyes, and absorbed the sun's rays. Sometime later, she heard him groaning. When she gazed down, she saw William stirring. He opened his eyes, only to notice that his wrists and ankles had been bound together with duct tape. He tried to scream, but only a muffled noise came out. Gwynn lifted her chair and moved it closer to him. Reaching over, she ripped the tape off his mouth and reclined back in the chair.

"What the hell do you think you're doing?" he asked in a trembling voice.

"I'm sorry, William, but I had no other choice," she said. "Okay, I have to be completely honest with you. I'm actually not *that* sorry."

William shouted for help, his voice echoing off the quarry walls.

"You're wasting your time. There's no one else out here."

"What have I done to deserve this?"

"For starters, you defend scumbags and profit handsomely from the pain and suffering of their victims. But that's not the real reason I'm going to kill you."

His eyelids flared.

"What do you have to say about the victims who were hurt because of your clients' crimes?"

His Adam's apple bobbed over the swells of his throat. "It's my job to defend them."

"You didn't seem to care for the victims, even when you knew that your clients were guilty."

He shook his head, trying to maintain his bearing. "I was merely protecting the individual from the overbearing vagaries of the state."

She laughed. "Oh, is that what you were doing?"

"Yes."

"What a swell guy."

"Okay, you've made your point. I'm an assassin who shields himself with a legal principle."

"And a lousy poker player to boot."

"I was getting dealt terrible hands all night," he shouted. "Besides, why would you kill me when there are so many other violent criminals deserving of death?"

"I agree. You're on a much lesser scale of evil. Unfortunately, your mistake was being in the wrong place at the wrong time."

"What are you talking about?"

"You arrived home at the worst possible moment."

"How so?"

"I drowned your wife, William. Believe me, I didn't want to, but I had no other choice."

"You killed Sandra?" His face went slack.

"Your lovely mermaid, as you referred to her, was planning to blackmail me if I didn't play ball with her. Obviously, I couldn't let that happen. Unlike the two of you DINKs, I have a young son to raise. And I certainly don't want him to be an immoral heel like you."

"I can't believe you killed my wife." He appeared on the verge of tears. "How did you do it?"

"I took your boat out while she was on her morning swim. Did you know that she saw me leaving the Custom House with that missing Boston man?"

"You mean you…killed him, too?"

"Now he really deserved it."

"What kind of monster are you?"

"Did Sandra ever tell you what that creep did to my friend back in college?" He shook his head.

"Sam Townsend date-raped her and walked away scot-free. Sandra knew about it, too, and planned on profiting from his criminal behavior. I assumed she told you the whole sordid story."

"She didn't."

"Knowing the vile crime he had done, can you believe she invited that rapist to her firm's event?"

He looked out over the quarry.

"Do you know what Sandra was planning to do to Townsend at her corporate event?"

"No."

"She was going to blackmail him in order to land a business deal with his firm. That's the amazing woman you married, William."

"You're blaming Sandra for your actions?"

"Do you really think it was a good idea to invite a rapist to a business function? And then blackmail him into doing a business deal, using my friend's rape as collateral?"

"Of course not, but don't blame me for my wife's actions. If you let me go, I swear I'll never say a word about this to anyone."

She pretended to consider this. "You swear on it?"

"Swear to God. Not only that, but I'll represent you in court if they ever arrest you for any of this—and I'm the best criminal defense lawyer in Maine."

She laughed. "That's so sweet of you."

"I promise, you'll be in safe hands with me as your attorney."

"You mean you'd defend the very person who killed your wife? Now that's true love."

He looked away in shame.

"No, I don't think I can take that risk, William. But thank you, anyway, for that generous offer."

"I swear on my mother's grave that I'll never utter a word of this to anyone. Please, I beg you to let me go."

"You've got such a terrible poker face. It doesn't surprise me that you lost five whole dollars."

"I swear to you that I'll never breathe a word of this to anyone."

"I Googled some of your cases, William. It's impressive how you won that stockbroker an acquittal after he ripped off the life savings of those three senior citizens."

Saliva trickled down the side of his mouth. "It was my job to represent him."

"You destroyed that sweet old lady on the stand, saying she willingly signed away her money. How could anyone with a conscience do that to an elderly woman who'd lost everything?"

"It's the state's responsibility...I was getting paid to...." He stopped when he saw that his words were having no effect on her, and, in fact, were making the situation worse.

"How about that teacher you got off for raping his student. Are you aware that she killed herself a year later?" She stood.

"Please," he said. "I'm begging you to have mercy on me."

"Mercy is exactly why I'm doing this," she said. "What you need, William, is a taste of your own medicine."

Gwynn leaned over and reapplied the duct tape over his mouth, trying not to look into his aggrieved eyes. His muffled groans filled the air as she stood back and took him in. She hesitated for a few seconds, not because she felt sorry for him, but because she wanted to revel in his pain for a few seconds longer.

She stepped behind him, grabbed his shirt by the shoulders, and dragged him kicking and screaming toward the edge. It was a struggle on account of the twenty-pound dumbbell attached to his waist and scraping the hard earth. William thrashed frantically, his movements dulled by the lingering effect of the Ambien in his system. With much effort, she positioned his body parallel to the edge of the quarry, stopping only to catch her breath.

Beads of sweat trickled down her forehead as William turned his head and gazed down at the blue-green water. Then he looked back up at her one last time, terrified, his eyes begging to be spared a watery death. "Goodbye, William," she said before pushing him over the edge. Leaning forward, she watched as he fell backward. Their eyes locked, and he landed backside against the water. A huge splash went up. His upper and lower body jackknifed as the dumbbell dragged him down to the watery depths.

She felt intoxicated, as if a chainsaw was buzzing inside her ribcage. For a brief second, she felt herself hovering over her body and looking down at herself. After taking a few minutes to reorient to her surroundings, she walked back to her SUV in a daze, carrying the lounge chair in hand.

As she was about to open the car door, she heard a noise up ahead. Like tires gripping dirt. She glanced over at the road and saw a young boy riding his bicycle up the hill. He had a fishing pole attached to the handlebars and a tackle box over the rim of his back tire. He pedaled toward her. Had he seen what happened? She stepped forward to say hello, praying she wouldn't have to take drastic action.

"Hey," the boy said.

"Hi there," she replied, trying to sound happy. "How's the fishing today?"

"Haven't dropped a line yet. There's a creek down the road where we like to catch trout. There's fish in the quarry, too, but I have to pedal all the way down the other side to get there." He appeared to her on the spectrum.

"Are you here all alone?"

"I usually fish by myself unless Teddy and Rusty want to come with me."

"Who's Teddy and Rusty?"

"Teddy's my best friend, and Rusty's my dog," the boy said. "I'm George."

"A pleasure to meet you, George." She realized she had a death grip on the roll of duct tape in her hand. "I'm Debbie."

"Don't usually see anyone up in this quarry. What are you doing here?"

"Just hiking while it's nice out," she said, hoping she could spare the boy. "This place is so pretty."

"It's just a stupid old quarry."

"I suppose," she said, turning to look at the spot where she pushed William over the edge. "Where do you live, George?"

"The old green house at the bottom of the hill with the red metal roof. I've lived there my whole life. We have two cats and a bunch of chickens."

"Lucky you, then."

"Why do you have that roll of tape in your hand?"

She looked down at the roll. "I was going to patch my lawn chair."

"Don't look broken to me." George hopped back onto his bicycle seat. "You shouldn't be up here."

"Why not?"

"You could slip and fall in that quarry. People have died in it, you know."

"Have you seen anyone else up here today?"

"Just you. Why? You looking for someone?"

"No. Just wondering."

"I gotta go before the fish stop biting." He pedaled away. "Bye."

"Bye, George."

Her nerves afire, Gwynn jumped in her car, hoping that she never laid eyes on that boy again. She was relieved that she didn't have to do the unthinkable, despite already having done it two times in the last twenty-four hours. Three times in the last month. Six times since she'd been alive.

Chapter Thirteen

The Victorian located in the West End wasn't directly on the Promenade, but it was an impressive home all the same. Through hungover eyes, Peters saw a turret and below it two circular porches. Beneath the porch was a hand-built stone wall and two massive lilacs that kept the front door out of view from street level. He looked down at his notes and wondered if he had the right address. Dr. Ezra Kaufman was not married and had no children. Attended Harvard and Harvard Medical School and even taught there for a number of years before coming up to Maine to take a position at the local university. Peters gazed back up at the house. So why would a single man need a huge home in the West End?

He staggered up the steps, trying to manage the debilitating hangover now plaguing him. A pulsating ringing chimed in his ears as he rapped on the door. The three Tylenols he'd gulped down earlier in the day had only managed to dull the sharp edges of his pain. He chastised himself for overindulging last night. Despite it, he was glad he'd called Gwynn this morning and arranged for them to meet later. If he didn't call her today, he feared he might never again work up the courage.

The door opened, and for a second, Peters didn't see the man. Kaufman was considerably shorter than he expected. Embarrassed, he stared down at him. The diminutive shrink was wearing Browline frames, and a gray three-piece suit that he could tell was made by Joseph's in the Old Port, the most exclusive tailor in town. Peters introduced himself, and the doctor nodded grimly before stepping aside to let him in.

The interior was as impressive as the exterior. Gridded ceilings. White pillars separated the various rooms. The walls were painted aqua blue. A gauzy painting of a wheat field hung on the wall. Kaufman invited him to sit on the opposite sofa. Above him, a tasteful chandelier hung from a decorative circle that looked like a Roman artifact. Between them, a coffee table supported the bronze sculpture of a bucking horse. Peters could go on admiring this house all day, but he had a job to do and a hangover to heal.

"Thank you for seeing me, Mr. Kaufman."

"It's Doctor."

Douche move, he thought. "Okay, Doctor."

"How can I help you?"

"As you know, I'm looking into the disappearance of that Boston man, Sam Townsend, and I saw your name on the list of attendees." He felt a wave of nausea pass over him, and he wished he hadn't drunk that last IPA after arriving home last night.

"I'm sorry to disappoint you, Detective, but I didn't know the man."

"No, I'm sure you didn't. It's just that I'm required to interview everyone who was at that Custom House event and try to piece things together."

"I understand. Unfortunately, I don't think I'll be of any help to you."

"Probably not, but let's give it a go anyway."

The doctor nodded as if acknowledging a lowly peasant and it reminded him of the dwarf on the show *Game of Thrones,* although Kaufman was certainly no dwarf.

"You said you didn't know Sam Townsend."

"No, but I did see him that evening."

"In what capacity?"

Kaufman paused for a few seconds. "He was holding forth with a group of people, and I happened to notice him from across the room."

"How did you know it was Townsend?"

"I didn't recognize him until the next day when I saw his picture in the newspaper."

"And you remembered that it was the same man?"

"To be honest, he was the type of man one notices when you walk into a room. I could see why he was so successful in the business realm."

"Maybe a bit too successful," Peters said, jotting everything down. "How did you get invited to the event?"

"My office is located across from Plumhurst Capital. I've been longtime friends with one of the senior partners, Saul Feldman. We used to go to the same synagogue together."

"Did you stay long?"

"No."

"Why is that?"

"Corporate outings are not my thing. I made the rounds, talked to Saul for a few minutes, and then came directly home."

Peters looked down at his notes. "You're a psychiatrist who went to Harvard?"

"Yes, Harvard Medical, as well. I taught in the Psychiatry Department for a few years and helped develop their curriculum on behavioral therapy."

Peters heard this last part as *blah, blah, blah.*

"I moved up here over thirty years ago and taught at the medical college before opening my own practice."

Just what the world needs: more shrinks. "So you left the Custom House early that evening?"

"Yes. And then I took an Uber straight home. The receipt is on my phone."

"You keep all your Uber receipts?"

"Yes."

"Was Townsend still at the Custom House when you left?"

"I don't know."

"And you didn't see anything unusual before you made your way out?"

"No, nothing at all."

He closed his notebook and stood. "I guess that's all the questions I have, then."

Dr. Kaufman stood.

"I love your crib, by the way."

"Crib?"

"Home."

"Thank you," Kaufman said, escorting him a little too quickly toward the front door. He grabbed the ornate handle and opened it for him to leave.

Peters glanced around at his surroundings and noticed four black-and-white photos of a young girl on the wall near the door. "She's quite the looker. Who is she?"

Kaufman turned and stared wistfully at the photos. "That's my mother six months after leaving Auschwitz. She was fifteen years old when that picture was taken."

"Wow. Is she still alive?"

"Yes. She lives in a nursing home down in Massachusetts."

"Your mother is fortunate to have survived her ordeal."

"Of the fifteen thousand children who were sent to Auschwitz, she's one of a hundred kids to make it out of that camp alive."

"Your mother must be an amazing woman."

"She is, but that's for another time," he said. "Look, Detective, I have much work to do this afternoon."

"Of course, thank you for your time, Doctor. Take care."

"You as well."

Peters walked out the front door and staggered down the path, happy to be out of the man's stifling presence. With his dour and depressing disposition, it was no wonder Kaufman never married. Men like that preferred to live in their heads rather than in the real world.

Peters sat quietly in his car and tried to give his stomach and head time to settle. Having made little progress in this investigation, he decided to go home and get some rest before his 'interview' with Gwynn tonight. Although he felt like shit, he couldn't wait to see her. He was determined not to let this precious opportunity slip through his fingers. He only needed to come up with a few novel questions that he hadn't previously asked her. Then, after some friendly banter, maybe they could break the ice and establish a deeper connection.

Chapter Fourteen

Gwynn stared in the mirror and once again didn't recognize herself. It always alarmed her when this happened. The woman in the mirror looked normal, but she knew the truth; she was a vampire in hiding. She turned away and ran the faucet, leaning over the sink to splash cold water on her face. The sensation didn't register. When she gazed up again, she got the same result: a strange and unfamiliar woman was staring back at her. Kaufman claimed this happened because her mind was trying to separate itself from the body, causing gaps in her memory. The process was induced by stress or trauma and was usually temporary.

Peters would be over in less than an hour, but she couldn't pull herself away from the mirror. She placed her hand on her cheek. Ran her hands through her hair. Pinched the skin over the bridge of her nose and then her upper lip. She still felt nothing. Studied the blue eyes staring back at her and studied the faded freckles dotted over the bridge of the nose. She took a few deep breaths, inhaling and exhaling, before her body and mind started to slowly merge together.

It astounded her to realize that she had killed three people in less than a month. They were all terrible people, leaving pain and destruction in their wake. So why did she feel so conflicted? So guilty? And why was she constantly asking God to forgive her trespasses when she believed what she was doing was just?

She looked away and then back in the mirror, and there she was again. Full recognition now. Gwynn Denning. Loving mother of her son, Jack, and the wife (at least for a little while) of Tom Denning. Adopted daughter of David and Anita Preston. The only missing piece from her life was her biological parents. She had always wanted to know her real mother and father, but never had the stones to pursue the matter, knowing how much it would upset her dad. He'd warned her that this might not be a good idea and that the possibility existed that she might be rejected a second time. Only now, she didn't care; her father's dementia had progressed to the point where he'd never know if she went looking for them.

The doorbell rang, and she realized it was Peters. She straightened out her white blouse, thinking it looked good contrasted against her denim jeans and pink sneakers. Satisfied with her appearance, she walked out to the living room, turned up the volume on her wireless speaker, and opened the door. Peters stood there holding a bottle of wine in one hand and a pizza box in the other. He looked handsome this evening, his face sandpapered in stubble. She laughed when she saw that he had on a white button-down shirt with denim jeans.

"I think we should have coordinated our outfits." He handed her the bottle.

"Nonsense," she said, taking the bottle from him. "Great minds think alike." She thought it risky that he'd brought wine to a police interview.

"Wow. 'Captivity'. That's one of my favorite John Mayer songs."

"Really?"

"Yeah. I've seen him two times in concert."

"Me too." She giggled like a schoolgirl. "Well, not two times, but my girlfriend and I once took the train down to Boston to see him at the Garden. It was one of the best shows I've ever seen." An awkward silence passed between them.

"I thought wine might pair better with pizza."

"Everything pairs better with pizza," she said.

"Did you know that pizza contains the entire food pyramid in one slice?"

"Never thought of it that way," she said, staring at the bottle of wine in her hand. "No offense, but I think I'd rather have a beer with my pizza."

"Me too. Let's ditch the wine."

"Do I even have beer?" She laughed as she walked toward the refrigerator.

"Wait. Should you even be drinking on the job?"

"I just got off shift," he said. "Let's just say I'm going above and beyond my usual duties."

"Above and beyond, huh?"

"Of course," he said. "So what would you like to do first: answer my questions or drink beer and eat pizza?"

"I'm perfectly capable of walking and chewing gum at the same time, Detective." She grabbed two cold bottles of Tom's Heineken out of the fridge and placed them down on the granite countertop. "I might be forced to report you to your superiors for flirting with a suspect."

"So now you're a suspect?" He sat at the island.

"What else am I to think if you're paying me a second visit?"

"Maybe I'm just conducting a follow-up interview because the last one was so much fun."

"Is that what you're calling this now? A fun follow-up?" She rested her chin on her knuckles and studied him.

"If I asked you out on a date, you might have turned me down."

"True."

"So now you understand where I'm coming from?"

"Totally. It's all in how you word things."

"Exactly."

"Maybe we should call this an interview instead of a date. That way, it will take all the pressure off us."

"Good idea," he said. "So let's just get past the formalities and make this interview official. Are you responsible for that man's disappearance?"

"I find your interrogation tactics quite harsh, Detective. You're practically beating the confession right out of me."

"Please answer the question, ma'am."

"And what if I invoke my constitutional right and take the Fifth?" She opened the pizza box, and a puff of steam billowed out.

"You have every right to invoke that as long as you pass me a beer and a slice of pizza."

Gwynn grabbed a slice and served it to him on a plate. Then she slid the green bottle over the granite countertop until it rested in his awaiting palm.

"Have you made any progress on the case?"

"Very little, ma'am. This man's disappearance is a complete and utter mystery to me." He bit into his pizza.

"What are we, actors in a nineteen-forties noir movie?" Gwynn laughed, grabbing some napkins.

"I was sort of enjoying my role as Dashiell Hammett."

"So, Dashiell, how does a man just disappear from plain sight?"

"I was hoping you might enlighten me." He uncapped the beer.

"Nice try, Detective."

"Call me Mike."

"I think I like Peters better."

"Wow, you remembered my last name. I'm impressed."

"You should consider hiring me as your sidekick. I'd make a great Watson." She cracked open her beer and took a sip. It tasted cold and delicious.

"I must admit, you'd look lovely in blue."

"Butter the suspect up and make her fall for your line of BS. I see what you're up to," she said, biting off the tip of her pizza slice and nearly burning the roof of her mouth. "Have you considered the possibility that this missing person might have had enemies down in Boston?"

"I didn't find a shred of evidence of that when I went down there and talked to his friends and coworkers."

"People often have mysterious pasts."

"Are you speaking from personal experience?"

"I guess you'll have to find out."

"How's the pizza?" he asked, holding up his slice. "On a scale of one to ten?"

"Great. I'd give it an eight-point-seven. Where'd you get it?"

"Little place on Washington Avenue called Montes. Roman style, they tell me."

"I'll have to remember that."

"For our next interview?"

"If there even is a next interview."

"I managed to get this one. That's a good sign, wouldn't you say?"

"Sure, but you're going to need to work a lot harder for another," she said, enjoying this back-and-forth. "So tell me about yourself."

"Not much to tell. Been with the Portland PD for seventeen years and a detective for seven. Live by myself. Enjoy pizza and long walks on Higgins Beach."

"Ever been married?" She took another bite, keeping her eyes on him.

"For about six years. Divorced with no kids. You?"

"Recently separated. I have a five-year-old son named Jack, and he's the light of my life."

"That's cool."

"Have you ever fired your gun while on the job?" she asked, instantly realizing from his expression that she'd asked the wrong question. "I'm sorry. Did I say the wrong thing?"

"No, it's okay. It's just a touchy subject with me."

"Sorry. Sometimes, my sense of humor gets the best of me."

"It's perfectly alright. Besides, I like a woman with a warped sense of humor."

"Unfortunately, that's me," she said. "So what happened?"

"I shot a guy three years ago. Looked like a routine traffic stop, but then he got out of his car and started coming toward me in a threatening manner. He reached for something, which turned out to be a gun."

She listened but didn't say anything, cursing herself for ruining the good mood.

"I was placed on administrative leave while Internal Affairs reviewed the case. The victim's family and friends swore up and down that he wasn't carrying a weapon, but I knew firsthand that wasn't the case. Turns out the guy had a long and violent rap sheet. Internal eventually cleared me, but it was touch and go there for a while."

"That's awful."

"It was a pretty ugly situation, but that's what us cops face on a daily basis."

"You were only defending yourself."

"That's what I thought, but then the victim's family and the media make

99

you out to be this monster, and you start second-guessing yourself every time you make an arrest. I'll be honest, it's probably why my wife left me." He clutched his beer bottle and stared down at the counter. "It's why I badly need to solve this case."

She paused to consider this. "Because of what happened three years ago?"

"Precisely because of it. I need to reestablish my reputation in the department. Admittedly, I've got a long way to go."

"Why is that?"

He shrugged. "Don't really know. I've been seeing a counselor off and on, trying to figure things out. She thinks I might have developed PTSD from that shooting."

"I feel for you," she said. "At least that's another thing we have in common. We're both seeing shrinks."

He laughed. "You a little screwed up, too?"

"I may look like I have my shit together, but let me warn you, I can get batshit crazy at times." She felt much closer to him now that he had admitted to killing a man. "Can I ask you another question?"

"Who's the one asking the questions around here?"

"I am. But you don't have to answer it if you don't want to."

"Go right ahead."

"What did it feel like when you killed him?"

He sipped his beer and seemed to think it over.

"We don't have to talk about it if you don't want to."

"No, it's okay." He grabbed another slice of pizza. "I was scared shitless after I shot him. Then relieved when I saw the gun and realized it was him lying dead on the pavement and not me. I pretty much knew as soon as I shot him that he was dead. We're trained to shoot to kill."

"That must have been hard on you."

"You don't even know. I felt guilty about it for months afterward, running that situation over and over through my mind, wondering if I'd made the right decision. But then I realized I wouldn't be here today if I hadn't pulled that trigger."

"What crimes had he committed?"

"Armed robbery. Drug charges. Sexual assault against a minor, and numerous domestic abuse charges."

"Sounded like he was no altar boy."

"Far from it."

"I have little sympathy for violent criminals, especially those who hurt children." She gently tore apart her pizza crust using her fingers, turning it inside out, picking off the basil and charred crust. "Everything happens for a reason."

"You think?"

"I do; what goes around comes around."

"There are people out there who say he didn't deserve to die."

"What if it was you lying dead on the pavement? Would you have deserved to die for merely doing your job?"

"I don't believe so."

"Neither do I." She sipped her beer, wondering if she had pushed him too far. "How about we change the subject and talk about something more pleasant?"

"Sounds good to me."

"I'll get us a few more beers while we're at it," she said. "And by the way, this pizza is legit."

"I told you."

Gwynn was happy the conversation had transitioned and put him in a better mood. Surprisingly, she enjoyed talking to him. He was considerate and kind, good traits for a potential boyfriend. Their conversation flowed naturally, especially after the two beers they'd consumed, and in a short time, they were laughing and telling each other jokes. She was having so much fun that she wondered how she could ever go back to being with Tom.

An hour passed, and Gwynn realized she had drunk more beer than she had in a long time, and she didn't even like Heineken. But with Peters, it was the best beer she'd ever tasted. She checked her phone to see if there were any impending crises at work and was relieved to see that everything was quiet at The Loft.

They laughed, and she touched his forearm, hanging on his every word. Her cheeks felt warm and rosy, the alcohol running laps around her brain. Peters seemed much more relaxed than before.

What she wouldn't give to tell Peters everything about herself. Tell him about the six murders she'd committed during the course of her life and how every one of them seemed justified. Now, they had killing in common, even if he claimed to have killed that thug in self-defense.

Before she knew it, two hours had passed. Where had the time gone? Laughing at one of his jokes, she went to get him another beer, but he held up his hand; he had to drive home. He stood to leave, and she got up and escorted him to the door. She badly wanted for him to kiss her goodnight before he departed, but under no circumstances would she be the one who initiated it.

They made small talk by the front door.

Her entire body trembled as she stared up at him. She hadn't had sex in a long time, and the last encounter she had was a miserable quickie she'd had with Tom down in the basement. He'd cornered her by the washing machine and wouldn't let her leave until she agreed to have sex with him. Even back in college, sex with Tom had been dull and forgettable. Making love to him felt like being stuck in a Bulgarian wrestling move that she desperately wanted to escape from. Tom always rushed things, paying more attention to his own needs rather than hers. Sex with him seemed staged, as if they were following a script. Looking back, she'd fooled herself into thinking that she enjoyed their intimacy. At the time, she hadn't even known the meaning of mind-blowing sex; Tom was the first boy she'd ever slept with. In her early twenties, she'd engaged in a few one-night stands that made her hate herself and never want to have sex again.

Peters opened the door, and they stood for a second, staring into each other's eyes. It should have felt awkward, but it didn't. 'In Your Eyes' by Peter Gabriel played over the speaker. Gwynn noticed that he had a tiny speck of tomato sauce stuck to his lower lip. She badly wanted to use her thumbnail to scrape it off, but instead resisted the temptation. Then, without warning, Peters leaned over and kissed her. She could smell the pungent aroma of garlic and basil on his breath. His hand gently reached behind her back and rested nicely on the base of her spine. Her entire body quivered at his touch. She closed her eyes as his lips pressed gently into hers, and she felt her hands balled into fists up by her chest. Then, just as quickly as the kiss began, his lips drew back. She opened her eyes and saw him smiling down at her as he shuffled backward and out the door. Once he hit the walkway, he turned and strode with purpose toward his car.

Watching him drive away, Gwynn felt as if she was floating on air. She closed the door and retreated to the kitchen island. Could Peters be the one? The one who took her to Hot Suppa on Sunday mornings and then to concerts later in the evening at Thompson's Point. She imagined picking out furniture with him at Ethan Allen, then returning home to drink cold beer and eat Empire Chinese food out of white boxes.

She snapped back to reality, promising herself to not get too attached to this police detective. Not yet, anyways.

Once back in the kitchen, she gathered up the remaining slices of pizza and put them on a plate. She placed the empty bottles in the recycling bin. Sitting at the counter, she considered all the good things that were happening in her life. A possible new love interest. A meaningful and fulfilling job. An end in sight to her unsatisfying marriage. And the fact that she'd eliminated three unscrupulous people from this world in the last month. Hopefully, she could put an end to that chapter of her life and move on. Live like a normal person. Spread kindness and cheer.

Come Monday, she planned on starting out in a new direction. She would begin to look for her biological parents. Maybe learning who they were would help her come to terms with the dark thoughts that had plagued her from a young age. And with her father's dementia getting worse by the day, he'd never have to know that she was pursuing this matter.

Chapter Fifteen

Gwynn awoke the next morning to the sound of the doorbell ringing. She dragged herself out of bed and stumbled down the stairs, her head pounding and her tongue dry as cotton. After opening the front door, she let Tom and Jack inside, giving Jack a big welcome hug home. He ran into the living room and started playing with his toys in the bin. Then she and Tom sat down at the kitchen island and made small talk for a few minutes before she decided to inform him of her decision.

"I'm sorry to say, Tom, but it's over between us. I plan on filing for divorce," she said as Jack ran happily around the room, playing loudly with one of his action figures.

"You don't really mean that," Tom said.

"I'm afraid I do." Jack made loud explosion noises in the background.

"It's a big decision. You should give it more thought."

"Trust me, I've given it a lot of thought, and I can't see us going forward as a married couple."

"Look how happy Jack is when we're together."

"Jack will be fine. Besides, I'm sure he wouldn't want his mother to stay in an unhappy marriage."

Tom picked up an empty envelope on the island and began to aggressively tear it into strips. "Are you really that unhappy?"

"You became overbearing and insecure, Tom. It felt like you were always keeping tabs on me."

"I'm sorry. I didn't realize I was doing that."

"Besides, we were drunk when we made that silly pact back in college. Then we made an even bigger mistake when we acted upon it after meeting at Gritty's."

"Are you saying that Jack was a mistake?"

"Of course, Jack wasn't a mistake. I wouldn't trade him for anything."

"Neither would I," he said. "Nor would I change the fact that I fell in love with you and we got married."

"I'm not changing my mind, Tom." She went over to the refrigerator and pulled out the plate with the cold pizza slices, placing it on the island between them. "Are you hungry?"

"Fuck your pizza," he mumbled under his breath.

"There's no point in being mean."

Tom leaned over the counter and started to cry into his hands, which startled her. "You'd better get a good lawyer," he said, shooting her a sinister look she'd never quite seen before.

"Don't worry about me, Tom. You better start worrying about yourself from now on."

"You can be such a bitch," he whispered. "I wish I had known you were like this when I first met you."

"I wish I had known that you jumped into bed with Sandra Clayborn the minute we broke up."

Tom appeared stunned by this.

"Don't act so surprised. I've known about it for a couple of years now."

"You had broken up with me at the time. I didn't owe you anything."

"Maybe not, but of all the girls at Brooks to sleep with, you had to jump in the sack with *her*?"

"What do you want me to say? It just happened."

"You had to have known how much that would hurt me."

"You know what, Gwynn? I'm glad I slept with Sandra. Serves you right for how you treated me."

"Be careful, Tom. Don't say anything you might regret."

"And what are you going to do about it?"

She laughed, thinking how satisfying it would be to plunge a steak knife through his eye. Or wrap an electric cord around his fat throat and choke him out. But she'd never kill Tom—or at least she felt that way at the moment. And even if she did want to kill him, which she didn't, she had to think of Jack. Jack would definitely be worse off without his father around. He loved Tom dearly.

"Jack, come say goodbye to your dad," she said.

"Bye, Daddy," Jack shouted, still playing with his action figures.

Tom walked over and gave his son a bear hug goodbye. His belly hung over his belt buckle, and his longish hair fell into his son's eyes. He looked sickly and had obviously been drinking and eating more since they broke up. She watched him amble over to the front door and let himself out without even a goodbye. Thankfully, Jack continued to play, not noticing the hostility simmering between them.

She turned and saw her son gripping an action figure in his stubby fingers, using it to beat on another action figure. She didn't feel the need to discipline him for this, seeing as how boys were biologically programmed to play more aggressively than girls. She figured he'd eventually grow out of it and be the man she hoped him to grow into, strong and decent.

"Would you like to go to the park, buddy?"

"Yeeeeeah! Will you push me on the swings, Mommy?"

"Of course, I'll push you."

Jack sprinted over to her, shoved his little hand into hers, pulling her toward the door.

Once at the park, she and Jack played tag, laughing and chasing after one another. He asked her to push him on the swings, and she happily agreed, pushing him higher and higher until she feared he might go over the top. The peal of his laughter made it all worthwhile, and when he jumped off the swing mid-arc, she thought he might fly away and leave her forever. Instead, he landed like a paratrooper descending on Normandy and then ran over to the slide. He scrambled up the ladder and then slid down it headfirst, and she caught him in her arms each and every time. Then he went to the merry-go-round and she spun him continually until he got so dizzy that he walked off it like a sailor at last call. She laughed hysterically at the sight of him falling to the ground. Jack laughed, too. When it was time to go home, she grabbed Jack in her arms and tackled him to the grass, tickling his belly. She kissed his warm cheek, listening to the delightful peel of his laughter. It was like a symphony in her ears and one that she would never get tired of hearing. It reaffirmed her decision to do everything in her power to stay in her son's life. It was the primary reason she had to kill William Clayborn.

"I love you so much, Wiggleworm."

"Love you too, Mama," the boy said. "Can we get some ice cream cones now?"

"Of course we can."

Chapter Sixteen

Three Days Later

D espite the added bounce in his step, Peters had made little progress in the case of the missing Boston man. So when he arrived at the station and heard that two more people had gone missing, he couldn't quite believe his ears. It seemed as if someone was playing a cruel joke on him. And on the city of Portland.

He read the report and learned that Sandra Clayborn and her husband, William, hadn't shown up for work on Monday morning. Quite unusual, seeing as how William had a big trial starting that day, which the judge had to postpone on account of his absence. It had been totally out of character for William not to show up in court. People assumed they'd jetted off to Europe and had simply missed their flight. But wouldn't they have called someone at the office and told them about this? When Tuesday rolled around, neither of them appeared for work that day, either.

Why did the name Clayborn ring a bell? Peters had interviewed so many people now that he'd lost track of names and associations. Not that he'd been dwelling much on the case after his 'interview' with Gwynn. It surprised him when, against his better judgment, he leaned over and kissed her before he left her house. It pleased him even more to learn that she was equally receptive to his advance. But this new development perplexed him. Three people were now missing in little old Portland, Maine, and he had not a clue what happened.

Disappearances like this didn't happen here. They took place in bigger, more populated cities. Dangerous cities with evil lurking around every corner. The only other prominent case he could think of was the Muddy River Killer, who terrorized the women of Portland back in the eighties, nineties, and early aughts. The first few bodies were discovered on the Muddy River, and then the rest were found along the banks of the Presumpscot. All the victims were young, some were prostitutes, and most had varying degrees of substance abuse and mental health issues. He was a young boy the first time he learned about it. The thought of a serial killer in town terrified him, until his father sat him down one day and assured him that the Muddy River Killer wasn't interested in dumb kids like him, but 'young whores no one gave a shit about'. It was the Muddy River Killer that piqued his interest in serial killers and made him want to be a detective someday.

Could the Clayborns have gotten sick of the rat race and fled town without telling anyone? He doubted it. William Clayborn relished his role as the state's top criminal defense attorney and had been featured prominently on TV and in newsprint. His wife was an ambitious businesswoman and the vice president of Plumhurst Capital, earning an MBA at Harvard Business School. A power couple like that didn't just up and leave without telling anyone. His gut instinct told him that they ended up the same way that Sam Townsend did. Maybe even in the same place. But where was that? And who did them in?

Something troubled him, and he couldn't understand what it was. Sitting at his desk, he took out all the files he'd collected on Sam Townsend and pored over them. Then, he read his notes and experienced an unusual sense of dread. Sandra and Gwynn both attended Brooks College, graduating the same year. Worse, Sam Townsend went to Crawford, graduating a year earlier. Did any of this add up to anything? Why did this connection to two elite Maine colleges strike him as significant? Because Brooks College was roughly fifty miles from Crawford?

He sat back and thought about how ridiculous he was being. There was no way a woman like Gwynn Denning had anything to do with the disappearance of these three persons. Besides, he doubted a slender woman like her would even be capable of overtaking a hulking man like Sam Townsend. He cursed himself for being so suspicious all the time and undermining his own confidence.

The nagging doubts he experienced had ended his first marriage. He couldn't keep himself from thinking that his wife was cheating on him while he worked the three-to-eleven beat. Beth denied it vehemently, but he would call her at night while he was cruising around town, and she wouldn't answer. Many nights, she'd come home well after he'd come off shift, a little tipsy, saying she'd gone out with friends. His nagging suspicions began to eat away at him until he couldn't take it anymore. He began to lash out at her for no apparent reason, accusing her of all kinds of malicious behaviors, knowing in his heart that he was out of line. By the time he got promoted to detective and started working the day shift, the damage had already been done to their marriage. Not long after that, she informed him that she wanted a divorce.

Peters planned on making more calls, talking to people who knew the couple. The possibility even existed that one of William Clayborn's former clients might have killed him. Either that or one of the victims William interrogated—more like harassed—on the stand during one of his brutal cross-examinations. But even that seemed remote. Wouldn't an angry client or victim ambush the lawyer and use a gun to kill him?

He decided to hold off on making any calls until he visited the Clayborns' home and got a better feel for the crime scene.

Chapter Seventeen

Peters walked inside the waterfront home, and it didn't fail to disappoint. Two technicians stood nearby collecting evidence. Nothing looked out of place. He detected no signs of a struggle and saw no suggestion of blood, although testing with luminol would be the most comprehensive search. He stopped at the patio door and gazed out over the swirling, turbulent bay. A thick mist hovered over the choppy surface of the water. All of this normalcy confounded him.

"Come up with anything yet, Chuck?" he asked.

"There's a dog locked in the bedroom. Looks like a Miniature Poodle."

"Anything else?"

"Almost done here, but I'm not detecting anything. No sign of blood or foul play."

"This is a really strange crime scene. Did you notice that both cars are still parked in the driveway?"

"Yeah, it's like those two disappeared into thin air, same as that Townsend guy," Chuck said, still examining whatever he was looking at.

"William's friend in Falmouth said that the four of them played Texas Hold'em, drank scotch, and smoked cigars well into the early morning. Then William returned home. Supposedly, he had to get ready for a trial he was starting on Monday. He said the same group of guys had been getting together like that for years. And none of them seemed like the type who would commit murder. A fellow lawyer, a doctor, and a CPA."

"That means the perpetrator must have been waiting for him when he returned home. Whoever did this could have taken care of Sandra first and then killed William."

"There appears to be no security breach," Peters said, walking around the living room, looking for anything that might help him. "Could they have known the person who did this?"

"Anything's possible," Chuck said, standing.

"No Ring Cam videos?"

"Surprisingly, no."

"You would have thought a defense lawyer would have had all kinds of security cameras installed in his house."

"Yeah, especially a lawyer who represents the kind of dirtbags he does," the man said. "Check this out, Peters. There were still grinds in the Breville. Looks like a full pot, meaning that maybe there was more than one person here."

"What's a Breville?"

"A fancy coffeemaker for rich people. It's on the kitchen counter."

Peters walked over and studied the contraption. "How much does this thing cost?"

"That one probably runs just under three grand. Everything in this kitchen is high-end, which tells me that either one of them, or both, had made coffee before they disappeared."

"Could have been sitting there for a while."

"It's just starting to get moldy, which fits in perfectly with the timeline."

"Where are the coffee cups?" he asked, peering into the empty sink and then the empty dishwasher.

"Your guess is as good as mine."

Peters glanced around for an errant cup. He never would have thought of that detail because he purchased his coffee every morning at Tony's Donuts.

"What about their cell phones," Peters asked.

"William's phone is on the coffee table. And Sandra left hers on the kitchen island."

A woman walked down the stairs, and he recognized her as another evidence tech.

"Looks like you've got your work cut out for you, Peters," Chuck said as he and his partner walked into another room.

Peters took out his pad and stared down at his notes, noticing something interesting in them. Sandra had competed on the swim team back at Brooks and was known to take long swims each morning before work, assuming the weather was decent and the bay relatively calm. He took out his phone and did a quick search of the weather the weekend Sandra went missing; it had been clear and sunny. He moved to the window and looked out at the choppy surface of the water, wondering if her body was somewhere on the ocean floor, along with her husband's—and Sam Townsend's.

Chapter Eighteen

I n the afternoon, the gray clouds parted, and the sun-drenched Portland in sunlight. Gwynn had been toiling in her office all morning, filling out paperwork and trying to get a new client installed into one of their residential homes. She pored over the girl's file, shaking her head in disgust at all the abuse the child had been through these last few years. Gwynn had read similar accounts thousands of times before, but never ceased to be appalled every time she encountered a new client. Last year, the girl had started to cut herself. She'd been given a dual diagnosis of PTSD and bipolar disorder. Gwynn's heart broke as she continued to read the file. She'd come to believe that being born on this planet was often the luck of the draw. It's why she considered herself so lucky to have been adopted by such loving and kind parents.

It was part of the reason she wanted to track down her biological parents. She'd made a few initial calls that morning to get the ball rolling. One source at the state capital said she would call her back later in the day with some information. Now, every time the phone rang, she nearly fell off her chair answering it.

An hour later, a nurse called to inform her that Ivy was resting comfortably in her bed at the group home on campus. Gwynn debated walking over to the home, which was only two hundred yards from the administrative building, but decided against it for now. The last thing the girl needed was a bunch of adults hovering over her and asking her a series of annoying questions. Somehow, Gwynn knew that she had to sit down with Ivy at some point and try to persuade her from moving back home with her family, assuming the judge ruled in their favor.

Gwynn picked up the newspaper and walked toward the window. Outside, the children ran around on the playground. They looked so happy and normal that an outsider might not realize just how troubled they were. She promised herself to go out and play with them before she started back on her administrative duties.

Her attention returned to the headline story about the Clayborns' disappearance. The police had no clue as to what might have happened to them, meaning she sufficiently covered all of her tracks. They hinted that the case might be related to the missing Boston man. Her heart skipped a beat when she read the quote by Detective Peters, and she briefly recalled the moment he'd kissed her.

Never in her life had she felt this happy. Soon, she would be free from Tom and be able to live her life accordingly, without him watching her every move. He was a CPA by trade, but sometimes she believed his real job was accounting for her every action. She and Peters shared a chemistry that neither of them could deny. Furthermore, she doubted that the police would find any compelling evidence to pin these murders on her.

Having killed six times up to this point in her life, she hoped to put that part behind her and fulfill her potential as a person. Despite just meeting Peters, she envisioned having a long-term relationship whereby she could finally find happiness and joy, and live her life accordingly. Maybe he could be the elixir that quelled these occasional urges that came over her. And maybe reconnecting with her biological parents might help facilitate the healing process, assuming they were still alive and would agree to meet with her.

She had hoped for this outcome before, particularly when she decided to marry Tom. Then the dark thoughts returned, and it was all she could focus on until they eventually passed, like a fast-moving thunderstorm. She likened her situation to an alcoholic who quit booze for a few months only to burn with the desire to consume one more drink.

Feeling invigorated, she exchanged her heels for Sketchers and headed outside to play. A few of the smaller children cheered when she ran onto the field, rushing over to hug her. One of the kids tossed her a Frisbee, and she flung it back and forth with the girl. After tossing it around for a while, she joined some boys for a game of three-on-three basketball. When she hit a long jumper for the win, they all broke out into peals of laughter, not able to believe that this slender woman had such mad hoop skills. After the game, she moved over to the tetherball pole and played a vigorous game with two girls. In the middle of the game, her phone rang, so she excused herself to answer it.

"I discovered something about your biological mother that might interest you," the woman at the state capital said.

"Wonderful."

"Don't get your hopes up, though. It's no guarantee."

"No, of course not. But anything you can do will help."

"There's an elderly woman who used to work for the Little Wanderers adoption agency. Her name is Lillian Belson, and she lives in Limerick. She might or might not be able to help you locate your parents."

"Thank you so much. Would you mind texting me her name and number when you get a chance?"

The woman agreed before ending the call. Gwynn felt everything in her life finally starting to come together: work, romance, finding her biological parents. Still, she couldn't help but experience a pang of guilt about betraying her father's wishes. He'd made her promise that she would never go looking for them and now she was going back on her word.

The bell rang for the children to return to their classrooms. The smaller ones surrounded her on either side as she escorted them back to class. She knew all their names, knew what was in their file cases, and what they liked to do for fun. After exchanging goodbyes with them, she watched the kids disappear inside the school building. The empty playground left a void in her heart, but interacting with the children made her work here all the more meaningful.

Her phone pinged as she made her way up to her office, and the name and number of the woman from the Little Wanderers agency appeared on-screen. It unnerved her to see it. Tonight, she would drive over to her father's house, even if he didn't remember much these days. As depressing as it was to see him in his condition, Gwynn knew she had to spend as much time as possible with him before he left this world. She prayed that he might experience one last moment of joy before their time together passed.

Chapter Nineteen

Gwynn's father appeared in good spirits when she sat across from him at his kitchen table. It wouldn't last long, however. She'd read up on the illness, and medical studies had consistently shown that mental acuity in patients with dementia declined rapidly as the day wore on. Her father was no exception.

He sat flipping through a sailing magazine and staring down at the glossy photos on the pages. Gwynn tried not to focus on the boats because it reminded her of what she'd done to Sandra. At one point, he turned the page, revealing a Boston Whaler, the rig similar to the one she'd used to motor out to Sandra.

Her father mumbled something under his breath while turning the pages. His caretaker shuffled around the living room, tidying things up. Thank God he'd had the wherewithal to purchase disability insurance when he was younger. She felt grateful for the amazing staff who looked after him and treated him with the compassion and respect he once bestowed on the homeless people he served. They fed and washed her father, helping him with his daily routines. Otherwise, he might have had to live in one of those dirty, underfunded nursing homes where the staff didn't care about the clients' well-being.

"How are you, Dad?"

"Wonderful, sweetheart. How are you?" He gazed into her eyes like he used to when she was a little girl. Did he still recognize her?

"I'm good."

"Glad to hear that. Your mother's in the other room with Jesus. She'll be so happy to see you."

"I'm sure she will." She'd long ago given up telling him that his wife was dead. "Those are some beautiful boats you're looking at. Remember when you had that little skiff? You used to take me out in it and teach me how to be a captain."

"Sure do." He didn't.

"You used to love cruising around Sebago Lake."

"I did?"

She nodded.

"Well, I'll be damned."

"Jack said to say hi."

"Jack?" He wrinkled his brow.

"Your grandson." She took out her phone and showed him the same photo as always.

"I have a grandson?"

"Yup. Isn't he cute?"

"Sure is." He smiled, his eyes still icy blue. He'd lost most of his blond hair on top, but he still resembled the charismatic street minister from her youth. "Your mother will be so happy to see you."

She patted his knotted hand.

"What's your name again?"

"Gwynn."

"Nice to meet you."

She couldn't go on like this, week after week, watching him slowly waste away, repeating the same lines over and over. Sometimes, she believed it would be better if he just died. Then, there were times when she was not yet ready to let him go.

She kissed him on the forehead and stood. He continued to gaze down at his magazine as if she wasn't even there. Gwynn went into the living room and thanked his caretaker before leaving. Instead of driving away, she sat in her car and had a good cry.

Until her phone pinged.

"Did you hear the news?" Peters asked.

119

"No, I've been too busy."

"Sandra Clayborn and her husband have gone missing."

"Oh my God," she said, trying to remain calm. "Do the police have any idea what happened to them?"

"We don't, but I'm not optimistic about finding them alive."

"Why is that?"

"Sam Townsend, and now these two? Something's not right in this town."

"Sandra and I used to be friends back in college, but I haven't spoken to her in quite some time. I didn't even get a chance to talk to her at that Custom House event."

"I know, that's why I called—to give you a heads-up."

"Thanks for telling me," she said, trying to sound sad. "Do you really think their disappearance is connected to that Boston man's case?"

"It's too much of a coincidence not to be. Three people who were at that Custom House event have now gone missing. What other conclusion am I to draw?"

"I suppose it does look rather fishy," she said, her mind calculating what he and the police might know. "It's still hard for me to believe that Sandra's dead."

Peters hesitated. "She's missing, but we haven't found her body yet. That doesn't necessarily mean she's dead."

"Yes, you're right." She scolded herself for inferring as much. *Think before you speak, Gwynn, or you'll end up in prison.*

"I wanted to tell you that I had a wonderful time the other night," he said.

"Pizza and beer, what else could be better?"

"That was nice, too, but it wasn't the pizza and beer I was referring to."

"Then it must have been the John Mayer song I put on."

"Yeah, that must be it." He laughed. "I'd really like to see you again."

"All you gotta do is ask, fella."

"I'd like to, but this development with the Clayborns might keep me tied up for a while. Can I get a rain check?"

"Of course," she said. "Good luck, Peters. I hope you find out what happened to them."

"Me too."

Gwynn ended the call, trying to remember everything she did after each incident. Did she sufficiently cover her tracks? And what about the captain of the *Lilly*? Did he see anything as he piloted his lobster boat out to sea? He obviously hadn't said anything to the police yet, which boded well for her.

She took out her laptop and started working on the manuscript she planned on sending to Tift. In some form or another, all this intrigue would make for an amazing story. Maybe even a movie. Of course, she'd have to change all the names and hide her complicity in everything. But that shouldn't be a problem. The mere act of writing helped her process her emotions and keep the demons at bay. Kaufman recommended she keep at it, saying that journaling what was going on in her life was therapeutic. Gwynn wondered what Tift would think about the script once she read it. Would she connect the dots and conclude that Gwynn was a serial killer and that she had paid Sam Townsend back for what he had done to Tift back at Brooks?

Dr. Ezra Kaufman

I nearly spit out my coffee this morning when I read the headlines. People are wondering what happened to Sandra and William Clayborn. The news both disturbs and intrigues me, especially when I learn that Sandra graduated from Brooks College the same year as Gwynn. I can't help wondering why three people who attended the same event with Gwynn have disappeared.

Knowing her as well as I do, I keep asking myself why I haven't yet turned her in to the police.

I think of my mother and the hellish existence she had to endure in order to survive that death camp. The evils forced upon her make my blood boil. She endured days on end when she and her fellow survivors barely had any water or food. I can't even imagine the terror she must have felt, wondering if she, too, would end up at the bottom of a mass grave.

It's why I understand vengeance on a personal level. I'm not saying it's right, but I do get why it happens. When once asked at a cocktail party whether I would have killed the adolescent Hitler, knowing the evil he would one day commit as an adult and knowing the consequences I would face, I unequivocally said yes. But in reality, I lied. I would never have been able to do it. It's just not in me to take another person's life.

Is Gwynn able to kill without experiencing crippling guilt? I've asked myself this question countless times. To all appearances, she appears to be a decent and caring person. But I've gotten to know her better than most people. I've observed these black holes in her personality that briefly pop up from time to time. On the other hand, I've seen the love and tenderness she shows to the children in her care. She adores her son, as well as her father. Yes, she suffers from a variety of personality disorders that, on occasion, affect her decision-making, but she takes medication for her condition. It's why she's been seeing me all these years.

I can understand, even sympathize, why she may have pushed that teacher to his death back in high school. I can even understand why she might have killed that drug-addict father who perished before her very eyes. The way she explained it, she showed up to check in on the child and found squalor and neglect. The two-year-old boy was crying hysterically, had cigarette burns all over his malnourished body, and was covered in feces and urine. I can only imagine the sorrow and outrage Gwynn must have felt upon coming across that horrific scene. It must have been similar to the way the liberators felt upon seeing the survivors at Mauthausen before the camp was freed.

I can picture it in my own mind. The boy's father was passed out on the sofa, the elastic band still wrapped around his emaciated bicep. His inner forearm resembled one of those silly connect-the-dot puzzles we used to pass the time on as children. Gwynn knew how to administer heroin, having seen the process performed many times as a social worker. She grabbed the spoon and lighter, and put in enough of the drug in the syringe to drop an elephant. Lit it and then injected the dark fluid into his veins, and no one knew any better.

Is the world a better place now that he's gone? There can be no doubt. Certainly, the neglected child is better off. I struggle at times to deny such harsh truths, but there can be no question that justice was served that day. I only hope the boy was placed with a good family and that he turned out okay.

So what could this Boston man have done to warrant a death sentence? Or the Clayborns? Knowing Gwynn, it must have been pretty serious.

I don't understand how she keeps her faith after witnessing all the evil in this world. I wish I could say I believe in God after everything that's happened to my family and after all the wars and atrocities that have occurred throughout history. I'm stuck in the middle somewhere, one day a believer and the next, a doubting Thomas. What kind of God allows the horrors of Nazi Germany to happen? Or watches as young children are abused and neglected by their own parents?

What puzzles me most is that my mother bears no ill will toward anyone, past or present, whereas it's all I can do some days to face humanity. It just doesn't seem fair. Why should her hardships bother me more than it does her? I'm sure she hasn't forgotten her trespassers, but has she forgiven those who wronged her?

I think about her treatment at the hands of those cruel camp guards and wonder why I must suffer in silence, a victim of my first-world privilege. My life has been nothing if not entitled. My parents sacrificed and scrimped so I could attend the finest schools and live a good life. I could have chosen any career path I wanted, but I picked psychology. My goal was to learn about human behavior and what makes people tick. I have also wanted to understand my own convoluted mindset. This quest for knowledge has consumed me to the point where I've never made any close friends or lovers. The intellectual walls I've constructed around myself in pursuit of knowledge are as daunting as the ones that once encircled the Polish ghetto.

There it is. Me in a nutshell. Despite my strict rules, and seeming lack of affection toward humanity, Gwynn's probably the closest thing I have to a daughter. What I feel for her goes far beyond a mere client/therapist relationship.

She's a fascinating individual and I want to know more about her. I've kept detailed notes about her behavior, chronicling her life and developmental thought processes. As a student of human behavior, I've never broken any new ground in the field, but this might be my one chance to prove or disprove the nature versus nurture debate. Selfishly, it's why I've prodded her to locate her biological parents. Maybe her dark nature is a genetic predisposition passed down from them. Or maybe the answer is much simpler: she enjoys it, rationalizing her behavior by killing only bad people.

I've come to the depressing conclusion that Gwynn has committed murder. Maybe more than one. Somehow, she's managed to convince herself that what she's done, illegal and immoral as it may be, was wholly justified.

And though it pains me to say it, she might be right. I hope she'll open herself up to me in future sessions and tell me why she does what she does, and how she justifies her actions.

Chapter Twenty

Two days had gone by since Peters broke the news to Gwynn about the Clayborns' disappearance, and still, there had been no new discoveries. The fact that the police were baffled about what happened relieved Gwynn, but she knew sooner or later that Sandra's body would wash ashore.

Two days ago, Gwynn called the elderly woman who once worked at the Little Wanderers adoption agency and spoke to her. Yesterday, following the woman's lead, she took the day off and ventured up to Augusta and spent the day there doing research. The woman had told her exactly where to look in the files, and she did as instructed, finally coming up with the names of fourteen women who could potentially be her mother. She was surprised that she found the names so quickly. But that was thirty-seven years ago, and she had no idea where to find these women, or even if they were still alive.

Gwynn had called the retired woman from the adoption agency and asked for additional assistance, and the woman had agreed to meet with her. That was her plan for today: drive over to Limerick and hear what the woman named Lillian might say. Hopefully, finding her biological mother would give her some insight into her genetic and psychological makeup, and she could decide whether it was nature or nurture that caused her to be this way.

Forty-five minutes later, she pulled into the woman's driveway and saw the house set back in the woods. Off in the distance, she saw a red barn with a green tractor parked in front of it. It reminded her of the landscape near her cabin. She'd brought a fruit basket with her as a token of her appreciation. After walking up to the woman's front porch, she knocked on the door, and in seconds, the woman appeared, looking small and frail.

"You must be Gwynn," the woman said with a welcoming smile. "I'm Lillian."

"Please to meet you, Lillian. I brought you this as a show of my appreciation." She handed the woman the fruit basket.

"How beautiful. You didn't have to do that."

"It's my way of saying thanks."

"But I haven't done anything for you yet."

She smiled. "You will. I just know it."

Gwynn followed her into the living room. The woman placed the basket down on the coffee table and sat on the sofa. The inside of the house looked exactly the way Gwynn pictured an old woman's home to look like. Dated wallpaper in the dining room, tan shag carpet, and lots of photographs of kids hung everywhere, which Gwynn assumed were Lillian's grandchildren. There was a pink sofa and a recliner in the living room, which was separated from the dining room by an alcove. She noticed a fireplace with an outdated mirror over the mantel, supporting a series of tiny statuettes. She sat down across from the woman, noticing the black and white photograph of a man wearing glasses, possibly Lillian's deceased husband.

"Before we get started, I need to ask you something."

"Of course. Anything."

"Are you sure you want to go through with this?"

"I wouldn't be here if I didn't."

"It's just that I've helped others in the past, and with few exceptions, it rarely goes the way people planned."

"Don't worry about me. I'm a social worker and understand the risks involved with this sort of thing."

"Did you end up getting adopted by loving parents?"

"I couldn't have asked for a better mother and father growing up."

"You don't know how happy that makes me," Lillian said. "So, how do they feel about you looking for your biological parents? Because you have to consider their feelings in all this, too."

"My parents don't mind," she lied.

"Really?"

She laughed nervously. "Really. They're quite supportive, in fact."

"Well, if you're absolutely sure."

"I am." Gwynn took out her legal pad with the fourteen names written on it. "How long did you work at the Little Wanderers agency, Lillian?"

"Thirty-nine years. They closed their doors five years after I retired."

"Wow. You must have found the work very rewarding."

"I did, but it was also sad in many ways, watching those poor young girls part with their babies."

"How did most of them react when they handed their newborns over to you?"

"Some of the girls became quite attached during their pregnancy and sobbed uncontrollably, not wanting to give their baby up. Others simply allowed me to take their child without a care in the world."

"That must have been tough to watch."

"What did you say your name was?"

"It's Gwynn Denning now. My parents' last name was Preston. My father was a minister in town."

"I remember him now. Your father was an extremely nice man. Your mother was a bit reserved, if my memory serves me correctly."

"Yes, that's right. I'm impressed that you actually remember them."

"They had no children and were extremely happy when I handed you over. How are they doing?"

"Great. My father retired from his ministry a few years ago."

"Please give them my best."

"I certainly will," she said. "Do you remember anything about my biological parents?"

The woman glanced down at her knobby, arthritic fingers.

"Really, Lillian. Nothing you say will bother me. And it's not like I have high expectations of finding them, like some of the other people you've helped."

"I didn't know your biological father. But your mother was young, maybe sixteen or seventeen, when she gave birth to you. And she had quite a troubled past."

"Troubled in what way?"

Lillian sighed and fingered her wedding ring. "She was a runaway and a...a...?"

"A what?"

"A streetwalker."

"A prostitute?" This surprised her.

"Yes. It was so sad. She was such a pretty girl, too."

All of this information fascinated her. "You actually remember her after all these years?"

"How could I not? It was probably one of the saddest cases I've ever dealt with."

"Why?"

"Because she was so smart. And beautiful. She could have been one of those models you see on TV," Lillian said, placing a hand on her cheek. "Looking at you now, I can see some of her in you."

Gwynn felt self-conscious, but she was anxious to hear more.

"The poor girl had so many issues."

"What kind of issues?"

"Anger problems, for one. She accused her mother's boyfriend of molesting her when she was twelve. He got off on the charge but eventually ended up doing time for sexual assault of a minor. She got into fights at school with the other girls. Finally, she just dropped out and took to the streets."

"And that's when she became a prostitute?"

"I'm not sure when it happened. I do know that a few years after giving you up for adoption, she ended up going to prison for stabbing a man."

"She stabbed a man?" This revelation excited her.

"She claimed he raped her, so the judge sentenced her to a five-year term. I heard she got heavily hooked on drugs after that, but to be honest, I lost track of her."

The news that her mother had stabbed a man sent a chill down Gwynn's spine. Was this the connection she'd been waiting all these years to hear? It still didn't excuse the six murders she'd committed, but it would at least provide her with an explanation for why she felt the way she did.

"If I give you this list of names, would you be able to recognize hers?"

"I don't need a list. I remember that girl like it was yesterday," Lillian said, fiddling with the charm bracelet around her wrist. "Her name was Daisy Tuttle, but I doubt she kept her maiden name."

Gwynn examined her list and was excited to see the name Daisy Tuttle on it. "Why is that?"

"She got very attached to men. She struck me as the kind of girl who would marry early and often."

"Do you think she's still alive?"

"I have no idea."

"It shouldn't be too difficult to find her if she's alive. There can't be a lot of fifty-three-year-old Daisys walking around."

"Are you really sure you want to find her, Gwynn? It might not be a pretty sight."

"I've been mentally preparing for this for a long time now. So yes, I am ready to meet my biological mother."

"I wish you the best, then," Lillian said, standing. "My sister is coming over in a few minutes."

"Thank you, Lillian. You've been a big help."

"Glad to do it. And it's a good thing the agency shut its doors, or I would have been bound by that confidentiality agreement I signed."

"Let's hope I can track her down."

"If you do manage to find her, please don't mention you talked to me. It might bring back some painful memories."

"I promise you I won't."

"It's funny, but all of a sudden, I feel guilty about giving out her name."

"I'll be respectful at all times."

Lillian smiled. "If you need anything else, feel free to call."

"Will do."

Gwynn thanked the woman one last time before leaving. Once she arrived home, she set about looking up her mother's name.

* * *

The first thing Gwynn did when she returned home was boot up the computer and look for the best people-searching website. After scanning through them, she settled on one called FindersKeepers because it had the highest and most positive reviewer ratings. She inputted the information about Daisy, and the site began to process. While waiting, she opened the newspaper and read the latest on the three missing people, occasionally eyeing the screen in case it kicked something back. Oddly, she couldn't learn enough about these disappearances. It thrilled her to know that she was the only person in the world who knew who killed them and where their bodies were. But she needed to keep her eyes and ears open for any new information about these cases in the event the evidence pointed to her.

Ten minutes later, the screen blinked, and she saw a name pop up. Daisy Carson, aged fifty-three, and living at 62 Shelby Way in Westbrook. The site asked if she wanted to put in her credit card and learn more about Daisy, but she declined. Maybe later, she'd do it if the woman refused to tell her anything about herself. For now, she was just happy to have the address, assuming this was the same woman who gave her up for adoption all those years ago.

Gwynn decided to pay her a visit. Just the thought of being face-to-face with her biological mother gave her goosebumps. Maybe she'd finally get to know whether or not she inherited the dark thoughts that plagued her.

Her phone buzzed. It was Peters texting to say he missed her. Then he asked when he could see her again. She texted him back, telling him that she missed him too. *Possibly this weekend?* She typed back before hitting send.

Can't wait to see you, he texted back.

Chapter Twenty-One

P eters stood on the deserted, rocky beach above what appeared to be the body of Sandra Clayborn. She had been discovered by a recreational boater who was motoring close to the shore, almost a mile and a half from Sandra's home. The tide had carried her from her regular swim route and deposited it here. He waited patiently while the police photographer snapped pictures of the corpse from every angle. When the man finished, Peters walked over for a better view.

He squatted down like the all-star catcher he was in high school and examined her. The briny odor of death instantly punched him in the nose, forcing him to cover the bottom half of his face with a handkerchief. It took all his willpower not to throw up over the clump of seaweed covering her bloated, exposed foot.

There was nothing unusual to see because she was covered head to toe in a black wet suit, with the exception of her left foot and face, both of which had been exposed to the salt water. Her face had turned a greenish-brown, and the pimpled surface had begun to detach, which meant that the fat deposits had loosened under the skin.

But what interested him most was her exposed left foot. Using his pen, he removed the seaweed covering it. Why was the boot on the right foot still attached, but the left one had come undone? He reached down with a gloved hand and tugged down on the right boot, observing that it was snug around her waterlogged foot. The skin and flesh on the left ankle had almost been stripped to the bone, as if something had been wrapped around it. A chain? A wire or rope? Maybe her boot came off when her body came

132

in contact with a rock or heavy object. But he doubted it.

So what to think? Maybe she had suffered a medical condition while swimming, and the simple explanation was that she'd drowned. Okay, he could understand that happening. But then, what about William? And how did all this tie in to Townsend?

The medical examiner's staff arrived. He motioned for them to take her away. Walking back through the woods, he took out his notebook and glanced at what he'd written. A neighbor who lived a half a mile away claimed that Sandra took her morning swim at roughly the same time every morning, which was around six-thirty. Had any boaters or fishermen seen her swimming?

When Peters emerged from the woods, he saw three reporters standing in front of the officers maintaining the perimeter. No sense whitewashing it. He told them exactly what he had found and hoped that someone would come forward with some helpful information when the news hit this afternoon.

Something about that missing boot troubled him. The one remaining boot had a distinctive white stripe along the side and a checker-patterned loop near the back of the ankle. A loop that could be used to thread a rope through?

Peters returned to his desk, only to discover that the chief had added another detective to the case. A promising young woman named Janet Nguyen, who'd graduated from the University of Maine with a degree in electrical engineering, but then decided she wanted to become a police officer instead. Great. Like he needed another headache to worry about. He was a detective on a murder case, not a babysitter.

The only good thing happening in his life was Gwynn. The prospect of a romantic relationship with her was what motivated him to solve this case.

* * *

Peters sat down at his desk and reviewed all his notes again. Something about Townsend attending college fifty miles from Sandra Clayborn nagged at him. He decided to call one of Sandra's old college friends living in the area. After a brief conversation, the woman told him to call another woman who had been closer to Sandra back at Brooks. He called the woman, now living in Atlanta, and she gave him the name of another woman named Elizabeth Wells, who knew Sandra even better than she had. They were on the Brooks swim team together, and both went to graduate school in Boston. He thanked the woman and punched in the Manhattan number.

"Yes, Sandra and I were friends in college. We also went to Harvard Business School together," Elizabeth responded. "What's this about?"

"I'm sorry to tell you this, but Sandra is dead."

"Dead?" He heard silence at the other end of the line. "What happened?"

"She washed up on a beach near her house. We believe she drowned during her morning swim."

"Oh my god, that's terrible. But why are you contacting me? I live in Manhattan."

"We're looking into whether she was a victim of foul play."

"It had to have been foul play if she drowned."

This surprised him. "Why do you say that?"

"Sandra was easily the best swimmer on our college team and super competitive. There is no way that woman would have failed to make it back to shore. And I know for a fact that she often wore a wet suit while she swam, because we still talked from time to time."

"Yes, she had one on when we found her."

"There you go, then."

"What does that have to do with anything?"

"Sandra had plenty of money and bought the best of everything. That wet suit she purchased would have given her enough buoyancy to make it to shore."

"She could have developed cramps."

"You don't know how competitive she was back at Brooks. And at Harvard Business School, as well. She hated to lose, whether that be at swimming or anything else she pursued. No way will I ever believe that she wouldn't have made it back to shore safely."

He believed her. He'd also researched that brand of wet suit and saw that it cost over five hundred dollars.

"She told me a few months back that she was training for the Peaks-to-Portland swim," she said. "Does that sound like someone who drowned?"

"Not really, unless she had an undiagnosed medical problem."

"Did you see the shape that woman was in? I seriously doubt it," she said. "We used to commiserate that it was highly competitive for a woman in the world of high finance. Dog eat bitch, we used to joke."

"What about back at Brooks?"

"Back at Brooks?"

"Yeah. What was she like on campus?"

"Sandra was a polarizing figure, to say the least."

"Did you know Sam Townsend?"

"Name doesn't sound familiar. Should I?"

"He went to Crawford College around the same time as you and Sandra."

"I have no recollection of a Sam Townsend," she said. "Is there anything else I can help you with, Detective? Because I really need to get back to work."

"Just a few more questions. Did Sandra have issues with anyone back in college?"

"I wouldn't say it was an issue, but like a lot of the other girls at school, she was obsessed with Tift Ainsley. I couldn't have cared less about that stuck-up bitch, but Sandra really wanted to be a part of her clique."

"*The* Tift Ainsley? I didn't know she went to Brooks."

"She most certainly did. Sandra used to bemoan the fact that Tift roomed with someone other than her. For whatever reason, it really pissed her off."

"Who did Tift room with?"

"Gwynn Preston."

Gwynn? His heart began to hammer in his chest.

"Sandra became friends with Gwynn in order to get close to Tift, but behind Gwynn's back, she made fun of her all the time."

Peters could barely hold the phone his hand was shaking so badly.

"I really have to run, Detective. I'm sorry about Sandra, but I have nothing else to add to your case. Good luck finding out what happened to her."

His suspicious nature might end up being the death of him, even if Sandra Clayborn did sound like a backstabbing, ambitious bitch who used people to advance her career. He felt like he was inching toward a truth he did not want to know. Why did he feel so distrustful of everyone? This character flaw of his pissed him off. That deadly shooting changed him. It made him more cynical and paranoid, questioning everything and everyone. The ghost of that motorist-thug reaching into his jacket haunted him every day.

But Gwynn was different. Despite having just met her, he sensed that she had a good heart and would never hurt another living creature. Although a bit premature, he even believed he might be in love with her.

He sat procrastinating on his computer when his phone rang. The front desk had forwarded a call to him. He answered it and realized that he was talking to a man named Ben Davis, who operated his lobster boat north of Portland. The man explained that he set off at six-thirty every morning and that he'd observed a small outboard motor cruising through the harbor around the same time that rich woman went missing.

"Did you get a good look at the person steering the boat?" Peters asked, frantically flipping through his notes.

"No, I didn't think twice about it at the time."

"Do you know what make of boat it was?"

"Oh, sure. It was a Boston Whaler with a Mercury engine. I know that because I owned a similar one when I was a kid."

"Did you notice anyone swimming in the bay at the time?"

"No, sir. It was a quick glance, and then I was off to check my traps."

"Thanks," he said, his mind trying to remember what else was in his notes. And then he located what he was looking for. Sandra and William Clayborn owned a Boston Whaler that they kept tied to the dock.

He reclined in his chair and theorized what might have happened. It all started to make sense now. Sam Townsend and Sandra Clayborn were having an affair. William Clayborn found out about it and killed them. He obviously knew that Townsend would be coming up for Sandra's event, so he meticulously planned the murders. After killing them, he fled town. It was a stupid plan, especially for someone who made his living as a criminal defense attorney. But Peters knew that scorned men often do desperate things.

He called his superiors and explained to them what he'd theorized. No other scenario made sense. It felt good to solve these murders, and he couldn't wait to call Gwynn and tell her the good news. Now, all they had to do was find William Clayborn, get him to confess, and case closed.

Chapter Twenty-Two

Tom had a late Friday night business meeting, so Gwynn had agreed to hand Jack over to him in the morning. It was a wordless transaction and not a good omen for their future dealings, although Jack seemed oblivious to their estrangement, happily rambling on during their tense swap. She felt bad that she no longer loved Tom, despite his flaws, but she couldn't afford to spend any more emotional currency worrying about it. Had it not been for Jack, her break with Tom would have been easier. Surgical. Clean.

Tom's mother and sister would not be happy about her divorcing him, but when were they ever happy with her? The two had been cool to her ever since she first met them back in college. Gwynn felt that Tom's mother was as controlling with him as he was with her. And Tom always joked that no girl had ever met with his mother's approval. Listening to Tom talk about his mother throughout the years, she got the impression that the woman was high-handed and tyrannical toward her kids. Was it the reason Tom was so intrusive in their marriage? Had he been henpecked from a young age, forced to repress his true nature? It didn't matter now. Gwynn would still have to deal with the two women at all of Jack's major life events.

She had a busy day planned. Tonight, she and Peters would be getting together for their next 'interview.' She was so eager to see him that she couldn't decide which outfit to wear. Even better, Peters texted her, believing he'd solved the mystery of the three missing people. His theory was that William Clayborn had killed both his wife and Sam Townsend before fleeing the state. According to his theory, Sandra and Townsend had been having an affair and William found out about it. Had Gwynn not known any better, she would have thought it a reasonable hypothesis. Now, she only had to bolster his theory and congratulate Peters on a job well done, and hopefully, she'd be in the clear.

Later in the afternoon she would travel to Westbrook to see if she could locate her biological mother. Hopefully, Daisy was still alive and would agree to meet with her. She had no reason to believe otherwise, not finding any death notices after hours of searching the obituary pages in the local newspapers. The woman must have lived a hard life, but at the age of fifty-three, she was still relatively young. Maybe she'd turned her life around and would be happy to finally meet her long-lost daughter. Or maybe not.

Gwynn had another session scheduled with Kaufman next week. She'd been doing so well lately that she thought she might stop therapy altogether. She'd still need her prescription meds for when she began to dissociate, but she could use a nurse practitioner for that. For quite some time now, she'd been tired of his strict adherence to the same old practices. She'd grown wary of never being able to connect with him on a deeper level. His persona was so calculated and cold that he wouldn't even allow her to give him a hug when she needed one. In all the years that had passed between them, she realized she knew next to nothing anything about Kaufman as a person. Then again, that was what he was paid to do: attend to her needs. In his own strange way, she really did believe that he was looking out for her best interests.

Gwynn's father had been the one who recognized her mental health struggles at an early age. How did he know? And why did he choose Kaufman out of all the other psychiatrists in Portland? Her relationship with Kaufman had been the most meaningful one she'd ever had with another person. Much more so than with Tom. And even more so than with her father, a man she loved more than any other man in her life, and who provided her with guidance and direction, but rarely sought to understand her as a person.

Before leaving the house, she placed her cellphone on the kitchen island and then drove over to Westbrook. Her nerves began to act up the closer she got to the town line. But then she heard the news come over the radio, and she had to pull over to the side of the road to collect herself.

Sandra's body had washed ashore just north of her waterfront home.

It was not like she hadn't expected this to happen. It was the sole reason she'd loosened the boot around the woman's ankle, so rescue divers wouldn't find her along the ocean floor, a knot tied through the loop of her boot and connected to that kettlebell.

All the same, the discovery of her classmate washing ashore was an alarming development. Hopefully, there was nothing on Sandra's body that could implicate her.

* * *

Gwynn turned into a decrepit trailer park, following the chipped and faded numbers until she arrived at an ugly unit numbered 62. It resembled a cargo container, tan and dirty, with chipped blue trim painted over the top. Gwynn parked in front of it and walked over to the rickety stairway along the side. The railing wobbled as she climbed the steps. She knocked on the door and waited. After a few minutes passed, she decided to return and try again at another time. She walked back to her car and opened the door. Just then, a raspy voice called out to her. She turned and saw a woman with frizzy gray hair sticking out in all directions.

"Who the hell are you, and what do you want?" the woman shouted.

"My name is Gwynn. Can I come in and talk to you?"

The woman stared at her for a few seconds. "You got any booze or smokes?"

"I don't."

"Then get the hell out of here."

"If I go get you a bottle and a pack of cigarettes, will you talk to me?"

Her expression softened. "What kind you getting?"

"What kind do you want?"

"Vodka. And not that fancy shit. The good kind. And a pack of Virginia Slims."

"Smirnoff okay?"

"That'll do."

"I'll be right back."

"Oh, and get me some scratch tickets while you're at it.

* * *

Gwynn was struck by the possibility that this woman could actually be her mother.

The inside of her trailer looked much worse than the outside. A bunch of old magazines sat piled against one side of the wall next to a stack of books. The woman returned from the kitchen holding two red plastic cups and the bottle of vodka. She handed one to Gwynn before pouring orange juice into her own cup. Then Daisy added a generous amount of vodka. On the cluttered coffee table sat various fast-food wrappers, tabloid magazines, and an ashtray with a crack pipe in it.

"I'm sorry to trouble you, Daisy."

"What does a fancy pants like you want from me, anyway?" she asked before taking a healthy sip of her drink. Most of her teeth were either missing or rotted. "Come on, lady. I ain't got all day."

"Before I continue, I want to say that I don't expect anything from you," she said.

"Good, 'cause I ain't in the giving mood today," Daisy said, tearing through the five scratch tickets. "Not a winner in the bunch. Thanks for nothing."

"The reason I'm here," Gwynn said, taking a small sip of her drink and trying not to gag. "is that I believe you're my mother."

The woman froze mid-drink and stared at her.

"I'm sorry to spring this on you. I just had to know for sure."

The woman said nothing for a few seconds before breaking out into a fit of laughter.

"What's so funny?"

"That you think I'm your mother."

"Look, I'm not here to harass you or make any demands."

141

"Harass me all you want as long as you keep bringing booze and smokes."

"So, is it true?"

"Even assuming I am, there'll be none of that mother-daughter crap between us. We won't be going out for tea and cucumber sandwiches."

"No, I don't expect that to happen."

"Then what the hell do you want?"

"Just for you to explain why you gave me up for adoption."

"I was sixteen and pregnant and wanted an abortion, but he convinced me not to do it."

"Who convinced you?"

"Who do you think? The dude who knocked me up."

"Why did he want you to keep the baby? Were you two planning on getting married?"

She broke out laughing again. "Married? Are you for real?"

"I'm just curious."

"Look, sweetheart, I met him on the street. He was one of my…. Let's just say he didn't believe in that sort of thing."

"Is the man still alive?"

"How the hell should I know?" Daisy took another gulp of her cocktail.

"Can you at least tell me who he is?"

"Let's see how nice you are to me first."

"I heard you once stabbed a man."

"Who told you that?" Daisy stopped drinking and stared at her. After a few seconds passed, she slammed her fist down on the coffee table, causing everything on it to jump. "That piece of shit tried to rape me. I only wish I finished the job."

"Do you often feel this way?"

She made a face. "What way?"

"Like killing people?"

"Oh, no. I'm a lover, honey, not a killer."

Gwynn felt the wind go out of her sails.

"I stabbed the asshole because he pinned me down and tried to stick his dick in me. I grabbed a pencil off the bed and shivved him in the ribs a few times until he rolled off me. And to think I was the one who had to do jail time."

"I'm sorry that happened to you."

"I didn't ask for pity. Bring more booze if you want to cheer me up."

Gwynn could barely control her anger. Daisy's long-lost daughter was sitting right here in this trailer, and the woman couldn't care less about her. Although she'd repeatedly braced herself for this kind of reaction, experiencing it in person was an altogether different thing, and she was surprised to realize the woman—her mother—had hurt her feelings.

"Could you tell me something about my father? Anything at all would help. Then I promise I'll leave you alone and never bother you again."

"How much money you got on you?"

She realized she was being played. "How much do you need?"

"Give me a thousand bucks, and I'll tell you whatever you want to know."

The woman's demand infuriated her, but Gwynn realized she had no other choice. "Okay, but you won't get a dime until you tell me everything."

"You bring the cash; you'll get what you want."

"Deal."

"Here's what we'll do," she slurred. "You give me half up front when you come by tomorrow. Then, when I tell you who he is, you give me the rest."

"That will work," Gwynn said, holding her hand out to shake. "But just to let you know, I'll be really upset if you don't keep your end of the deal."

"What are you gonna do? Kill me?" She laughed, waving off Gwynn's handshake. "Don't worry, I'll tell you the deadbeat's name."

Gwynn strode toward the door and opened it.

"And bring more booze," Daisy said. "I'm kind of enjoying these family reunions."

Gwynn stormed back to her car, disappointed that this witch was not the cold-blooded killer she'd expected her to be. Yes, she would return with the money and vodka tomorrow, but she'd better get answers. The man who impregnated her biological mother just might hold the key to her psychological freedom. His identity and life history could open a Pandora's box about her complicated psyche. After meeting Daisy, however, she hoped to never spend another minute in the woman's presence.

Chapter Twenty-Three

Peters picked her up later that afternoon. It was a beautiful day, so they decided to go to an outdoor brewery in town that served wood-fired pizzas from a truck. They sat at a picnic bench and ordered pints of cold beer and a pepperoni pizza. They talked as they drank beer and waited for the pizza to come out. Gwynn told him about her childhood, leaving out all the bad stuff, of course. No sense starting their relationship off on a sour note by revealing that she'd spent her life harboring murderous urges. Finally, the piping-hot pizza came out of the brick oven, and they dug in.

When they finished, she suggested they walk along the Eastern Promenade. It was a beautiful night. Peters grabbed a blanket out of his trunk, and they strolled along the hill, admiring the ocean and islands far below. Gwynn viewed the bay in a different light now. She couldn't look at it without recalling Sandra's body sinking down into the murky depths, her hands the last to disappear into the ocean water.

Despite that depressing meeting with Daisy, Gwynn felt better now that she was with Peters. They walked and talked, and he reached for her hand at one point. They stopped where Congress Street intersected with the Eastern Promenade, and he flapped the blanket in the air, letting it settle over the cool grass. A gentle breeze blew in from the ocean. They sat down next to each other, their shoulders touching, the two of them staring out at the streaks of pink forming over the eastern sky. Peters put his arm around her, and it felt like the most natural thing in the world. She rested her head on his shoulder, and they sat quietly like that for a while, their bodies interlocking puzzle pieces that had finally come together.

She tried not to think of all the bad things she'd done. Nor the good things, either. Living in the moment was its own reward. And an escape hatch, as well.

Once the sun set and darkness settled in, they folded the blanket and headed back to the car. He asked if she wanted to return home, and she said she'd rather go back to his place. No way she wanted to go back to her empty house, a house that still reminded her of Tom and their depressing marriage. Peters warned her that his apartment was small and cluttered, but Gwynn didn't care what it looked like.

They went back to his place in Libbytown and she was not in the least bit turned off. Yes, it was tiny. And old. They sat on his battered sofa, drinking ice-cold Coronas from the bottle, and this made her happier than she'd been in some time. It reminded her of her college days when she was young and free to do whatever she wanted, without the stress of a failed marriage, a sick father, raising a child, and running an agency for abused children.

"Why did you break up with your husband?" he asked.

She rested her head on his shoulder. It felt warm and snug, as if made just for her. "Are we really going there?"

"I suppose we'll have to eventually."

"I suppose," she said, feeling tipsy from the beer. "But I'd hate to ruin the mood."

"You have the right to remain silent."

"Thanks, Miranda," she said, sitting up. "Since you raised the topic, why don't you go first."

"Okay." He tilted his beer and drained half of it. "Beth and I drifted apart. I know that sounds corny, but we didn't have kids, and we worked different schedules. And to be honest, it takes a special woman to be married to a cop."

"In what way?"

"The crazy hours. The stress. Look how that shooting affected me."

"True."

"And being a police officer is not exactly the most appreciated job these days. One small mistake, and they plaster your name all over the news, and then your reputation is set in stone for life."

"I feel sorry for police officers today."

"I was one of the lucky ones. At least I survived that ordeal and was able to keep my job."

"So, am I a special lady for wanting to be with a cop?"

"Time will tell, but I think you're special," he said. "What about you?"

"I do love Tom, but I'm not sure I was ever really *in* love with him. What happened to us was unfortunate. And funny in some ways, too."

"How so?"

"I don't mean laugh-out-loud funny, but funny in a poignant sort of way."

She relayed the story of how they dated back in college but decided they were better off as friends. And that drunken pact they'd made the night before graduating from Brooks, agreeing to marry one another if they were still single by the age of thirty. Then, meeting up at Gritty's years later, ending up in bed together, and getting married at city hall. It was too early to tell him about Tom's controlling nature.

"That really is comical," he said, catching himself, "though in a poignant sort of way."

"So you don't hate me?"

"How could I ever hate you?"

"My relationship with Tom would be movie fodder if it weren't so tragic." Saying this made her think about all the twisted stories she was writing in her spare time. "Tom's not taking the breakup well. And, of course, we have Jack to consider."

"Hell, if you broke up with me, I wouldn't be taking it well, either."

"Then you'd better be nice to me, buster." She punched him in the arm.

"I would never be anything but nice to you." He gazed into her eyes, and it filled her with a warm glow. "Besides, we're still in the 'interviewing' stage, so I don't want to get out over my skis."

"And go over the cliff?" The image of that rapist teacher plunging to his death came to mind.

"Exactly," he said. "You still think my interrogating technique is harsh?"

"Let's just say that you're getting better with practice."

"Good, because I'd hate to treat my number one suspect badly."

"Now I'm your number one suspect?" Was she really saying this?

"Of course. I'm a one-suspect kind of cop."

"Not to change the subject, Peters, but have you made any progress tracking down Sandra's husband?"

"Do we have to talk about work right now?" He placed his bottle down and caressed her cheek.

"You brought it up with that 'it takes a special woman' bit."

"So I did."

His knuckles felt warm against her skin.

"I've had no luck tracking down William Clayborn. There's not been a single credit card transaction, no sightings of him, and no bank withdrawals. The man has become a virtual ghost."

"Probably by design."

"No doubt."

"So you believe that he took his boat out into the bay and drowned her? Merely because she was having an affair with Sam Townsend?"

"It's a working supposition. The captain of that lobster boat mentioned seeing William's Boston Whaler motoring across the bay that morning, and I can only assume it was him piloting it."

This news about the captain of the lobster boat caught her attention. "And he definitively identified it as their rig?"

"No, but he knew the exact make and model. William obviously knew where the key was. Once Sandra dove into the water, he waited patiently and made his move.

"Then why did he go on the run?" she asked, wanting to learn as much as possible about what the police knew.

"Because he killed her. Why else?"

"He's a criminal defense lawyer. William could have just as easily denied having anything to do with her death and said she drowned."

"Except for that captain seeing the Whaler out in the bay. That's pretty damning evidence, and he must have realized it before it was too late. Then there's the fact of him leaving his friend's house early that morning. Oh, and now fleeing the state shows consciousness of guilt."

"Yeah, I suppose you're right," she said.

"Enough about murder and mayhem." He leaned over and kissed her. "You can't possibly drive home after all the pizza and beer you've had tonight."

"Was that your plan all along?" She smiled and kissed him back. "Stuff me with gourmet pizza and then get me drunk?"

"I would never," he whispered in her ear. "But if all the evidence points that way..."

"I'm not quite ready for that yet," she whispered, touching his lips with her finger. "I'm still married."

"No, I wasn't implying anything untoward. You take my bed, and I'll sleep out here on the couch."

"How about we snuggle on your bed? Fully clothed, of course."

"I wouldn't expect anything else."

"You'd make a terrible suspect, Peters. I can tell a mile away when you're lying."

He stood, grabbed her hand, and led her into his small bedroom. He lay down first and wiggled back on the mattress so that she could scoot in next to him. She turned and fit snugly into the crook of his frame. He wrapped his arm around her and grabbed hold of her wrist, and she thought she could lie like this forever.

Then, he ruined the mood by asking about Tift. Tift seemed to worm her way into every conversation.

"Why do you want to know about her?"

"I'm just wondering what she's like?"

"Can we talk about this later? I'm really tired right now."

"Sure. It's just that you never told me you roomed with her in college."

How had he learned about that? Had he been looking into her past? "There's a lot of things about me you don't know."

"So it seems," he replied. "She's one of my favorite actresses."

"I bet she is, if you're like most hornballs out there."

"What's that supposed to mean?"

"Nothing. Just go to sleep." All the good feelings she had for him had now evaporated.

"You're a mystery to me," he whispered.

You don't know the half of it.

* * *

Morning arrived, and Gwynn woke before the sun came up. Glancing at her watch, she saw that it was just after six thirty. Peters lay facing away from her, his long body stretched out over the bed. Her head felt blurry from all the beer she'd drank last night. She wanted to give him a kiss before leaving but decided against it. Besides, she didn't want him to know that she'd slipped out without him knowing.

That conversation about Tift still circulated in her head, and it irritated her. But she needed to learn what he was up to.

Despite Peters bringing Tift's name up in conversation, he'd been the perfect gentleman last night. It was one of the best dates she'd had in a long time. Always better to leave a man wanting, she thought. Besides, she needed to keep him close and find out what he was learning about these cases.

She grabbed her bag in the living room. But first, she took a pen out of her bag and drew a heart on a slip of paper. Returning to the bedroom, she placed it down on the spot where she'd slept. Then she tiptoed out of the apartment before he heard her leave, gripping the railing as she made her way down the flimsy stairs. The first rays of sunlight streaked across the sky as she made her way to her car. The fog in her head had not yet dissipated. The first thing she planned on doing upon arriving home was making a pot of coffee and taking some aspirin. Then, she would go to church.

Driving through the empty Portland streets, she was happy to have her life back from Tom and not have to account for her whereabouts. It appeared as if fate had set things up that way. As if killing Townsend had all been predetermined so she could meet her soul mate and be free again.

In some ways, despite having just met him, she felt they were meant to be together. Like her, he'd killed a man, shot the guy in cold blood on a dark Portland street. Not any man, but a longtime criminal undeserving of the gift of life. But hadn't she committed all her murders in the name of self-defense and, in the process, made the world a safer place?

She parked in the driveway and sprinted inside. Started a pot of coffee before settling down at the kitchen table with her laptop. She typed in Peters's name along with the shooting incident and discovered a slew of news articles about it. After opening the first tab, she read through it and learned that the department had put him on paid administrative leave for two months after that shooting.

The victim's family was quoted in the story, and she could tell by the reporter's tone that he sympathized with their version of events, even though none of them were at the scene. But to a person, every one of Cordell James's family said he didn't own a gun. Considering his long list of violent crimes, she found that hard to believe. Cordell's mother claimed that her son had recently turned his life around. He'd stopped drinking and taking drugs and had started attending Bible classes at Grace Community Church. Peters's vehicle had been unmarked, and there seemed to be no valid reason for an off-duty detective to pull him over. Internal Investigations spent weeks poring over every detail in the case and had no reason to doubt Detective Peters's version of the incident, especially considering Cordell's long and violent criminal history.

Citizens in the community erupted in protest after the report's findings. Activists gathered in front of city hall, demanding accountability and justice. She remembered watching the protester march on the local news.

The firearm found on James was a Rohm .38 snub nose, and there were no fingerprints discovered on it. She researched the Rohm and learned that it was often used by cops as a throwaway gun. It was a cheap and easy firearm to obtain. Small enough to conceal, too. Had Internal Investigations overlooked this detail? It came down to the simple fact that Peters had a clean police record, while James's history was anything but clean. For that reason, the benefit of the doubt was given to the officer.

Then she read about the crimes Cordell James had been found guilty of, and she had no doubt that he deserved what happened to him. At least now, he couldn't hurt anyone else. Or make more babies he couldn't support. He would never again beat up another girlfriend the way he did Lyssa Owens, putting her in the hospital for three weeks. Or sell drugs to kids and addicts.

All this new information about Peters excited her more than she realized. Gwynn closed the laptop and considered what he might have done, and it made him even more desirous of her. Yes, people had their inalienable rights, even the worst of criminals. And, on occasion, some violent offenders did change their lives for the better. But what about the victims? What about their rights and their emotional well-being? Those murdered by such violent scumbags would never get their lives back.

She imagined what really happened that night. Peters pulled the speeding car over, instantly recognizing James behind the wheel. James refused to comply. Maybe Peters really did believe the man had pulled out a gun. She envisioned him pulling the trigger. James lying dead on the pavement, blood pooling around his body. A shiver of pleasure rumbled through her, followed by a sharp pang of guilt.

She moved to the washing machine and transferred the damp clothes to the dryer. Then she added a new load to the wash. It felt good to get back to a normal routine and keep herself occupied. It helped her forget about the three people she had recently killed.

Dr. Ezra Kaufman

T his is bad, I think, as I drive down to Boston to visit my mother. I turn on the radio and learn that Sandra Clayborn's body was found washed up on a sandy beach not far from her home. Everyone familiar with the woman knew she took long swims in the bay each morning before she left for work. Not to mention that she was a champion swimmer back at Brooks College. Does anyone really believe that a healthy, perfectly fit woman like that drowned in calm seas?

What have you done, my precious Gwynn?

I imagine William being in the wrong place at the wrong time. Then again, I can't muster up much sympathy for the man, even knowing that his actions didn't warrant the death sentence. William was a much sought-after criminal defense lawyer, but one with few, if any, scruples. I won't be the least bit surprised if they also find his corpse somewhere. Wouldn't that be an ironic form of justice?

I keep coming back to a particular incident in Gwynn's life when she was in her teens. It hadn't struck me as unusual until recently. She was walking the family's small spaniel one morning when it got attacked by a neighboring dog. The German shepherd came racing out, growling and completely unprovoked. Without hesitation, Gwynn jumped on the aggressor's back and maneuvered it into a choke hold, holding it there until the dog fell unconscious. Her father had gotten her into martial arts at a young age, knowing the value of self-defense in a world filled with predators and villains. He'd been a decorated Marine and welterweight boxer in his early twenties, well before he became a man of God.

Gwynn didn't merely stop when the shepherd went limp in her arms; she continued to choke the dog until the owner came out and saw the two of them lying twisted on the ground. By then, the animal had been so deprived of oxygen that his heart stopped. Seeing the bloodied and dead spaniel on the sidewalk, the owner had no legal recourse. His dog had clearly been the aggressor.

I didn't think much of the story back then, other than to be impressed with her bravery, but now I remember the look on her face while she recalled that attack to me. Her eyes had glossed over, and she seemed to go into a trance. What courage the girl possessed, I remember thinking at the time. Rather than coming to any psychoanalytic conclusions, I allowed her to get everything out of her system, fearing she might develop post-traumatic shock if she was unable to talk openly about it. Yet she seemed to revel in what she had done. Surprisingly, she had no remorse for killing that dog. The death of her spaniel, however, had devastated her. In hindsight, everything is starting to make sense. Could that one act from her youth have caused her current state of mind? Or did it result from it?

I pull up to my mother's assisted facility and go inside. I've brought her some of her favorite pastries, as well as a bagel and some lox. Entering her tiny efficiency, I waltz happily into her presence, and she smiles when she sees me. She's such an upbeat and optimistic person. How does that happen after everything she's been through?

All these questions continue to weigh on me. Like why are there so many bad people in this world intent on causing pain and suffering? If they one day disappeared from this planet, would it make the world a better place?

More intriguing is whether Gwynn convinced herself that what she's doing is justified and worth the risk.

Chapter Twenty-Four

When Peters woke up, he noticed that Gwynn was gone. On the bed next to him was a piece of paper with a heart drawn on it. Seeing it made him miss her even more. At least she left something for him before she took off.

He recalled how irritated Gwynn had gotten when he mentioned Tift's name. Why would she get so mad about it? He would have thought she'd be honored to have such a famous actress as a close friend. Unless something bad happened between Gwynn and Tift that caused them to have a fallout.

He thought about calling Tift and asking her himself. But Gwynn might get mad if she found out that he'd called her old roommate and asked about her. Yet the opportunity to speak to Tift Ainsley seemed too good to turn down. He remembered watching her in the movie *Safe Haven* as she ran around that tropical island half-naked, all the while getting chased by murderous cannibals, and then killing them off one by one.

After a shower and shave, he headed over to the police station. Because it was Saturday, he figured it would be quiet, and he'd be able to get some work done. His mind, however, couldn't stop thinking about his night spent with Gwynn. If he'd ever imagined a perfect date—'interview'—that was it. How wonderful it had been to sip microbrews and then sit on the Eastern Promenade with his arm around her shoulder, watching the sunset over Casco Bay. Then, kissing her on his couch while she caressed his cheek and stared into his eyes. It was all he could do not to rip her clothes off while she lay next to him. He'd even had to scoot his hips away from her backside so she wouldn't notice the erection threatening to bust through the seam of

155

his pants.

Peters settled in at his desk and examined the list of calls he needed to make. The first one he made was to the LA police department to find out how to contact Tift. They took his name and number and promised to get back to him with some information. Then he called the next name on his list: Charles Cyr. Cyr and William were once partners at the same law firm before William struck out on his own. William had spent the night at Cyr's house, returning early the morning his wife had disappeared. During their first interview, Cyr said he was absolutely certain that William left his house at six thirty-five because he had a tennis match at the Portland Country Club scheduled for quarter to seven.

Peters was baffled by this answer and asked him again, sure that Cyr must be wrong about the time, but Cyr was so adamant about when William left his house that Peters had no choice but to believe him. After hanging up, he glanced at his notes; the captain of the *Lilly* claimed to see the motorboat at precisely six thirty-nine am. Someone's account must have been wrong because Cyr lived a good fifteen minutes from the Clayborns' home. Yet the lobsterman insisted he arrived at that part of the bay at exactly the same time each morning after picking up his bait. He then called the bait shop, and they backed up the lobsterman's claim.

If these accounts were true, that meant William could not have killed Sandra. This development depressed him, but he didn't give up believing his theory that William committed the crime. The alternate theory seemed too depressing. His gut told him that Townsend, Sandra, and William were all murdered by someone else, and their bodies disposed of somewhere. But where? In the bay? Somewhere else? And who would have wanted all three of them dead? And why?

As he mulled over these questions, his phone buzzed. He picked it up and heard a silky voice on the other end of the line. It took him a few seconds before he realized that it was Tift Ainsley. He imagined her at her Hollywood mansion high up in the hills, outfitted in a floss bikini while sitting in an infinity pool overlooking the city. She probably had a Margarita in hand as she busied herself reading the new script sent over to her by

Marty or Quentin.

"They said you wanted to speak to me about a murder," Tift said.

"Yes, if you can spare the time."

"I'm extremely busy right now, Detective. And to be honest, I'm not sure I can help you."

"This should only take a minute," he said, flipping nervously through his notes. "By the way, I loved your performance in *Blue River*."

"Thanks," she said, "but that experience left a bad taste in my mouth."

"Yeah, but you and Bradley Cooper had such amazing chemistry."

"God, I love Coop. I wish I could be in every movie with that dude."

"Honestly, your performance blew me away."

"You don't know how hard it was trying to recite my lines while paddling over those fast-moving rapids," she snapped, bringing him back to reality. "What is it you need from me?"

"I've been told that you knew Sandra Clayborn and Gwynn Preston back at Brooks College."

"Yes. Gwynn and I roomed together, and I love that girl to death. Sandra was a friend, although not one of my closest."

"I hate to be the one to tell you this, but Sandra was found dead a few days ago."

"Oh my god. That's terrible," she said. "What happened?"

"We discovered her body along the banks of the Casco Bay. Her husband has gone missing, as well."

"That's hard to believe. She was always so confident and self-assured in the water."

"Yes, it's a real tragedy," he said.

"Did you know she was captain of the swim team at Brooks?"

"I did," he said. "Did you know her husband?"

"I was introduced to him once. Sandra met him well after we graduated."

"Did you know a Sam Townsend?"

Tift paused for a few seconds. "The name doesn't ring a bell."

"He went to nearby Crawford College."

"Crawford is not exactly close to Brooks," she said as if irritated. "It's nearly fifty miles away."

"I understand, but did you know him?"

"If I did, it was a long time ago. But no, I don't ever recall meeting a Sam Townsend. Why?"

"He attended a corporate event at the Custom House in Portland and never returned home."

"Okay, but I don't see how that really concerns me."

"Gwynn, Sandra, and William were all at the same event the night in question."

"Again, I don't see how that concerns me."

"No, I guess it doesn't. I'm just trying to gather as much information as possible."

"Of course you are. Police officers have a difficult time these days."

"Thanks for understanding, Ms. Ainsley."

"It's Tift. And I'm always willing to help the police in any way I can," she said. "Did you see me in *Code Blue*, Detective?"

"I did not." He'd never heard of the movie.

"It didn't do that well at the box office," she added. "Anyway, it's about a female cop who gets railroaded by the system and has to mete out justice the hard way."

"Sounds interesting. I will certainly put it on my list of movies to watch."

"I hope you do. Then you'll see how sympathetic I am to the wonderful men and women of law enforcement." The line went dead.

Could Tift Ainsley have been any more cliche? Still, he'd gotten a secret thrill talking to her.

He sat back and thought about these cases. Again, his mind returned to Gwynn. In some tenuous way, she had a connection to all three victims. But why did she get so angry when he'd brought Tift's name up last night? He recalled Tift's noticeable pause when he asked if she knew Sam Townsend. Did something happen between Tift and Townsend back at Brooks? Tift and Gwynn? It seemed so convoluted and crazy that he believed there was something hidden in all this that he couldn't quite see.

After flipping through the pages of his notebook, he found the name and number of the mutual college friend the three women shared. Elizabeth from Manhattan. He punched in her number and she answered on the first ring. Was she working even though the stock market was closed today?

"Detective Peters from Maine again," he said.

"What is it you want from me now, Detective-From-Maine? I'm expecting an important call."

"I have another question about Tift."

"The overrated actress?"

"Actually, I think she's pretty talented."

"Pretty, is what you really mean to say."

Had he detected a note of jealousy in her voice? "Did something happen to her at Brooks? Or to either Sandra or Gwynn?"

"Not to my knowledge."

"What were they like back then?"

"I've already told you, Sandra was super competitive, always looking out for number one. I thought Gwynn was a little strange, although I never knew why. She was kind and well-liked by her classmates, but a little odd. Something might have happened to Tift her sophomore year, now that you mention it. I remember she grew a bit sullen for a short time and required lots of attention from the other girls. Not me, mind you. I could never stand that needy drama queen."

"Do you have any idea what might have happened to Tift?"

"Maybe realizing that she would one day star in *Prom Queen Massacre* with Wynn Purdue?" She laughed. "Honestly, I have no idea. A lot of girls back in college went through these dark periods. Some became bulimic while others drank like a fish and screwed every guy or girl they met."

He guessed that Elizabeth wasn't very popular at Brooks. "Did she recover quickly from her depressed state?"

"By her junior year, she was her same old bunny self. A dumb blonde who played the part to a tee. Go figure."

He thanked her and placed his phone down on the desk. He had a bad feeling in his gut. Something strange was going on and he couldn't quite put his finger on what it was. Did someone hurt Tift? Townsend? Sandra?

Gwynn?

Chapter Twenty-Five

Gwynn knocked on Daisy's door late that afternoon, eager to get in and out of her trailer as soon as possible. Inside her bag was a thousand dollars wrapped in an elastic band, along with a bottle of Smirnoff. After a second knock, the woman appeared. It took Gwynn a few seconds to recognize Daisy. She'd combed out her hair and put on way too much makeup, as if trying to make a good impression. In addition, she'd put on a flowery sundress that looked as if it had been purchased from a secondhand store. The effect was even more ghastly than when she was drunk.

Daisy turned and staggered back inside her trailer, not even inviting Gwynn in. Surprisingly, she'd made an attempt to tidy up her place. The magazines and newspapers, however, were still piled high against the far wall. At least she'd put the dishes away and gotten rid of all the fast-food wrappers on the counter.

Daisy sat on the soiled couch, and Gwynn sat across from her in the tattered armchair.

"Well?"

"Well, what?" Gwynn said.

"Where's my dough? And the bottle of hootch you promised?"

"What happened to the bottle I brought over yesterday?"

"I did my best Houdini impression and made it disappear."

Gwynn reached into her bag and pulled out the bottle, handing it to her. Then she removed the ten hundred-dollar bills she'd withdrawn from the bank, counting out five before giving them to Daisy. The woman practically snatched them out of her hand.

"Now, you need to keep your end of the bargain."

"Hold onto your horses, darling. This old girl needs a quick belt before we get started," Daisy said, twisting off the cap and flicking it behind her. Then she got up, went into the kitchen, and poured orange juice and vodka into a plastic cup. "Have a drink with mommy."

"I don't want one."

"It wasn't a question, kiddo."

"Don't you think it's a little too early for that?"

"It's happy hour somewhere. Now, I insist you have a drink with your dear old mother."

She paused to keep herself calm. "Okay, maybe just a small one."

Daisy walked back to the kitchen, returning with a beer mug filled to the brim with the orange juice and vodka concoction. Then she handed it to her and sat back down.

"So you want to know about your sperm donor?"

"Yes." Gwynn pretended to drink from her cup.

"I met him in town after I ran away from home at the age of fifteen. For whatever reason, he took pity on me and gave me a place to live."

"Why did you run away?"

"I got sick of dealing with my mother's drunk boyfriends every night. A lot of them would end up hitting on me whenever she passed out. Stupid bitch never believed me when I told her what those perverts were doing to me."

"I'm sorry that happened to you, Daisy."

"Keep the pity to yourself," she said. "One day, I took off like Rudolph the Red-Nosed Reindeer and ended up on the streets. That's where I met your daddy. He wasn't like the other losers I dated. He actually cared about me and paid me my cash beforehand."

"He cared about you?"

"As much as a john could care about his whore."

"You're saying he was one of your customers?"

"He sure wasn't Santa Claus." She laughed. "But like I said, he treated me nice. He felt bad that a young kid like me had to run away from home. So he helped get me an apartment and gave me money to stay off the streets."

"Did you tell him what had happened to you at home?"

"Of course, I told him. Sometimes, we wouldn't even do it when he picked me up, but just sit and talk. And he always paid me whether we did anything or not." She took a healthy swig of her drink. "This is good stuff."

"Glad you like it."

"Mommy loves her vodka."

"So what happened next?"

"I stayed in the apartment and watched every TV show known to mankind until I was blue in the face. Anyway, he said I was pretty and smart, and he wanted me to go back to school and get my diploma. I laughed when he said that and told him that hell would freeze over before I went back to school."

"Did he stay being your boyfriend?"

"For a while. Dude couldn't get enough of me, and he liked it rough in the sack. Sometimes, he'd put tape over my mouth while we did it. Or tie my hands and feet to the bedposts. There were other crazy things we did, too. I never asked about his personal life, but I assumed he had a family like most of the guys I dated."

"So, how did you get pregnant?" Gwynn asked, not wanting to get into the intimate details of Daisy's sex life.

"I got careless with the pill. After a month or so, I became bored sitting around that stupid apartment all day, watching reruns and soap operas. I started drinking and smoking weed to fight off the boredom, and because of that, we began to fight."

"What were you two fighting about?"

"The fact that I forgot to take my birth control. We had this big blowup after I told him I was preggers and planning on getting an abortion. He got so mad about it that for a second, I thought he was going to hit me."

"I take it that it was me you wanted to abort?"

"You're still here, aren't you? So stop your bitching," she said, her words becoming sloppier the more she drank. "There was no way I was raising some snotty-nosed kid. I had no steady income, I was tricking on the side, and I was the wild child from hell. I wanted to party all the time, not be stuck at home changing some rugrat's diapers."

"My diapers."

Daisy shrugged.

"So, how did you decide to give me up for adoption?"

"Wasn't my idea. Dude said he'd pay me a thousand dollars a month if I had the kid. In the meantime, all I had to do was be a good girl. Hell, a thousand bucks a month for doing nothing seemed like a sweet deal at the time, especially considering that he'd take care of everything."

"So you did as you were told until you gave birth?"

"I drank a little and smoked some weed during the pregnancy. Not every day, mind you, but enough to fight off the boredom. I usually knew the days he was coming over and had enough time to clean myself up. And we still fooled around on occasion."

"While you were pregnant?"

"Sure. Whatever floated his boat. He liked doing it up until the last few weeks."

Gwynn wondered if Daisy's alcohol and drug use might have contributed to her mental health struggles—and desire to kill.

"But he was nice at times, too. Sometimes he'd rub my belly and feel the little shit kicking inside me. I didn't care either way as long as it made him happy."

Gwynn reminded herself that 'the little shit' inside Daisy's belly was her.

"Did you have any remorse after you handed me off?"

"Remorse? Are you kidding?" She laughed, and her mascara and eyeliner started to run. "Ecstatic is more like it. I couldn't wait to get back out on the street and start kicking it with my homies."

"What happened to the man who impregnated you?"

"Your pops came to the hospital one last time to pay me my money. Then I never saw him again."

"Did you ever wonder how I turned out?"

"No offense, lady, but I never gave two shits. I could barely even take care of myself back then."

Gwynn stared at the woman, trying to muster up sympathy for her.

"You've barely touched your drinky-poo. I thought this was supposed to be a family reunion."

Gwynn tipped the cup and pretended to drink.

"I got a picture of him. Wanna see it?"

"I'd love to."

"Then you can pay your old lady the rest of her money," she said, struggling to stand. She left her cup on the table and staggered toward the back of the trailer and toward the bedroom.

Gwynn walked over and dumped her drink in the sink before returning to her seat. It depressed her to sit in this trashy trailer with this trashy woman who had delivered her into this world. Once she saw what her father looked like and got his name, she would never return here again. Maybe it had been a mistake to track down Daisy. The woman had absolutely no maternal feelings.

Ten minutes went by. Gwynn wondered if the woman had passed out drunk in her bedroom. She was about to go and check on her when Daisy came staggering back, bouncing off the walls of the hallway during her return. She collapsed on the couch in a drunken heap and began laughing hysterically. Once done, Daisy sat up and grabbed her pack of smokes off the table. After lighting one, she passed a photograph to Gwynn and sat back, waiting for a reaction.

"He was a pretty good-looking dude," Daisy said, pouring Gwynn another shot.

Gwynn held her cup out for Daisy to fill, the photograph face down in her hand.

"Go on now. Take a look at him," Daisy said, puffing on her cigarette. "You really do look like him."

Gwynn flipped the photograph over and stared at it.

Chapter Twenty-Six

G wynn's entire life felt like a complete and utter lie. The man in the photo was her father, the same one who adopted her. The young, attractive girl sitting on his lap was Daisy. She looked to be around sixteen at the time and was absolutely gorgeous. Lillian was right when she said she could have been a model or Hollywood actress. She had on a two-piece, white bathing suit that left nothing to the imagination. Gwynn's father appeared behind her, one forearm on the armrest of the chair and his hand pressed against her smooth belly button. Gwynn felt every muscle in her body go numb as she stared down at the photo.

She couldn't quite wrap her head around this. Her biological father and her adopted father were one and the same. She stared in disbelief as he gazed into the camera's lens—as if he were looking into her very soul. A cigarette stuck out of Daisy's snarling young lips, her feathered blonde hair parted down the middle. Although Daisy's looks had faded considerably, Gwynn could see how attractive she'd been back in the day.

Gwynn's life was crashing down before her eyes, and she felt dead inside. Her father, the beloved pastor and dedicated husband, had been a lying, cheating scoundrel. Had he patronized other prostitutes? Did he suffer from some kind of sexual addiction?

Maybe she'd been wrong all this time about there being a god. It wasn't the first time she'd wrestled with her faith. And it wouldn't be the last.

"Pretty suave, wouldn't you say?" Daisy said, exhaling smoke out the side of her mouth. The butt of her cigarette was smudged with lipstick.

Gwynn kept silent, simmering with barely suppressed rage.

"His name was Dave. When I met him, he told me it was Gerry, but I found his wallet one day."

"What did he say when you found out?"

"Dave? Gerry? I didn't give a shit what he called himself. Most of the Johns used an alias anyway."

"This man is my father," Gwynn muttered under her breath.

"Of course, he's your father, kiddo," Daisy said, stubbing her cigarette out in the ashtray. She smacked the box against her palm, but nothing came out. "Goddammit, I'm all out of smokes."

Daisy pushed herself off the couch and teetered away.

"Where are you going?" Gwynn asked.

"I need to bum a few smokes off my neighbor."

"What should I do in the meantime?"

She held out her palm. "I don't care what you do, lady. But I want the rest of my money before you split."

Gwynn reached into her purse, removed the remaining five hundred-dollar bills, and handed them to her. Daisy took the money and tucked them into her bra.

She wondered if Daisy knew that the man who gave her life was the very same man who ended up adopting her. How could she know this?

"Mind if I stay and have another drink?" Gwynn said.

"Suit yourself, but I want that photograph back when you're done with it."

Gwynn handed it to her. "All done."

"Now you listen here, Miss Fancy-Pants. My life is good these days, so I don't want you coming around here and bothering Mommy anymore. Understand?"

"Perfectly."

The woman left out the front door. Gwynn moved to the window and saw Daisy shuffling down the dirt path and toward another trailer. Certain the woman wouldn't be returning anytime soon, she made her way to the bedroom to see if she could find more photographs of her father.

She entered the cluttered room and searched around for more evidence of his infidelity. Booze bottles and fast-food wrappers littered the floor. Even the mattress was covered in junk, allowing only a small space for Daisy to sleep on. She was about to leave when she caught sight of a tattered shoe box sitting in the corner. The cover sat slightly askew over the box. In it, she saw photographs and various other items. She picked up the box, removed the cover, and saw at least a dozen Polaroid photographs along with a stack of news clippings. She took a few out and flipped through them. The images in the Polaroids made her skin crawl. Many were pornographic photos of Daisy in various sexual positions. Why had she kept these disgusting photographs? Then she saw one of her father completely naked and positioned behind Daisy. Repulsed, she turned the Polaroid the other way.

It made sense why he never wanted her to track down her biological parents.

She was about to put the photos back in the box when she caught sight of a news clipping. She took it out and read it; it was an article about the Muddy River Killer. Glancing into the box, she realized that there were lots of articles like this. She picked out a second one about the killer's victim. Then another and another. Every photo was of a young girl with blonde hair, similar in many respects to Daisy, but none quite as beautiful.

A frightening thought occurred to her. Was her father the Muddy River Killer? The possibility both horrified and intrigued her. Had Daisy known the entire time that her child's father had been a serial killer—and she never told anyone?

She whipped out her phone and looked up the Muddy River Killer. The first body was discovered in 1980. His reign of terror ended around 2010. Her father had been in a car accident that year and shattered his hip and left leg. It was so bad that he couldn't walk without a cane for the next eighteen months. She buried her face in her hands and wept. No wonder he didn't have the physical strength to track down and kill any more young women.

Gwynn returned to the living room, dazed by these revelations. She had no intention of leaving this trailer until she learned the truth straight from Daisy's mouth. The woman's cup sat on the table between them. She filled it with vodka and a spritz of orange juice. Out of her bag, she took two Ambien and ground them up on the coffee table. Scooping the powder into her palm, she emptied it into the woman's drink. Then, she sat down and waited for Daisy to return.

Fifteen minutes passed before Daisy staggered back into her trailer and collapsed on the couch. Upon seeing Gwynn, she lit a cigarette.

"I thought I told you to beat it."

"I refreshed your drink."

Daisy stared down at her plastic cup. "So you did. Such a considerate daughter I have. Now get lost."

"I need to show you something, Daisy."

"Show me what?" She lifted the cup and downed half of her drink.

"This." Gwynn reached into her bag, pulling out five twenties. She placed them on the coffee table and then sat back to study the woman's expression.

"That'll certainly help your dear old mom." Daisy snatched the bills up and wedged them in her bra. "Now hurry up and tell me whatever it is you want."

"The man in that photograph was the same man who raised me."

Daisy puffed on her cigarette and stared at her.

"He and his wife—my mother—were the ones who adopted me. My father was a beloved pastor in town who ministered to homeless people and runaways. When he found out that you were pregnant, he must have decided to adopt the child and raise me as his own."

"What's your point?" Daisy said.

"All those years growing up, he never once told me he was my biological father. He made it a point to tell me that I was adopted and that he and my mother loved me with all their heart."

"Daddy's little pride and joy."

"Did you know all this time that he was the Muddy River Killer?"

Daisy lifted her cup to her lips and froze.

"So you did know," Gwynn said.

"I didn't know nothing," Daisy said.

"Why didn't you tell anyone? You could have saved so many lives."

"Get outta here before I call the cops."

"Go ahead and call the cops," Gwynn said. "I'll tell them you knew all along that my father was a serial killer. That would make you an accessory to murder. Many murders, in fact."

Daisy gave her a death stare.

"You should have gone to the police and told them what you knew."

Daisy took a long sip of her drink and dropped her head to her chest before snapping it back up. "He threatened to kill me if I told anyone. What did you expect me to do?"

"So you kept silent all those years and allowed young girls to die, knowing the entire time that he was the one killing them?"

"Don't you judge me. I'm the one who brought you into this world."

"You wanted to get rid of me."

"But I didn't. I gave you life."

"Only because my father stopped you. Or else I never would have been born."

"I had no idea what that man did when he wasn't with me."

Gwynn laughed. "Oh no, you knew. It's why you kept all those articles about his victims."

"Did you go through my stuff?" she said, her eyelids fluttering.

"Yes, and I saw all the disgusting photographs you saved."

"I wish I'd aborted you when I had the chance."

Gwynn managed to stay calm. "Why didn't my father kill you?"

"Because I was different from all the other sluts he paid to fuck. I was the mother of the only child he would ever have." Daisy struggled to stand.

"How did you know he would never have more children?"

"Because he said his wife couldn't have kids," Daisy said, picking up her phone. "Bitch was sterile."

"What are you doing?"

"Calling the cops."

Gwynn jumped up and grabbed the phone out of her hand. Not that it mattered now, because Daisy could barely move now that the Ambien had wormed its way into her system.

CHAPTER TWENTY-SIX

"Sorry, but I can't let you do that."

Daisy opened her mouth, but nothing came out.

"I'll have you know, I'm my father's daughter."

Daisy struggled to keep her eyes open.

"Don't worry, Mother, I spiked your drink. You won't feel a thing when I kill you."

Daisy's eyes widened, and she tried one last time to stand. Gwynn sat for a few minutes until the woman closed her eyes and fell unconscious over the sofa. She snatched the cigarette out of the ashtray, took a few quick puffs off it, and then grabbed the cash out of Daisy's bra. Feeling the urge come over her, she placed the lit end of the cigarette against Daisy's sundress. In less than a minute, the material caught on fire.

Gwynn turned to leave and saw Daisy's body consumed by the flames. Kaufman would have a psychological field day with this scene. She would have loved to stay and watch her mother turn to ashes, but she had to get out of there before someone identified her and called the police. She reminded herself that Daisy was not her real mother. No, her mother was the woman who raised her all those years and who had died of breast cancer a few years after Gwynn graduated from college.

As she sped out of the trailer park, she stopped near the entrance and noticed a familiar car parked along the side of the road with a man asleep behind the wheel. She got out of her idling SUV, walked over to the driver's side window, and peered inside. The sight of him alarmed her. Had he followed her here? Did he know the terrible things she'd been doing all these years? She tiptoed back to her car, wondering if she'd need to kill him, too. In the rear view mirror, she caught the first hint of flames flickering out of Daisy's trailer.

The woman who gave birth to her was now out of her misery. But what should she do about her father?

And what to do about this little stalker of hers.

Dr. Ezra Kaufman

I did something very unlike myself yesterday. I followed Gwynn on two separate occasions after she left the house. Honestly, I felt like a common gumshoe. Me, a Harvard-trained psychiatrist, resorting to spying on my patient. But it paid off. What happened left me reeling and confirmed all my suspicions about her.

I left the house early and parked at the end of Gwynn's cul-de-sac, determined to see what she was up to. Instead, I sat in my car for three hours, perusing old editions of the *American Journal of Psychiatry* that I had fallen behind on. At various intervals, I had to get out of the car and stretch my legs.

The first time she left the house, I followed her to the church she regularly attends. I parked in the back and then waited a few minutes after she entered. I hadn't been to temple for some time, so I felt slightly guilty about attending a Christian service. Then, I reminded myself that Jesus was a Jew like me. I waited a few minutes before slipping in the side door, peeking into the nave to see where Gwynn had settled. It was a beautiful place of worship. The oak ceiling resembled an upside-down arc. Christian-themed, stained-glass windows lined either side of the walls, most of them depicting scenes of Jesus. Fortunately for me, Gwynn had taken a pew in the front row.

I sat off to the side, near the exit, so I could make a quick escape. I'd been in other Christian churches before, but never of my own volition. Usually, it was to attend a colleague's wedding or a child's baptism.

The pastor's sermon was called the Parable of the Talents and was about the biblical passage from Matthew 25:14–30. It's an instructive story where the master goes away for a period of time and leaves each servant a sum of silver based on their level of ability. Upon his return, two of the servants put their silver to good use and made nice increases in their investment. But the lowly servant buried his silver in a hole in order to protect it, fearing his master's wrath if he lost it in a risky business deal. On the surface, this parable sounds like a classic venture capital story. But the meaning is much deeper than that. The return God expects from us in life is commensurate with the gifts we've been given. The point of the parable is that we are to use whatever talents we have for God's purposes.

After the sermon, I slipped out of the church and waited in my car for her to leave. I couldn't help wondering if Gwynn was using religion as a crutch to justify her actions. Or maybe she was asking God for forgiveness for the terrible things she had done.

She returned home after the services, and I parked at the end of the street and waited. I debated abandoning this project, but what else did I have to do but sit around and read old journals? The waiting paid off; Gwynn drove past me. I ducked down so as not to be seen, waited a minute, and then followed her.

It could have been a routine grocery trip, but I somehow doubted it. Her husband had their son for the weekend. It hadn't surprised me when she announced that she was separating from Tom. Gwynn had admitted in our sessions that she'd been unhappy in her marriage for a long time. She explained how Tom had become more controlling and insecure as the years wore on and that he was terrified she might leave him. She'd seemed anxious and scattered, as if something heavy had been weighing on her mind.

So it surprised me when she pulled into what looked to be a run-down trailer park. Not that I've visited many trailer parks in my life, but it was like no other park I'd ever seen. Each trailer was set back into the woods, and there was plenty of room between the units. I pulled up to the entrance and watched Gwynn cruise slowly down the lane, as if looking for a specific address. Her car pulled up at the last trailer, and she parked behind it and out of view.

I sat back and listened to a talk show where the host advised people about their financial problems. Are people really this ignorant about money? After about an hour, my eyelids began to droop. Roughly forty minutes later, I heard a woman's raspy voice. I opened my eyes and saw a woman staggering down the road. She kept going until she stopped at another trailer, where she spent ten minutes with an obese man with long red hair and a red beard. Then she returned to the trailer Gwynn had entered. Who was this woman, and why had Gwynn driven out to Westbrook to see her?

I sat back, closed my eyes again, and fell asleep. The older I get, the more I find this happening to me. Sometime later, I was awakened by the wail of sirens. I opened my eyes and saw flames consuming the woman's trailer. What happened? Was the woman inside?

Rather than stick around, I performed a U-turn and headed home, hoping to learn more about this tragedy come morning. What about Gwynn? Had she escaped? Or had she been the one who...

Chapter Twenty-Seven

Peters's phone went off while he sat at his desk. Gwynn had sent him a message saying that she badly wanted to see him. At first, he was excited about the prospect of meeting up with Gwynn, but then he got to thinking about his cases, and it gave him pause. Could she really have committed these murders?

The absurdity of such a thought reminded him of why he was alone in this world. He had a bad habit of always thinking the worst of people.

He texted Gwynn and informed her that he wanted to see her this evening.

Too bad she'd left his apartment so early the other morning. Nothing would have made him happier than to wake up next to her, smelling her hair and feeling her slim body up against his. Then, going out to breakfast at Becky's Diner, sipping coffees and noshing on blueberry pancakes while staring into her blue eyes.

Something came to his attention while he was sitting at his desk. He heard one of the other officers talking about a fire in Westbrook that took a woman's life. He didn't know why this news struck him as odd. Normally, he wouldn't think twice about something like this, but with two people missing and one dead, he thought it plausible that this fire in Westbrook could be in some way connected to these three cases.

"Can I speak to you for a second, Detective?" a woman's voice called out to him in a deadpan voice.

Peters glanced up and saw Detective Nguyen standing beside his desk. He gestured for her to sit, which she did. It pained him that an experienced detective like himself needed to be paired with a woman who barely looked old enough to drink.

"I might have a suspect," she said.

"And who might that be?"

She adjusted the black glasses on her nose. "Robert Durkan. William Clayborn represented his son five years ago on a drug charge. It was one of the few cases where Clayborn didn't win an acquittal for his client."

"Why does this guy warrant any attention?"

"Look," she said, holding out a piece of paper for him to see. "William took out a restraining order on him a year ago. Seems that Mr. Durkan sent him a series of threatening letters and emails, promising to do bodily harm to him and his family. Mr. Durkan also has a bit of a criminal history himself."

"Such as?"

"He owns a successful body shop, but he's got a couple of violent assaults on his record. He rides in a local motorcycle gang and was busted for breaking-and-entering six years ago."

"Nice work, Nguyen, but that still doesn't connect this case to Townsend," he said, worried that she might actually solve these cases before him.

"I know. I'm still trying to figure all this out."

"Good. Keep hammering away on it." He stood to leave.

"Where are you going?"

"To check out a death in Westbrook. Apparently, a woman died in a trailer park fire."

"What does that have to do with our case?"

He shrugged. "There's been a lot of suspicious cases lately, which is unusual for our neck of the woods. We need to be tracking down every possible lead, even the ones that don't appear on our radar."

"How about we meet up later and compare notes?"

"We definitely should."

"One other thing," she said as he turned to leave.

"What?"

She gazed into her phone. "Have you looked into this woman, Gwynn Denning? I know it's probably a long shot, but I see that she's connected to all three of these missing individuals."

The sound of Gwynn's name coming out of his partner's mouth startled him. "I've interviewed Gwynn Denning twice, and there's nothing there. She went to Brooks College with Sandra, but they rarely socialized. And she barely knew Sandra's husband. As for Townsend, she has no connection to him whatsoever."

"I read where they attended college fifty miles apart. Could they have dated or met at a party somewhere along the line?"

"Maybe," he said. "But have you seen Gwynn Denning? No way she fits the profile of a killer. She's slender and not someone who could overpower a guy as big and strong as Sam Townsend."

"You're probably right."

"Furthermore, she's the director of The Loft. Do you even know what that place does?" he said, wondering if he was trying to convince himself of her innocence more than he was trying to convince Nguyen.

"It's a children's welfare agency."

"Precisely. You think a woman who runs a home for abused children would commit murder?"

"If only we could locate the two other bodies, that would tell us a lot."

"We'll have a better idea of what happened to Sandra Clayborn once the ME finishes his autopsy." He turned and left before Nguyen asked him any more pesky questions.

* * *

Peters pulled up to where the trailer once stood and saw that it had burned to the ground. A police cruiser sat parked nearby. He got out and approached the officer's vehicle. After a quick chat, the cop directed him to the detective walking around in the rubble. Peters approached the heavyset man and introduced himself. Then he told him the reason for his visit.

"What's this got to do with those missing persons?"

"I'm not sure it has anything to do with them. I'm just trying to turn over every stone."

"I'm afraid this stone ain't going to yield much, Detective. The woman who died in this fire was a well-known alcoholic and drug addict. It appears she passed out drunk with a lit cigarette in hand."

"You think?"

"I do. Sorry to disappoint."

"What was her name?" Peters took out his pen and pad.

"Daisy Carson. Fifty-three and unemployed. A real piece of work, according to the people who knew her."

"Smoke inhalation?"

"Like my wife's pot roast; well done." The detective laughed.

"Any family?"

"None that we could find. Neighbor said she had no husband or kids that anyone knew of. If this was intentionally set, we'll know soon enough, but the arson investigator told me he found no sign of any accelerants being used. And the people who knew her said she was a big-time chain smoker. And hoarder."

"Can you ask the medical examiner to check and see what was in her system at the time of death?"

"I'm pretty sure they'll find every substance under the sun."

"Mind if I talk to a few of the neighbors?"

"Knock yourself out. Not sure you're going to learn much."

Peters thanked the man and started at the first trailer. After that, he moved on to the next one. None of the neighbors told him anything that had any bearing on the woman's death. He arrived at the last unit and knocked. The occupant appeared at the door, fat and sloth-like. He had long red hair and a beard and seemed to be on some heavy medications. The man took several seconds to lift a cigarette up to his lips. His fingers were nicotine-stained and ended in long, dirty nails. Peters asked the usual questions, but cocked his head up at one response, so he asked it again.

"Yeah, Daisy was here before her trailer burned down."

"What did she want?"

"Bummed a few smokes off me. Oh, and we had a quick drink," the man said. "Daisy's never got any money on her."

"And you say she visited you right before her trailer burned to the ground?"

"Yeah."

"Did she say anything else?"

"Daisy liked to talk," he said, blowing out smoke.

"What was she talking to you about?"

"Said she had company over and was waiting for them to leave."

This got his attention. "Did she say who this person was?"

"She laughed and said it was her daughter. I didn't know if she was joking or not. She never talked about having a daughter, but then again, she didn't talk a lot about her past." The man took another drag on his cigarette and then blew it out the side of his mouth. "Not many of us here do."

"Join the club," Peters said, jotting something down in his notebook. "Did she say what her daughter's name was?"

"No. I just assumed she talking shit like she usually does when she gets drunk. I didn't want to set her off. That woman could get psycho when she was boozing."

"She get like that a lot?"

"All the time. Whenever she came over, I would sit quietly and keep my mouth shut, waiting for her to leave."

"And in all these years, she's never mentioned a daughter to you?"

He shook his head. "Not that I can remember."

"One more question. Do you remember seeing an unfamiliar car parked near her trailer that night? Coming or going?"

"Sorry, I don't."

Peters thanked the man and shut his notebook. Somehow, he seriously doubted that Nguyen's theory about Gwynn held any water. He only hoped she stayed out of his hair long enough so that he could solve this case on his own.

Despite his suspicions, he couldn't wait to see Gwynn tonight. He knew for a fact that she was not Daisy's daughter. She had told him that her father had once been a minister in town. No way a caring and compassionate woman like Gwynn would ever resort to murder.

He knew her to be a loving mother to a little boy.

A tireless advocate for abused and neglected children.

A minister's daughter.

In no way did she fit the profile of a serial killer. Gwynn was good. And kind.

These were the things he kept telling himself as he drove back to Portland.

Chapter Twenty-Eight

Gwynn was ready for bed by the time Tom pulled into the driveway. He'd brought Jack home later than usual because they went down to Boston and visited the Science Museum and New England Aquarium. She unlocked the door and let them in. Tom said a quick hello before carrying their son up to his bedroom.

Tom returned downstairs, looking exhausted from his long day. She asked if he wanted something to eat before he returned to his apartment, and he asked for a cold beer. He looked so down in the dumps that she actually felt sorry for him. Maybe getting a divorce would allow him to find a woman who would truly love him the way he wanted, and the thought of it briefly made her jealous.

But then she remembered how unhappy she was in her marriage and how wonderful she felt when she was with Peters, and she knew that she was making the right decision. Jack didn't deserve two unhappy parents bickering and fighting all the time. And now that she knew the brutal truth about herself and her father's twisted, hidden past, her life had forever changed.

Watching Tom drink his beer, she half expected the police to show up at her door, especially after seeing Kaufman at that trailer park, asleep behind the wheel. Had he been following her the entire time, keeping track of her like when they'd been together? Did he know what she had done?

"Thanks so much for taking Jack down to Boston," she said, placing a bowl of chips down in front of him. "You guys have a good time?"

"We had a blast. I couldn't get him out of the Children's Museum. And you should have seen him at the aquarium. Kid couldn't stop talking about the sharks." He sipped his beer and sighed pleasurably. "Still buying Heineken, I see?"

"No, it's yours from the case you left behind," she said. "You want what's left of it?"

"Nah. I should be cutting back, anyway," he said, patting his gut.

"Where did you guys eat?"

"Regina's in the North End. Split a pepperoni and sausage."

"You shouldn't be eating spicy meats, Tom. You know it gives you indigestion."

Tom laughed. "Why do you even give a shit?"

"You're the father of our child. I still care about you."

"Right," he said, chugging the rest of his beer. "But you're not in love with me anymore."

Gwynn clutched her neck and looked away from him. "Can we not talk about this right now?"

"Sure. How about getting me another Heine?"

"You drank that one pretty fast."

"Are you going to lecture or get me another beer?"

She grabbed him another bottle out of the fridge.

He held out his empty, and she took it from him and put it in the bottle return bag. "I know this sounds ridiculous, but I thought you might be rethinking your decision to divorce me."

She laughed at this. "Trust me, Tom. I'm not."

"A guy can hope, can't he?"

"You're only making things worse by pressuring me."

"You always knew all the little things I liked, like buying my favorite brand of beer and chips."

"Sour cream ripple." She picked a chip out of the bowl and held it up to show him.

"With French Onion dip."

"Always—except I'm out today." She bit off part of the chip.

"Sometimes I think you know me better than I know myself."

"We know practically everything about each other," she said, wishing she had known the real Tom when she married him.

"We were the best of friends back at Brooks." He swallowed half his beer in one gulp.

"We're still good friends. Unfortunately, we grew apart. It happens."

"That's where you're wrong. I've always loved you and always will."

"I'm sorry, Tom, but I can't help that I don't feel the same way."

"Were you ever in love with me? I won't be mad if you say no."

"Of course, I was in love with you." She wondered if she really was.

"It doesn't really matter at this point. Because I believe that we'll get back together again someday."

She didn't know how to respond to this or convince him that it would never happen. His unrealistic and rosy view of their relationship was another flaw she couldn't overlook.

"I'd move back in with you guys in a heartbeat if you just said the word."

"You need to stop torturing yourself like this."

"You're the love of my life, Gwynn," he said, gazing into her eyes. "I'll never give up on you."

"You might want to go easy on those beers. No sense getting a DUI."

"Look at this spare tire I've put on. Do you really think two Heinekens will have any effect on me?" He stood. "Mind if I grab one for later?"

"Take whatever you want. Just wait until you get home to drink it."

"Sure, Mom." He moved toward the fridge, not understanding how he'd just slighted her by calling her mom.

"You might as well take what's left of the twelve-pack."

"No, I'll save it for the next time I'm here." He grabbed a bottle and shut the refrigerator door. "Just to let you know, this has been really hard on me."

"It's been hard on all of us."

"You don't look too broken up about it."

"I don't show it as much as you do."

He stood by the front door, holding the knob. "As long as we focus on Jack, we should be okay for the time being."

"I couldn't agree more. Everything we do should be for our son."

She watched him leave out the door. Heard the roar of his Mercedes speeding away. Despite his words, she didn't trust Tom. What if he fought tooth and nail for custody of Jack? Or looked into her past and dug up all the dirt on her? She wouldn't put it past him, knowing how controlling he could be.

She recalled her meeting with Daisy. Remembering the way her sundress caught fire as she held the smoldering cigarette up to the fabric. It all seemed like a strange, exotic dream. She had no doubt now that her father was the dreaded Muddy River Killer. Tomorrow, she planned on leaving work early and paying him a visit. If she got the chance, she would show him the photographs she took from Daisy's house and see if they jogged his memory. She doubted he would remember anything, but what if he did?

* * *

After dropping Jack off early at preschool, she arrived at her office and got to work. She had three new client intake forms to fill out, a federal grant she had to have completed by the end of the week, as well as numerous other tasks related to her role as director. She couldn't help wondering how she'd be able to make up the loss of donation money now that the Clayborns were dead.

She ignored all the phone calls and continued to work through the morning so that she could leave for a short time and visit her father. Just after ten, she received an email that caught her attention. It was from an estate attorney at Sandra's law firm. Part of her wanted to delete it and continue working, but the email intrigued her so much that she clicked it open.

Goldstein & Herd
110 Commercial Street
Portland, Maine 04101

CHAPTER TWENTY-EIGHT

Dear: The Loft Educational and Behavioral Services of Maine

BENEFICIARY NOTICE LETTER

Under the Clayborn Trust, your agency has been named as one of the beneficiaries. However, since William Rayford Clayborn is still listed as a missing person, the trust does not take effect until seven years after the date William Rayford Clayborn has been declared a missing person. At that point, the court will declare William Rayford Clayborn deceased, which means that the funds will be released.

THE LOFT's share of the contribution is $250,000 per annum for three years. You may withdraw your share within thirty (30) days from the date of the contribution to the trust by notifying me in writing of your request. This withdrawal right is noncumulative, so any withdrawal not made cannot be carried forward into a future year. However, if you decide not to exercise your withdrawal right when the funds become available, the right to demand a withdrawal for any future contributions is not lost.

If you have any questions or if I can be of any assistance to you, please contact me. Additionally, kindly sign your name on the copy of this letter in the place designated for acknowledgment of receipt of this letter and return the signed copy to me.

RECEIPT ACKNOWLEDGED: _____
_

Very truly yours,
  William Goldstein, esq.

Gwynn stared at the email, not quite believing that the Clayborns had left The Loft two hundred and fifty thousand dollars per year. The generosity of such a gift astounded her. It would have made a huge difference if not for the fact that seven years had to pass before the trust released the funds. The Loft might not even make it that long without the money. She kicked herself for dumping William's body into the quarry. If only she had disposed of it where it could have been found, thousands of kids' lives might have been saved.

Rattled by this unexpected turn of events, she stared at the words on her screen. She rapped her palm down on the desk, and the sound echoed off the walls of her office.

She e-signed the document and sent it back to the law firm.

The grant she'd been working on would have to wait. She pressed her eyelids together and thought of the sermon given last Sunday by their minister. How people were to use their unique gifts to the best of their abilities. Maybe killing bad people was her talent in life.

Her phone rang, and she answered it. It was Sue at the Fellow House. Ivy was acting up in class again and demanding to speak to her. Could this day get any worse?

Chapter Twenty-Nine

W ell, that came as a surprise to Peters. The Westbrook police called and informed him that an occupant of the trailer park had observed an unusual car parked at the end of the street the night Daisy Carson died in that trailer fire. A Mercedes S-Class sedan. A vehicle like that cost nearly a hundred thousand dollars, depending on the options. The neighbor had written down the license plate number. Peters typed it into the database and saw that it belonged to a Dr. Ezra Kaufman of Portland.

Now, there was a name he couldn't forget.

He flipped through his notes until he found it. Dr. Kaufman had also attended the same corporate event at the Custom House that Townsend, Sandra, and Gwynn were present at. Peters remembered interviewing the stuffy doctor inside his Victorian home in the West End and the brief conversation they had. Kaufman had seemed preoccupied and uncomfortable the entire time. Peters recalled the photographs of the man's mother hung on the wall. She'd been a prisoner in the death camp at Auschwitz and had been one of the few survivors.

Why would Dr. Kaufman be in that trailer park the night Daisy Carson perished? It seemed so strange that he couldn't fully process the news. For that reason, he decided to go over to Kaufman's house and ask the man himself. Maybe showing up unannounced would catch him by surprise and get that old windbag to open up.

* * *

Kaufman was not home when he pulled up, so Peters waited in his car, flipping through the sports page and studying the football lines. He couldn't, however, stop thinking about Gwynn, hoping she felt the same way about him.

Forty minutes later, the Mercedes S-Class pulled into the driveway and disappeared behind the house. Peters put down his pencil and gave the man a few minutes to go inside and get settled. Then, when he felt ready, he strode up to the front door and rang the bell.

Kaufman looked flustered when he opened the door and laid eyes on him. Reluctantly, he allowed Peters inside. They sat down in the living room and across from one another. Peters noticed that Kaufman had quickly regained his composure. He had to admit, despite being short, the man had gravitas. He carried himself with the bearing of a much taller and more confident man. And there was a somberness about him, as if he were hefting the weight of the world on his shoulders.

"Are you having any more luck solving these cases, Detective?"

"Unfortunately not. The leads have been few and far between."

"That's too bad, but I'm afraid I've told you everything I know."

"I'm sure you did, Doctor. As you must know, every little detail in these matters helps."

"Of course. So, how can I assist you?"

"There was a fire in a trailer park the other night," he said, noticing a subtle change in the man's expression. "A woman died."

"Tragic."

"Yes, very."

"But how does that concern me?"

Peters scratched his head as if confused. "Well, Doctor, here's the rub. Someone in one of the trailers saw you asleep at the wheel of your Mercedes. They thought it odd and took down your license plate number."

Kaufman stared at him with a blank expression before taking his glasses off and pinching the bridge of his nose.

"So, is it true?"

"Yes, I'm afraid it is. I had a few drinks that day and pulled over to collect myself."

"Where did you have these drinks?"

"Look, Detective, I often get restless and go out for long drives to calm myself. I had two glasses of bourbon at some nameless bar. I started to become tired, so I pulled into that trailer park to close my eyes for a few minutes."

"You could have killed someone, driving impaired like that."

"I know, and I deeply regret my actions."

"So you pulled into the very same trailer park the night a woman died in a fire? What are the odds?"

"Quite an unfortunate coincidence."

"I'll say." He suspected that Kaufman was lying and needed to get him to slip up.

"I read about that fire in the newspaper the next day. Not only did I not know the woman who died, but I never even got out of my car."

"Yes, that's what the person who was watching you said."

Peters couldn't help thinking about the fact that Kaufman, the Clayborns, and Sam Townsend were all at the same function as Gwynn.

"You were seen driving away just after the woman's trailer went up in flames."

"I woke up, saw the blaze, and then drove out of there."

"Why didn't you call the fire department and report the incident?"

"I'd consumed two glasses of bourbon and had gotten behind the wheel, something I rarely, if ever, do. Also, I heard the sirens approaching soon after I woke up."

"Did you not think that the woman inside might be trapped and needed help?"

"I didn't know if anyone was in there. And in the shape I was in, I could barely even take care of myself."

"What would your mother think if she knew you'd bailed on someone who might have needed assistance?"

Kaufman's lips turned white, and for a moment, he looked like he wanted to punch him.

"Especially when you consider all the people in this world who helped her along the way," he said, trying to throw Kaufman off his game.

"What would you like me to say?"

He glanced at his notes. "Did you see or hear any unusual activity before the fire started?"

"Like I said, I was asleep at the wheel much of the time."

Peters laughed.

"Why are you laughing?"

"You don't park a Mercedes S-Class in a trailer park and expect not to get noticed."

"This is no laughing matter, Detective."

"I know. I was laughing at the irony of a car like yours in a run-down trailer park."

"Would you have preferred I drive home in that state?"

"No," Peters said, rethinking his strategy. "Was there a reason why you were so restless?"

Kaufman threw off a stare so cold and unwavering that, for a moment, it frightened him.

"I mean, you've got a beautiful home, you drive a Mercedes-Benz, and obviously have a good deal of money. I don't get it."

"You should never assume things about a person based on their financial status."

"If you saw the dump I live in, you might think otherwise."

"You mentioned my mother earlier. Yes, she survived that death camp, but she is also the happiest person I've ever known. My father was a tailor, and they both sacrificed and scrimped so that I could get the finest education possible and live a better life than they did."

"She sounds like an amazing woman."

"She is, but the point I'm trying to make is that happiness is in many ways subjective."

"How do you figure?"

"I've learned that being happy is not necessarily what drives us as human beings. It's about having a passion and knowing that you're making a difference."

"Easy to say when you're loaded."

"Money has nothing to do with it."

"Sorry, Doc, but I beg to differ."

"My mother's experience in that camp made her appreciate life more than the average person, because death was always lurking around the corner. She strove every day to make things better for the people around her."

"What's your point?"

"She raised a family and worked in a school cafeteria. Neither of my parents had any great expectations for their lives, knowing that simply being happy was a gift in and of itself. Their only goal was to be responsible citizens and leave the world a better place than they left it."

Peters looked away and sighed, not expecting to be lectured to.

"They put exceedingly high expectations on me and my brother. Then, when my brother died, all their expectations were placed onto my shoulders."

This caught his attention. "How did your brother die?"

"Vietnam."

"I'm sorry for your loss."

Kaufman nodded. "He was only twenty when a South Vietnamese soldier tossed a grenade into his bunker."

"That must have been hard on you."

"It devastated us, especially my mother. It's part of the reason I became a psychiatrist."

"I imagine you've helped a lot of people over the years."

"Do you remember in *The Wizard of Oz* when the Wizard says, 'A heart is shown not by how much you love, but by how much you are loved by others?'"

He nodded.

"That's how I want to be remembered."

The line hit so close to home that Peters didn't know how to respond. It made him think of Gwynn and how she could make him happy. He thanked the man and left.

Sitting in his car, he realized that he wanted Gwynn in his life more than anything. No way he planned on ending up like Kaufman, living all alone in a big house and wishing his life had turned out differently.

* * *

He made his way to the West End market and picked out a dozen roses and a box of assorted candies at the outdoor market. After calling in his bet on the Steelers, he made his way to The Loft.

He pulled up to the campus entrance and cruised down the driveway, heeding all the signs warning him that there were children at play. To his right and left, he saw playgrounds and endless fields and rows upon rows of raised vegetable beds. He continued driving until the administration building appeared. The ornate brick structure looked old and impressive and was surrounded by a satellite of pod classrooms. As he parked in the visitors' lot, his heart rate ticked up at the prospect of surprising Gwynn with the gifts he'd purchased for her. He hobbled up the wooden stairs, stopping to ask someone where Gwynn's office was located. A woman with neon purple hair and a nose ring directed him to the top floor. He sprinted up the remaining stairs, his footsteps echoing off the plaster walls and hardwood floor. Out of breath, he could barely control his excitement.

At the top, he circled around until he located her office. It was easy to find because it was the largest office on the floor. Also, her name was printed on a big brass plate hung on the wall. The door stood slightly ajar. He rapped his knuckles against it, and it creaked open. Such a cheery and spacious office with tall ceilings and a low-hanging chandelier.

Stepping inside, he noticed her empty desk. Behind the desk sat three massive windows, giving him an amazing view of the ocean off in the distance. He knew he shouldn't be in here without her permission, but he couldn't help himself. He inhaled the scent of her essence and allowed it to fill him with optimism.

Peters walked over to the large window behind her desk and peered out it. The sun shone brightly above. He glanced down at the playground and saw two figures strolling side by side. It took him a second to realize that Gwynn was walking alongside a teenage girl. They seemed to be discussing something as they made their way around the grounds. The girl punched the tetherball and sent it flying through the air. At one point, they stopped, and the girl turned to Gwynn. They talked for a minute or two before the girl threw herself into Gwynn's arms.

A loud ping went off behind him. He turned and saw a message on Gwynn's computer screen. Reflexively, despite his better judgment, he leaned over the desk and read what it said. After reading it a second time, he did a double-take. It couldn't be. The message was from Dr. Kaufman. It said, 'This is a reminder that we have a session tomorrow at ten. See you then, Gwynn.'

He turned back to the window and stared down at Gwynn in shock. She still had the girl in her arms.

His ears turned red hot, and his head felt like it was going to explode. His suspicions roared like a fire-breathing dragon in his ears.

He ran out of the office, gripping the flowers and candy, and sprinted back to his car. Sweating profusely, he gasped for air as if suffering from a panic attack. Once inside his car, he gunned it out of the parking lot before Gwynn caught sight of him and wondered why he showed up to her work.

Back on the road, he shoved the candies into his mouth, one after another. Had Kaufman followed Gwynn to that trailer park? And if so, why? Did Kaufman have the same suspicions about his beautiful patient as Peters did? Depressed, he couldn't help but think that his ridiculous suspicions would put an end to their budding relationship.

Chapter Thirty

Gwynn knocked on the door and saw Ivy sitting in the back of the classroom with her back turned away from the teacher. The girl was hugging her knees to her chest and looked upset. The rims of her eyes were shadowed in dark eyeliner, and her ears had multiple piercings down the lobe. She also had a silver septum ring that drooped down over her philtrum. Three other girls sat slumped in their chairs, staring down at some silly word search puzzle handout their teacher had assigned them.

With a nod of her head, Gwynn motioned for Ivy to come with her. The girl jumped out of her seat, flipping off the teacher. It was nothing Gwynn hadn't seen a million times before. Ivy followed her outside and slammed the classroom door shut behind her. They walked in silence toward the field, past the basketball court, tetherball pole—Ivy punched the ball hooked to the string—and then onto the soccer field. They moved onto the lawn and began circling the outer perimeter. Gwynn waited a few minutes before deciding to speak.

"Having a rough day?"

"I hate this fucking place."

Gwynn said nothing and continued to walk alongside her.

"The teachers here suck. And all the kids are fucked up, too."

"You may not believe this, but everyone here is doing their best to help you."

"I'm really sick and tired of these idiots. They piss me off so much."

"You don't really mean that."

"Oh yes, I do. I hate everyone in this place."

"You're fourteen and have lots of anger inside you, which is understandable. Most kids who have gone through what you have feel the exact same way."

"Most fourteen-year-olds get to live with their family and not in some shitty group home."

"Do you really want to go back to that life? Living with your abusive parents?"

"At least they love me."

"Is that what you think love is? A drug-addicted mother and a father who abuses you?"

"You don't know that."

"Oh, but I do."

"My father said he was sorry for what he did to me and is trying to get help. My mother has a back injury and needs to take medicine to ease the pain. People can change, you know."

"I know they can. But do you really believe yours will?"

"He said he made a mistake and that he's trying to clean up his act. My father has a sickness."

"Hurting your child is a sickness?" she said. "He's only sorry because he got caught."

"My parents care about me way more than you or anyone else here."

Gwynn did not want to get into a power struggle with the girl.

"Sometimes I get so mad I just want to kill everyone," Ivy said.

"I felt the same way when I was your age," she said, which wasn't exactly a lie. "A lot of kids do."

"You felt like killing people?"

"Yup. And it's okay to feel that way at times. It's part of growing up and becoming a mature adult."

"Bet you didn't have a messed-up father like I do."

Gwynn laughed. "Trust me, my father was worse in many ways."

"Did he hurt you?"

"Very much so, although in a different way than your father hurt you. But

195

that's not what's important here. What's important is to forgive yourself and to forgive others, and then try to move on in life."

Ivy put her hands in her jacket as she walked ahead. "Do these feelings ever go away?"

"Depends."

"On what?"

"On whether you're willing to accept help. Some people are able to move past their abuse and go on to live wonderful and fulfilling lives, while others stay stuck in the past and remain bitter and angry all the time. It depends on what you want out of life and the work you're willing to put in."

"How do I get over feeling this way?"

"By staying in school and continuing on with your therapy. The key to healing is learning how to process everything. Those bad feelings will never go away if you let them take control over your life."

"I don't want to feel like this forever."

"You won't, I promise. Feeling sad and depressed is emotionally draining. It saps your ability to do great things, like your artwork."

"How do you deal with it?"

I kill bad people, she wanted to say. "I see a therapist. It helps me deal with my issues."

"Do you still feel like killing people?"

"Not everyone." She laughed. "And not all the time."

Ivy laughed, her dark mood beginning to lift. "I really want to forgive my parents, but I feel like such a loser for feeling this way. In my head, I know they're the ones who messed me up."

"Forgiveness is your ticket to freedom. Otherwise, you'll be giving those abusive people all the power over you."

"I don't know if I can forgive them right now."

"It won't happen overnight. Maybe not even tomorrow. It's a slow process that takes time and patience."

"Maybe if I'd been a better person, my parents wouldn't have turned to drugs and alcohol, and taken out all their shit on me and my brother."

"Their problems are not your fault," Gwynn said. "Your parents are adults and responsible for their own actions. Survivors like you and me have to be strong and support each other. We have to do everything we can to rid ourselves of the negative influences in our lives so that they can never hurt us again."

"What do you mean rid ourselves?"

"Write them off. Move on. People like that are toxic and will never rest until they destroy everything and everyone in their path."

They arrived full circle and pulled up in front of Ivy's classroom. Gwynn noticed that the girl was crying, so she pulled Ivy into her arms and allowed her to take solace in the embrace.

"What's wrong?"

"I know that what my parents did was wrong. So why do I still love them?"

"Because it's hard to let go of those who are closest to you," Gwynn said, her hand around the girl's head. "As you get older, you'll see that there are lots of wonderful people out there who are willing to love you for who you are."

"Even if I turn out to be a loser?"

"You will most definitely not turn out to be a loser."

"Maybe I can be like you someday and get a job helping people?"

"Oh, girl, you'll be way better at that than I am."

"I can't imagine anyone ever falling in love with me."

"You wait and see how many people will fall in love with you," she said, knowing that she was one of those people. "Why don't you go back inside now? Sit in the back and read quietly while you compose yourself. I'll let your teacher know it's okay."

Ivy turned and walked inside the classroom, wiping the tears from her eyes as she did. Gwynn glanced at her watch and realized she was running late. She had a meeting with a social worker later in the afternoon to talk about a child slated to enter the program. If she wanted to see her father and return in time, she had to leave now.

She heard an engine roaring, and when she turned, Gwynn saw a car speeding too fast down the road.

197

Chapter Thirty-One

Gwynn knocked on her father's door despite having her own key. Aria, one of her father's caretakers, opened it and let her in. The woman had taken amazing care of her father these last ten months, as his mental health had steadily declined.

"How is he today?" Gwynn asked.

"Not too bad. He's watching a television show right now."

"Is it okay if I go in and talk to him?"

"Of course, dear. He's your father."

She paused. "Would you mind if we had a little privacy? I shouldn't be more than thirty minutes."

"Sure, if that's what you want. I'll run to the store and grab him some of those butter cookies he likes."

Gwynn took her purse out and handed the woman a twenty. "Get yourself a coffee and pastry while you're at it."

"I've got my own money."

"Take it. I insist."

Aria took the money and put it in her purse. "Want me to bring you back anything?"

Gwynn shook her head and watched as Aria departed. It took every ounce of energy to act normal around the caretaker, knowing the monster waiting for her in the other room. Once the woman backed out of the driveway, Gwynn turned and walked toward her father. A game show played on the television. Her father sat slumped in his chair, watching with a blank expression as a contestant answered a question. Fighting back the tears, she grabbed the footstool and pulled it up next to him, sitting down on it. She stared at his blank face, still unable to believe all the horrific things he'd done to those poor girls.

"Hi, Dad."

"Hi," her father whispered, his eyes glued to the game show.

"I've got something to show you." She opened her purse and removed the photographs taken from Daisy's trailer. Her hand trembling, she held up each one for him to see. "Do you know who any of these girls are?"

He glanced briefly at the photographs and then returned his attention to *The Price is Right*. Judging by his nonplussed reaction, she concluded that he had no recollection of anything he'd done.

"Do you know who this girl is?"

He stared at the photo for a few seconds before saying, "Daisy."

This startled her. "So you do remember her?"

"Of course. We were married for fifty years."

"No, Dad, you were never married to Daisy."

He looked at her. "I wasn't?"

"No, you most certainly were not. This is the woman you cheated on Mom with."

"I cheated on Mom?"

"Yes, with this little tramp."

He stared ahead.

"How many girls did you end up killing?"

"Killing?"

"Yes, Dad. Did you hunt for them while you were out preaching the Gospel?"

He turned toward *The Price is Right* and stared at the screen.

"Just tell me how many you killed." Tears streamed down her cheeks.

"I don't..." He turned to her, looking as if he was about to cry.

Sadly, she knew she was her father's daughter. Killing was in their genes, although she vowed to never kill the weak and vulnerable like he had done. A sense of loss overcame her while staring at the man she once loved and idolized. He looked so harmless now. This was the man all the parishioners came to in their time of need. The man who raised considerable sums of money and then used it to feed the homeless, and help street people get back on their feet. But it was also how he met all those young, vulnerable girls he deposited along the banks of the rivers. She was the only person in the world who knew the truth about him.

What to do now? Her life felt upended. Part of her wanted to stuff a pillow over his face and be done with this monster. But this was not for her to decide.

Gwynn thought about her poor mother. Thankfully, she never found out about the terrible things her husband had done. She would have been devastated to learn the truth.

Gwynn left her father's side and went downstairs and into the basement, where her parents kept all their records. She pulled the chain above her head, and the bulb illuminated the cardboard boxes scattered along the floor. Starting with the first one, she began to rifle through it. Most contained old financial documents that her father meticulously saved in green file folders. Electric and water bills. Tax records. Church documents. There were photo albums of her and her family in better times.

Fifteen minutes later, she came across a box buried way in the back. It was duct-taped and shut on all sides. She moved to the tool bench, grabbed an old utility knife, and sliced through the layers of tape, mindful that duct tape was a serial killer's best friend. Inside sat a series of gauzy Ziploc bags containing strands of hair, bits of jewelry, and various personal items that a young girl from that era might own. It stunned her to realize that her father had kept these items in order to remember his victims. Her hands shook as she pulled out a yellowing newspaper article detailing the death of the girl in question. Horrified, she stuffed it back inside the bag. Then she proceeded to count the number of Ziploc bags in the box. Eighteen in all. Recalling the Muddy River Killer's reign of terror, she remembered that there were only thirteen victims recovered, which meant that five of the girls were never found. With her father in mental decline, the police might never know the full extent of his crimes.

Dazed by this discovery, she secured the box and wedged it under her arm, intending to take it home and burn it in the fireplace. As she headed upstairs, her phone rang.

"Tift? Why are you calling me in the middle of the day?" she said, surprised to hear her friend's voice.

"My wonderful Gwynn, do you have a minute, darling?"

"Of course," she said, heading back down the rickety stairs so as not to upset her father. "How are you?"

"Couldn't be better. It's been a long time since we've spoken."

"We talked last month, remember?"

"Of course we did, but a month is way too long not to speak to my BFF."

"How've you been?"

"Wonderful. I just found out that I'm being considered for the main role in David Fincher's new film. Oh, and I'm reading a script for a possible series, which sounds really exciting."

"That's awesome, Tift. What's it about?"

"A serial killing nurse. Really creepy script, and I'm dying to do more edgy work after starring in *Cry Me Blood*."

"That was a dark film," Gwynn said, her pulse racing at the thought of a cable show based on a serial killing nurse.

"Oh, and I'm appearing on Kelly Clarkson's show next week. Then Jimmy Fallon the week after."

"Wow. Sounds like things are really clicking for you out there," she said, trying her best to stay positive.

"For the most part, although I was a little disappointed when I didn't get the role in the newest Scorsese film, but you can't win them all."

"No, I suppose not."

"And I just purchased this really nice house out in West Hollywood. It's a little big for me, but it's in a great location and has one of those infinity pools and a hot tub. It's a wonderful place to entertain, and I got it at a great price."

"I've always wanted to swim in one of those pools."

"Then you guys should come out sometime. I miss seeing you so much."

"I miss you too."

"I bet Jack would love to spend a week out here. We could take him to Disneyland, and I could introduce him to Ben and Leo."

"Ben and Leo?"

Tift laughed. "Affleck and DiCaprio."

"Oh, those two. Jack might not care to meet them, but I certainly wouldn't mind an introduction," she said, pacing frantically back and forth.

"Those two are the best."

"I do know that Jack would love to visit Disneyland and go on all the rides." She looked around the dark and moldy basement, wanting to get out of there as soon as possible.

"How's Tom doing?"

"Tom and I have decided to separate for the time being."

"Oh no. I'm sorry to hear that. And his band played a rocking version of 'Creep.'"

"That's because it's my favorite song."

"He sang it mostly to impress you."

"No, he sang it because he knew I was a creep."

"You were so not," Tift said. "I always liked Tom."

Gwynn knew this was not true. Tift always tried to undermine her relationship with Tom, wanting her all to herself. Maybe Tift knew they weren't right for each other. Or maybe it was a case of Tift being a self-absorbed bitch, and in many ways as controlling and domineering as Tom.

"Remember that crazy house party we attended where Tom's band played? The drummer got so drunk during their set that he collapsed over his drum kit."

The thought transported her back to a more innocent time in life, and she smiled at the recollection. "Yeah, that was pretty funny. They had to carry him up to the bathroom, where he made a mess all over the floor."

"And then Tom and the rest of the band continued playing as if nothing happened. They were really good that night."

"They were."

"Is Tom in a band out there?"

"God, no. Tom hasn't picked up a guitar in years. He's too busy slaving

202

away at that CPA firm he works at."

"Maybe it's for the better. You weren't meant to marry a bean counter."

Gwynn didn't know how to respond to this.

"Any word yet about what might have happened to Sandra and Townsend?"

She stopped pacing and pressed the box against her side, the pit in her stomach growing. "The police still have no clue about what happened to them."

"I bet Townsend hurt someone else and finally got the payback he so richly deserved."

"It's possible. But then, how do you account for Sandra drowning and her husband going missing?"

"All I know is that Sam Townsend deserved whatever happened to him," she snapped. "I hope you'll keep your word and never tell a soul about what he did to me that night."

"You know I never would."

"It's good to know that I can trust you."

"Don't worry about me, Tift."

"It's just that people change as they get older, and I'm someone who struggles with change."

Gwynn wanted to laugh at this, from a woman who changed films every six months. Boyfriends, too. And now homes. "I'm still the same girl you roomed with back at Brooks."

"Remember how we used to play 'Planet Claire' at full volume in our dorm room and dance around like lunatics?"

"I most certainly do. We adored The B-52's back then."

"Totally," she said. "I would hate for the tabloids to find out what Townsend did to me and make a big stink of it. It could jeopardize my career if something like that ever came to light, especially since I'm starting to get some decent roles now."

"How would it jeopardize your career?"

"The powers-that-be in Hollywood are terrified of the #MeToo movement and the backlash that has occurred over the last few years. They'd be very reluctant to hire someone who might file a complaint against them and create a scene."

"Makes sense."

"I have a wonderful idea, Gwynn. Why don't you come to Hollywood for a few weeks and hang out with me? It'll give you a chance to relax and write to your heart's delight. We'll sip cocktails by the pool, munch on hot dogs at Pink's for lunch, and dine at The Apple Pan in the evening. We could have so much fun."

"I couldn't possibly drop everything now. There's my work to consider. And Jack."

"You must have some vacation time saved up. And bring that adorable little boy with you. My neighbor, Kate, has a wonderful babysitter, and she'll give me her name if I ask."

"As much as I'd love to, Tift, I really can't right now," Gwynn said, not wanting to mention her father's declining health or these investigations.

"Now that you're divorcing Tom, you should consider moving out here. You were always such an amazing writer back at Brooks, and Hollywood could use more talented writers like you."

"I never said we were getting divorced," she said, knowing she was headed in that direction.

"Sorry, I just assumed as much, seeing as how you're separated from him," she said. "How's the writing going?"

"Great. When I'm finished, I'd like to send you what I've been working on. I think my scripts would make an amazing TV show."

"Maybe we could pitch it to some producers once you're done."

"Yes, I'd love that," she said, recalling what Sandra had told her. "Can I ask you something, Tift? And please be honest with me."

"Of course."

"Why did you tell Sandra what Townsend did to you? You said I was the only person you confided in."

There was a silence at the end of the line. "Did she tell you that?"

"Yes. Years ago."

Another brief silence. "That woman betrayed my trust."

CHAPTER THIRTY-ONE

"She's dead, Tift. Don't be upset with her."

"She swore that she would never tell anyone what Townsend did to me."

"Why did you lie to me?"

"You should have called me as soon as Sandra told you that. That way I could have explained my reason for telling her."

"Don't blame this on me."

"You know how badly that incident messed me up. I wasn't thinking straight when I blurted it out to her one night. You, of all people, should be more sympathetic to my needs."

Gwynn couldn't believe her friend's self-centeredness.

"What did Sandra tell you?"

"Forget it, Tift. I have to get going."

"Okay, but you and I must discuss this when you come out to visit. And I will not take no for an answer."

"Sure."

"And make sure you send me your script. The edgier, the better."

The line went dead, and it took Gwynn a few seconds before she could compose herself. Conversations with Tift always left her emotionally spent.

By the time she made her way back up to the living room, she realized that her father was not in his chair. Figuring he must be in the bathroom, she walked down the hallway and noticed that he was not there, either. Nor in any of the bedrooms. For a brief moment, she began to panic, knowing that her serial-killing father was not anywhere in this house. She bolted outside and looked up and down the street, not seeing him. Just then, Aria pulled up and parked in the driveway. Seeing the stunned look on Gwynn's face, Aria jumped out and asked what was wrong.

"I can't find him."

"What do you mean you can't find him?" Aria said.

"He must have wandered off."

"Weren't you watching him? You can't just leave your father alone and let him fend for himself."

"I...I...I was in the bathroom," she lied, trying to conceal the box under her arm.

"Get in. We'll drive around the neighborhood until we locate him."

"One second." Gwynn ran over to her SUV and placed the box on the seat while Aria waited for her to return. Gwynn got in Aria's vehicle, and the woman backed out of the driveway.

"Call 911, Gwynn."

"Do we really need to get the police involved?"

"Honey, calling the police is as much about saving my ass as it is finding your father. I could get fired for your screw-up."

"I'll call them right now."

When they got two streets over, she saw her father standing on someone's doorstep and banging his fist against the door. In his free hand, he was holding a steak knife. Aria pulled up against the curb. She opened the car door and ran up to her father as he pummeled away. He was shouting something unintelligible at the top of his lungs. His behavior scared Gwynn. She'd never seen him so worked up.

"Open the damn door," he shouted. "Let me in."

Stunned, Gwynn grabbed her frail father by the arm, gently took the knife out of his hand, and led him back to the car. He was huffing and puffing and looked visibly upset. A police cruiser pulled up as soon as they reached the curb. She tucked him in the back seat and closed the door, then approached the officer. Aria walked around to her side.

"I'm sorry, Officer, but David is my patient and suffers from dementia. He slipped away from me while I wasn't looking," Aria said, glancing over at Gwynn.

"And who are you?" the officer asked.

"I'm Aria Burrows, his caretaker, and this is his daughter, Gwynn."

"I suggest you keep a closer eye on him, Ms. Burrows. People in his condition are prone to wandering off and getting lost."

"I promise you I'll never let him out of my sight again," Aria said.

"Okay, I'll go explain the situation to the homeowner. Best to get him home as soon as possible."

"Thank you, sir," Gwynn said.

The police officer walked up to the front door as they returned to the car.

Aria started the car and pulled away. The woman on the doorstep looked down and waved to them, almost as if she were the one who should have been apologizing.

"Are you okay, Dad?" Gwynn turned and asked her father.

He grunted something unintelligible and stared out the window.

"You must never do that to me again," Aria barked. Gwynn couldn't be sure if the caretaker was talking to her or her father.

"Why do you think he became so angry back there?" Gwynn asked, wondering if she'd set off his memory with those photographs.

"It happens with this disease. I've had other clients who have become even more violent than your dad."

"Has this happened with him before?"

"On occasion."

"You don't think anything upset him this time, do you?"

Aria shrugged. "Hard to tell with these cases. But I will say this, some of the most aggressive patients I've ever cared for were the sweetest people you'd ever want to know before coming down with this shitty disease."

"It's almost as if they were hiding some inner rage?"

Aria shrugged, not interested in arriving at some deeper meaning.

Gwynn considered this explanation as Aria turned into the driveway. Aria's description fit her father perfectly. And in other ways, the aggression he displayed was a natural manifestation of his true self. The self he kept hidden from everyone around him.

Chapter Thirty-Two

P eters examined the Daisy Carson file again, unable to put his finger on what was bugging him. Nothing in the file seemed remotely tied to either Townsend or the Clayborns. Nor could he see any connection to Gwynn other than the fact that her therapist happened to be asleep in his car inside the very same park where Daisy perished. Initial findings by the fire marshal discovered no accelerants inside her trailer. And everyone knew that Daisy was not only a heavy drinker and chain smoker, but a crackhead, too.

Clearly, the woman had lived a rough life. Arrested multiple times in Portland for prostitution when she was a teenager. Arrested also for petty theft, drug use, and using with intent to distribute. There was an arrest for forgery, as well. She spent some time at Windham Correctional Facility. In her twenties, she was diagnosed with oppositional disorder and put on medication. In her thirties, unable to work, she went on permanent disability and moved into public housing. Drunken arrests and domestics followed, both as a victim and aggressor. A couple of marriages but no kids.

Maybe Kaufman stopping in that trailer park really was a coincidence, but Peters couldn't escape the nagging feeling that it was connected to something larger, and possibly connected to his cases. He remembered what Albert Einstein said: Coincidence is God's way of remaining anonymous.

He glanced up at the clock, excited to see Gwynn tonight, despite this new development. The Steelers were playing the Bucs at eight, and he had five hundred bucks riding on the game.

Why did Gwynn need to see a therapist? Not that seeing one was unusual in this day and age. He'd been in therapy, required by the department after he shot that motorist, as had just about every other cop in the department. So why did Dr. Kaufman tell him he was retired? Was Gwynn the only patient he counseled?

His jumbled thoughts ricocheted all over the place.

As for tonight, he'd reserved a table at an Indian restaurant in Portland, thinking it would make him look sophisticated and urbane, even though he'd never in his life eaten Indian food. How should he dress? He decided to wear a suit jacket and tie. Maybe he should have picked something safer, like Chinese or Italian. Too late now.

The clock couldn't spin fast enough. He picked up his notes and casually flipped through the pages. While reading them, he heard someone approaching his desk. Nguyen plunked down across from him and appraised him with a dead-eye stare. She was not very good-looking or particularly memorable. She dressed in drab clothes and wore glasses that made her look like the engineer she'd initially studied to be. Despite being tall and thin, her face had a peculiar fleshiness to it that one would ascribe to a heavier woman. The prospect of her nosing around, in his case, annoyed him more than it should have, but he couldn't let on that it did.

"What's up?" he asked, sighing.

"I can't help but wonder why everything about these cases points back to Gwynn Denning."

"I just reread the case file on Daisy Carson and concluded that her death had absolutely no connection to any of this."

Nguyen ignored this remark. "I did a Google search on the man they found asleep in his car the night of the fire."

Peters made a show of looking at his notes. "Dr. Ezra Kaufman."

"That's him," she said, repositioning the glasses on her flat nose. "He's quite an interesting character."

"I know. I interviewed him twice."

"His mother survived the Holocaust," she said as if he wasn't even there. "Graduated from Harvard and Harvard Medical School. He was once very active in his synagogue, as well as in the civil rights movement. Did you know that he's been arrested numerous times?"

"He failed to mention that in our interviews," he said, surprised at this oversight. "What for?"

"Civil disobedience. He and a group of protesters once chained themselves to the fence of a nuclear power plant. But that was a long time ago."

"Okay, that's a big nothing burger, then."

"I kept digging around and found this," she said, passing him a black-and-white photograph that had once appeared in the local newspaper. "It was taken back in the late eighties."

Annoyed, and ready to leave for his date with Gwynn, Peters took the photograph in hand and stared at it. It captured a dozen people standing in front of a youth shelter. He read the article and realized that the people in the photo were pastors, rabbis, priests, and various laypeople gathered to do community work. The article detailed the story of a young girl they helped rescue from a sex-trafficking ring. Under the photograph, he read all the names and saw that one said Dr. Ezra Kaufman. He handed it back to her.

"So he liked to give back to the community. Big deal."

"Did you see the other name on the list?"

He shook his head.

"One of them is the Reverend David Preston."

"Am I supposed to know him?"

"You should. It's Gwynn Denning's father."

"Let me see that again," he said, jolted by this news. He took the page back from her, feeling his face turn red at the embarrassment of such an oversight. "So the two men once knew each other. Portland's a small town."

"Just seems like a strange coincidence, doesn't it, especially when you combine that with Kaufman showing up at that trailer park?"

"An educated man like Kaufman must know a lot of people in town," he said, trying to mask his nervousness. Had Nguyen also learned that Gwynn was his patient?

"Yeah, I suppose." She sat back and stared blankly at the photograph. "I'd guess that if your parents survived something as horrific as the

Holocaust, you too would feel compelled to give back."

She looked up at him with deadpan eyes. "My parents are boat people, Peters."

"So what? A lot of people in town own boats."

"No. It means they fled Vietnam in a trawler along with eighty-six others. My mother's sister and brother drowned, and other passengers were killed by pirates. They landed in Malaysia and spent six months in a United Nations refugee camp before they emigrated here. So don't you lecture me on hardship."

"Sorry, I didn't know."

"It's one of the reasons I became a police officer. To ensure that people get justice and we have a country of rules and laws."

"Good enough reason to join the force."

"That's why I'm going to do everything in my power to find who killed these people."

Peters had enough of this upstart trying to show him up. He felt embarrassed that he didn't know his partner's family history, know what the term 'boat people' meant, or wasn't the one who discovered the connection between Gwynn's father and her therapist. Snatching his jacket off the chair, he stormed off without saying goodbye.

"Where are you going?" Nguyen called out after him.

"I'm done for the day."

"I'll call you if something comes up."

"You do that, Nguyen."

Chapter Thirty-Three

Gwynn looked so beautiful when the door opened that he could barely catch his breath. At first, he thought she was going to rush over and kiss him, but instead, she reached up and tightened the tie around his neck. For a moment, it felt like she was strangling him, and he was slightly taken aback by the feeling of her hands around his throat. He pictured her doing the same thing to Townsend and William Clayborn, and it freaked him out a little. Was he being paranoid? He relaxed when he saw her smiling at him.

They made their way to his car. He opened the door and tried not to stare at the bare leg she exhibited while slipping into the passenger seat. She had on high heels and a black dress that revealed a good deal of cleavage.

She was quiet during the ride over, and the lull in conversation made him nervous. But once they were seated at the restaurant, their conversation flowed so naturally that he forgot all about his suspicions. The sexual chemistry between them sizzled. At one point during the conversation, as he reached for his Kingfisher beer, she grabbed his hand. Her touch felt soft and firm at the same time, and he imagined her body to be spectacular under that black dress.

He excused himself and went inside the bar. The Steelers were playing on the big screen and were up by two touchdowns in the first half. If the score stayed the same, he figured he should have a nice payout come tomorrow. Feeling good about the way the night was going, he headed back to his table.

His phone vibrated against his thigh, but he ignored it, swearing to forget about work for the remainder of the evening. He listened to the story

Gwynn told about some crazy woman she'd encountered at the supermarket. His phone vibrated again, and he decided to shut it off the first chance he got. He watched her closely, pretending to hang on her every word, when what he really was doing was admiring the contours of her face. Her blue eyes radiated warmth and were rendered even more stunning by the subtle outline of charcoal drawn around the edges. Her lips were painted a gentle shade of pink. Silver earrings dangled from her lobes, which were partially hidden by her shimmering hair.

Their plates arrived, aloo gobi for her and lamb vindaloo for him, even though he had no idea what vindaloo was. It tasted strange and looked like an exotic version of beef stew, filled with bitter spices that defied description. He thought the flatbread called naan tasted good, so he filled up on that and the Jasmine rice.

Gwynn laughed. "Are you okay?"

"Sorry, just lost in thought."

"You need to chill and take your mind off work, Peters."

"I know," he said, realizing that he was not spending *enough* time at work. He pictured Nguyen back at the station, fueled by the injustice perpetrated against her mother country, burning the midnight oil and trying to solve these cases before he did.

"I, more than anyone, want you to catch the person responsible for Sandra's death, assuming it wasn't an accident. But you have to allow yourself time to relax and have some fun."

"You're right. I've been working way too hard lately. How about we put all the bad stuff aside for the evening and talk about you?"

"Me?"

"I want to know more about you, Gwynn."

"What's more to know?"

"Anything you want to tell me."

"You first."

"I grew up in Biddeford. My father worked in a warehouse, and my mother was a secretary at a law firm. I have two older sisters. I knew in high school that I wanted to be a cop, but I wasted two forgettable years at

213

the community college, bored out of my mind. One bad marriage and no kids. Just my cat."

"You never wanted kids?"

"With my crazy schedule and all, it just never happened. And then things started getting rocky between me and my wife, so we figured it best not to complicate matters by having children."

"Yes, I suppose that was the right thing to do, although I don't know what I'd do without Jack."

"I guess it just wasn't meant to be. At least not with her, anyway."

"Are your parents still alive?"

"Yeah. They have a small place in Bridgton and spend winters down in Fort Myers," he said. "What about you?"

"I've probably already told you this, but my father was a minister in town for many years and is now retired. My mom worked for the church, doing administrative stuff and caring for my father. She passed away from cancer when I was in my early twenties."

"Sorry to hear that. Any brothers or sisters?"

Gwynn paused for a moment to take a sip of water. "No, it was just me."

"A minister and his wife didn't want more kids? Go forth and multiply sort of thing?" He laughed.

"Obviously not."

"Kids are a lot of work. And the people who absolutely shouldn't have them are the ones reproducing like rabbits."

"Tell me about it. I work with troubled kids every day and see the damage bad parenting has done to society."

"There's no bad kids, just bad parents," he said, parroting what a social worker once told him.

"I was so lucky to have such a loving mother and father growing up," she said, standing. "Will you excuse me while I use the restroom?"

"Of course." He stood in courtesy.

While she was gone, he pulled out his phone and opened the text message sent to him from Nguyen.

The medical examiner report came back on Sandra Clayborn and Daisy Carson. Ambien was found in Carson's system, along with alcohol, meth, and marijuana. They determined that Clayborn had a small amount of water in her lungs, which seems unusual considering that she drowned. Otherwise, all her vital organs were in good condition. It's possible we might have two murders on our hands now. Maybe three.

Peters considered this message and agreed with his partner's assessment. Experienced swimmers like Sandra Clayborn didn't just drown in calm seas unless they were experiencing a medical emergency. Combine that with her missing husband and the small amount of water in her lungs, and it added up to murder.

He typed back.

Okay. Thanks for letting me know. Message me back if you hear anything else.

He hit send just as Gwynn stepped out of the hallway, looking lovely as ever. She walked back to their table and sat across from him.

"Did I just catch you looking at your phone?"

"Guilty as charged. But that's it; no more work tonight."

"Listen here, Peters. You can choose to keep working, or you can choose to be with me."

"That's a no-brainer."

She reached across the table for his hand. "Isn't it funny how things turned out?"

"How so?"

"Not that I'm saying that this missing Boston man is a good thing, but if it hadn't happened, we might never have met."

He found it a strange thing to say, but he couldn't argue with the logic. At least something good came out of all this murder and mayhem. Oddly enough, things often happened that way.

* * *

Gwynn picked up the tab when the waitress delivered their check. That surprised him, seeing as how he had just come back from the bar and saw that the Steelers had lost their big lead. The prospect of losing five hundred bucks soured his mood, especially now that Gwynn had paid their bill. It made him feel less like a man. They headed out to where he'd parked. Once they'd settled into their seats, she leaned over and kissed him.

"You okay?" she asked.

"Couldn't be better."

"I thought maybe you didn't like your vindaloo."

"It was spicy, but tasted okay," he said, knowing he'd toss his doggy bag in the trash come morning. "How about I drive you home."

"How about we go back to your place instead."

"Really?" He couldn't believe his ears.

"Really. I think I'm ready."

"You sure?"

"Yes, but I can't stay long. Jack's got a babysitter."

"Then that will be the worst part of my night, watching you leave."

"I'll be sure to make it up to you beforehand."

He accelerated back to his building. Once he parked, they ran upstairs to his apartment, which he'd cleaned beforehand. She was already undressing by the time they reached the bedroom, and he could barely believe his good fortune. He felt like a teenager experiencing sex for the first time; his anticipation was so great. And she looked even better once she'd stepped out of her dress and was standing naked before him. He didn't have time to admire her figure because she quickly dove under the covers, beckoning for him to do the same. Every bit of energy gravitated toward his crotch, and he thought for a second he might prematurely explode. As soon as he joined her in bed, she snuggled next to him and smothered his neck with kisses. Her breasts and pelvic bones pressed up against him, and he felt as if he could stay like this forever. His fingertips massaged her body as she raised her head up and kissed him on the lips.

* * *

Gwynn hopped out of bed and dressed quickly, almost falling as she slipped into her high heels. Giggling like a happy schoolgirl, she leaned over and kissed him on the lips, whispering that she couldn't wait to see him again. For a brief second, he almost spit out the dreaded three words, but wisely, he stepped back from that precipitous ledge. It was way too early in the relationship for the L-word.

Having sex with Gwynn had totally made up for the fact that he was five hundred bucks lighter in the wallet. Maybe she could help him quit his gambling and put that bad habit in the rearview mirror.

Two times in one hour? At the age of thirty-seven? And he probably could have gone another round if she would have stayed overnight. More than anything, he wished he could fall asleep in her arms. Then wake up in the morning and breakfast on sausage, eggs, and hot coffee. That way, he could enjoy her presence for a few minutes longer. She was the best thing that had ever happened to him, and he vowed not to screw things up with his paranoia and nagging self-doubts.

"Do you have to leave so soon?" he asked, resting his head on his palm.

"Jack's got a babysitter, remember?" she said, buttoning her blouse.

"Okay, I'll get dressed and drive you home."

"You stay in bed, Romeo. I've already called for an Uber."

"Why'd you do that? I could have driven you."

She kissed him on the lips. "Go back to sleep, Peters. I'll call you in the morning." She grabbed her bag and slipped out of his apartment.

Exhilarated, he laid his head back down on the pillow. Tomorrow he would return to the investigation and try to solve these cases. But now sleep beckoned.

He grabbed his phone off the nightstand and checked his messages one last time. He noticed there was one from Nguyen. How late did that woman work?

I've been doing some digging around and found out something interesting. Did you know that Daisy Carson gave birth to a child when she was sixteen and gave it up for adoption? At least that's what an old friend of hers claimed. Think it means anything?

Peters sat up and read the message again. Then, one more time. Daisy gave up a baby for adoption at the age of sixteen? He estimated Daisy's age and then Gwynn's age, and it perfectly fit the timeline. He recalled the conversation he had with Gwynn over dinner and her mentioning that she was an only child. Was that because her parents couldn't have children? And just like that, those damned suspicions returned in full. Was Gwynn adopted? Did he dare ask her and ruin what could be the best relationship he'd ever been involved in?

For the first time since he started on this case, he seriously suspected that Gwynn Denning, the woman he'd fallen deeply and madly in love with, might know something about these four mysterious cases. He felt like he needed to be sure before he got deeper into this relationship.

Dr. Ezra Kaufman

Gwynn sits in my waiting room while I fret in my office. A part of me wishes I had dropped her as a patient when I retired. Of course, I know why I didn't. It's this curious nature of mine. It's why I continue to pay for office space on Portland's pricey waterfront and tend to her needs.

How could I have been so reckless as to fall asleep in that trailer park? For someone with two Harvard degrees, I'm not that smart. Did I really think that a Mercedes wouldn't stick out in that park like a sore thumb? Now the police are onto me, and it's only a matter of time before they realize that Gwynn is my patient.

I have no doubt now that Gwynn Denning is a killer. So why am I not in any hurry to rush to judgment? Throughout my life, I've had my own secret thirst for vengeance. How many nights have I lain awake, fantasizing about what I'd like to do to those Nazi bastards who committed genocide against my people? It's always angered me that my mother was all too willing to move on in life. Not necessarily to forgive and forget, but look to the future. How can I possibly help my patients overcome their problems when I can't even understand my own?

I spent a good deal of my early life trying to advance civil rights and fight the war on poverty. But after years of supporting these causes, I kept asking myself what good has it done? The world's problems appear to be growing worse despite my considerable efforts. The war on poverty seems like a misnomer, because at least wars end at some point. Drug use and addiction are worse than ever.

Somewhere along the way, I noticed that my thinking began to shift, and I secretly (and with much guilt) began to consider the idea of addressing these societal problems from a different angle. What about getting rid of the people who are responsible for causing the world's endless suffering? Admittedly, it's a dangerous idea. And I fully realized the paradox I'd boxed myself into. I would become just like the followers of the Third Reich. Israel transformed into Nazi-like Zionism. The French and Bolshevik Revolutionists. Sometimes, the best intentions lead to the greatest acts of evil.

But what if, in the right hands, capital punishment worked the way it was intended to?

Is this how Gwynn feels about the acts she's committed? If so, I think I understand her mindset. Not that I'm condoning what she's done, but even I feel no remorse for the two reprobates she murdered earlier in her life.

Now, after all these years of counseling her, I feel like I don't even know Gwynn Denning. Yet, in some ways, I feel I know her better than ever. So why did she kill Sam Townsend? And Sandra and William Clayborn? What about the poor woman in that trailer park? What grave crimes had all of these people committed? Had she meted out her own form of justice?

Do I broach the subject with her in therapy? Would I be putting my own life in jeopardy if I brought up my concerns? I seriously doubt she would try to harm me after all the years we've spent together.

Or would she?

I mentally steel myself for this session. I put on my game face and lift the notepad off my desk. Take a few deep breaths before I open the door to greet her. Any deviation from the norm might send the wrong impression. She smiles brightly when she sees me. I invite her in and then sit down behind my desk, noticing the glow of contentment on her face. Is it because she's gotten away with murder and knows it? Four murders, to be exact? No, five, if my assumptions are correct.

"How have you been, Dr. Kaufman?"

"Just fine, thank you."

"Been sleeping well?"

What does she mean by this?

She stares at me for a few seconds. "I saw you recently."

"Oh? Why didn't you come over and say hello?"

"Well, I tried, but you were indisposed at the time."

"Indisposed?"

"Let's just say that you were asleep at the wheel."

My heart leaps up against my ribs like a caged tiger.

"It's rare that you see a Mercedes in a trailer park."

She knows that I followed her to that park. And that she killed that woman.

"Don't worry," she says. "I'm actually quite relieved that you know."

"You're relieved?"

"Yes. I've been dying to unburden myself of all this," she says. "Are you going to tell the police you saw me there?"

I shake my head, but I'm not really sure.

"Are you certain about that?"

"Yes, I am."

She nods as if satisfied with my response.

"Are you planning to kill me, Gwynn?"

She seems to think this over. "I don't want to, if that makes you feel any better. You've been so wonderful to me all these years, helping me deal with my issues."

I sit quietly, wondering what kind of monster I've enabled all these years.

"Besides, you would have already turned me in by now if you were so inclined." She crosses her bare legs and stares at me. "So why haven't you?"

"I think you know why."

"Please enlighten me."

I consider my words. "I've had...my suspicions about you for years now."

"Suspicions?" she says, looking surprised.

"It started with that dog you killed when you were a teenager. Then, my curiosity began to snowball after that gym teacher fell to his death. And that drug addict who died in your presence."

"The death of that heroin addict must have really cinched it for you."

221

"Let's just say I didn't chalk it up to coincidence."

"And after all these years of being suspicious of me, you've never rushed to judgment."

"I've been strict on you in therapy because I wanted to understand your mindset. I gave you the benefit of the doubt, knowing what an accomplished and compassionate woman you are, especially with the children in your care. I think I know why you do this."

"You do?"

"I can't be totally sure, but it's my belief that you believe that what you're doing is just and right."

"So that is the conclusion you arrived at after all these years?"

I don't understand what she means by this.

"Okay, you at least understand part of the reason why I do what I do."

"There's another reason?"

Gwynn sits back in her chair, not responding to this question, and we sit quietly like this for a few moments. She gazes at me with those icy blue eyes, looking so alone and vulnerable that it causes a lump to form in my throat.

"I didn't ask to be like this." Her eyes go moist.

"Of course you didn't."

"All I ever wanted in life was to be normal like everyone else. I just didn't know how."

"I believe I can help you now that I know the full extent of your issues."

"You really think you can help me?"

"I do."

It seems like a good time to embrace, but we don't. Instead, she turns on her heels and leaves my office.

Alone with my thoughts, I consider what I've done. And what I'm prepared to do for her, my very last client. I'm in too deep now, I realize. I've crossed an ethical line and can never go back. The only way forward is reforming Gwynn Denning.

Chapter Thirty-Four

Gwynn felt a load lift off her chest after meeting with Kaufman. She sat shaking in her car, trying to collect herself. All her life, she'd been waiting to confess to someone about this sick, hidden desire of hers, and now she'd done it. But what was even more surprising was that Kaufman intuited it all along. He understood why she had killed those people and didn't judge her for it.

She didn't need to worry about Kaufman. If he hadn't reported her to the police by now, he'd never do it.

She drove back to The Loft, thinking about all the goodwill that had come her way in the last few months. The sex last night with Peters had been amazing, in fact, the best she'd ever experienced. It was all she could do to pry herself away from him and return home. Even the people at her office noticed the glow on her face this morning. It made her laugh to think that she was falling for the same detective who was in charge of solving the four murders that she had committed. Knowing this gave her a secret, perverse pleasure and made her wonder if her feelings for Peters were genuine.

Her phone rang while she was driving. She pulled over to answer it.

"Gwynn," an elderly woman's voice said.

"This is her."

"It's Lillian. You visited me recently about your biological mother?"

"Yes, I remember."

"I don't know if you've heard the news, but the woman who died in that Westbrook trailer *was* your mother."

"What? Oh no." She tried to sound sad.

"I'm sorry for your loss. Did you ever get a chance to meet her?"

"No. I've been so busy with work lately that I hadn't been able to set anything up."

"That's such a shame," the woman said. "The reason I'm contacting you is that a police detective called and left me a message."

This alarmed her. "What did they want?"

"They said they wanted to talk to me about Daisy."

Had she slipped up? "Why do they want to talk to you?"

"They must have found my number on her phone records."

"Why would your number be on her phone?"

Lillian hesitated a few seconds. "I called her the day before she died and left a message about the possibility of you coming over to see her."

"Why in the world would you do that?"

"I felt guilty about giving her name out because of that confidentiality agreement I signed years ago."

"But you said that the agreement became null and void after the agency closed," Gwynn said, nervous that the old woman might have given the police her name.

"It did, but I felt guilty about going back on my word. So I thought that giving her a heads-up was the right thing to do."

Gwynn smoldered, angry that this woman might have messed things up for her.

"Because of that, I'll need to tell the police that you contacted me if they ask."

"I was really hoping we could keep this between us. I don't want my father to find out that I'd been searching for my biological mother. He'd be heartbroken if he knew."

"I thought you said they were okay with you looking for your real parents."

"I did, Lillian, but I wasn't telling you the truth."

"I can't lie to the police, Gwynn. I only called to give you a heads-up in the event they contact you about her death."

Gwynn said nothing, trying to find a way out of this mess. There was no way she could allow the police to find out that Daisy was her biological mother. Yet she didn't want to do the unthinkable to this old lady. It would go against everything she stood for when she acted on these urges. Maybe a few heartfelt words of encouragement might persuade her otherwise.

"When do they plan on coming over and talking to you?"

"Tomorrow morning."

"Okay, Lillian, thanks for letting me know."

"No problem. And I'm very sorry that you never got to meet her."

"Me too," she said, abruptly ending the call.

There was no sense going back to the office. Instead, she turned around and drove straight to Lillian's house. Every fiber in her body told her not to do the unthinkable. But Lillian held the power to ruin her life and separate her from Jack. And that could never happen. She would make sure of it.

***

Lillian looked surprised when she opened the door.

"Gwynn, what are you doing here?"

"I got to thinking," she said. "Can I come inside so we can talk?"

"But I was just heading out."

"This should only take a minute."

Lillian looked around in confusion, not sure what to make of this unexpected visit. "You should have called me before coming over."

"I know, and I'm sorry, Lillian. My phone died. And your call really shook me up."

"Well, okay, but please make it quick."

"I will."

Lillian sat on the sofa, and Gwynn sat across from her, praying that this woman would change her mind.

"What would you like to talk about?"

"I was wondering if you could do me a really big favor."

"Of course. Within reason."

She leaned over and took the woman's veiny hands in her own. "I'd rather you not tell the police about why I came over here to see you."

"Why not?" she said. "You had nothing to do with that woman's death. The newspaper said the fire was an accident and that she fell asleep while smoking a cigarette."

"Yes, I read that."

"I can't lie to the police, Gwynn. Besides, you told me that you never even got a chance to meet her."

She pictured herself getting arrested and being separated from Jack, and her eyes started to water at the thought. "It's true, but I absolutely swore to my father that I would never go looking for my biological mother. He'd disown me if he knew what I was doing."

"The police won't release your name. You had nothing to do with her death."

"I agree, Lillian, but what if, by chance, the press found out and put my name in one of their stories, and then my father read about it? It would devastate him."

"Why would they do that?"

Gwynn wiped the tears out of her eyes. "Why does the news media do anything? To sell newspapers. And this would be quite a story."

"It would?"

"Possibly. And maybe the police might suspect foul play."

Lillian pinched her lips. "Are you implying that someone set fire to that woman's trailer? Is that why the police want to question you?"

Gwynn shrugged. "Who knows?"

"Even assuming her trailer was intentionally set, which I doubt it was, you'll be able to tell the police that you were nowhere near that park when it burned down."

Gwynn felt the walls creeping in. Glancing around for a pillow, she wondered why this old fool was being so stubborn. She tried to convince herself that Lillian had lived a long and fruitful life. Her head pounded at the prospect of what she might do to this woman if she refused such a simple request. If she did kill her, she'd have to take her phone and destroy the SIM card. But hopefully, it wouldn't come to that.

"Now, if you'll excuse me, I have to go out and meet with my sister." The

226

woman stood to see her out.

"Sit down, Lillian."

"Excuse me?"

"I said sit down," she said in a firm voice.

Lillian registered this new tone and sat back down.

"I'm begging you with all my heart not to tell the police why I came here. Can't you see it in your heart to do me this one favor?" she said, hoping this last plea worked and she wouldn't have to take matters into her own hands.

Lillian's expression changed. Was she reconsidering?

"Please," Gwynn said, tears falling down her cheeks. "So that my father can live out the remainder of his life in peace."

"Well..."

"Don't destroy my family and what little time I have left with my dad."

Lillian stared at her for a few seconds. "Okay, Gwynn, I won't say anything. But only because I respect your father so much."

"Thank you so much, Lillian. You don't know how much this means to me," Gwynn said, breathing a sigh of relief. She released the woman's hands and stood. Confident that Lillian wouldn't speak to the police, she walked over and gave her a hug, more for herself than for the old woman. It would have destroyed her if she had to snuff out this sweet old lady's life.

Chapter Thirty-Five

Gwynn climbed her office stairs and, at the top floor, saw an unassuming Vietnamese woman waiting on the wooden bench next to her office. The woman stood when she saw her and took out her police badge. Who was this? And what had happened to Peters?

"Hello, Mrs. Denning. My name is Detective Nguyen. I'm one of the Portland detectives working on the disappearances of Sam Townsend and William Clayborn, as well as the death of Sandra Clayborn. And we are also looking into the death of a Daisy Carson in Westbrook, as well."

Peters never told her about a second detective working on the case. Was this a new development? It seemed as if one hurdle fell to the wayside only to give way to another.

"What happened to the other detective who interviewed me?" she asked.

"Detective Peters is still on the case. We're working together now."

"Oh, okay," she said, hiding her disappointment. "Would you like to talk in my office?"

The woman walked inside, sitting across from her desk.

"I've answered all the other detective's questions, so I'm not sure what else I can add."

"You told him that you didn't know the woman who died in that trailer fire."

"It's true. I don't know anything about her."

Nguyen looked at her notes. "Did you know that Daisy Carson gave up a child for adoption many years ago? I did the math and discovered that it was around the same time you were born."

Gwynn froze.

"Were you adopted, Mrs. Denning?"

How did she know about this? There was no way Gwynn could deny it because it would be very easy to find out.

"Yes, I was adopted."

"Do you know your biological mother?"

"No, and I have no desire to ever meet her. My mother and father were wonderful parents, and I promised them I would never go looking for the woman who gave birth to me."

She noted this. "Do you have any other residences?"

"My husband and I purchased a cabin a few years ago in Western Maine."

"Do you use it often?"

"No, not that much. Our schedules have been very busy as of late. Also, we recently separated."

Nguyen wrote this down. "I see you have a son."

"Yes, Jack is five years old," she said. "Do you have any children, Detective?"

The detective ignored her question and continued to look down at her notes. "Did you know that Sam Townsend once visited your dorm?"

Alarms went off in her head, but she managed to stay calm. How did this cop know all of this? And would she push the envelope and uncover what really happened?

"I never knew him, so I wouldn't have any knowledge of that."

"I took a ride to Brooks College and learned that they keep detailed logs of all the visitors who went in and out of the dorms. The older records are stored in the library's database."

"I have no reason to doubt you."

"Sam Townsend signed into your dorm at 7:22 at night and signed out at 7:27. Do you think he was going out on a date with someone?"

She shrugged. "I have no idea."

"Could it have been your roommate? The actress?"

"Again, I have no idea."

Nguyen stared at her notes. "Did you know that Tift Ainsley vacationed in Maine this summer?"

"No, I didn't know about that," Gwynn said, wondering why Tift hadn't told her about her visit to Maine. "Do you know where she stayed while she was here?"

"She rented a house in Phippsburg. A place on the water."

"Oh, okay," Gwynn said. "Tift and I are obviously not as close as we once were."

"You seem distracted, Mrs. Denning. Are you okay?"

"I have a girl in my care who's been having a hard time lately. On top of that, I have tons of paperwork to fill out."

"Okay, I'll try to wrap this up as soon as possible," Nguyen said. "Did you know that Sandra Clayborn and her husband spent the night with Tift while she was here?"

Her head felt as if it was about to explode. "No, but it doesn't surprise me. They were friends at Brooks, and Tift's free to do whatever she wants."

"I spoke to some of your old college friends. It seems that there was some competition between you and Sandra for Tift's friendship."

"That's absolutely not true. Sure, Tift was popular at Brooks, but she was also my roommate. As to your other point, I was never in competition with anyone for Tift's friendship, especially Sandra." Gwynn took a deep breath. "Besides, that was many years ago when we were college kids."

"Did Sandra tell you that she left a good sum of money to The Loft in the unlikely event that she and William passed away?"

"God, no. She would have never discussed something that personal with me. I only found out about it after she died."

"How did you find that out?"

"The Clayborns' lawyer sent me an email about the trust they set up for The Loft."

"She never mentioned to you that the agency would cease to get any money if certain conditions were not met?"

"Never. We barely spoke, and when we did, it was never about money." Gwynn stood, pushing the chair behind her.

"That's all the questions I have for now, Mrs. Denning." Nguyen stood to leave, her face expressionless. "Thank you for your time."

"Am I a suspect?" Gwynn said. "Because the way you've questioned me makes it sound like I am."

"Oh no, these are just routine questions I'm required to ask."

Nguyen smiled, or what passed for a smile, her unwavering eyes betraying her pale lips. The cop walked out of her office as Gwynn thought back to the four murders she'd committed, and she prayed that she had sufficiently covered her tracks. But the circumstantial evidence against her could raise eyebrows, and she didn't want things to get that far. No, she would ensure that things never did.

None of this drama would have happened if Sandra hadn't seen her walking away from the Custom House with Townsend that night. Had she not killed Sandra and her husband, maybe Gwynn wouldn't have felt so compelled to track down her biological mother. She couldn't help to think how one crime led to another, until she had arrived at this point in time.

Something must be done before this new detective discovered the truth about her.

Before Gwynn started in on her paperwork, she called Tift and left her a detailed message. Not only was she upset with Tift for coming to Maine this past summer without telling her, but that Tift had invited Sandra and her husband to her home, and not her.

Why?

Had Sandra asked Tift for help with her charity while visiting her vacation home, and had Tift turned her down?

Could she persuade Detective Peters to help deflect suspicion from her? Convince him to get this pesky cop to look in other directions?

Gwynn called Kaufman and asked if she could see him as soon as possible. He agreed, but he informed her that she would need to come to his house this time for their session. She hung up, scared, her mind racing. Then she realized that she had no idea where Kaufman lived. She texted him back and asked for directions, and he texted back with his address. How had she not known he lived in Portland's stately West End?

Dr. Ezra Kaufman

I'm in my office journaling about all this when Gwynn calls, asking to see me. By all means, I want to see her, but I don't let on that I'm as anxious about this session as she is. I tell her to come over to my house on account that I'm not up for traveling across town for a one-hour meeting, and I certainly don't want anyone to see her walking into my office. My hands become clammy at the prospect of seeing this murderess, and I realize I need to be cool and calm and keep my head on straight. With everything that's been happening, I'm more eager than ever to learn more about her mind's inner workings.

Minutes later, she texts back, asking for my address. It seems odd that in all these years, I've never told her where I live. But upon further reflection, maybe that was a good idea.

But is it safe for me to tell her my address? I'm sure she could find out if she really wanted to.

I text her back.

Ten minutes later, Gwynn shows up at my doorstep, tears running down her cheeks, staring at me like a long-lost relative. She looks like she wants to cry on my shoulder, but she knows the rules I've set down about physical affection. I move aside to let her in, escorting her to my office just off the parlor. Gwynn doesn't comment on my home, or even seem to notice the expensive paintings and rare sculptures I've collected throughout the years. She enters the office and collapses in the beaded leather armchair. I settle behind my desk, journal open, and hand her a tissue, remaining the consummate professional. My heart beats twice its normal rate. With my hands clasped over the desk, I sit forward and wait for her to compose herself.

Once she does, she tells me how one of the detectives on the case believes she might be responsible for all the mayhem that's been happening around town. I ask her if it's Detective Peters, and she says no, and that it's a Vietnamese woman who's been asking all these vexing questions.

The news of this second detective worries me. How would that look if people discovered that I was her therapist? Would I deny having any knowledge about her illicit activities?

"Why did you kill that woman in the trailer, Gwynn?"

"You really don't know?"

"I have no idea," I say, feeling on shaky ground here. "And anything you say will never leave this room. We've long ago established patient-client confidentiality."

"My father never told you the reason for how I ended up getting adopted?"

"Why would he?"

"I assumed the two of you were tight."

"We were friends, yes, but tight might be too strong a word," I say, neglecting to tell her that he was also my patient for a few years. "As popular as he was in the community, I don't ever recall him having any close friends. To be honest, he was a hard person to get to know."

"He was my father, and I often felt the same way about him."

"Much of our time together was spent working in the community and talking about poverty, social justice, and theological issues. I guess you could say we had a very good working relationship."

"I remember my father spending a lot of time preaching to the people on the street. He seemed a bit obsessed with it, and I had no idea why at the time."

"Your father was one of the most decent men I've ever known. I'm sorry about what he's going through right now."

"Thanks." She nibbles on her thumbnail.

"To be perfectly honest with you, Gwynn, your father and I rarely socialized or talked about our personal lives."

"There were times, when I was a little girl, when I thought he cared more about those street people than he did his own family."

"That's not true. He was always going on about how much he loved you and your mother."

"Then you couldn't have known that he adopted me from one of the street prostitutes he ministered to."

This revelation shocks me. "Are you saying that your...your biological mother was a prostitute?"

"That's what I'm saying. Thanks to you, I tracked her down recently and learned the truth. She was sixteen when she became pregnant with me."

"I'm sorry, Gwynn. I had no idea."

"How could you have known?" she says. "It's obviously why he never wanted me to go looking for her."

"He was trying to protect you from the truth."

"Anyway, the girl wanted to have an abortion, but my father talked her out of it."

"Despite his progressive tendencies, he was a firm believer in the sanctity of life," I say. "We once marched arm in arm protesting the death penalty. Your father was a man of faith and conviction."

She breaks out laughing, which confounds me.

"What's so funny?"

"You obviously didn't know my father as well as you think you did. But don't blame yourself, Doctor, because neither did I."

"Admittedly, he was a complex man, but he was also compassionate and caring to those less fortunate."

"That might be the understatement of the century."

"Why do you say that?"

"Because it was my father who impregnated her."

Did I mishear her?

"Yes, you heard me right. Come to find out, my father had a weakness for pretty young streetwalkers, and he happened to get this one pregnant—with me."

"You mean..."

234

"Yes, he's both my adopted and biological father."

I try to make sense of what she's saying. Surely, this cannot be the same man I knew and counseled. It just doesn't seem to fit in with what I know about him. I'm a psychiatrist. He was my patient for two years. How could I have not known this about him?

"The woman who died in that trailer park was my biological mother."

I try to process all this and match it with what I know about her father.

"I've never seen you at a loss for words," Gwynn says.

"It's shocking news," he says. "I'm sorry you had to learn this about him. But why did you feel the need to kill her?"

"She said she wished she'd aborted me."

"That's a cruel thing to say."

"You think?"

"People change as they get older and often regret the decisions they made earlier in life. And from what I read in the newspaper, that woman had a whole host of substance and mental health issues."

"She was planning on blackmailing me by releasing photographs of my father in compromising positions."

"But why? Your mother's deceased, and your father has dementia. Who would even care at this point?"

"Can you imagine the shame that would cause my family? I have a young son to think about."

"I suppose."

"But the real reason I killed her was the photographs and news articles she had saved in a shoebox. They proved beyond a doubt that my father was the Muddy River Killer."

"The Muddy River Killer?" My blood turns cold.

"He gained access to his victims through his street ministry."

"Are you sure about this, Gwynn? It doesn't at all sound like the man I knew."

"I'm beyond sure. Daisy collected photographs and news clippings of every woman the police found dumped along that river."

"It just doesn't add up."

"It does if you think about it. Do you remember when my father got in that car accident?"

"Of course. He was laid up for a long time after that."

"He suffered a shattered leg and a severe concussion, which the doctors believe led to his dementia."

"What does that have to do with any of this?"

"The first bodies started appearing in the early eighties, soon after my father started his church and street ministry. The police stopped finding victims right around the time of my father's accident."

I sit back, unable to breathe, both devastated and in denial of her father's deeds.

"And I found a cardboard box down in his basement. Apparently, he liked to keep souvenirs of his victims."

She leans forward and shows me the photos on her phone. As I study them, there can be no doubt what he'd done. I feel ready to faint. I think of all the times I spent with Pastor Dave working with runaways, alcoholics, prostitutes, and drug addicts. Had I been facilitating his murderous spree the entire time? Enabling him with praise that assuaged his conscience? All that goodwill and preaching had been merely a ruse to cover his true nature. I feel like such a fool.

Is it happening all over again with his daughter? And am I also rationalizing her murderous behavior?

This changes everything. She's both a perpetrator and a victim. It's no wonder she enjoys killing; the trait was passed down to her from her father. And what's sad is that she's been trying all these years to repress it and keep her murderous impulses in check. Somehow, the dam burst when she caught sight of her friend's rapist at the Custom House, and it brought out the worst in her. Academically, this a huge discovery. Personally, it's a heartbreaking development in this family's tragic saga, and it needs to stop here and now.

"This must be hard on you," I say.

"It is hard, but it's also a relief as well."

"A relief?"

"It's like suffering from a debilitating illness for years without a diagnosis. At least I know now why I'm like this."

"What will you do about it?"

"Whatever possible in order to stay in my son's life."

I understand this to mean that she will continue to kill, if need be, in order to stay out of prison. Somehow, I need to get her to end this vicious cycle and move on in life.

"You have to change your ways, Gwynn. You don't want to end up like your father."

"Do you think I want to be this way, constantly fighting off these dark thoughts that come into my head?"

"No, of course not. We need to ramp up your therapy and keep trying to get at the root of the problem."

Gwynn looks around at her surroundings. "My years of therapy probably paid for this expensive home. Is making money all you care about?"

"How could you say that?" I say. "I didn't get into this profession for the money."

"That's probably what Daisy said to my father."

"Now you've hurt my feelings."

"The hell with your feelings," she said in a stern voice. "How much do you really care about me?"

"I care greatly about you and always have. I'll even waive my usual fee if money's so important to you."

"I don't need your charity."

"What do you want, then?"

She focuses her steely blue eyes on me. "Do I have to worry about you going to the police?"

"No," I say, shaking my head. "I want to help you end this destructive behavior. I want you to be able to trust me enough to be completely open and honest during our sessions."

"I've never felt comfortable discussing my feelings with anyone, including you."

"You need to alter your behavior, even if you believe the people you've punished deserved it."

"It's all I've been trying to do since I was a young girl." Tears drip down her cheeks. "I hate being like this. If I could stop, don't you think I would have by now?" She sits quietly, obviously in pain, waiting for me to comfort her.

"So what will you do about this new detective?"

"I don't know yet," she says, grabbing tissue after tissue out of my Kleenex box. "I'm hoping I won't have to do anything drastic unless she becomes a threat."

She stands and, without even a goodbye, leaves. And just like that, she's out the front door, leaving me to pick up the pieces of my fractured mental state.

Everything in my life has changed. I'm a different man than I was thirty minutes ago. Insecure. Less sure of myself. Reevaluating everything I've ever known about people and my ability to help them.

Chapter Thirty-Six

Peters opened the door to his car, happy that it was Friday. He was about to get inside when Nguyen pulled up next to him. Just the sight of this dour woman made his skin crawl. She'd been working around the clock on this case, hunched over her desk while he'd been home watching football and screwing his new girlfriend. What would Nguyen think if she knew he'd been dating a possible suspect? For whatever reason, Nguyen seemed to think that Gwynn Denning might have had something to do with these four cases. Maybe he'd feel the same way if he hadn't fallen so crazy, madly in love with her. In his heart, knowing what a wonderful woman she was, he'd convinced himself that she would never hurt anyone.

"Leaving so soon?" Nguyen said, dark circles under her eyes.

"It's Friday, and I'm beat."

"Just to let you know, I'm requesting a search warrant for the cell phone records of Gwynn Denning."

"I think you're way off on this. There's not a chance in hell she could have done it."

"You're probably right about that. I just want to be on the safe side and rule her out as a suspect."

"Why are you so focused on this woman, Nguyen?"

"I spent all day yesterday in Augusta doing some research. Did you know that Daisy Carson gave birth right around the time Gwynn Denning was born? Because of privacy issues, I wasn't able to prove that the two are related, but a DNA analysis would certainly confirm it."

"Even if it's true, it doesn't prove she murdered her or had anything to do with the three other cases."

"Why do you continue to defend this woman, Peters? It seems very strange to me that you're not even curious about learning more about her."

"I'm not defending her. I just think you're wasting valuable time when you could be out looking for the real killer. Someone with means and motive and who checks off all the boxes."

"Wasting my time? I've been putting in way more hours on this case than you have."

"All the same, Gwynn Denning can't weigh more than a hundred and twenty pounds soaking wet. In addition, she in no way fits the profile of a serial killer. Added to that, she could never have overtaken Townsend or William Clayborn."

"Did you know that she's been seeing a therapist?"

His heart skipped a beat. "A lot of people see therapists, including me. Maybe you should consider seeing one."

"Very funny," she said. "But what if I told you that her therapist is none other than Dr. Ezra Kaufman, the man they found asleep in his car the night of that trailer fire?"

He couldn't believe his ears. How did Nguyen find out about that? Had she been following Gwynn? Still, he knew it didn't prove anything.

"That's solid police work," he said, trying to sound impressed, "but it still doesn't prove anything."

"Maybe. Maybe not."

"Look, Nguyen, I think you're doing great things in the department. But maybe it's best to slow down and not rush to judgment."

She looked away, as if embarrassed at the compliment.

He stood awkwardly, unsure of what to do or say next. "Is there anything else you need to tell me?"

"Lieutenant Reddick called and asked me how we're doing on these cases."

More alarms went off in his head. "Why?"

"He wanted to know how much time you've been putting in on them and what you've learned."

"I hope you told him that everything's fine between us, right?"

"I told him that I'm working one hundred hours to your forty. To be honest, I told him that I don't think you're up to the task of solving these cases."

He felt a murderous rage toward his younger partner, but he knew she was right. Sometimes, he wished he had just stayed on as a beat cop, doing his rounds and going home at night, no other worries except keeping the streets clean from criminals and reprobates.

"I don't think that's a fair assessment of the situation," he said, knowing that the powers-that-be would side all day with an ambitious, young Vietnamese woman over a white has-been with a sketchy work history.

"It is more than fair," she said, turning toward her car. She stopped at the driver's side door and stared at him. "I still don't understand why you're so intent on defending this Denning woman."

"I am not defending her. It's just that she doesn't fit the profile of a serial killer, and I don't like wasting valuable time."

"Is there something going on between the two of you?"

"Fuck off," he said, getting in his car and slamming the door shut. Furious, he raced out of the parking lot before he said something he might regret—something that might get him in trouble with his superiors.

Chapter Thirty-Seven

He stood there inside of himself. Gwynn opened the door before he even had the chance to ring the doorbell. She looked stunning with her hair up in a ponytail and her face lightly made up. Those lips and eyes made his heart skip a beat, yet he couldn't shake the feeling that she was keeping something hidden from him.

She wrapped her arms around his waist and kissed him, smelling of citrus and freshly picked roses. Her glossy lips practically dissolved into his own like the sweetest of cotton candies.

"Are you okay?" she asked.

"It's been a long week." He handed her the six-pack of beer he'd brought for the movie they were planning to watch. "Where's your son?"

"At his babysitter's house. Luckily, she was available tonight."

"I bet he's a great kid."

"Jack's the best," Gwynn said, placing the beer down on the kitchen island. "Maybe you'll get to meet him someday."

"I'd love to."

"Have you learned any more about your cases?"

He massaged his jaw. "Can we sit down and talk?"

"Is there something wrong?" She sat on the sofa, and he sat next to her.

"I don't know how to tell you this, Gwynn, but my partner is asking all these crazy questions about you. She's got it in her head that you may know something."

"Me?" She laughed. "Are you serious?"

"Her parents were boat people, and now she wants to right every wrong and catch every bad guy," he said. "The woman is too ambitious for her own good."

"I spend all my time caring for my son and the children living at The Loft."

"I told him that, but she has a hair across her ass for you."

"Sure, Sandra and I were old college friends, but I barely knew her after we graduated from Brooks. As for the other two people, I never even met them."

He gazed down at the floor, shaking his head.

"Look at me, Peters. You know I wouldn't hurt anyone, right?"

He glanced at her. "I tried to tell her this, but she's got it in that head of hers that you're somehow involved in those those deaths and the two missing men."

She crossed her arms. "You don't believe her, do you?"

"You think I'd be here if I did?"

"I hear a but coming."

"She's trying to get a search warrant on your phone and GPS records."

"Let her. I have nothing to hide," she said. "In fact, my phone records will definitely prove that I was here on the days in question."

He studied Gwynn's face for a tell. "As much as I despise this partner of mine, she told me some other things that put you in a bad light."

"Like what?"

"She told me that Dr. Ezra Kaufman is your therapist," he said.

She stared at him for a few seconds. "Since when is it a crime to see a therapist?"

"It's not. Even I've been known to see one from time to time."

"Then what's the problem?"

He took her hand. "Did you know that Kaufman was at that trailer park the night the woman died?"

"Why in the world would he be there?"

"He said he was tired and had a few drinks and turned into the park to rest."

"There you go, then. I don't know what he does in his spare time."

"Of course, you don't," he said, hating himself for telling her all this.

"Supposedly, the woman who died in that fire gave a child up for adoption in 1984."

"And your partner has it in her head that I'm the child she gave up?"

He struggled to choose his words, not wanting to tell her the rest of what he knew. "She claims that you were adopted the same year."

"I was, but I have no idea who my mother is, nor do I care to find out. I had the best parents a child could ever ask for growing up. My father was a minister, for God's sake. They loved me more than life itself."

"Look, I just wanted to give you a heads-up about what this lunatic is saying about you," he said. "She's even trying to get me kicked off the case."

"Why would she do that?"

"To get ahead in the department. The fact that she's a young Vietnamese woman completely works against a guy like me in this day and age."

"She can investigate me all she wants, but she'll find nothing to back her ridiculous claims, because I didn't do anything wrong."

"I tried to tell her this, but she wouldn't listen. It's no wonder she's single."

"It's the silliest thing I've ever heard."

"I know. I'm just relaying what she told me."

"Look, Peters, I've dedicated my life to helping abused children and making the world a better place. My father was a beloved minister in town. I have a beautiful five-year-old son, a nice home, and an all-around wonderful life. Why in the world would I jeopardize all this by killing people I barely know?"

"She's a backstabbing ladder climber who will do or say anything to get ahead."

"And does she really believe that I could physically overtake a guy as big as Sam Townsend? I read where he was a star linebacker in college."

"Exactly what I told her."

She rested her head in his lap and looked up at him. He cupped her chin in his hand and felt the silky smoothness of her skin.

"Be honest, Peters. Do you have any doubts about me? If so, you should tell me now before this gets serious between us."

"Absolutely not, Gwynn. I've never once doubted you."

"Are you sure? Because I can't possibly date a man who believes I committed such heinous crimes."

"Being with you these last few weeks, I've seen the kind of wonderful person you are, and I know you would never hurt another soul."

She reached up and caressed his cheek. "I don't want to get you in any trouble."

"You won't."

"Thanks for standing by me," she said, sitting up and kissing him.

But Peters did have his doubts, and they continually whispered in his ear, trying to undermine his relationship with Gwynn and ruin everything good in his life. He knew the doubts would always be there unless he confirmed one way or another whether she committed these crimes.

As she streamed Tift's first feature-length movie, he thought of a way to find out if she'd killed Sandra Clayborn. If, by some crazy chance, she took the bait, he would know for sure and be able to continue on with his life. If not....

"I hate interrupting a good movie, but I might have to check my messages from time to time."

"Oh?"

"Nguyen said she might have some important information about the cause of Sandra Clayborn's death. She also said there was someone on the water that day who might have witnessed what happened to her."

"Do what you need to do," she said as she sat back down next to him.

"Thanks for being so understanding."

She leaned over and kissed him. "That's me, the most understanding woman you'll ever meet."

He placed his phone down on the coffee table while she went over to the kitchen and grabbed them some beers. After a few minutes passed, she brought them back in tall, chilled pilsner glasses. Then she kissed him again before starting the movie, and Tift's face appeared on the screen.

Halfway through the movie, he excused himself to use the bathroom. While inside, he took out his burner phone and sent a text message to his department phone sitting on the coffee table, certain that she would hear it ringing. The message would pop up on his phone's screen, where Gwynn could easily see it. He waited a few minutes to make sure she had time to read it. When he came out moments later, Gwynn was not there. He called out for her, but she didn't reply. Where had she gone? Had she read the message?

He downed his beer.

Finally, he heard her coming up the basement stairs, carrying a basket of laundry. He scolded himself for being so paranoid, then picked up his department phone and pretended to check the messages on it. A frightening thought came to him. Was he afraid of his own girlfriend? She placed the basket down behind the sofa. Then she went into the kitchen to get them two more beers.

He now felt certain that he didn't need to be concerned about Gwynn. She had absolutely nothing to hide.

After a few minutes passed, she returned with his beer and handed the tall Pilsner glass to him. He took a healthy sip as she cuddled next to him, her feet tucked beneath herself. An hour passed, and he felt himself becoming drowsy. The alcohol and long work hours were taking their toll on him. He almost nodded off, but then Tift appeared topless on the screen, and his attention shifted to her supple breasts.

Chapter Thirty-Eight

He woke up in the dark, in only his boxers, and wondered where he was. His mind felt blurry and disconnected from his body, and it was all he could do to maintain his equilibrium. How many beers had he knocked back during that movie? It took him a few seconds to realize that he was in Gwynn's bed and under her sheets. He knew he'd been tired last night, but he never expected to fall asleep during the film, especially an action-packed movie featuring a half-naked Tift Ainsley. He turned but didn't see Gwynn beside him. A sinking feeling overcame him as soon as he remembered the fake text message he'd sent to his departmental phone last night. He jumped out of bed, unsteady on his feet, his head spinning. Dressing haphazardly, he wondered if he'd be able to keep his car from veering off the road.

His phone beeped as he searched for his keys. Through blurry eyes, he saw a text message from his bank informing him that his account was overdrawn. He also noticed that Nguyen had left him a message last night. He opened it.

Unless you're doing a late-night interview, Peters, you have some explaining to do. Good luck telling Lt. Reddick about how you spent the night at Gwynn Denning's house.

That bitch had been spying on him. He should have suspected as much from her.

He needed to get out of this house. But where was Gwynn? Then he remembered the text message he had sent to his phone, and he knew exactly where she went.

Now he knew the truth: Gwynn had killed those four people.

He ran around searching for his car keys but couldn't find them. Where did he put them last night? Glancing out the window, he noticed that his car was gone. His gun was not in its holster, either. He'd severely underestimated her. He'd set a trap for Gwynn, but she'd managed to pull a fast one on him. Now, he had to rush over to the dock before she did the unthinkable.

Fortunately, she'd left the keys to her SUV on the kitchen island, not expecting him to wake before she returned home. And now he knew why. Gwynn had spiked his beer. No way he'd ever pass out after four beers, especially with Tift Ainsley running around onscreen in a floss bikini while shooting an AK 47.

A horrifying thought occurred to him: his girlfriend was a serial killer.

Chapter Thirty-Nine

Gwynn didn't want to spike Peters's beer, but what other choice did she have? She'd read the brief message Nguyen had sent to his phone and knew she had to act before this murder investigation got out of her control. She'd only put a small dose of Ambien powder in his beer, enough to put him asleep until morning. But it actually took a lot longer for him to pass out than expected. The man had an extremely high tolerance. She helped him stumble woozily to her bed, where he collapsed onto her mattress and fell into a deep slumber. Certain that he would not wake until later the next morning, she grabbed his handgun and searched in his phone until she found the message. She reread it a couple of times to make sure she was doing the right thing.

Peters,

Ben Davis, the captain of the Lilly, just called me to say he remembered snapping a photograph of that Boston Whaler. If the tech team can blow up the image, we might be able to identify the person who was piloting it. I'm going to meet with him when he returns to the dock tomorrow afternoon.

Nguyen

Gwynn dressed in black before making her way to the kitchen, fully expecting Peters to still be asleep when she returned home. Then she would snuggle up next to him as if nothing had ever happened. She pocketed his Glock, knowing that the poor lobsterman didn't deserve to die because of a random picture he'd taken of her. He probably had a wonderful wife at home and some beautiful kids that loved him. Yet there was no way she could leave her only son without his mom and with only Tom to raise him. Tom, with his passive/aggressive personality concealing a whole host of deeper flaws that she hoped to never learn about. She needed to raise Jack right and make sure that he didn't turn out like her.

She jumped in Peters's car and headed out to where the *Lilly* left port each morning. The weather was warm, the ocean smooth and glasslike. Ben Davis would surely go out lobstering on a gorgeous day like today. Whereas before, she enjoyed killing the scum of the earth, the prospect of ending this good man's life filled her with despair, and she drove in tears, trying to think of another way out of her dilemma.

She reached the dock in Yarmouth and parked Peters's car near the pier, pounding the steering wheel in frustration. She asked God for a way out of this mess, but it was as if God was ignoring her. Slipping the black ski mask over her head, she exited the car and retrieved his handgun out of the trunk. She have to catch the lobsterman by surprise if she hoped to kill him and steal his phone. Then what? Dump his body in the ocean?

Was there any other way out of this situation without having to end his life? If only she could render him unconscious and snatch his phone away, she might not have to do the unthinkable. But then he might put up a struggle and identify her. And he was a big guy and strong as an ox, as most lobstermen were. Judging by his occasional social media posts, he looked to be well over three hundred pounds. After giving it more thought, she realized that killing him was her only option.

After thirty minutes of waiting and praying, she saw him parking his F-250 in the lot. Her pulse raced as she waited until he got out of his truck. Then she walked briskly toward where the *Lilly* was docked. Luckily for him and for her, he was wearing wireless headphones. With gun in hand, she moved stealthily forward, her heartbeat pulsating in her ears. Davis turned onto the dock and waddled toward his boat, and she skulked a few yards behind.

"Gwynn, don't do it," a voice called out in the darkness.

She turned, and to her surprise saw Peters standing behind her in the shadows. How could he still be conscious? He looked tired and scared, his hair sticking up at all angles.

"That lobsterman didn't take any pictures of you, Gwynn."

"I read that text message your partner sent to you."

"No, I was the one who sent that message. I sent it to myself, hoping you would see it, never in a million years expecting that you had…"

"I had what?"

"I had to know for sure, Gwynn. Now I know that you killed those four people."

"So you lied to me."

"Yes. And unfortunately, my suspicions turned out to be true."

She turned and watched as Ben Davis approached the *Lilly* and then climbed aboard the vessel, no worse for the wear.

"I set you up in order to learn the truth," he said. "That lobsterman has no idea you were in Willam's boat that day."

She turned and walked toward Peters, pointing the gun at him.

"Why did you kill them?" Tears bubbled in his eyes.

"Get in the car."

"I loved you, Gwynn."

"So now you don't love me?"

"I can't just shut off my feelings for you, even knowing the terrible things you did."

"The terrible things I did?" She laughed, although laughter was the last emotion she felt right now. "You don't know anything about me or the things I've done."

"Maybe not, but I know I still love you."

"Get in." She tossed him the keys. "You're driving."

Peters got behind the wheel. She sat in the back, the barrel of the Glock pressed against the driver's seat.

"Where are we going?"

"Make your way toward Cousins Island."

"What's there?"

"Just drive, and I'll tell you where to go. And don't do anything rash."

"I had to know, Gwynn."

She didn't respond to this, instead directing him to drive the rest of the way in silence. The road took them over a narrow bridge that connected the mainland to Cousins Island. The island was quiet and remote, the roads empty at this hour. Gray clouds blanketed the dark morning sky, and a slight mist began to fall. He took a left onto Sea Meadow Lane until he arrived at the spot she had in mind. Waves lapped against the rocky shoreline as he pulled up next to the water. Massive rocks lined either side of the cove. As much as she tried to deny it, this spot was perfectly suited for what she was planning to do.

"Shut off the engine."

Peters did as instructed.

"If you do anything stupid, I won't hesitate to kill you."

"I believe you, Gwynn."

"My initial plan was to get rid of Townsend. That's it. The others I had to do in order to cover my tracks."

"What reasons could you have had for killing four people?"

"What reason did you have for killing that violent criminal?"

"He was reaching for his gun. I shot him in self-defense."

"I could say the same thing about what I did."

"You killed them in self-defense?"

"In a way," she said, having convinced herself of this twisted logic. "I felt terrible about lying to you. In fact, I never intended to fall in love with you in the first place."

"Neither did I. It just happened."

"And knowing that you killed that motorist made me appreciate you even more. I felt as if we'd made a connection."

"Because we both killed people?"

"Yes."

"But I didn't murder him, Gwynn. I did it in self-defense."

"It's still taking a life."

"My gut instinct kept telling me to be careful around you. Maybe I didn't want to believe all the evidence pointing toward you," he said, staring at her eyes in the rearview mirror. "My love for you completely blinded me to the truth."

She wiped away a tear. "I'm sorry you had to find out the hard way."

"Is that why you stayed with me all this time? So you could wean information out of me and stay one step ahead of the law?"

She sniffed up a tear. "You think that I was using you?"

"What else am I to believe?"

"It pains me that you think this way, because I did no such thing."

"I'm sorry, Gwynn, but I don't believe you."

"Then, that's your problem," she said.

"I should have never got involved with you."

"Maybe not, but I can't help it that we made a connection that day you came over to interview me. It was nice while it lasted."

"And now you're going to kill me? For merely doing my job?"

"What other choice do I have? I'm sure as hell not going away to prison and let my asshole husband raise my son."

"I swear I won't tell anyone what you've done?"

She thought about it for a few seconds, wondering if his response was genuine, or a way to save his skin. "Sorry, Peters, but I just can't take that chance."

"Do you think I'd screw you over like that? Especially all that we went through?"

"Trust me, I've been screwed over by people a lot closer to me than you."

"You'll never get away with it. My partner knows that I spent the night at your house."

"I will get away with it. I'll make it look like you took your own life," she said.

"Suicide?"

"Why not? You've been depressed after your divorce and from the shooting that took that motorist's life. You've been struggling at your job.

And what about all those dire messages on your phone?"

"What dire messages?"

"You never told me you had a bad gambling habit and that you owed money to your bookie."

His eyes moved from the rearview mirror to the ocean.

"I can't risk being separated from Jack."

"Can you at least explain why you killed them?"

"Stalling is not going to work."

"You owe me an explanation if you're going to take my life."

Gwynn hesitated a few seconds before saying, "Yes, I owe you at least that."

She told him how Townsend date-raped Tift back in college and how emotionally draining it was for the two of them that semester. How they supported each other emotionally and academically throughout their college years, which was why they remained best of friends to this day. Or at least she thought they still remained friends. She told him that Sandra had witnessed her leaving the Custom House with Townsend, and then tried to blackmail her when she stayed over her house. How she took the Boston Whaler and ambushed Sandra while she swam in the bay, only to return to the woman's home and practically bump into William as he made his way inside. Then, discovering that Daisy Carson, as a sixteen-year-old prostitute, had been paid by her biological and adopted father to sleep with her. She might not have killed Daisy had the woman not also blackmailed her with those disgusting photos of her father.

"Holy shit!"

"I might as well be totally honest with you, Peters. These murders are not the first time I've killed."

"You've done it before?"

"Three times, in fact. Seven people in total."

"Seven times?" He whistled. "Who else did you kill?"

"The first victim was my gym teacher. He sexually molested some of my classmates, one of whom ended up taking her own life. The next person was a guy in Paris who attacked me while I was walking along the Seine. I was in college and living there for the summer. It was late at night, and like a dummy, I thought I would be safe walking alone in Paris. I ventured off the path and went downstairs to stroll along the banks, carrying a bottle of wine. That's when he jumped out of the shadows and wrestled me to the ground. As he mounted me, I grabbed the bottle by the neck and smashed it over his head. He fell back in a daze. I might have been able to run away if I'd wanted, but why take the chance? So I stabbed the jagged shard into his neck and rolled him into the Seine."

"Damn!"

"They found his body the next morning on the banks of the river. Come to find out, he had a long record of assaulting women."

"And the third victim?"

"It had been my third month on the job as a social worker. I went inside the apartment I was assigned to visit and saw a two-year-old boy running around naked and unsupervised. There were cigarette burns all over the poor child's body; he'd clearly been malnourished and abused. I was so distraught about the child's condition that it brought me to tears."

"That must have been horrible."

"Trust me, it was one of the worst things I've ever seen," she said. "The boy's father started to nod off during our interview. So I waited until he passed out; then, I shot him up with a lethal dose of heroin. I sat back and watched as his breathing shallowed, knowing the little boy would be better off without him. After feeling no pulse, I scooped the boy up in my arms and called the authorities."

"Sounds like he had it coming to him," Peters said.

"I won't lie to you. I enjoyed watching that piece of shit die," she said, staring out the rain-splattered windshield. Waves lapped against the layers of shale and foam sprayed into the air.

"You like killing?"

"I have a...a disorder."

"What kind of disorder?"

"More like a condition," she said. "Ever since I was a young girl, I've been trying to resist these dark urges that occasionally come over me. I'd been doing a good job as of late until I saw Townsend that night at the Custom House."

"Does that mean you're going to take pleasure in killing me?"

"No. This will haunt me."

"Then don't do it. There must be some other way we can handle this situation."

"There might be, but I can't think of one right now."

"Despite everything you've just told me, I still love you. As a cop, I've seen the worst in people, and sometimes, I wish the system did a better job of removing dirtbags from society. So a part of me really does understand why you did it."

"If only I could really trust you, Peters, I would."

"You can. I swear I won't ever say a word about this to anyone."

"Unfortunately, that's not enough of a guarantee for me. I have my son to think about, and he comes first in my life."

"Please, Gwynn. I'm begging you."

"Maybe if I didn't have Jack, I'd reconsider, but I have his future to consider. And if Tom ends up raising him, my son's life will be ruined, and then he'll turn out just like him. Or me."

"What's wrong with his father raising him?"

"Tom has his own issues."

They sat quietly for a few minutes.

"You're not the only one who has a secret," Peters finally said.

"What secret could you possibly have?"

"One that could cost me my job and land me in prison if the truth ever came to light. Maybe even get me killed."

"Gambling debts?"

"Oh no. Those are nothing compared to what I'm about to tell you."

"Then what?"

"Turn your cellphone onto record, and I'll tell you," he said. "If you go down for for your crimes, then you can take me down with you."

"Are you suggesting that we—"

"Yes, we blackmail each other. Doing this will prove beyond a doubt that you can trust me."

She thought about it for a few seconds. "What do we have to lose?"

"We have everything to gain," he said. "Are you recording me yet?"

"Turn around and face me, Peters. Slowly." He unbuckled his seatbelt and turned between the seats until his face was above the neckrest. "Are you ready?"

"Ready." She placed the gun down on her lap and held her phone up to film him.

"The motorist I shot during that routine traffic stop was not carrying a gun. I knew it the entire time, and yet I shot him anyway."

She glanced over the phone, surprised that he had just admitted to committing murder. For some reason, it relieved her to hear this, knowing that he was a cold-blooded killer just like her.

"Are you admitting on camera to murdering that man in cold blood?"

"Yes. I'd arrested him three years earlier on a domestic abuse charge, and it was one of the worst cases I'd ever seen. He beat up his mother and put his girlfriend in the hospital with five broken ribs and a bad concussion. The lowlife served only eight months in prison and then was right back on the street, dealing drugs and robbing people. He'd committed numerous offenses, starting at the age of twelve, and had fathered four children by four different women. Even after I shot the bastard, knowing he wasn't armed, I'd convinced myself that I'd done the world a big favor."

She felt a rush of euphoria sweep through her.

"Not only did I murder him in cold blood, but I planted that gun on him afterward. I thought of myself as one of the good guys, keeping people safe from thugs like him. Why should I be the one to pay for his violent and sadistic behavior?"

"Do you regret doing it?"

"Hell no. I'd kill him again if I knew I could get away with it."

She glanced over her phone and stared at him. It took a second to realize her mistake. Peters lunged for the gun in her lap, managing to rip it out of her hands. Once he had it, he pointed it at her.

"What are you doing?" Gwynn asked, cursing herself for being so careless.

"Give me your phone."

Reluctantly, she handed it over to him.

"I thought you loved me, Peters."

"I do love you. More than you know."

"Then let's be together. No one ever has to know the awful things we did."

"I would love nothing more than to be with you, Gwynn, but how will it look when Nguyen solves these cases and then tells everyone about us falling in love?"

"You can tell her she's wrong."

"It's not that easy. She followed me last night and knows that I spent the night at your house. She probably took photographs of my car parked in your driveway."

"She won't be able to solve these cases if we keep our mouths shut and work together."

"It only takes one murder case for her to solve, and we're both screwed. And have you forgotten about the phone call you took from when you stayed over at Sandra Clayborn's house? It was the same weekend the two of them went missing."

Gwynn cursed her stupidity. She had meant to destroy her phone and get a new one, but she hadn't done it yet.

"I'm sorry, Gwynn, but I can't let that video you took of me go public. I have to look out for myself."

"I can't believe you're doing this to me."

"What other choice do I have?"

"I'd rather you kill me than send me to prison."

"As much as it breaks my heart to see you behind bars, solving this case will be a huge boost to my career."

She punched the seat in front of her. "Is that all you care about, Peters? Your damn career? What about the love we have for each other?"

"Sorry, but I'm broke with no prospects of making a decent living outside of being a cop. I live in a dump and drive a lemon with over a hundred thousand miles on it. And as you know, I like to gamble on football games and horses. So unless you have a better idea of how we can beat these raps, I'm afraid I have no other choice but to take you in."

"Loving me is not enough?"

"What good will our love be if we're both found guilty of murder? And you do realize what happens to cops in prison? Especially cops who have shot and killed a gang member in cold blood?"

She needed to think quickly before he handcuffed her and took her into the station.

"There must be some way we can work this out."

"There isn't, Gwynn. It's over," he said, ordering her out of the car. "Now put your hands behind your back, and don't make this any harder on me than it already is."

She got out of the car and placed her hands behind her back. The mist dampened her hair as he locked the cuffs around her wrists. Tears streaked down her eyes at the thought of never seeing her son again.

Peters stuffed her into the back seat and closed the door. He settled behind the wheel, turned the ignition on, and headed toward the police station. As they crossed the bridge, an idea came to her that was so genius it just might work.

"Pull over," she said once they reached the other side. He hit the brakes and pulled over to the side of the road. "Do you really and truly love me, Peters? Or were you just saying all that to save your hide?"

"You know I do." He turned to look at her.

"Good. I have an idea that could solve all our problems."

"Stop torturing yourself, Gwynn; it's over."

"Just hear me out. I have a plan that will allow us to be together until death do us part."

"I doubt there's anything you could do or say now that would make me change my mind."

"That's where you're wrong, Peters," she said. "I'm going to make you rich and famous."

Chapter Forty

You're going to make me rich and famous?" He wiped his eyes and laughed. "I'd love to hear how you're going to do that."

"Trust me, you'll be a household name after I'm done with you."

"Keep talking."

"Do you remember the Muddy River Killer?"

"Sure. The guy committed a string of murders in the eighties, nineties, and aughts and never got caught."

"Well, I know who did it, and I want you to be the one who solves the case."

The offer intrigued him, but he knew not to underestimate this woman. "I'm still listening."

"Do you know any of the primary suspects from that time? Someone who could take the fall for those murders?"

"Wait. You mean I'm not even going to arrest the real killer?"

"No."

"That doesn't seem right, especially considering that the person who committed those crimes might still be out there."

"Trust me, the Muddy River Killer will never hurt anyone else again."

"How can you be so sure?"

She stared out the window. "Because the man who committed those murders is my father."

He couldn't believe his ears. "I thought you told me your father was a minister."

"He was, but now he's got dementia and can't even remember his own name."

"So you're telling me that your father killed those prostitutes and dumped their bodies along the banks of the river?"

"That's exactly what I'm saying."

"Holy shit."

"You can imagine how shocked I was when I found out about his secret life. It's the reason I had to kill that woman in the trailer park. She knew what my father had done and never said a word about it to the police. In fact, she kept a box of photographs in her bedroom that proved beyond a doubt that he killed them."

"Is that how she was going to blackmail you? By handing those photographs over to the police?"

"Yes, and I could never let that happen."

"Sounds like your father deserves to be in prison for what he's done."

"I couldn't agree more, but think of all the negative publicity my son would be forced to deal with if that information ever came to light. It's not Jack's fault that his grandfather was a vile serial killer."

And his mother. "I'd probably do the same thing if I had a kid, but I need proof, Gwynn."

"Come over to my house, and I'll show you. He kept souvenirs of all his victims in a shoebox," she said. "You can even keep me in handcuffs while you examine the evidence."

He thought it over, wondering if she was telling the truth. Then again, what did he have to lose?

"So, do you want to be a hero and 'solve' this important cold case? Or do you want to go back to your old life, single and miserable?"

"I want nothing more than to have you back in my life."

"And you in mine," she said. "Hear me out."

"I'm all ears."

"We offer Nguyen a deal to keep her mouth shut. Then the two of you solve this cold case together and go on to achieve fame and national recognition."

"But what if she doesn't agree to this?"

"Trust me, she'll have no other choice. And even if she still believes that

I'm the one who committed these murders, she'll never in a million years be able to prove it. Only you and I will know the real truth."

"What about my phone call you took at Sandra Clayborn's house?"

"Admittedly, it doesn't look good, but it's not absolute proof of my guilt. I'll just say she invited me over for dinner the night before, and I left it there. You could even back me up and provide me with an alibi. Tell people that you were surveilling me that morning, watched me leave, thereby proving that there was no way I could have killed the two of them and disposed of their bodies."

"It might actually work."

"Then, after you've solved the Muddy River Killer case, you go on all the cable news shows and reiterate that William Clayborn murdered both his wife and Townsend. Theorize that they were having a torrid love affair, and then he went on the lam. Who will ever doubt you, the brilliant detective who arrested the Muddy River Killer?"

"Wow. You've thought this whole thing through."

She beamed with pride. "Furthermore, since all three of them are dead, they'll never be able to deny the affair."

"What about your husband?"

"Don't worry about Tom. I can deal with him."

"I'm still not sure that Nguyen will agree to this."

"She will if she knows what's good for her. And if she doesn't, you'll be the one who gets all the fame and glory. This solution is going to make everyone happy: you, me, Nguyen." She leaned over the seat and kissed him. "This way, you and I can be together when all this blows over."

"I want that more than anything."

"You're going to be a hero, Peters. You'll be rich and famous and finally able to pay off all your debts."

"I especially like the sound of that."

"We love each other and have both committed murder."

"In all honesty, Gwynn, I have no desire to ever kill again."

"Neither do I," she said. "I'm prepared to leave all that behind me now that I have you by my side."

"If we're to be together, you need to stop this behavior. Losing you would be too great for me to bear."

"You will never lose me again. I promise."

"I'd rather have you in my life than any fame or fortune that might come my way."

"That's sweet of you, but now you get to have both."

"Come up here and sit next to me," he said. He got out, opened the back door, and then opened the passenger door.

She got out of the back seat and sidled up next to him. After removing the cuffs, he gathered her in his arms.

"Are we good now?" she asked.

"We're more than good."

He couldn't believe his luck. Not only did he have Gwynn back in his life, but he would also get to solve the Muddy River Killer case. All he needed to do was research the case and decide whom to pin these murders on. He didn't care that he had to cheat the system in order to get ahead. A lucky break like this could advance his career.

They kissed, reveling in each other's company. That Gwynn was a serial killer didn't bother him in the least now, knowing the real reasons why she did it. The people she killed had no respect for life. She killed because she *valued* life.

It took a while to pry himself away from her. They needed to go somewhere and finalize their plans. The two of them had a lot of work to do if they wanted to clear her name and make a new one for himself. A name that people in this town would never forget. And respect.

* * *

The next day, he went into the office early and started researching the case of the Muddy River Killer. He pored over each and every file and read everything he could get his hands on. It amazed him that Gwynn's father never became a person of interest. The lead detective on the case was a guy named Eddie Purchase. He checked around and learned that Purchase was retired, still alive, and lived in Old Orchard Beach with his wife, Peggy. He decided to call the guy, but before he got a chance to do so, Nguyen sat down at her desk, instantly ruining his good mood.

"Good to see you're showing some initiative this morning," she said, staring down at her phone's screen.

"For your information, I was interviewing Gwynn Denning the evening you were spying on me. It happened to be the only time I could talk to her. My car wouldn't start, so I left it there and took an Uber home. And you can call and ask her yourself if you don't believe me."

"You're such a liar."

"I swear to you that I'm not."

"Are you sleeping with her?"

"God, no. What a terrible thing to say."

"You do know that she's a suspect in four murders. Think of the trouble you'd be in if it came out that you were involved with her."

"You think I don't know that?" He shook his head in frustration. "She's not even my type."

"Please don't tell me your type, because I don't care."

"I went back and looked at all the evidence, and I'm now one hundred percent certain that she had nothing to do with any of this."

"What a surprise," she said. "You're lucky Lieutenant Reddick is on vacation. I'm going to meet with him as soon as he returns to work."

"You do that, Nguyen. And you tell Steve that for all the long hours you've been putting in on this case, you've got nothing to show for your efforts."

"I don't know how or why, but I'll prove that your girlfriend had something to do with all this."

"She's not my girlfriend, so I would appreciate if you would stop saying that."

Nguyen pulled out a file.

"The problem with you, Nguyen, is that you work hard, but not smart."

"Underestimate me at your own peril."

"Gwynn Denning didn't even know Sam Townsend."

"Then why did he sign into her dorm that day?"

"He was probably dating Sandra Clayborn back then. That's where their relationship first started," he said. "And I called Tift Ainsley, and she said she had no recollection of ever meeting him."

"That dumb Hollywood actress gets paid to lie."

"As far as Daisy Carson is concerned, Gwynn was home the entire evening."

"How would you know?"

"I staked out her house that night and saw that she never left home. It's in my notes."

"How convenient." Nguyen continued to stare down at the file. "I don't believe you."

"Believe what you will."

Nguyen looked up at him. "There was something about Sandra Clayborn's body that is still troubling me."

"Like what?"

"The missing boot. The skin from her ankle had partially come off. It was almost as if something had been wrapped around it, like a rope."

"Her leg could have gotten tangled up in a line. There's lots of lobster traps out there in the bay."

"I suppose."

"Use your head, Nguyen."

"What if someone motored out there and tied a rope or chain around her foot, then tied it to a heavy object. It could have caused her to sink to the bottom. Then, at some point, the boot slipped off her ankle and took the loose skin with it. I researched those boots she had on and learned that they aren't designed to come off so easily."

"I still think William murdered her and fled the state."

"No way a fit woman like that drowns in a calm sea. And she was a champion swimmer back at Brooks."

"If we can just track down William and bring him in, we can solve this case once and for all. My guess is that he became enraged when he learned that Townsend was banging his wife. Didn't you read in the file that they had lunch together earlier in the day? Reservation for two at Dimillo's."

"I still don't buy your stupid theory."

"That's because it makes too much sense."

Nguyen grumbled under her breath.

"The killer has to be William. He was the only one who knew where the key to the boat was, and he had the motive and means."

Nguyen stood to leave, clutching her phone. "Seems rather stupid to kill his wife and her boyfriend, especially when he's one of the top criminal defense attorneys in the state."

"Think about it, Nguyen. Townsend visited that dorm back at Brooks so he could take Sandra out on a date. They were in a passionate on-and-off relationship for years now, on the q.t. Did you even look at Townsend? Not only was the guy rich, but he looked like a model."

"William left no paper trail, which is almost impossible to do in this day and age. There's not been a single trace of him anywhere. No credit card purchases or bank withdrawals."

"That's because the search for him hasn't gone national yet. Maybe the guy planned this murder for years, stashing away enough cash and gold to support himself, preparing for the day when he could kill them. And as you know, it's very easy to get lost in Alaska."

"Say what you like, but I still think Gwynn Denning is our number one suspect," she said, staring back down at her phone. "And I'm talking to Lieutenant Reddick as soon as he comes back from vacation, and getting his take on all this."

"Let me ask you this, Nguyen. What are your career goals?"

"My career goals?" She looked up from her phone. "I want to be the best cop I can be."

"How old are you?"

"Thirty," she said, which surprised him. She looked much younger.

"A cop like you has a bright future in law enforcement."

"You're so out of line with that comment that I don't even know where to begin."

"Maybe so, but we both know that you'll be able to write your own ticket in this department."

"I'm going to solve this case because I'm smart and hardworking, not because of my gender—or ethnicity."

"Throwing your partner under the bus is not a good look. Steve, and all the other cops, will see right through you."

"Steve?"

"Yeah, my good friend Steve Reddick. We graduated from the Academy together."

"The good old-boy network won't save your ass," she said, looking away in disgust. "I'll make sure of it."

Nguyen stormed off. Good. He'd finally gotten under her skin. It would make things easier when he offered to share credit with her for solving the Muddy River Killer case. If she turned down that offer, then so be it. Once he became famous, he'd do everything in his power to destroy Nguyen and run her off the force. She wouldn't get hired as a dogcatcher if she turned him down.

* * *

The conversation with Purchase was short and terse, the complete opposite of what he'd expected. He'd probably feel the same way if he'd spent much of his career chasing a ghost that never materialized. At least he got a solid lead from the conversation with him: an old loser named Vinny Lazzara.

He spent the next hour trying to find out if Vinny Lazzara was still alive and where he lived. Finally, he discovered that Lazzara owned a little ramshackle house tucked away amid the industrial sprawl between Marginal Way and Congress Street. Lazzara had never married or had children. His primary occupation for the last forty years had been driving a taxi cab in town, but he had slowed considerably after suffering a heart attack two years ago. Lazzara seemed like an odd duck. Purchase claimed that Lazzara used to pick up street girls and transport them around, sometimes in trade, which meant that the girls would provide him with sex in exchange for fare. Some of the girls even claimed that he paid them to have sex with him in his cab. There was an arrest thirty years ago for assaulting a prostitute, but the case had been dropped by the prosecutor when the girl failed to show up in court. In fact, no one had ever seen her again.

Peters checked out the location of Lazzara's home on the map. It was nestled between the homeless shelter and the soup kitchen and well-suited for what he and Gwynn planned on doing. He looked up some photographs of Lazzara and saw a greasy old Italian guy with a hunched posture, nervous eyes, and wavy black hair. Lazzara would be the perfect fall guy for the killings that Gwynn's father had committed.

Only problem was, Peters had no desire to share any credit with that ambitious little backstabber. What he really wanted to do was to take all the glory for himself and ruin Nguyen's life. Just like he wanted Gwynn all to himself and not have to share her with that fat bastard of a husband.

Later that day, Gwynn texted him with a plan. He only hoped it went off without a hitch.

Dr. Ezra Kaufman

I go over to Pastor David's house to see for myself what the face of evil looks like. Sometimes, I think I should have been an FBI profiler, but my parents would never have approved of that career choice. They didn't scrimp and sacrifice so I could become a government enforcer like those Nazis. They wanted more for me.

In my coat pocket sits the 1938 Czech pistol that my father received in exchange for food. I'm not even sure it works. I had to go on the internet to learn how to expel the magazine. There are still bullets inside it, although they are old and rusty.

I knock on the door and am let in by his caretaker. I've brought with me an expensive box of Haven's chocolates. It's my upbringing that's to blame. She asks if I'll watch Pastor Dave for a few minutes while she runs to the store, and I tell her that will be fine.

He's sitting at the table when I make my way into the kitchen. David looks up at me with those twinkling blue eyes, faded considerably by time's arrow, and it nearly makes me sick. The man is still handsome, and I can now clearly see how much Gwynn resembles him. His hair, surprisingly, still has glints of blond in it. He smiles, and it reminds me of when we marched against oppression and injustice. It's easy to picture him charming those young girls and telling them about how Jesus transformed Mary Magdalene from a prostitute into a devout follower.

"Hello, David."

"Hey, how are you?"

"I've been better," I say, pushing the box toward him. "I've brought you a present."

"Thanks."

"They're Haven's," I say, hearing the caretaker leave out the side door. I gently lift the cover off the box, revealing the assortment of treats. "Go on. Have one."

He dips his finger in the squares and plucks out a coconut cream. Gazes at it for a few seconds before taking a bite. He slowly chews on it, as if tasting chocolate for the first time.

"Good."

"I'm so glad you like it."

"What's your name?"

"Ezra. You don't remember me?"

He stares, still chewing.

"We worked together thirty years ago. I'm your daughter's therapist. I even helped you back in the day."

He continues to chew.

"Do you remember all those innocent girls you tortured and killed? The ones you ministered to on the street?"

He swallows his treat and then finishes what's left between his chocolate-stained fingers.

"Do you remember that sixteen-year-old prostitute you impregnated?"

"When did this happen?"

"Thirty-six years ago. She gave birth to your daughter."

"I have a daughter?"

"Yes, and she's a serial killer just like you, David, but definitely not as cruel," I say, pulling the gun out of my pocket and placing it on the table. His eyes gravitate toward it, but he doesn't appear frightened.

"I have to go to the...to the bathroom," he says, standing. "Do you know where it is?"

"Yes. Do you need help?"

He nods.

I lead him down the narrow hallway until I find the bathroom. He stands in front of the toilet, looking at me for direction. Am I really going to help him with this? I go inside and undo his belt buckle, pulling down his trousers and underwear. The flow is weak, and I have to position his hand around his member in order to aim his stream into the bowl. Never in my life have I done this type of thing.

After he washes his hands, we return to the kitchen table. The gun is still there, looking old and toylike. I despise guns and always have. Pastor Dave and I once marched down Congress Street lobbying for stricter gun control legislation. My only reason for holding onto this weapon is to keep my connection to my father. I pick it up and point it at Pastor Dave's temple, my hand trembling. He simply turns toward me and smiles, the barrel now pressed between his eyes.

I hold it there for a few seconds before putting it back down on the table. People who kill are a different breed than I am, and I realize I don't have what it takes to do it.

Minutes later, the caretaker's car pulls up in the driveway. I stash the gun back into my pocket. Once she returns inside, I tell her to help herself to the box of chocolates. Then I leave, hoping to never see this man again.

But what about Gwynn? What do I do about her?

Chapter Forty-One

Peters paced back and forth, waiting for Nguyen to show up for their agreed-upon meeting this evening. Hopefully, she'd agree to sharing the credit with him and putting all this behind him. He'd parked in the dilapidated lot behind Bruno's Restaurant, but closer to the Portland Boxing Club. A light mist fell over his windshield as he thought about his current financial woes. But he knew all of that would change once he solved the Muddy River Killer case.

Naively, Gwynn believed that Nguyen would agree to share credit for Lazzara's capture, but knowing his partner as he did, he doubted it. She was stubborn and hardheaded. Too idealistic in her beliefs to take a deal. He was once that way, but not anymore. Not after seeing how many violent scumbags slipped through the cracks of justice.

He glanced over and saw Gwynn sitting in her car, watching from a distance. He'd asked Gwynn to hold onto his gun while he dealt with Nguyen, in the event she feared being ambushed.

Earlier in the day, the two of them had driven over to the Bayside neighborhood where Lazzara lived. They waited until Lazzara left his house, watching as the enfeebled man shuffled out to his Buick with the aid of a cane. Once he drove off, Gwynn snuck around the back and broke in through an open window. It took her fifteen minutes to plant her father's "souvenirs" in one of his closets down in the basement. Now all Peters had to do was get a judge to issue a search warrant, discover the box, and the case would be solved. Then, he and Gwynn could start building their lives together and planning for the future.

Ten minutes had passed since their agreed-upon meeting time. Had Nguyen decided not to show up? He paced around the weedy lot, nervous that she might not appear. Just when he was about to walk back to Gwynn's car, two headlights whipped around the corner. The car approached, stopped, with the headlights on. Burying his hands in his pockets, he watched as Nguyen stepped out of her vehicle, one hand on her holster.

"Why did you call me here?" Nguyen said, looking around nervously. "And where is your car?"

"I had dinner at Bruno's and parked over by the restaurant."

"You said you had some information you wanted to share with me."

"I do."

"Why didn't you tell me over the phone?"

"I needed to do it in person, Nguyen. No one else can know about what I'm about to tell you."

"Okay, let's hear it."

"I've just discovered some explosive new evidence that will rock this town to the core."

"No offense, Peters, but would you mind putting your gun on the hood where I can see it."

"You don't trust me?"

"I don't trust anyone." She took her gun out and pointed it at him, moving into a shooter's stance.

"Jesus, Nguyen. Is this really necessary?"

"Do as I say, or I'm out of here."

"I didn't even bring my gun," he said, arms up to show her his empty holster. "Besides, you're out of your mind if you think I'd dust a fellow cop."

"Start talking, or I'm leaving."

"Look, the reason I haven't been spending a lot of time on this case is that I've been working on something way more important."

"What?"

"Have you heard of the Muddy River Killer?"

"Sure. He killed a bunch of young women and dumped them along the river and has never been caught. I don't know any more than that."

"That's because you were too young when it all went down."

"So what about it?"

"I've been doing some digging around in my spare time, and I figured out who committed those murders."

"You're supposed to be focusing on our investigations, not any cold cases."

"I know, I know, but some fascinating developments recently came to my attention, and I just had to look into them."

"What kind of developments?"

"I spoke to an informant the other day who provided me with irrefutable evidence that an older suspect is our killer. This could be huge for us, Nguyen."

"Sounds like bullshit to me."

"This woman I talked to claimed to have seen the photographs he took of his victims, as well as the personal items he kept as souvenirs. Seemed the old pervert liked to relive his crimes to the prostitutes he hired."

Nguyen shifted her weight, eying him curiously. "Who is the woman you spoke to?"

"I'm not at liberty to say right now, but she's legit. She's even willing to speak to the judge issuing the search warrant."

"Why do I find this hard to believe?"

"I've spent every second of my free time researching this case, and I'm certain beyond a doubt that I've uncovered the real killer."

"Maybe you brought me here because I figured out that your girlfriend is a murderer."

"I'm offering to share credit with you when we arrest this guy. With this collar on your record, you're guaranteed to advance in the department."

"Why would you want to help me?"

"You may not believe this, Nguyen, but I think you're a talented cop with a bright future in front of you. I want to see you get the recognition you so rightly deserve."

"There's no way a cop like you could solve such a complex case as the Muddy River Killer. And I know for a fact that you lied to me about your relationship with Gwynn Denning."

CHAPTER FORTY-ONE

"I was not lying."

"Then why did I see the two of you kissing."

"Don't ruin your career, Nguyen. I'm trying to help you."

"Help me?" She laughed. "I don't need your help."

"I'm offering you the opportunity of a lifetime."

"You're offering me shit."

Nguyen made him want to pull out his hair.

"I also read the case file of that shooting you were involved in. The victim was carrying a Rohm .38 with no serial number. We both know that James wasn't packing the night you murdered him."

"Internal Investigations cleared me of all wrongdoing. Besides, the guy was a dirtbag with a long and violent criminal history. Why do you even care about him?"

"I don't. I care about the truth. Always have and always will. It's why I became a police officer in the first place."

"Then take the deal and help me bring this guy to justice."

"I don't trust you, Peters," she said, her engine still idling.

"Listen to me, Nguyen, Gwynn Denning is not our killer. Trust me on that."

"When I get a search warrant for her phone, I'm sure it will reveal some interesting things. As will her DNA when it matches up with Daisy's."

"Go ahead. Make a fool out of yourself."

"I guess we'll just have to see who the real fool is."

"Are you turning me down? Because I'm only offering this to you once."

"Do whatever you want. I'm going to build my own case against your girlfriend. Then I'll be coming for you next."

"It will be your word against mine."

"We'll see about that."

He badly wanted to kill her right now and leave her body in the nearby gully. That simple act would solve all his problems. But for now, Nguyen held the upper hand. She controlled both his and Gwynn's fate, and he hated feeling powerless to do anything about it.

He was about to try reasoning with her one last time when he saw Gwynn crouching behind Nguyen's vehicle. What was she doing? Gwynn tiptoed forward before standing and pointing the gun at Nguyen.

"Drop the gun, Detective, or I'll kill you."

Nguyen felt the barrel press into her back. She squatted and dropped her own gun onto the pavement. "I should have suspected something was up when Peters asked to meet me out here."

"Don't be too hard on yourself, Detective," Gwynn said. "Even assuming I were to let you go, you'd never be able to prove anything."

"Maybe. Maybe not," she said. "But you wouldn't be holding a gun to my back if you believed that."

"She wouldn't take the deal," Peters said to Gwynn.

"I figured as much," Gwynn said. "That was a bad career decision, Detective."

"I'll never compromise my ethics like your dirty boyfriend here," Nguyen said.

"Even if your life depended on it?"

Nguyen didn't reply.

"You'll get credit for arresting a ruthless serial killer and will forever be known as one of the cops who captured the Muddy River Killer. If that happens, you'll be able to have any job in the department you want."

A car approached. Had Nguyen called in backup? The high beams remained on as the car pulled up. Temporarily blinded, Peters glanced over and saw a driver holding a phone out the window. Was the person filming them?

A shout went up. When he looked over, he saw Nguyen sprinting toward Forest Avenue. Gwynn lay sprawled on the pavement, clutching her head, Nguyen's gun still on the pavement. He scooped it up off the ground and gave chase, but his partner was a lot faster than he was. Firing off a round would only attract unwanted attention from the diners and staff inside Bruno's, and he couldn't possibly shoot his partner while in pursuit.

He gasped for air, slowing in exhaustion, his lungs searing with pain. Nguyen's car sped past him with Gwynn behind the wheel. What was she doing?

As he tried to catch his breath, the other car pulled up in front of him. He squinted from the headlights, shielding his face with his arm. Breathing heavily, he started toward the driver's side door.

"License and registration, pal," he said.

"Fuck off, pig," the man behind the phone shouted.

"Who the hell do you think are you?"

The car sped past him.

Chapter Forty-Two

The attack on her happened so quick that Gwynn never saw it coming. Tom pulled up in his sister's car, distracting her. Then Nguyen did some kind of spinning backkick that knocked her upside the head. By the time she stood up, Peters had grabbed his partner's gun and had taken off in pursuit of Nguyen.

Without thinking, Gwynn jumped into Nguyen's idling car and accelerated past Peters, who was still giving chase on foot but slowing considerably. Although her head hurt, she stopped at the end of the driveway, desperate to stop Nguyen from destroying their lives. When she glanced in the other direction, she saw her nemesis sprinting down the sidewalk and heading south on Forest Avenue. Fortunately, Nguyen had left her cell phone on the passenger seat, meaning she couldn't call for help.

Gwynn turned left onto Forest Ave and accelerated. Swerving to the opposite lane, she parked in the wrong direction on the wrong side of the street and then jumped out to pursue Nguyen on foot. Despite the pounding in her head, she knew she could catch up to her.

She picked up her pace, legs and arms pumping, and gained ground on her mark. Cars screamed past her on Forest Ave, their headlights flashing. Up ahead, she saw a box truck pulling out of the liquor store's parking lot. Nguyen had no choice but to slow down and go around it. The detective glanced over her shoulder and saw Gwynn gaining ground on her. Nguyen turned and bolted across the street, hoping to disappear into Baxter Woods. If that happened, it would be virtually impossible to find her.

The truck inched out into the road as Gwynn bolted past it. A car appeared from the opposite direction. The front end of the car smashed into Nguyen, and she flew over the hood. Her body flipped in the air like a platform diver. The driver hit the brakes and swerved across the road and in the path of an oncoming car. The two cars collided as Nguyen fell hard against the pavement. The blistering sound of metal on metal echoed in the air. Car horns blared, and steam billowed out of the hoods. Gwynn stopped running and saw Nguyen's twisted body lying over the yellow line. Blood poured out of her ears and nose, and her leg was bent at an odd angle.

Was Nguyen dead? She debated going over and checking the cop's pulse, but decided against it after one of the motorists exited his smashed-up vehicle.

Panicked, she pivoted and changed direction, sprinting back toward the liquor store and disappearing into the woods behind it. Once she found the set of train tracks, she headed north over them, jogging at a steady pace, her feet meeting the timber planks at regular intervals. Her heart chainsawed in her chest, and she wondered if Nguyen had survived that horrific crash.

But then she remembered the sudden and unexpected appearance of that other car in the parking lot. Why had Tom followed her here and filmed their encounter? She knew he was curious about her whereabouts and who she spent time with, but she had no idea the lengths he would go to keep track of her. Had he been following her the entire time? Was he hoping to win custody of Jack? Or was he jealous of her relationship with Peters?

She could handle Tom. Tom was weak and malleable, a jealous husband who would do anything to get her back in his life. He had no idea about the kind of woman he'd married.

Or did he?

$$* * *$$

Upon returning to the parking lot, she saw Peters sitting in her car and staring red-faced out the window. She opened the door and sat next to him. Then she turned the ignition and accelerated away.

"Why are you taking a right here?" Peters asked. "Isn't it faster to go down

Forest Ave?"

"Trust me, you don't want to see what happened to your partner."

He stayed quiet for a second. "Did you—"

"If I did, it wasn't intentional."

"What do you mean?"

"Nguyen ran out into the street while I was chasing her and got hit by a car."

"Holy shit. Is she dead?"

"Not sure, but I don't see how she could have survived that collision. It was bad."

"Did you push her?"

"Come on, Peters. Do you think I'm that much of a monster," Gwynn said, fully knowing that she would have if given the chance. "I was chasing her. She ran out into the street. A car hit her. End of story."

"Who was that other person who showed up in the parking lot?"

"That was my husband, Tom. I have no idea why he came there."

"Every time we clear up one problem, it seems another one pops up."

"I wonder what he wanted."

"Maybe he found out about our relationship and was trying to get some dirt on you."

"If so, he didn't stick around long enough for us to find out."

"If he saw what happened to Nguyen, you and I are screwed."

"Don't worry. I'll take care of Tom," she said, knowing she was doing all this for Jack's future.

She steered the car off Washington Avenue and headed up the ramp onto 295, heading back toward Peters's apartment. The Portland skyline passed on her left. The Back Cove and Southern Maine University on her right.

"You need to get that search warrant and bring Lazzara in ASAP," she said.

"That's a given. I paid this prostitute to say that Lazzara hired her for sex. She'll testify to seeing those incriminating photos inside his house, which means we might be able to arrest him tonight."

"Good. We need to make this happen sooner than later."

"Once I get that search warrant, we'll be home free."

"Do this the right, and you're going to be famous, Peters. You'll be on every news station and every true crime show in the country," she said. "They might even make a movie out of the case."

"Who do you think should play me?"

"You're much better looking than those pretty boys in Hollywood," she said, parking three blocks away from his apartment.

"Maybe Tift can play you."

"Oh no, I don't want that happening."

"Why not?"

"It's complicated between us; let's just leave it at that."

She turned off the ignition and kissed him. They sat like this for a few minutes, fogging up the windows. She wanted to stay with him so badly that it hurt. His hand slipped under her shirt, but she pulled it down before they did something they might regret.

"You need to go home. Officially, you never left your apartment tonight."

"Got it."

"And we need to stop seeing each other for a while."

Peters sighed. "How am I going to live without you for the foreseeable future?"

"You'll manage. You have for the last thirty-seven years."

"True, but I'll go crazy thinking about you, wondering when we can be together again."

"Trust me, you'll be way too busy giving interviews and making TV appearances. If you handle this case right, you're not going to have time for anything else in the next few weeks. Now get out of here before I rip off all your clothes and jump your bones in this car."

He leaned over and kissed her one last time before sprinting out the door. She watched as he disappeared into the darkness. Gwynn turned the car around and raced back to Falmouth. Once home, she would call Tom and have a long talk with him. Try to find out what he was up to and why. Then decide what to do about it. And him.

The horribleness of what she had done plagued her. Nguyen was not supposed to be harmed. Nguyen had caused her to go against all her principles when it came to killing, assuming the stubborn cop succumbed to her injuries. Only bad people deserve to die. But she couldn't allow herself to get sent to prison and leave Jack with Tom, especially after seeing what he had done tonight. Jack needed her for moral guidance. Jack needed her in his life if he was going to grow into a decent, law-abiding man. For all these reasons, she knew she needed to stop committing murder and be a good role model. She needed to stop this self-destructive behavior and follow her better angels.

Dr. Ezra Kaufman

For the entire weekend weekend, I hid inside my home and lamented the fact that I did not have the courage to kill Gwynn's father. What a cowardly and weak person I am. Had someone given up their life to kill Hitler when he was a young boy, the death camps and genocide might have never happened. Surely, I'd like to think that I would have had the pluck to do it. But the truth is, I know I wouldn't have.

In the end, I remain true to the oath that I took as a physician. I'm here to save lives, not take them.

Imagine my surprise when I woke up and read the headlines. They're calling Detective Peters a bona fide hero for arresting the Muddy River Killer. The photograph of Vinny Lazzara shows him to be a decrepit old man, feeble and bent over. Apparently, he kept pictures and DNA evidence of his victims down in his basement for when he wanted to recall the murders he most certainly did not commit.

I'm to meet with Gwynn today for another session, and I doubt this subject will come up. It's obvious that she's trying to protect her father from prosecution, as well as having his legacy exposed for all the world to seed. His true self, if uncovered, would negatively affect her and her family. Who wants to be known as the child or grandchild of a brutal serial killer?

The other big story is about the injured police detective. The Vietnamese cop was also working on the murder and disappearance cases. Apparently, she was struck by a car while crossing Forest Avenue late in the evening. The driver of the car claimed that she bolted out in front of him near Baxter Woods. Detective Nguyen was rushed to Maine Medical and is now in a coma. The doctors are unsure if she'll recover from the grave injuries she sustained in that pedestrian crash.

I read about her history. Her parents were boat people who fled the horrors of Vietnam and nearly died on that ocean voyage. After staying in UN refugee camps, they arrived in the United States and settled here in Portland, Maine, where her parents opened up a small Chinese restaurant on Brighton Avenue. Detective Nguyen is single and has never been married.

I can't get over how much she reminds me of myself. Is she as bitter about her parents' arduous ordeal as I am about mine?

* * *

Gwynn comes into my office, and we pretend that nothing unusual has happened. It feels as if we're playing a game. I ask how her weekend went and she says that it was quiet and uneventful. She asks me the same question, and I reply in a similar fashion, although I wonder how she would react if she knew I held a gun to her father's head and debated pulling the trigger.

My gut instinct tells me she's responsible for what happened to that detective. I just need to understand why. But now is not the time. I don't want to scare her off with my probing questions. Knowing Gwynn, she'll tell me everything when she's good and ready, especially now that she knows she can trust me.

Something has changed between us. Maybe a wall has been torn down. And another one put up. Either way, the balance of power has shifted in her favor.

I feel protective of her, knowing that she needs to be reined in order to make better decisions. These urges she experiences are not her fault, but passed down to her from her father. She's as much a victim in all this as everyone else.

Assuredly, her father had no one who could serve this same function for him. He was too proud to admit his flaws. Too stubborn and vainglorious. After two years in therapy, he decided that he no longer needed my services, believing that God would take care of him. Had I known about his murderous predilection from the beginning, I might have been able to help him steer his compulsions in a more meaningful direction.

Or at least turn him in to the police.

I feel something for Gwynn that I've never felt for anyone else in my life, despite all that she's done. Is it possible she could end up like her father? I doubt she's capable of such cruelty. She possesses a deep and abiding conscience. She wants murderers and rapists to be held accountable for their crimes. I tell these things to myself because I desperately need to believe them. But killing begets killing and leads to greater acts of evil. It's just the way it happens with these kinds of people.

Chapter Forty-Three

Three Days Later

Tom refused to answer her calls despite all the messages she'd left for him. She stayed inside her house all weekend, doing chores and trying to keep busy, worried about what Tom might do with the information he'd recorded on his phone. But all she could think about was Peters. They'd agreed not to meet for the foreseeable future, and it pained her to know that she wouldn't be able to see him.

She opened the newspaper and learned that Nguyen didn't die from her injuries but was lying in a coma at Maine Medical. How in the world had she survived that brutal collision? The news articles stated that Nguyen had suffered broken bones all over her body, internal bleeding, liver and spleen damage, brain trauma, as well as considerable trauma to her neck and spine. Even though her prognosis looked grim, the fact that she was still alive both amazed and worried Gwynn.

What if Nguyen someday woke from her coma and told the police everything that had happened that night? The police were puzzled about the accident and were trying to understand why she had been running down Forest Avenue so late in the evening. Was she being chased? Or maybe chasing a suspect? Everyone who knew Nguyen knew she lived for her job and worked around the clock. As a cop, she was as idealistic as they got.

Gwynn waited anxiously for Tom to return Jack home, calling him repeatedly, worried that he might have kidnapped their son. She phoned

Tom's sister and mother, but they didn't answer her calls. For a brief moment, she debated calling the police, but then decided against it. The mere thought of bringing them into all of this made her queasy. She thought it best to take a deep breath and stay calm. *Everything will work itself out*, she told herself.

She stayed up late that night, watching the movie *Bridesmaids,* one of her favorites. She thought it would lift her spirits. Instead, it filled her with even more dread. She went straight to bed after a glass of wine and tried to sleep, but Nguyen's horrific accident replayed in her head. She heard the bone-crunching sound made when that car made contact with Nguyen's body. Saw Nguyen flying through the air, and then heard the sickening thud when she landed on the pavement. Observed the spinal fluid and blood oozing out of her ears and nose. Recalled that unnaturally twisted leg.

At some point in the night, Gwynn sat up covered in sweat. Had she intended to kill Nguyen or just send her a message? Good thing that speeding motorist did it for her—or almost did it. Still, she'd been the one who caused the accident. And she'd do it again if that meant staying in Jack's life.

It gave her comfort knowing she had another session with Kaufman. She needed him now more than ever. Would he know that she was responsible for Nguyen's injuries? Kaufman's only request going forward was that she be honest with him. But would she?

* * *

Gwynn woke up early, made coffee, and went out to get the paper. She was both surprised and happy to see Lazzara's face plastered on the front page of the paper. Beneath it was the article detailing his arrest and capture, as well as his personal history as a cab driver in town. Beneath that was a photograph of Peters. She marveled at how handsome he looked. As she settled down to read the article, the doorbell rang.

She walked over to answer it, hoping to see Tom and Jack. When she opened the door, however, she saw Tom's sister, Trish. Jack scampered inside and gave her a quick hug before running up to his room.

"Where's Tom?" Gwynn said.

Trish glared at her in silence. Did she know something about what had happened?

"I don't appreciate you bringing my son home this morning when Tom should have done it."

"Shut your mouth, Gwynn. The way you've been treating my brother lately, you don't deserve an explanation for anything he does," Trish said, pointing a finger in her face.

Gwynn felt a wave of indignation wash over her but managed to stay calm. Rather than argue, Trish turned and walked back to her car.

She had to get Jack ready for school. So many things to do and not enough time to do them all. No one told her that being a working, single parent would be so hard.

Jack was asleep in his bed when she went upstairs to check on him. She roused him up and asked why he was so tired.

"Aunt Trish let me stay up late last night to play video games," he said as he sat up in bed.

"Were you at Daddy's house last night or Aunt Trish's?"

"Aunt Trish's." His eyelids fell over his eyes.

"Why were you not at Daddy's?"

"I don't know."

Jack shrugged sleepily and she decided to ignore it for now and get him dressed. But she planned on having a word with Tom when she got around to it. Mostly, though, she wanted to know why he had followed her and what he'd captured on film. She couldn't figure out what kind of game Tom was playing.

* * *

The meeting with the client's parents went way over schedule, causing Gwynn to miss lunch. The mother blamed her and all the staff for her daughter's emotional outbursts and anger problems, even though the state had been required to remove the girl from the family home. Relieved when the meeting finished, Gwynn sat back in her chair to finish the granola bar she had started on earlier. Her phone pinged. She opened it and saw that it was a Snapchat message from Peters.

I miss you so much and need to see you. Can you meet me at the Baymont Motor Inn tonight? 7?

It seemed like a bad idea so soon after Nguyen's accident, but she really wanted to see him. They needed to talk about what had happened and how they would proceed from here. They needed to be careful, because Peters was practically a celebrity in town after solving the Muddy River Killer case. She typed back.

I want to see you, too. If I can get a babysitter for a couple of hours, then I'll meet you there. If not, it won't be for lack of trying.

She hit send just as Peters's first message disappeared.

I love you, Gwynn. I can't wait to see you.

She heard footsteps coming up the hallway stairs and knew it was the next social worker ready to fill her in on a potential new client.

I love you, too, Peters. And congrats on solving the case.

She exited out of the service and returned to the main menu, trying to prepare herself for this meeting. It didn't bother her in the least that Peters had received all the credit for Lazzara's arrest. Him doing so solved all her problems. It also made it possible for her father to die in peace, despite all the horrible, evil things he'd done.

The social worker walked in with the young girl in tow. Staring into the poor child's eyes, Gwynn wanted to rush over and hug her. She knew the girl had been mistreated by the ones she'd loved most. She'd seen that look a million times before. The child would struggle initially while living here, before getting accustomed to the program's structure and rules. She'd be taught to deal with her anger and abandonment issues. And with medication and lots of therapy, nutritious food, and a roof over her head, she might have a decent shot at living a normal life. Oftentimes, Gwynn made these intake decisions without even reading the social worker's report. She could look into the child's eyes and know the truth. Today would be one of those days, and she knew she would accept this girl into The Loft's care. It was an opportunity to save another young person's life, and this, she believed, was her true calling.

Chapter Forty-Four

The interviews kept coming one after another: Fox, CBS, NBC. It wasn't that he didn't enjoy all the fame and publicity, but he felt guilty on account that he'd done very little to solve the case. Still, he'd take his one lucky break in life and run with it. Compared to the shit he'd taken in the department all these years, this was like winning the lottery.

He sensed that his living conditions would soon change once his bank account grew. He'd always dreamt about having a place on the water. Already, there'd been book and film offers sent his way. Did he need an agent? It didn't really matter. As long as he had Gwynn by his side, he'd be happy.

By the fourth interview, his mind was a blur, and he could barely concentrate on the questions being asked of him. So many thoughts ran through his mind that he couldn't possibly process them all, especially after what he'd been put through these past few weeks. Like Nguyen's accident. Or the troubling fact that she was still clinging to life. Nguyen's doctor stated that in the unlikely event she woke from her coma, there might be extensive brain damage. Hearing this pleased him. Would she even remember the deal he offered her? Or Gwynn chasing her down Forest Avenue? Or getting hit by that car?

"How long had you been working on this case?" the woman from *Court TV* asked.

"A long time. And mostly in my spare time when I wasn't working on my other cases."

"What turned the corner in your investigation?"

"Lazzara was always the number one suspect, but the previous detectives could never get enough evidence to pin it on him. I'd been reading everything I could get my hands on and knew most of the details about these cases. I just needed a lucky break. Then I got it when this brave woman stepped forward with some explosive new information. But if it hadn't been for all the hard work by the detectives before me, I never would have solved it."

"What was it that convinced you Vinny Lazzara was the killer?"

"There were many factors that pointed to him, the most important being a tip I received from the woman who ventured inside Lazzara's home. The old man bragged to her about killing those poor girls. When she said she didn't believe him, he tried to impress her with his hidden box of souvenirs."

"What was inside the box?"

"I can't get into much detail except to say that he liked to keep some his victims personal items."

The interview finished, and another came in and asked him variations of the same questions, which he answered the same way as before.

For some reason, he couldn't get Gwynn's husband out of his head. He wouldn't be as worried about what had happened to Nguyen had it not been for Tom showing up unexpectedly in that parking and filming them.

After the last interview finished up, he left the room, breathing a sigh of relief. How many times could he answer the same question? He'd wanted nothing more than to see Gwynn, but knew he had to be careful, which was why he made arrangements to stay at the Baymont Motor Inn off Riverside Avenue. It was not that he didn't want to stay at a nicer place, or couldn't afford it, more that they needed to be as discreet as possible in the coming days. If they were seen together, it could ruin all their plans.

Fellow officers congratulated him as he made his way through the station, but he ignored them all. They never paid him any attention before he solved the case. So why should he care about them now? He slipped past everyone and into the parking garage. As he headed out, he felt relieved not to see any media waiting for him by the exit. He drove straight to the Baymont

Inn, but before he made it over there, he picked up a six-pack of beer.

Now, he just had to wait until Gwynn arrived, assuming she could find a babysitter on such short notice. The last thing he wanted to do was sit in a rundown hotel room by himself, with only his cold beers keeping him company.

He got his card key from the front desk and headed straight to his second-floor room. Once upstairs, he stuck the card in the slot and opened the door. The room didn't look as ratty as he thought it might. They wouldn't be there long, and no one knew he'd rented it. He shut the door behind him and collapsed onto the hard mattress. Turned on the flatscreen sitting on the bureau and saw his face plastered on *Law & Order TV*. Thought he looked better on television than he did in his mind's eye.

His thoughts began to spiral as he drank more beer. Did he still have his doubts about Gwynn? Killing seven people was nothing to sneeze at, but he knew she was a good person, a person who took the law into her own hands when society refused to.

Was it only a matter of time before she got tired of him and....

He cracked open another beer and clicked to the next channel. Another interview of himself on *Law & Crime*. Saw Lazzara doing the perp walk, knowing the guy was completely innocent of the murders he was accused of committing.

More than anything, he couldn't wait to see Gwynn tonight. Despite the voice in his head whispering to be cautious, he couldn't deny that he loved her.

He finished his beer and cracked open another, tossing the empty on the floor. Glanced at the newspaper and perused the football lines, debating whether or not to bet on the Jets tonight. Clicked to an old sitcom that usually made him laugh. Sitting back against the headboard, he forgot all his worries while listening to the canned laughter. Drank more beer and maintained his buzz. Looked at his watch and saw that Gwynn was running late.

An hour passed before he realized she wouldn't be coming. He had a nice glow to him now, especially since he hadn't eaten anything for the last few hours. He debated walking to one of those fast-food restaurants down the street and grabbing a few cheeseburgers. Be a mistake to drive home in his condition and get pinched for a DUI. Instead, he fell back against the pillow and clicked to the football game, disappointed that Gwynn hadn't made it. But there would be other nights for them to be together. Many more nights, he hoped.

Grabbing his phone, he called for a pizza delivery.

Someday soon, they would be reunited for good. Maybe even married. This is what he hoped for more than anything.

Chapter Forty-Five

G wynn didn't bother to call her babysitter. It was not that she didn't want to be with Peters, but she was thoroughly enjoying her time with Jack. She'd made them both hot cocoas with marshmallows, and they resumed playing one of Jack's video games. Jack giggled whenever he got one up on her, and each time he did, she reached over and tickled him, enthralled by the peal of his little boy laughter.

She realized she loved Jack so much that it physically hurt. The thought of something bad happening to him often kept her up at night, and she knew she would happily give her own life to protect him. Having a child was both a blessing and a curse. Had her parents felt the same way about her? Is that why her father was so careful about not getting caught? Because he didn't want to bring shame and humiliation to the ones he loved.

Pressing the buttons on her controller, she wondered what Peters was doing right now. Was he thinking about her? As much as she missed being with him, she was glad she didn't go over and meet with him tonight. Making love at the Baymont Inn was not her idea of romance.

Sometime later, she put on *Toy Story*. Jack loved this movie, but by nine, he was out like a light. She carried his limp body up to his room, noticing how heavy he was getting. Once back downstairs, she poured herself a glass of wine and turned on the television, trying to get her mind off everything.

Although there was nothing she could do about Nguyen, she was starting to worry about Tom. His controlling and overbearing nature had reared its head in the worst possible way. Why had he showed up at that parking lot? And why did he have Trish hand Jack over to her instead of doing it himself? She knew Tom was deeply unhappy that she'd broken up with him, but how could she stay with a man who wanted her to be something she wasn't? Who wanted to know her every move and keep constant tabs on her spending and who she befriended. He still loved her and wanted more than anything to get her back in his life, if that was how he defined love. Thankfully, he hadn't gone to the police yet and told them what he knew about that incident behind Bruno's. What would she do if he did?

Blackmailing her was not in Tom's character. Or at least it hadn't been before all this happened. Maybe his true nature was finally emerging.

She closed her eyes and prayed that she wouldn't have to resort to killing Tom. If he tried to get full custody of Jack, her life would be ruined. She loved him, if only as a friend. Jack loved his father, not knowing the true nature of his personality. Why couldn't Tom just accept the inevitable and move on? Because there was no way she would let another human dictate how she should behave.

Chapter Forty-Six

The next weekend she opened the door, expecting to see Tom, but again it was Trish. Jack stood behind Gwynn, wearing his coat and with his bags packed. She didn't want him to leave with his aunt. The sight of Trish made her furious, and for a brief second, she imagined tying a Honda knot around her neck and squeezing the life out of her. She quickly caught herself mid-fantasy and snapped out of it, wishing she wouldn't experience such bad thoughts about her sister-in-law.

"Where's Tom?"

"He doesn't want to see you."

"Why?"

"I think you know why, Gwynn. You broke my poor brother's heart."

"I'd prefer to hand Jack over to him instead of you."

"Fortunately, you don't get to decide."

"We'll see about that."

"From the first moment my brother introduced us, you had it in for me."

"That's not true at all, Trish. It was you who never liked me."

"There you go again, rewriting history."

"I tried so hard to be friends with you and your mother. Get you guys to do things with me and Tom, but you two never had any desire to be a part of my life."

"I only wish Tom had listened to my mother that day when she told him not to get married. He was always smart about most things, except when it came to you."

"We shouldn't be talking like this in front of Jack," Gwynn whispered.

Trish sidestepped her and squatted down to welcome her nephew. "Come on, Jack. You ready to hang out with Aunty Trish for a while?"

Jack ran into his aunt's arms and hugged her. He clearly loved Trish. And Trish loved him. Still, Gwynn would rather have Tom pick him up. That way, she could sit down with him and iron out their differences.

Her sister-in-law walked hand in hand with Jack to her car. They got inside, and Trish glanced up one last time before backing out of the driveway and into the cul-de-sac. Then, the car accelerated and disappeared down the road.

The thought of spending the night alone depressed her. She wished she could call Peters and ask him to come over, but that was too risky. No, tonight she would go over to her father's house and spend the evening with him. With his disease progressing, his days on earth were numbered. No sense living the rest of her life bitter and resentful. She wanted to remember the good side of her father and leave it at that. Hopefully, before he'd lost all his cognitive ability, he'd confessed his sins to God and received forgiveness.

An idea came to her as she put on her jacket. She sent Peters a Snapchat message. He messaged her right back, saying that he would meet her anywhere, anytime. She typed in the address where to meet her and then added,

I can't wait to see you tomorrow!

He typed back.

I can't wait to see you, too. All this fame and celebrity means nothing without you by my side.

Chapter Forty-Seven

Gwynn walked into her father's house carrying the bouquet of flowers she bought for Delia, his most devoted and trusted caretaker. Delia hugged Gwynn before taking the flowers and placing them in a vase. Her father was sitting on the couch and watching television when she made her way into the living room. Delia walked in behind her, placed the flowers on the coffee table, then picked up her knitting needles and sat in the rocker across from him. Despite being in her seventies, Delia still enjoyed helping out her memory-impaired patients. Gwynn knew these women by their first names, the shifts they worked, and all their likes and dislikes. She put her hand on her father's shoulder and sat down next to him. The first thing she noticed was the silver cross dangling from his neck. Delia must have put it on when she helped him get dressed this morning.

"Hi, Dad."

"Well, hello," he said, smiling. For a brief second, he looked like her father of old. "How are you?"

"Wonderful. Jack also said to say hi," she said.

"Who's Jack?"

"Your grandson." How many more times would she need to repeat this?

He looked over at Delia, his caretaker, and then back at her. "I have a grandson?"

"Yes, David, and he's an adorable little boy," Delia said as if irritated.

Gwynn took out her phone and showed him the same photograph she always showed him. "That's Jack, Dad. He's five."

"Wow." He returned his attention to the television, where the six o'clock news was playing.

The first story was about Lazzara's arraignment. She watched as the old man stood hunched over in court, looking confused. Charged with thirteen murders, the judge had denied him bail. A few of the victims' families were interviewed. The story continued with old photographs of some of the victims.

"I know that girl," her father said, pointing at the screen.

Gwynn's entire body convulsed as if she'd been given an electric shock. Had he really remembered?

"No, you don't, David," Delia said, rocking in her chair and continuing to knit. "You were a man of God."

"I was?"

"Yes," Delia said. "The woman in that photo was a prostitute who was killed many years ago."

"Oh."

Gwynn sat quietly, almost paralyzed with fear. Maybe her father really did have a brief memory of the girl. If so, did the memory fill him with guilt? She wondered if she would ever be haunted by the murders she'd committed.

The next story was about Nguyen. Nguyen was in critical condition with swelling and bleeding in the brain. The police still had no eyewitnesses to the accident. Nguyen's immigrant parents appeared on-screen, speaking in broken English. To Gwynn's surprise, she saw Peters's face come into view, and her heart skipped a beat. He described Nguyen as a consummate and dedicated professional, a cop any officer would be proud to call their partner. He told the reporter how much of an asset she was to the city and that she had a bright future ahead of her in law enforcement once she recovered from her injuries.

"I wouldn't complain if he put me in handcuffs," Delia said while manipulating her knitting needles.

"What's that supposed to mean?" Gwynn said, offended by the innocuous comment.

"He's a fine-looking specimen." She turned to Gwynn. "You don't think so?"

It took her a second to compose herself. "He's okay, I guess."

"Tall, dark, and handsome? What's not to like?"

Gwynn wished the woman would stop talking about him.

"I'd like to know why that cop was running around Morrill's Corner that late at night."

Gwynn remembered the sickening thud of Nguyen's body landing on the pavement.

"Such a shame seeing those parents in so much pain."

Something about this visit didn't seem right. She just wanted to sit quietly with her father and remember the good times. Remember him for being the kind and compassionate minister he was and not the serial-killing monster he turned out to be. She just couldn't summon up the emotion necessary to hate him. And yet, part of her did hate him.

She looked over and studied her father. A trickle of saliva trickled down the side of his unshaven mouth. It wouldn't take much to press a pillow over his face and put him out of his misery. No one should have to live their last days like this, imprisoned in their broken-down body, forever living in the present. Maybe this deteriorating illness was actually a blessing in disguise. It would prevent him from ever having any dark thoughts in his golden years.

She kissed her father on the cheek, said a quick prayer for him, and bid him and Delia goodbye. Once in her SUV, she hightailed it out of there before she suffered a nervous breakdown. Before she actually considered returning to her father's house some night and burying his face under a pillow.

Chapter Forty-Eight

Peters slept in after tossing and turning most of the night. With the arrest of Lazzara, combined with his newfound fame, he knew he should be happy. His various dreams alternated between Nguyen waking from her coma and Gwynn chasing her down Forest Avenue.

In the first dream, Nguyen bolted upright from her coma and appeared ready to tell the world about what had happened to her. He'd tried desperately to find her and convince her to keep her mouth shut, but he kept running from hospital room to hospital room, unable to locate her.

As for Gwynn, he dreamt that he had accompanied her on a violent murder spree. He didn't take part in any of it, but he stood by and watched as she killed indiscriminately, laughing each time she murdered someone. Afterward, the two of them went out to dinner to celebrate her killing binge. She sat across from him at Bruno's restaurant, her face and dress splattered in blood. Or maybe it was tomato sauce; he couldn't be sure. Then their entrees came out, and they ate heartily. A shared Tiramisu for dessert. Afterward, they went back to her place. In this dream, he woke up later in the night to discover that his wrists and ankles were bound to the bedposts. A bloodied and naked Gwynn straddled him, bucking up and down and moaning pleasurably. Just as he got close to orgasming, she pulled out a noose and slipped it over his head. He remembered experiencing the most amazing orgasm as he stared up into Gwynn's eyes while struggling to breathe. When he woke from the dream, his body was covered in sweat, and his underwear was soaked in semen.

He sat at the kitchen table, drinking coffee, exhausted from everything that had happened to him in the last few months. Despite the nightmares that had been plaguing him, he looked forward to seeing Gwynn today. It was her husband's turn to have Jack, meaning she wouldn't need to find a babysitter.

Flipping through the newspaper, he saw that there was no change to Nguyen's health, which was both good news and bad news. He hoped she would die as soon as possible so he and Gwynn could finally get on with their lives.

He spent the day doing laundry and tidying up his shitty little apartment. Someday, hopefully soon, he planned on moving out of this place and buying a nice house, preferably away from Portland, nestled in the woods where it was peaceful and quiet. Either that or a pricey condo on the waterfront, within walking distance of all the restaurants and trendy bars along the pier. Or maybe he'd have one place in the boonies and one in the city.

Later that afternoon, he got himself ready for his date with Gwynn. He looked up the address she'd given him and noticed that it was at least a ninety-minute drive. The reality of spending the weekend with her finally hit him, and he became feverish with excitement.

He got in his car and headed out. Such a beautiful day to drive through the Maine countryside. Thirty minutes later, he turned onto a deserted county road. He drove past streams, old historic houses, stately country barns, and gentle rolling pastures with grazing cows. The smell of freshly mowed grass was like perfume to his nose. Something told him he could get used to this way of life.

* * *

Sometime later, he turned onto another dirt trail. Where was his GPS taking him? He cruised slowly up it, careful of the boy with the fishing rod pedaling up the side of the road. Once he reached the clearing, he noticed Gwynn's SUV parked in front of an unassuming cabin. What he wouldn't give to have a place like this, a private spot where he could commune with nature and enjoy some peace and quiet. Grab his fishing pole and catch a few Rainbow trout. Fry them in pads of butter and then wash them down with some cold ales. Return home afterward and cuddle up next to Gwynn in front of a blazing fire.

He popped two mints in his mouth before making his way up the path, lugging the case of beer under his arm. Gwynn sprinted out the front door with a big smile on her face, greeting him with a hug and kiss. The smell of pine cones saturated his nostrils as he reached around and cupped her spine. She felt so soft and vulnerable that he found it difficult to believe that this beautiful creature had killed a total of seven people, and very nearly an eighth.

"I've missed you so much, Gwynn. I can't believe we're finally together."

"I've missed you too. It's been too long."

"I can't live without you."

"Don't think that way. Let's just enjoy our time together while we have it."

"This is such a beautiful cabin," he said, stepping back to admire it. "I had no idea you owned a place out here in the country."

"There's a lot about me you don't know."

"I'll say," he said, fingering a strand of hair over her ear. "How long have you had it?"

"Tom and I purchased it a year after we got married. He didn't really want to buy it, but I insisted we make an offer. I wanted a place where we could take Jack and introduce him to nature."

"What will happen to it now that you and your husband are getting divorced?"

"Let's not talk about that right now." She grabbed his hand and pulled him up toward the house. "You're going to die when you see the view from the back deck."

He found himself bristling when he heard the word *die,* and that erotic dream came rushing back to him. Maybe he should turn around and drive home and never see her again. No, he was being foolish; Gwynn would never hurt him.

He walked up the steps and made his way inside the cabin, taking it all in. The place was not huge, but it was impressive all the same. The walls, floors, and ceiling were all made out of solid pine. Along the far wall was a magnificent stone fireplace that looked right out of one of those glossy home magazines. But the most spectacular feature was the massive window that looked out over the valley. He stared up at the cathedral ceiling behind him and the spacious loft behind that. An enormous porch made of pressure-treated lumber wrapped around the side of the cabin and was topped with deck chairs, tables, and grills.

"Oh my God, Gwynn. This place is spectacular."

"I know."

"I think I could quit my job and live up here forever."

"It only has two bedrooms, but there are some mattresses up in the loft if we ever have guests."

He turned and caught her beaming. Did she mean the two of them when she said 'we'? Or had she been referring to her and Tom? He turned and stared out at the valley, thinking he could look at it all day. Beyond it, he saw rolling hills and a clear blue sky. He imagined the sunsets here to be breathtaking. His shitty little apartment back in Portland came to mind, and he felt a hot sense of shame. But Gwynn didn't appear to judge him because of his sorry financial state. With her by his side, he might finally get another chance at love.

This cabin was exactly the kind of place he'd like to own. Hopefully, Gwynn wouldn't need to relinquish it once she and Tom divorced. It didn't really matter. He knew that there'd be plenty of money coming in now that he'd solved the Muddy River case. Maybe he'd reach out to Tom and make him an offer on this place. He envisioned himself vacationing up here with Gwynn, hiking the trails, and then snuggling up next to her near the fireplace, sipping Irish coffees and allowing the crackle of flames to warm their naked bodies.

He walked back to where she was standing and put his arm around her shoulder. They stood quietly for a few minutes, staring out at the valley. It felt a million miles removed from the streets of Portland and all the other departmental bullshit he faced on a daily basis.

"So you like it up here, huh?"

"Like it?" He turned and planted a kiss on her cheek. "I love it."

"Do you love it more than me?" She smiled up at him.

"I don't think I could love anything in the world more than you."

"Good answer," she said, touching his nose with her fingertip. "We've sworn to be completely honest with each other, right?"

"Yes."

"Keep your jacket on. I need to show you something else."

Gwynn took his hand and led him downstairs. What else had she planned on showing him? She directed him into her SUV, and he got into the passenger seat. She climbed behind the wheel and drove down the dirt road. The road ascended the further they traveled. Eventually, the road forked, and she took the steeper trail off to the left. This stretch was rockier than the main road, and she had to go slow in order to traverse it. They eventually reached a clearing. Gwynn pulled up and parked, shutting off the ignition. She nodded for him to get out, and they exited the vehicle.

He followed her up the path until he saw the full scope of the quarry. Gwynn walked a few steps ahead of him, stopping at the precipice of a large boulder that jutted out over the water. Afraid of heights, Peters stopped a few feet behind her and stared down at the calm green water. He reckoned it must have been well over a hundred-foot drop. Maybe more. When he peeked over the rim, he noticed that the tips of Gwynn's boots hung perilously over the edge. Anxious, he wanted to move further back, but he didn't want to appear scared in front of the woman he loved. A woman who seemed to fear nothing.

Why had she brought him up here? To kill him?

They stood like this for a few minutes, allowing the silence to envelop them. A gentle breeze blew in from the north, whistling in his ears.

"This is the primary reason I convinced Tom to buy that cabin."

"You like quarries, huh?" He laughed nervously.

"After seeing this massive hole in the ground, I just knew I had to have it."

"I'm sorry, Gwynn. I don't understand why this quarry would interest you so much."

She held her arms out as if to balance herself. "I pushed Sam Townsend and William Clayborn over the edge."

The words shocked him. "No shit?"

She nodded.

He studied her expression, and for a moment, it frightened him. Did he really want to get into a relationship with a beautiful serial killer, knowing all that she'd done? Knowing all that she could do.

"That was pretty smart."

"I know," she said, turning to face him. "Now that you know where the bodies are buried, you can never leave me."

She grabbed his face in her cold hands and kissed him, and all his fears and doubts evaporated into the ether. The kiss combined with the dizzying height left him breathless. Gwynn wrapped her arms around him.

"Isn't this life crazy and unpredictable?" she said, staring up at him.

"It is with you in it."

"You and I are soulmates, Peters. You are the only person in this world I can be totally and completely honest with."

"I feel the same way about you, Gwynn."

"I'm really a good person," she said. "All those people I got rid of deserved what they had coming to them, just like the man you killed."

"I couldn't agree more."

"The world is a better place without them."

She spun him around so fast that he was not quite sure what was happening. Before he knew it, his back was facing the quarry. For a second, he thought he might join Townsend and Clayborn in the watery depths below. Instead, she held his face in her hands and kissed him on the lips. Afraid to open his eyes, he felt both terror and arousal like never before. The heels of his shoes hung perilously over the edge. Before he could ponder the possibility of an untimely death, Gwynn wrapped one of her arms around his torso. The other moved to his crotch. He opened his eyes and looked down, feeling weak and powerless as she unzipped his fly. Feeling as if he might explode down there.

Chapter Forty-Nine

Gwynn woke up and yawned. She turned toward Peters, still asleep on his back, and rested her arm over his hairy chest. Through the loft's wooden spindles, she could see the first glints of sunlight rising in the sky. Above her stretched the massive wooden beams supporting the cathedral ceiling. She kissed Peters's leathery cheek before slipping out from under the warm comforter. As she made her way downstairs, she remembered how they'd made love last night on the sheepskin rug in front of the fireplace.

Once downstairs, she prepared a pot of coffee. She poured herself a cup once it finished brewing and sat on the sofa facing the window, her legs tucked beneath her. With daylight spreading over the valley, she'd never been happier. She'd opened herself up last night, and Peters had accepted her in full.

She remembered being on the edge of that quarry and holding him tight. His back faced the quarry, and if she wanted, she could have ended his life at any moment. It reminded her of that gym teacher, only better. Peters was scared, but he quickly surrendered to her. Trusted her with his life. The power she'd felt on that ledge was beyond anything she'd ever experienced. She couldn't deny the slightest urge to push him in.

Did she really love Peters, or had she confused her love for him with the thrill of her bad deeds?

She was lost in thought when Peters walked down the stairs, wrapped in Tom's white robe. It was too small on him, exposing his pale shins, and this made her laugh. He kissed her before going into the kitchen and pouring himself a cup of coffee. He returned with a cup in hand and snuggled next to her. Gwynn stretched out, laying her head in his lap, laughing when she saw the cup in his hand. It had Yoda's image on it, and the words *Coffee I Need Or Kill You I Will* scrawled over the surface.

"What are you laughing at?"

"Did you look at the cup you grabbed?"

He lifted his cup, read the phrase, and laughed. They sat quietly like this for a few minutes as they stared out at the morning sky.

Peters eventually built a fire and beckoned her to join him on the sheepskin rug. She tiptoed over and dove into his awaiting arms. The heat given off by the flames, combined with Peters's body, provided her with warmth. She finally felt protected and safe. Worth loving. It was not long, however, before he slipped off her robe and nuzzled his lips against her pale neck. She arched her back, unable to get enough of him as his lips move to her breasts. He stripped off his shorts and T-shirt and climbed on top of her.

They moved in unison, and it felt glorious. She was close to orgasming when she heard a loud banging at the front door. His hands had pinned her wrists on the rug behind her head, and his face was beet red and twisted up in pleasure. He looked nervously over at the stairway leading to the main entrance. The front door opened, and she heard footsteps coming up the stairs. Peters let go of her wrists and moved up to his knees. She rolled out from under him and turned on her stomach and saw Tom standing at the top of the stairway, staring at the two of them.

"Well, well," Tom said, moving over to the couch. "What a sorry sight to behold."

She couldn't believe her eyes. "Tom, what are you doing here?"

"Looks like someone got lucky this morning," Tom said.

Peters fell to his stomach. Gwynn searched for her robe but found Peters's white T-shirt instead. She slipped it over herself, letting it fall mid-thigh. Despite being separated from Tom, she felt ashamed that she'd been caught sleeping with another man inside the cabin they purchased as a married couple.

"I'll ask you again, Tom. What the hell are you doing here?" she said, stunned that he would do something so awful.

"How much did you have to pay her?" Tom asked Peters.

"Shut your mouth," Peters shot back.

"I'd like to see you make me," Tom said, turning to her. "This is my cabin, too, Gwynn. Or have you forgotten that we're still married?"

"Get the hell out of here," Peters said, pointing toward the door.

"Fuck off, dickhead," Tom shouted, standing up from the couch as if challenging Peters to a fight. "You should be kicked off the force for screwing one of your suspects."

Gwynn did a double take, confused by Tom's hurtful accusation.

"She was the one who wanted this place," Tom said, sitting back down. "Then again, I never thought she'd be fucking another dude in it."

"We bought this cabin together," she said.

"Oh yeah, Gwynn. With that huge salary you earn at The Loft."

"I'm warning you, Tom, you'd better leave right now," Peters said as he slipped into his boxers. He stood and looked as if ready to pummel Tom.

"What are you going to do about it? Or maybe I should tell the world about how the two of you put that Asian cop in the hospital." Tom laughed as Peters approached. "Sit down, tough guy. You don't scare me."

Peters hesitated for a few seconds and then backed away.

"If you ever fuck my wife again, asshole, I promise you'll regret it," Tom said, pointing a finger at him.

"Leave him out of this, Tom. What is it you want from me?" Gwynn asked.

"What I want, my dear, is for you to admit all the crazy shit you've been doing."

"What are you talking about?" she said.

"Let's not play games, Gwynn. I've known about you for a very long time," Tom said, turning to Peters. "Did you know that she was the girl every guy wanted to date at Brooks?"

"That's not true," she said. "It was Tift the boys wanted."

"That's where you're wrong, my dear. Tift was the girl every guy wanted to fuck," Tom said. "You two were like Ginger and Mary Ann; guys lusted after Ginger, but it was Mary Ann we all wanted to marry."

"What the hell is he talking about?" Peters said.

"Stay out of this," she said before returning back to her husband. "What is it you want, Tom? Do you want me to admit that I don't love you anymore? I'm very sorry about the way I feel, but I couldn't stand how you were treating me. I couldn't take a pee without you asking where I was going."

"It doesn't matter, because I know you'll love me again someday."

"Why are you torturing yourself like this? It's over between us."

He crossed his legs and placed his arm over the top of the couch. "I beg to differ."

"Nguyen's not coming out of that coma, meaning it's your word against ours, no matter what video you've taken of us," she said.

"Not if I tell the police about the bodies lying at the bottom of that quarry. Do you think they might find it interesting that the remains of William Clayborn and Sam Townsend are down there? Isn't Townsend the dude you met at that Custom House event?"

His words penetrated her like hollow-point bullets. How did Tom know about this? Had he been keeping tabs on her that night?

"Yes, your dutiful husband has been learning all your dirty little secrets. Did you forget that our phones are connected by our Life360 apps, and I know everywhere you've been?"

She cursed herself for that oversight.

"You didn't think I was going to let you off the hook so easily, did you? After a while, it all started to make sense to me why you wanted this cabin in the woods. I just had to be patient and make sure that I was right about you."

"Jesus, Tom. Are you okay? You sound a little unhinged."

"That's precious." Tom broke out laughing. "You're the one doing all the killing, and you're asking me if I'm unhinged?"

Phrased that way, he did have a valid point.

"You know what the strangest part about all this is? I don't even care about those dead assholes. Hasta la vista, baby. I never even liked Sandra

Clayborn. And her attorney husband was a complete scumbag."

"Does that mean you're not going to turn me in?"

"Now I didn't say anything about that," he said, enjoying the power he had over her. "I suppose it all depends on what you decide to do."

"Who's to say that I won't drop you in that quarry myself," Peters said.

"I wouldn't do that if I were you. First off, I recorded you and Nguyen in that parking lot and sent the thumb drive to a friend, instructing that friend that if anything should ever happen to me, they should take that thumb drive to the police. Furthermore, I recorded my beautiful wife walking arm in arm with Townsend the night he disappeared. Oh, and did you kill Sandra before or after her swim? I assumed that her husband walked in on you right afterwards, obviously in the wrong place at the wrong time."

She felt numb, knowing that Tom had her dead to rights.

"You know what else I know? I know the vile thing Sam Townsend did to Tift."

"How did you know about that?" Gwynn asked.

"You told me about it when we crossed paths at Gritty's. You said it made you so mad that you wanted to kill him. Then again, you were so drunk that night you probably forgot about that."

"Why are you doing all this, Tom?"

"Because I love you," he said, turning to Peters. "Who knew that my college sweetheart would turn out to be such a cold-blooded killer? Personally, I find it kind of hot."

"I've got news for you, Tom. I was a cold-blooded killer before I met you," she said, sitting next to him on the couch. "I'd killed three people by the time we got engaged."

Tom sighed. "You think you know someone, right?"

"Would you still have married me knowing that?" she said.

"I wouldn't be here otherwise."

His answer surprised her. Might she be able to stay out of prison and continue raising Jack?

"So what is it you want from me?"

"I want us to be a couple again. And to show that I'm serious, I'm willing to overlook everything that happened and forgive and forget."

She thought about it. "What if I say no?"

"Then the police get the tape of you chasing that brain-dead cop, and you two lovebirds go to prison."

"Is this what you really want, Tom? For us to be together?"

"I want the three of us to be a happy little family again," Tom said, turning to Peters. "And by the three of us, I don't mean you, shithead."

"But I don't love you," Gwynn said.

"You will learn to love me again. And I promise that I will change and be the man you always wanted."

"You're a good man, Tom. We just aren't meant to be."

"We are meant to be. And we always have been."

She gnawed on her thumbnail and tried to think of another way out.

"The way I see it, you really don't have any other choice."

"Gwynn loves me," Peters said, pounding his chest. "And I love her."

"Fuck off, Barney Fife. If I ever see you near my wife again, I'll make sure you spend the rest of your life picking up soap scraps in Windham Penitentiary."

Peters made an aggressive move toward Tom but stopped when Gwynn held out her arm.

"We have an amazing son. A beautiful home. Hell, we can even keep this cabin if you like. I don't expect you to fall in love with me right away. Sure, it will take time and lots of patience. But the love will return between us, Gwynn, I promise you that. And it will be stronger than ever."

She glanced at Peters and saw the defeated expression on his face. But she couldn't bear going away to prison and never seeing Jack again—and letting Tom raise him.

"Do you need some time to think about it?" Tom asked.

"No," she replied in a defeated tone. "I agree to your terms. We can be a family again."

"But what about us?" Peters complained, turning to her.

"It's over, Detective. I'm getting back with my husband."

"Be real, Gwynn. You don't even love him," Peters said.

"I'm sorry. It just wasn't meant to be," Gwynn said.

"I love you, and I know you feel the same way about me."

"Please leave," she said, pointing toward the door.

"And if you mention a word about this to anyone," Tom said, "I will send that video to your superiors and watch as you spend the rest of your miserable life being some gangbanger's bitch."

Peters stormed upstairs to grab his bag. While he was gathering his stuff, Tom slid over on the couch and kissed Gwynn's cheek.

"You watch and see, hon. We are going to be so happy this time around."

Dr. Ezra Kaufman

"I'm getting back together with Tom," Gwynn says after I ask what's going on in her life.

"That's a surprise." The news that Gwynn is getting back with her husband stuns me, especially knowing that he threatened to turn her in to the police. "I thought you were sick and tired of his controlling nature."

"Looking back, it wasn't really that bad," she says. "And Jack is better off with his parents together."

"How did he convince you to take him back?"

"Tom's love for me has no bounds."

"A man like that can be dangerous."

She laughs. "Tom is not dangerous. He just really cares about me."

"I'm concerned for your well-being."

"Don't be, because we've come to a mutual agreement about our relationship moving forward."

"What about your new boyfriend, that detective?"

"It just didn't work out between us."

"But you said that you loved him."

"I was obviously wrong about that," she says. "Tom has promised to change and be a better husband to me."

"How so?"

"He wants to know where I am at all times and what I'm doing. It shows that he really cares about my well-being."

"That doesn't sound healthy."

"You must remember, I did cheat on him," she says. "So, in that respect,

I'm in the wrong."

"A marriage should be an equal partnership."

"We're putting our relationship into the hands of God."

"And you're good with that?"

"I suppose I have to be," she says. "The Scriptures say that the husband is the head of his household and has God-given authority over his wife and children."

I stay silent, wondering if she's rationalizing this new arrangement because of what he knows about her.

"The other night, he decided we should have sex in his office after everyone had left for the night."

"You don't need to tell me this, Gwynn."

"It's liberating knowing that I can be completely open and honest with you."

I remain silent.

"My life is finally back to some semblance of normalcy, and as long as I have Jack in it, I'm going to be happy."

I study her.

"What?" She laughs.

"I'm just concerned about you."

"I'm a big girl."

I feel uncomfortable with this new arrangement but feel helpless to do anything. "How's the other thing going?"

"What other thing?"

"The urges?"

"I finally might be turning a new leaf in that regard, especially now that I'm back with Tom."

"At least that part of your life has improved."

"Tom feels the same way. He believes he can help keep me in check."

"You mean Tom knows about all the...things you've done?"

"Of course, he knows. We both realize that if we're to make a go of it, we need to be completely honest with each other," she says, looking down at her hands. "Like you and I are doing right now."

This revelation astonishes me, and for a second, I don't know how to respond. Tom knows about the murders she committed and is still okay taking her back? I understand why Gwynn might feel this way, but what does that make Tom? An accomplice to murder? To many murders? What influence does this woman have over men? And am I just another in a long line being played by her?

"I'm writing more these days, too, which is a good thing. I have all these crazy stories in my head just begging to come out."

"That's good. Keep journaling."

"It's not just journaling, but actual scripts. My friend, Tift Ainsley, said she'll pitch them to some Hollywood directors if they're any good." She stands. "Now that everything in my life is back to normal, I don't think I'll be needing your services anymore."

"Listen to me," I say, sitting forward in my chair. "I don't think it's a good idea for you to stop therapy."

"You've been absolutely wonderful to me throughout the years, but I have a much better handle on my life now."

"You've said this in the past, and look what happened, Gwynn. Continuing with your therapy has been beneficial to you."

"I've killed seven people while in your care. How beneficial could it really have been?"

I have no reply to this.

"But what if your dissociative disorder takes a turn for the worse? What will you do?"

"You should focus on yourself, Doctor. Why don't you sell that beautiful home of yours and retire somewhere nice and warm? Forget about me and start enjoying your life."

I've considered this option for many years now. But then, what would I do? I have no hobbies except this career I've chosen. I can't imagine living in the Villages with a bunch of old people playing Bingo and Pickleball while waiting to die.

"I'll be here for you if you ever need me," I say, staring at my watch. "If you care to return to therapy, just give me a ring."

Gwynn walks over to the door. "Thank you for everything you've done for me."

"I mean it," I say, holding out my hand. "Even if it's just to talk."

She shakes my hand. And just like that, she's out of my life. But I have the feeling that she'll be back someday. Something strange is happening to Gwynn Denning, and I'm betting it has something to do with her getting back with Tom.

I'll keep coming into this office despite having no patients. Paying the rent and keeping it tidy.

I pick up the newspaper and read that Detective Nguyen is still in a coma. The doctors don't know if she'll ever come out of it. The case of the Muddy River Killer has been solved, thanks to Gwynn's behind-the-scenes scheming. Detective Peters is now a star in his own right and has been appearing on all the true crime shows. He's managed to convince the world that William Clayborn was the person who committed these two murders, then fled Maine and went on the lam. Since he made that statement, there are calls coming in from all over the country claiming to have spotted the infamous criminal defense attorney.

I vow to come into the office each day, waiting for Gwynn to return. It's only a matter of time before she calls in tears, begging for my help. Begging me to take her back.

I drop my face into my palms in preparation for the tears. Only they never come. They never do.

Chapter Fifty

Gwynn left Kaufman's office and strolled down Commercial Street. It was a beautiful winter day, cold and sun-filled. The frozen, crusty bay to her left reflected brilliantly in the sun. She thanked God that He had taken mercy on her and allowed her to remain in Jack's life. And she promised to never kill again.

Tom had proved true to his word. He'd changed as soon as they arrived home. But he'd changed for the worse and became even more controlling, more domineering, dictating how she should behave and what she was allowed to do. In some ways, she felt like she was living under a totalitarian regime, every move she made scrutinized and closely watched. She could barely use the bathroom without asking for his permission. Or buy a cup of coffee.

Tom controlled the purse strings, as well as most everything else in her life. He informed her when and where they would have sex, the kind of kinky sex they would have, what vacations they would take, and where they would go. He even got to decide who her friends were and if she could visit with them.

The one consolation was that he allowed her to keep her job. She would have been lost without the children in her care. Tom's only concession was that she had to step down as director, which she did with much regret. The Loft had begun a national search for a new leader and that saddened her that she would no longer run the organization the way she saw fit.

More importantly, she was able to be with Jack every day, which made all her sacrifices worthwhile. If it were not for him, she would have killed herself. She'd do anything to be in her wiggleworm's life. Despite his defective genes, she swore to raise him to be a good and decent person and break the violent cycle of murder that he'd been born into.

She strolled along Maple Street, her heels clicking against the cobblestone lane. Old brick buildings appeared on either side of her. New buildings were going up every few months in this quaint town by the sea. Tom might scan his Life360 app and ask her about the route she'd taken, but she'd lie and say she needed some exercise, which was why she took the long way back to her office.

All she needed to do was get her hands on that thumb drive, and then she could dump Tom and live happily ever after. Until then, she planned on being the best wife possible. Pretend to love him. Make him happy every day. Perform his dark and twisted requests in the bedroom. Tell him whatever it was he wanted to hear. But she'd be thinking about Peters the entire time. And hopefully, he'd be thinking about her, too.

Just this morning, Gwynn had sent her pilot script to Tift. It was a story about a wife and mother who kills bad people, and she was anxious to see what Tift thought of it. Would it hit too close to home? Would Tift hate the idea of a serial-killing mother and wife? Would an audience hate the main character?

Her phone rang just as she neared The Loft. It was a message from Ivy's social worker. A family court judge had just ruled that Ivy could move back in with her parents. Gwynn tried not to let this depressing news affect her. How could the judicial system do this to Ivy and let another scumbag father off the hook for his perverted crimes? More than ever, Gwynn wanted to take the law into her own hands. She swore vengeance against Ivy's father and wished she could make him pay for what he'd done to his beautiful daughter.

Caring for the children in her care had been her calling, and now she felt like a complete failure. At least she had Jack back in her life, and she swore she would never let anything bad happen to him. Tonight, she would wrap her arms around Jack and tell him over and over how much she loved him. Protect him from Tom and make sure he didn't turn out like either of them.

When she walked onto the campus, the boys and girls, bundled in their winter coats, gloved, and wool caps, ran over and hugged her. She fell to one knee and accepted their embrace, grateful to be loved by them and to love them in return.

Acknowledgements

I'd like to thank the team at Level Best, especially Shawn Reilly Simmons and Deb Well. Thanks to my agent, Evan Marshall. And mostly, I give thanks to my wife, Marleigh, and two kids, Danny and Allie.

About the Author

Joseph Souza is the award-winning and bestselling author of eleven novels and a book of short stories. He's won the Maine Literary Award, the Andres Dubus Award and was a runner-up for the Al Blanchard Award. He's worked as a teacher, cabbie, social worker, truck driver, editor, bouncer, barber, wrestling coach, paralegal and intelligence analyst in the DEA (Organized Crime Unit), to name just a few jobs. He lives in Maine with his wife and has two children.

AUTHOR WEBSITE:
    josephsouzawriter.com

SOCIAL MEDIA HANDLES:
    Facebook: Joseph Souza, Author
    Twitter: @josephsouzafans
    Instagram: josephsouza2060

Also by Joseph Souza

Unpaved Surfaces (Kindle Press)

Need to Find You (Kindle Press)

The Neighbor (Kensington)

Pray For The Girl (Kensington)

The Perfect Daughter (Kensington)

The Anchorman's Wife (Level Best Books)